Dancing Magicians

Also by John Caris

Hermes Beckons,
A Tale of Alchemy and Magic

Reality Inspector,
A Tale of Computer-hacking and Chess

Foundation for a New Consciousness:
An Essay on Art, Science, and Meditation

Dancing Magicians

John Caris

Westgate House   San Francisco

Published by Westgate House, San Francisco, CA
Visit our web site Ye Olde Consciousness Shoppe
at westgatehouse.com

Cover image: bristlecone pines
Copyright © 2013 by Mary D. Caris

Library of Congress Control Number: 2013930741
ISBN 978-0-9607320-3-6

Manufactured in the United States of America

10 9 8 7 6 5 4 3 2 1

For Mary

Humpty Dumpty reveals a secret to Alice:
"When I use a word," Humpty Dumpty said, in rather a scornful tone, "it means just what I choose it to mean—neither more nor less."
"The question is," said Alice, "whether you can make words mean so many different things."
"The question is," said Humpty Dumpty, "which is to be master—that's all."
Lewis Carroll, *Through the Looking Glass*

Chapter 1

Walking down Sutro Steps to Cliffside Cafe where Philip was waiting, no doubt sipping coffee, I paused a moment to recall the previous night's affair. Shasta was fixing dinner, the kitties napping on the couch, and I was reading the recent issue of *MUM*, the Society of American Magicians' monthly journal. An article on mentalism had caught my attention. Suddenly an eerie sensation, a disturbing feeling, passed through me. I looked up. The kitties had their ears up and tuned in.

Shasta entered from the kitchen and commented, "I felt something strange like a low level vibrating sound or energy."

"I felt it too," I replied. "And Lucy and Karma were aware of it."

"Of course they would be." Shasta looked at them, now with their heads lifted staring at us.

A second time the strange phenomenon occurred.

"An earthquake? No, something else," I said.

Twice more we experienced the weirdness—an uneasy feeling resonating through our home. A quiet, more exactly a deep silence, not quite ominous, nor scary yet definitely strange filled the house. A lingering uncertainty pervaded our home, and we were still concerned this morning.

San Franciscans will realize their San Francisco isn't being described accurately. For in our beloved city, Sutro Steps leading to Cliffside Cafe don't exist. Thus imaginative readers will recognize the scene is existing in an alternate reality, a parallel universe. And too the story lives in a world its own. Yet its personal cosmos is directly and concretely linked to the readers' reality. Perceptive readers will notice along the way several parallel worlds have been laid upon each other, squeezed into a single universe with changing viewpoints. Whether this bit of dramatic magic reflects our daily world I will not judge.

Please forgive the break in the narrative, but I think it's necessary to shine light on the story's reality. So as I descended to Cliffside Cafe, I was puzzling over the strange phenomena my household experienced last night. It was in the forefront of my thoughts, and I planned to tell Philip about it.

Cliffside Cafe is situated about halfway down Sutro Heights Hill. Sutro Heights Park is located on top of the promontory. The stairs descend to the Great Highway that runs along Ocean Beach. Stepping onto the outdoor dining area, I saw Philip through a large glass window sipping coffee. He is a regular customer regardless of the weather. The cafe is close to the Institute and, even when crowded, gives him a private space for his contemplative moments.

Institute of Consciousness-Imagination-Nous or Institute of CIN is the full name. Philip bubbles with merriment when ultra-conservative critics call it Institute of SIN. Wondering if they're being ironic, he interprets their name as Institute of Sacred Imaginative Nous and believes it's a more accurate description of the work accomplished at the Institute. Most knowledgeable people just say the Institute.

Philip Austen is interested in occult activities and has spent the past forty years researching different areas in the broad spectrum of psychic happenings. His bibliography is fairly long, seven books and numerous articles. He is now studying the transformation of energy in psychological and, I suspect, spiritual processes. I don't think he would use the word 'spiritual,' yet he is fully open to such experiences. He performs his research at the Institute where he has an office and a two member team of like-minded investigators.

Last year Philip asked me to join his research project at the Institute with a position of consultant. He thinks the inner operation, structure, and processes of psychic power are revealed and become available for study during a magician's performance. Even though the mage is only acting the part, his act rests on the surface of psychic energy, and during his routines the energy will be perceived. His thesis certainly captured my interest, and I agreed to the position but without pay. I knew I would enjoy the project and could gather material for my next magic show.

I have been enchanted by magic since I was a child. After graduating with a BA from San Francisco State University, I decided to earn my living as a magician and have done fairly well.

So I, Ralph Garland, hastened to offer a personal experience for research. Whether Philip would consider it of scientific value or not was unclear.

Philip looked up when Ralph entered the cafe. Sensing a seriousness shrouding Ralph, he felt a troubling concern. He relaxed, sitting back into the chair, smiling as his friend sat down.

As they exchanged the usual pleasantries, Philip observed Ralph's behavior. "Any good dreams recently, Ralph?"

I laughed in an uneasy manner. Here was a typical Philip ploy. Discussing dreams was a portal to one's inner world and ultimately the collective unconsciousness.

"Well, I had an unusual experience. If I claimed it a dream, you would politely inquire and then soon forget it."

"Ah, the big IF. Not a dream then?"

"No. The Garland household experienced it. Perhaps a group hallucination but not a dream."

"Don't keep me in suspense, Ralph, with your misdirection. Lay it out."

I proceeded to describe the event in all its weirdness. Philip said very little during the telling of the twice-told tale. He only requested more details at a few points. Philip is fond of saying, "Truth resides in the details." I know he's not a poet seeking the right metaphor. He is a friend of chaos theory and its focus on forms within forms. I kid him he's actually stating an alchemical recipe: "as above, so below." We enjoy our quibbles and colorful retorts.

When Ralph had finished his report, Philip sat quietly, then called the waiter over and ordered a coffee refill.

After fresh coffee had been served, we talked about inconsequential things. A flock of pelicans flew overhead. We commented on their comeback after being on the endangered list. The recent storm had done less damage to the city than it had to the northern part of San Francisco Bay. So we remarked about that.

Finally Philip leaned forward indicating a tête-à-tête. "Ralph, this happening has the earmarks of a psychic event. I would like to investigate it further. It would tie in with an idea I'm working on."

"What's the idea?" I inquired.

"I don't want to say much at the moment. I can tell you it involves psychic energy exchange. I'm afraid I don't have a precise definition yet, so let's leave it vague."

I nodded. "Okay with me. Call it transformation of energy and I'm in." His proposal had an intimation of Hermes' craft attached to it.

"Yes, that's an apt phrase. Here's a possible catch though. I would like to involve Shasta and the kitties, if possible."

"I'll ask them though I can't guarantee anything."

"Accepted."

While mixing extra dry martinis for our happy hour, I mentioned to Shasta my conversation with Philip and his curiosity about our experiences. She was preparing dinner, an orzo dish with mixed vegetables. Later green salsa would be added.

"I don't know. I'm working on my novel and don't want to spend time on a research project. As for the kitties I don't want them hooked up to equipment and experimented on. I put myself in that category too. No experiments. But if you want to indulge, go ahead."

"I'll talk with Philip."

"Actually now I'm thinking about it, if he would like to make a social call between three to five some afternoon, I'd be happy to tell him my experiences. And if he can communicate with the kitties as we do, fine, if they're willing."

Chapter 2

John Ocean awoke with an enchanted vision: he was performing magic. Beside him was a small table with various magical props a stage magician uses. He had a wand in his right hand and a coin in his left. He was reminded of the tarot card Magician.

Getting out of bed, he walked over to the window and looked out at his garden. In the dream, he remembered, he had walked out on stage. Standing next to a table, he had picked up the coin and then the wand. The dream had dissolved leaving him with the vision of Mage. The image carried an intense feeling of power and confidence. He savored the feeling and decided he liked it. But he had a new client, who had contracted for his investigative services, so he put the vision out of his mind. Later when he had leisure time, he would revisit it. And perhaps his friends Mary Rainbow, proprietor of Rainbow Inn, and Od Tinker would have some insights.

Rainbow Inn was quiet, a lull after the busy lunchtime and before the dinner hour. The Inn was a well-known vegetarian restaurant and social center on Ocean Avenue. Aromas from the soup kettle mingled with fragrant odors from herbs hanging from the ceiling rafters and flowers nestled in the windowsills. Mary Rainbow had two large kettles the vegetable soup was prepared in. One kettle was used for lunch and the other for dinner. When the soup ran out, that was it until the next kettle was ready. The soup's ingredients changed daily. Besides vegetarian meals, a variety of teas and coffees were available. The seven herb tea was the Inn's specialty.

Mary was sitting at her private table with John and Od, the owner of Trading Shop. Her dark brown hair was rolled into a bun and fastened with barrettes. When hanging loose, it reached below her shoulder blades. Her brown eyes sparkled as a secret smile played upon her lips.

A pot of seven herb tea was located in the middle of the table ready to re-fill empty cups. A plate with small pieces of carrot cake was next to it. While they were enjoying the refreshments, John told them about the rather weird dream he had experienced several nights earlier. They both listened quietly. When he had finished, John looked at them, wondering, and asked, "Any thoughts or feelings about my vision?"

"Well," Mary commented, "the magic part certainly links to your own life and career as reality inspector."

Od laughed. "True. True. Your life is magical. Yet the dream suggests a different type of magic." He selected a piece of carrot cake and ate it.

"Yes," Mary rejoined. "I thought of the tarot card." Picking up the teapot, she refilled everyone's cup.

"Magician," Od added.

"A mystical quality." John nodded and spread his hands. "But, and here's the new element, a stage-performing mage." He sipped some tea.

"Yeah. Like vaudeville performers of olden times." Od was reminded of some magic posters in his shop. He suddenly realized they should be displayed more prominently.

"Houdini or Blackstone—those great magicians," Mary remarked. Nibbling on a piece of cake, she considered the potential of staging more acts like magic. The Inn had a small stage and hosted a variety of performances, although most were music or drama.

"Yes, I like the idea." John paused, sipping his tea. "But what is the sign here? What does the vision point me toward?"

"Okay, then, a new direction for you." Mary shone her light upon them. "A different stage, the pun intended, in your career." She felt a certainty all their lives were at a crossroads. They were being given the opportunity to make important choices.

Od chuckled. "Yep, a transformed reality inspector who creates a role in a new game."

"Of course. It's a game," Mary quipped. For her a game, especially chess games, was a basic metaphor for life.

"The master game," Od added. The cake was delicious, so he munched on another piece.

"And I'll be the master game player. Yes, that feels good." John beamed with approval. The idea appealed to him. He didn't perceive anything wrong with it at the moment, yet he would mulled it over and inspect its potential reality. Just in case there were any leaks.

"Every game has its rules and goals and equipment so what about the master game. What's its purpose?" Mary as usual went straight to the core of the issue.

"Is it going to be a board game or computer digital game?" Od replied.

"A mind game–that's what it'll be. The mage applies mind power to perform magical events. And he uses the magician's tools like a wand and coins and cards."

"So how does it differ from other types of magic? Magicians and wizards use wands and other tools too." Mary maintained focus.

"If it's real magic, not sleight-of-hand magic, what's the distinction?" Od's logic was lucid.

"Hmm. I know. It's psychic power." John had an aha.

"You mean like the force or something. Star Wars thing?" Od was back with his move.

"John, it's more of a mystical direction. Are you certain you want to go there?" Mary was concerned.

"Why shouldn't he? The force is similar to Chinese Tao. A basic power source," Od replied quickly.

John felt a little awed and his face brightened. "Of course. The master game fits with many of the new ideas in science. First I'll need to define the purpose and goal and then the rules. I would like you to help with the project. I'll start working on it now."

"You can count me in." Mary smiled back.

"And you can't keep me out." Od chuckled.

Chapter 3

Philip arrived with his team, Geraldine and Jerome Meadows, around 3:30 on Friday. Ralph ushered them into the living room. Shasta was seated at a circular wood table. Philip, whom she knew, clasped her hand gently. "Thank you for inviting us, Shasta. It's good seeing you again." He turned to his team and introduced them.

Geraldine, shaking hands with Shasta, said, "I go by Geri."

Jerome, following her, declared, "And I'm Jerry."

Shasta stifled a giggle. She pointed toward the kitties who were on the couch observing the proceedings. "The orange tiger is Lucy and the torby is Karma." The kitties sat up. Lucy smiled and Karma, after first yawning, smiled too.

Geri approached and greeted the kitties. "Hi Lucy and Karma," she said to them. She turned toward Shasta and asked, "What is a torby?"

"It's a tabby-tortoiseshell blend," Shasta replied. "Please find a comfy place to sit." She gestured at the couch and armchairs.

Geri and Jerry selected the couch and sat next to the kitties, who inspected them closely. Philip and Ralph took the upholstered armchairs.

"I'm curious. What's the purpose of your experiment?" Shasta inquired.

"Shasta, as I told Ralph, it's a new project, and I don't have a name for it or much of a definite set of criteria," Philip answered. "I will say it involves a type of transformation, using Ralph's term, and has analogies to energy flows of different substances like air and water."

"The experience did seem more on the level of movement through air, as vibrations are," Shasta remarked.

"Vibrations occur in all material forms although the more common are in air and water," Geri added.

"Don't forget earthquakes," Jerry noted.

"As you can tell, my team of specialists is ready for the project," Philip observed with a wry grin.

"Perhaps if Shasta and I relate our experiences, you can better understand the strangeness," Ralph proposed.

Philip nodded. "Fine. Please go first, Shasta, and tell us what happened."

Shasta smiled. "Yes, but the first thing actually is bringing out the refreshments that are now waiting in the kitchen." As she stood, she glanced at Ralph, who jumped up and excused himself for the moment. Once the drinks, a choice of tea or coffee, were served and two plates of cookies passed around, everyone settled down for tales of strangeness.

Philip asked whether the session could be video recorded, and the Garlands agreed. Philip sprinkled several questions throughout the narratives. Geri and Jerry played with the kitties or at least sat with them, each holding one and petting it.

After Shasta and Ralph had finished their descriptions of what they had felt and sensed, Philip and his team remained silent for a few moments. Philip sipped his coffee and then started to speak, but before he could, Geri declared, "This event fits tightly into our project."

"Actually," Jerry interjected, "it provides clear evidence for the energy exchange process."

Both Shasta and Ralph looked quizzical. "Can you explain the concept?" Ralph asked.

Geri and Jerry turned to Philip, who gestured at them to go ahead. "Simply," Geri stated, "the exchange involves an energy field on the psychic level with two poles, positive and negative."

"A clear analogy is air pressure," Jerry offered. "Like high and low air pressures caused by difference in temperatures and a flow occurs between them. High pressure flows into low pressure."

"And the exchange happens in the psychic zone," Geri commented.

Now intrigued, Shasta asked, "Can the pressure and flow be measured?"

Philip rubbed his chin, one of his nervous habits, especially when he was uncertain. "We think so. Problem is, we don't have sufficient evidence, which actually means experiments, to prove the energy is quantifiable."

"We're close though," Jerry added.

"You're too impatient," Geri reprimanded. "A lot more data are required before we can publish."

Philip was amused. Shaking his head, he said to Shasta and Ralph, "You have surmised that my team members are brother and sister."

"Sister and brother. I'm the oldest," Geri pronounced.

"We're twins. Would you believe it. She's only ten minutes older. That's not enough to shout about." Jerry acted disgusted.

Breaking the ensuing silence, Ralph remarked, "Waterfalls have a positive energy, a psychic force. I always feel good in their presence. Any negative energy I have dissipates."

Philip's eyebrows went up, but before he could reply, Geri commented, "Yes, many places in nature emit psi energy."

"Did you notice psychic power recently or were you aware as a child?" Jerry inquired.

"Oh, my, for a long time. Actually, when I was a child, I believed guardian spirits hovered around natural things, like waterfalls." He smiled, amusement graced his face. "Even now I speculate about sacred places and their spiritual presence. Sometimes I still search for the hiding spot of the waterfall's guardian spirit."

"Do you ever find it?" Geri asked.

"Surprisingly, I often do, usually a rock that's the spirit's abode."

Lucy and Karma decided the time was ripe for their performance. Jumping down from the couch, they began leaping into the air chasing a fly only they could see. All the two-leggeds started laughing.

Philip caught his breath and changed the focus. "We have recording devices we use to take readings. If we could go throughout your home with them."

"What type of readings?" Shasta had become quite inquisitive.

"These devices sense and record positive and negative energy pressures, remnants of recent past and present pressures. The twins can make the tour if Ralph will accompany them."

Shasta smiled. "Fine. You can tell me more about your project. I could use some ideas for thematic material in the novel I'm writing."

"Of course. And I'd enjoy hearing about the work in progress." Philip smiled back.

Ralph guided the tour with the kitties leading the way. As they were taking readings, Geri began watching the kitties. Lucy in particular snooped around the room, poking into corners and under tables and chairs. Karma contented herself with staying in one place although she did move to other locations in a room. Geri commented to Jerry that the kitties might have a special sensitivity for pressure levels and zones. Acknowledging her perceptive skills, she then turned to Ralph, "I'm a cat whisperer and quite sensitive to their behavior."

"And I'm a dog whisperer," Jerry announced. "Dogs and I communicate very well indeed."

After touring both the first and second floors, Ralph took them down to the basement. Karma became exceedingly curious and spent more time exploring than Lucy. Again Geri noticed the change in behavior.

"I think the kitties are definitely attuned to the energy pressure flow," Geri remarked.

"They're very special and perceptive people." Ralph beamed, very proud of them.

When the readings were concluded and the five members of the inspection team returned to the living room, Shasta was telling Philip about her writing activities. "I've been spending a lot of time with my poetry. I'm thinking about publishing a small book of it." She paused as the troupe entered.

Once they were all seated, Philip asked Shasta, "What will your new novel be about?"

"Ah, that's the million dollar query. The main challenge is selecting one central idea from several floating around in my mind. So of course this experience of ours and your interest in it provide more options."

"I really enjoyed the last novel where that San Francisco dealer of rare books and manuscripts is robbed of an alchemical work. Peaches is awesome, the way she got involved in esoteric culture," Geri remarked.

"*The Case of the Purloined Manuscript.* Yeah, I liked it too. And the one before about the magicians who had a serious conflict–that was great." Jerry added his approval.

"Shasta, what attracted you to alchemy?" Geri wondered.

"It was Ralph. I assisted with his recent magic show about alchemy," Shasta replied.

"She's my helpmeet and played the role of Queen in the performance," Ralph revealed.

The twins gave each other a knowing glance.

Eyes twinkling, Philip stated, "We're your fan club. I've read all your novels. Very fine."

Shasta blushed. "Thank you for the compliments. Writers like an appreciative audience."

In the momentary lull Ralph stood up and asked, "Who would like a refill?" They all agreed, and he took their cups into the kitchen. After he returned, the conversation moved back to Philip's project.

"If you'll give us approval, we'd like to place measuring devices around the house–four of them for the directions," Philip inquired. "These devices are wireless and will transmit data to the lab. The devices will be out of sight and unobtrusive."

"I'm quite fascinated with your research. It's rather exciting, so of course you may," Shasta affirmed.

"I'm in agreement, and if the kitties are okay with devices stationed here," Ralph declared, and he looked directly at Lucy and Karma who, by cleaning their paws, indicated it was a groovy idea.

Philip was delighted as were the twins. "Ralph, I have the preliminary results of today's readings. They're intriguing. Based on them, would you become a participant in the project? I have several experiments you could assist with."

"As one of your lab mice, Philip?" Ralph was amused.

"No. Instead of being a consultant, you would now be a partner although you would be a subject for tests, which will explore psychic energy fields and their potential application for practical purposes."

"What do the preliminary results indicate Ralph could assist with?" Shasta inquired.

"It's only a first analysis based on limited data, but Ralph seems to be linked with the changes in pressure levels. And," Philip stared at Shasta, "the kitties have an important part too."

"Well, am I left out then?"

"Of course not, Shasta, but your role is still to be identified. Remember, we haven't delved very far yet."

"Yeah, just on the surface," Jerry chimed in.

"These early readings are fantastic. Deep exploration is required now." Geri was quite enthusiastic.

"Shasta, if you would like to come to the Institute and join us in the tests, we'd be delighted. The kitties may participate too of course." Philip's invitation was alluring.

"No, the kitties and I will stay home and maintain a balance in the psychic pressure level," she graciously affirmed.

"If the twins can place the devices now, we can leave soon," Philip said.

"Please go ahead," Shasta responded.

Turning to Ralph, Philip remarked, "I'd like a peek at your studio, if you don't mind."

"Oh, yes, you should see his magic lair, Philip," Shasta announced with a grin.

Ralph laughed. "Right this way and I'll show you amazing feats."

After the devices had been installed, they gathered in the vestibule.

"Ralph, I'll phone in a few days, and we can set a date for your first test. Thank you, Shasta, for your refreshments and hospitality. And here's my card–as a reminder and memento," Philip remarked.

After the twins had thanked the Garlands, the psychic investigators left.

Shasta inspected Philip's business card. "Philip M. Austen. What does the middle initial stand for?"

"Marlowe. His parents were great fans of Raymond Chandler and his detective stories."

"Intriguing. Marlowe is the family name of a major Elizabethan playwright who led a mysterious and rather secret life."

"Yes. Christopher. And his famous play *Doctor Faustus.*"

"Perhaps, it is a sign."

Chapter 4

Sitting at his desk in Trading Shop, Odysseus Tinker thought about John Ocean's proposal for a master game. He was inspired by John's idea and the enthusiasm it generated. He decided it was time to devise his own game, one expressing his heart-felt thoughts about society. It too would raise awareness about human existence.

Od surveyed his shop. The contents were the essence of his wealth and joy, his treasure trove. His passion was trading, and he had built his business on that practice, yet he was a realist. Living in a society based on a common currency, Od accepted money for commercial transactions, and money was required by government agencies and most businesses. Trading Shop allowed him to indulge in his dominant pleasure and still support his lifestyle.

Od Tinker was a trader–by nature, by desire, and by profession. He traded objects, both antique and new; and he also traded services. If he didn't have an item or a skill someone wanted, he would put out a search for it. He was a member of the Bay Area Trading Community, a loosely knit group of trading associations. The BATC had a website for members to use whenever they were looking for a trade.

With the economic meltdown many small businesses were failing. He was fortunate. He was afloat and had sufficient funds to purchase goods at clearance sales. Many years ago before housing values rapidly escalated, he had bought the two story building that housed both his store at street level and upstairs his residence. He could endure the economic storm and survive.

Only large corporations had enough political punch to gain welfare subsides and tax breaks from the federal government. Billions of dollars of cheap or interest free money were daily handed out to the too-big-to-fail crowd.

Od remembered his father talking about the Great Depression–the total failure of the whole economic system. Thousands of Americans were made homeless when they were laid off. Unemployment surged. Food kitchens were set up in urban areas to feed the hungry. While organized crime syndicates were growing fat because of prohibition, decent Americans suddenly discovered the Great American Dream had vanished into nothingness.

From the way adults talked when he was young, he knew deep in his soul the present economic meltdown was as disastrous as the one in 1929. In the election year of 1932 Americans went to the polls and spoke loudly and clearly. They decisively rejected the economic policies of the Hoover administration and embraced the New Deal. The corporate ruling class was, of course, shocked by the audacious voters who wanted their share of the economic pie. The rulers called the people's demands socialistic and communistic. The great corporations had employed rent-a-cops to force their control on society. All those memories now arose in Od's mind as he watched American society fall into a third world nation and a corporate takeover in the offering.

Od had purchased many books from the bookstore on Ocean Avenue when it closed shop. While cataloging these books, he had perused each one, noting which ones he would read in the near future. Karl Marx's *Capital* had been in the stack. He had heard so much about it, mainly negative rants. He had looked forward to reading it and discover for himself what the truth was. He had learned long ago too many people relied on slogans and opinions of others, repeating endlessly the gossip spread by the corporate media, never seeking the truth for themselves, willing only to follow blindly the fashionable thoughts of the day.

Over the years he had developed his own economic theory based on the ancient system of barter. The use of currency was a recent development in the evolution of trade and it was filled with weaknesses and constantly reoccurring problems. Societies spent much of their time and energy trying to maintain a modicum of trade based on a commonly accepted currency.

He thought the present economic depression would continue for many years. He perceived an up-and-down rolling economic curve. A spurt of slow growth and then a worsening and downward spin. The process would repeat itself with another spurt of growth and a falling away. His reasoning was based on what the federal government had done in the face of the crisis. Its complete faith in policies supported by corporate leaders generated only a holding action for the oligarchy to restore some of its personal wealth but worsened the situation for the long run. Now the rulers expected to be bailed out and subsidized whenever they lost money playing their silly game. Yes, it was a game on the global scale. And it was a game against nature. The fundamental assumption of their voodoo economic theory rested on a childish and foolish view of nature: a fantasy notion that the economic marketplace should be free of any human regulation because it was natural and shouldn't be controlled, and so forth in an endless cycle. Yet the 2008 meltdown showed definitely the corporate players, when they lost against nature, wanted their workers to bail them out so they could start again. The adolescent leaders didn't like losing even if they praised an unregulated, natural marketplace. Of course, the people were first blamed for the difficulties and punished by the destruction of their wealth and security and finally forced to give more of their wealth to the oligarchy.

When he had finally read Marx's *Capital*, he found the work hard going. Besides the plodding nineteenth century prose, the presentation was dull although filled with a large amount of evidence Marx amassed to support his ideas. Much of the book Od skimmed, stopping where an idea caught his attention. Marx's popular work, rousing and fiery *The Communist Manifesto*, was something else entirely. It held his attention from beginning to end. In today's jargon it's a page turner. Its conclusion echoed in his mind: We have nothing to lose but our bondage to the corporate elite.

Od culled enough from both works to realize Karl Marx was the father of industrial capitalism with his incisive examination of industry and capital in the nineteenth century. One of his primary theses had been confirmed several times already, but the present economic meltdown proved its truth without any doubt: capitalism as an economic policy can remain viable only if it's supported and subsidized by the government. Otherwise, it will fail miserably as it has done today. The response of the federal government with its huge giveaways to the corporate oligarchy displayed the weakness hidden in capitalism and the free marketplace. An important prediction Marx had made was rapidly becoming true: the demise of the middle class. The United States was quickly becoming a society of one percent haves and ninety-nine percent have-nots.

Hearing the door chimes, Od paused in his musings and directed his attention to the front door. A lady of uncertain age entered the shop and waved at him.

"Good morning, Helen," he said.

"Beautiful day, it is," she replied as she walked toward him.

"I haven't seen you recently. How have you been?" he inquired.

"Oh, just the normal aches and complaints for my station in life. No more, no less."

"No serious health issues–that's good."

"I need a new comb and brush. Where would they be?"

Od led her to a table with personal grooming products. She set her bag down and began inspecting the combs and brushes while Od returned to his desk.

Helen was a longtime resident of the neighborhood, yet she had no permanent residence. She stayed with friends, a few days here and several days there, a round of temporary homes. Most residents of the neighborhood were delighted when she visited them. She received a small amount of social security and took part-time jobs. She frequently assisted Mary Rainbow at the Inn as a chef. Her dishes and soups were excellent, often prepared with ancient recipes she had learned from her grandmother. Helen owned few things, and all her worldly possessions were contained in a cloth bag she always carried with her. Her mind was agile and her thoughts clear– one of the sharper seniors Od knew. Like Hank, her male counterpart, she was a respected member of the community. Technically, according to the government, both Helen and Hank were homeless persons. But Od recognized them as itinerants, wanderers who journey through life on a personal quest.

With comb and brush in one hand and her bag in the other, Helen walked to Od sitting at the desk. Od conducted the financial part of the business there. He maintained his business records and transactions in a laptop located on the desk. For the few cash transactions he kept a metal cash box in a desk drawer.

Placing the comb-brush set on the desk, Helen said, "I don't have much to trade." Reaching into her coat pocket, she retrieved a small brooch. "I've had this for years, but I don't wear it much."

Od took the brooch and examined it. "This is an antique and quite valuable besides the many memories it holds for you. Do you still have your old comb and brush?" He returned the brooch.

"Only the brush. The comb had lost too many teeth, and I threw it away." She rummaged in the cloth bag and removed a brush, handing it to Od. The brush had some of its bristles missing.

Od took the brush and inspected it, holding it up to the light. "Okay. Your old brush for the comb-brush set you selected. I can use the brush for cleaning. What do you say?"

Helen laughed. "You're silly, Od. I do appreciate your kind offer. Yes, I'll trade." She placed the comb-brush set in the bag. "I'm chef at the Inn for lunch today. The soup will be based on a recipe my grandmother taught me. You best be there." She smiled and turned toward the door.

"Thanks for the invite. I'll plan to have two bowls." He waved as she left the store.

He smiled inwardly. Both Helen and Hank exuded a spiritual light. His musings started up with a religious flavor. He considered several of the books in the religious section that touched his mind deeply.

During the first, second, and third centuries CE many Christian denominations arose and spread their own interpretation of Jesus and his teachings. Some of the groups vied for leadership and control of the new faith. During the fourth century a set of beliefs became the official Christian creed supported by the Roman Emperor. The beliefs and teachings of all other Christian communities were declared heretical by the imperial religious establishment. The name 'Gnostic' was often applied to many of these 'heretical' Christian churches. And it was the heresy that captivated Od, having followed a less traveled path most of his life.

The word 'gnosis' is the basic term, derived from the Greek and meaning knowing or knowledge. The way these Christians applied the word was to denote an inner knowing, a direct spiritual knowing rather than a belief based on faith and worldly authority.

In the religion section were several books on Gnostic thought. One in particular had caught his attention, *The Secret Revelation of John* (or *Apocryphon of John*). It was an early Christian work, written in the second century CE, that gave a comprehensive account of the nature of God, origin of the world and human salvation. The cosmology was complex and, from Od's modern temperament, extravagant, yet he felt an affinity. Many of the work's ideas paralleled some of his social and economic concepts.

The Secret Revelation presented a cosmic system with a hierarchy of divine beings. The creator god Yaldabaoth, often imaged as a serpent with a lion's head, was also called Demiurge after the creator god in Plato's *Timaeus* and had many assistants or administrators. The cosmic system reflected the governing structure of the day, the Roman Empire and many small states with a king and aristocracy. The favorite form of government was a dictatorship pure and simple. The idea of democracy would have been considered treason and heresy.

At this nexus in time Od had a moment of enlightenment, the idea of a game. Because the political government reflected the religious cosmic governance, Od understood the parallel to the contemporary economic system. Those at the top, the one percent, controlled all those below, a pyramid structure, which has been the dominant social form for a long time.

As he considered a design for the game, a name for it emerged into his awareness: Archon Empire. Archon was the name for Demiurge's chief administrators, who were often viewed as the seven assistants involved in creating the cosmos and ruling it. But the Gnostics who used such symbolic allegory had a deity towering over Demiurge and its Archons: the true, unknown transcendental deity, the source and origin of all.

Here was the seed for his game; it would be not only a board and digital game but one that he would live. He had sought a new direction and he had found it.

Chapter 5

I stood observing the building carefully. It was a large two story frame dwelling built in the 1920s or earlier. It was an imposing structure. One of the oldest houses in the neighborhood, it had a feeling of ancestry and history.

The night was pleasant, a clear sky and waxing moon. A slight ocean breeze gently caressed me. I envisioned another night and different weather conditions: dense, wet fog creeping in from the ocean enveloping the houses in ghostly gossamer. An edge of suspense and a sense of danger lurking in the darkness would set the stage for a Dashiell Hammett mystery.

As I walked up the steps to the front stoop, I was ready for the strange and weird, perhaps perils hiding in the shadows, but the night played different music, that of science and the unknown. When the door opened to my bell ring, Jerry Meadows invited me in, and I began an adventure that changed my life.

As Jerry guided me around the first floor offices, I noted a quietness, not only because of the evening hour but of seriousness of purpose and dedication to knowledge. When we entered Philip's office, he was busy typing on his computer. Looking up at our entrance, he paused in his work.

"Welcome to our Institute where we're exploring the frontiers of knowledge, ye seeker of the truth."

Grinning at the levity, I sat down in a bulky, cushioned armchair meant more for a living room than a research office. At that point Jerry left to attend to his own activities.

"The first thing, Ralph, is a tour of the Institute and especially the testing labs. Shall we?" Philip rose and so did I, following him into the hallway.

"Jerry showed you the office layout of the first floor. The second floor is similar. Let's take a look."

There were more offices on the second floor. Jerry and Geri had theirs on that level. Philip mentioned the senior members of the Institute chose their office locations and most selected the first floor. Back to the first floor then, Philip lead me to an elevator.

"Now for the most important part. We have the testing labs in the basement area. With the type of experiments we do a quiet and secure environment is required."

Leaving the elevator, we proceeded along a corridor with labs on both sides. At the end of the corridor was a metal door, like a fire door to protect separate sections of a building. The door had a very special lock. It was a code and hand scan registry system. I was intrigued. What was so important behind the door? When we stepped through, I realized my life had branched into unknown territory. I would never be the same.

"No doubt you're wondering about the security. The labs in this section have highly sophisticated equipment which is expensive, astronomically so. We are outside of the building and in a subterranean structure in back of the house and adjacent to Sutro Heights Park. Overhead is undeveloped land. The labs are soundproof. Our most controversial experiments are conducted here, and of course the security is impeccable. Otherwise, our critics will complain that the results occurred because of faulty control. Leaks in security caused compromising information to become available to the subjects of the tests—that's a typical excuse for denying the results."

Philip showed Ralph several of the labs. "Our labs are equipped with a sound-video monitoring system. All activity is totally recorded from four angles. No part of the lab is hidden from view. When the subject enters the room and closes the door, it is locked automatically, so no one else can enter without unlocking it. The door can be unlocked manually from inside in case of an emergency. After the testing period ends, the door automatically unlocks."

"Where is the person conducting the test? Where would you be seated?" Ralph asked.

"As the tester I would be in my office working on other matters. I wouldn't be watching the test nor viewing any results yet."

Ralph was definitely puzzled. "Not watching? Why?"

"When you begin taking the tests, you'll understand directly so let me just say my watching might contaminate the results or at least some critics could say so. You'll be starting with simple ESP sessions, similar to those performed for more than seventy years, beginning at Duke University."

Philip peered at Ralph with an intensity that shone. "For example, psychic energy crosses many barriers and travels distances. We're talking about the essence of mind power. What if the tester unintentionally uses mind power to corrupt the results by sending mental content to the subject?"

Ralph was astounded. "You mean the tester telepathically communicates with the subject. Now that is a mind-altering concept. The notion sounds more like science fiction."

Philip realized Ralph was hooked and now was the time to reel him in. "Yes. In advanced psychic studies we must consider the reality of such power. If we don't, our critics will fry us."

"That's ironic. Critics who don't believe in psychic power say you mentally fixed the results."

"Actually, some critics do think such an energy exists, but they won't tolerate messy experiments. Everything must be neat, clean, and rigorous. Remember, we're at the frontier of science, and the dominant paradigm will not change easily. Science is still based on nineteenth century philosophy of materialism. Nothing exists except matter which is quantifiable. Many scientists believe psychic energy is only a superstition, a metaphysical hobgoblin."

Having received his BA in philosophy at San Francisco State University, Ralph felt he was in his own element. Of course, the older philosophy had grounded science, but it no longer provided a conceptual foundation. Findings in many branches of science could no longer be explained by materialism. The exotic, yet real, happenings in quantum physics, cosmology, and biology required a new set of concepts espousing a new paradigm. Two important holes in the traditional philosophy occurred toward the end of the nineteenth century and beginning of the twentieth: the Michelson–Morley experiment and the discovery of radioactive decay. Suddenly the basic elements, stable building blocks of matter, were found to be changeable. And light was behaving in peculiar ways.

"Philip, I'm on board for your project. One thing, though–is there a secrecy oath?"

Philip chuckled. "Well, certainly not like national security or anything of such a nature. But we don't want gossip going around about the project until the results are published. It's more like being silent until we're ready to go public. Is that okay?"

"Yes. I was thinking I might be able to use some ideas as thematic material for my new magic show."

"A new show? How much have you developed?"

"At the moment, I'm working on the basic design. I plan to take my interest in alchemy a step further. I want to explore the psychic level of reality more fully."

"Sounds great. Only promise you'll discuss any ideas you might apply to the show before you go too far."

"Agreed. Now when do we start?"

"No tests today. We're only at the introductory stage. Let's go back to my office. You need to fill out some forms, mainly your background including interests and hobbies. Part of the analysis correlates the subject's background with test results. I'll give you more details of the work the Institute is doing. And I believe you'll enjoy viewing our library, which you'll be able to borrow from."

Chapter 6

The cool ocean breeze was invigorating, tingling her senses. Feeling vibrant, Rafé Courbet strode along Holloway Avenue toward her apartment in Ingleside Terraces. The afternoon theater workshop had been exciting. Her mind was active, examining her performance and the perceptive comments given by her instructor and fellow students. Today had been the first hurdle, presenting the seed idea and a preliminary outline of her act. It had been a success. Now she was ready to begin the next stage, selecting traditional stories and preparing actual routines for the magic drama that would be her master's thesis. She turned on Alviso Street and walked to Urbano Drive. Her apartment was one of several in the large building, once a mansion in the 1920s for a wealthy San Franciscan family, at the corner of Urbano and Alviso.

Entering the two room apartment, Rafé set her bag on the couch, took off her jacket, and went into the kitchen area. She heated a pot of water and took a bag of green tea out of a basket containing an assortment of teas. After pouring steaming water into the cup, she carried the cup of tea into the social area and sat down in the comfy armchair facing the window.

From the view out over the neighborhood she could see the tall buildings at San Francisco State University. During the past year she had completed one stage of her life and started a new one. Rafé had received her BA with a major in theater arts in June. Now the real work and thrill of theater was only commencing with her enrollment in the MA program. Over the summer she had chosen the courses she would take and designed an outline of her master's thesis.

Her future was bright. She smiled. Once she had proven herself with academic success, she had applied for a scholarship for the MA program. Her people, the Citizen Potawatomi Nation in Shawnee, Oklahoma, provided scholarships and fellowships for many opportunities. Shortly before fall semester began, a letter had arrived, congratulating her for fine academic work and notifying her of the scholarship. Pleased, Rafé felt secure, knowing she had firm support of her people. With money from part-time magic performances and assisting Ralph Garland with his shows added to her resources, she wouldn't need to worry about finances but could concentrate fully on her studies and future career.

Another exciting change was her new roommate, Teri Rhodes. When her previous roommate Giulietta Firenze had received her degree in June, she had moved back to her home in Napa Valley where she planned to open a personal growth office. She thought the wineries and resort features of the region would provide enough people interested in her style of therapy and awareness development.

Now Rafé would share the apartment with Teri, who was a theater arts major in her senior year. Teri was a pleasant and quiet person, completely devoted to her studies and planning to enroll in the master's program the following year. If they got along, Rafé would have a roommate until she received her MA.

Setting the empty cup on the side table, Rafé got up and walked over to the desk and booted her laptop. Opening the thesis project document, she reviewed the ideas she had listed. The project was to design and execute a dramatic performance using magic routines that portrayed traditional Native American stories. She would become a Native storyteller, narrating Native People's stories with magic. Her inspiration for this style of magical performance was Ralph's Alchemical Light Show she had assisted with. It had been a daring and risky venture to portray occult themes and thoughts, yet it had worked well. Ralph had even produced a DVD of the show.

Last spring she had researched traditional Native American animal stories and chosen a few for routines. She had been performing them during her walk-around magic acts at Ocean Delights, a cafe on Ocean Avenue. She had shown two of these magical effects today at the theater workshop. Her teacher and the other students were amazed at her skill.

The first task involved selecting specific stories from different categories: creation, trickster, and self-affirming behavior that supported the community and nature. After the selection she could decide on particular routines and effects that best displayed the themes. She would allow part of her mind to catalog stories in the background while she studied for other courses. Because Teri was working tonight at a restaurant in Stonestown Galleria adjacent to the campus and wouldn't be home until after ten pm, she would have some serious study time.

After an hour of studying she had already lost her concentration. She wasn't tired–no, just the opposite. Her brain was buzzing with activity like a hive of honey bees. Something in the back of her consciousness wanted attention. Clearing her mind, Rafé went to the kitchen and heated water for tea. Walking over to the window, she peered out into the night. A raven. What about the raven, she wondered? Raven had spoken to her on her way home from campus. In fact, it had followed her and chattered constantly for several blocks.

She heard the water boiling and, returning to the stove, filled her cup with steaming liquid. With the cup of tea she moved into the living area and sat down. Yes, raven was announcing something of great importance. She would seek guidance from anhinga, her personal guide and Peyote Woman's water bird. Putting her cup on the side table, she went into the bedroom and retrieved her shawl and a cedar box containing sacred objects used during a Native American Church service. Wrapping the fringed shawl decorated with a water bird motif around her shoulders, she returned to the living area and opened the box.

Her *mIshomes*, grandfather, had been a Roadman, one who led the peyote ceremony, and his inner sight had told him several weeks before he was to pass over to the spirit world when the time was to come. She had made a special trip to be with him at his passage. He had presented her with the gift of his sacred possessions and a blessing to honor Peyote Woman forever. She was a member of the Native American Church and had her membership card that protected her from the mean spiritedness of the dominant society, in particular the federal and state governments. The card gave her the right to have an eagle feather and peyote in her possession. She often wondered why the government didn't require other churches to provide their members with cards so they could possess crosses or wine.

She selected the prayer feather. The shaft of the eagle feather was beaded using a peyote stitch. Twisted leather strips had been attached to the end of the shaft before the beadwork was stitched. Next she took the gourd rattle with an image of Peyote Woman painted on one side and a sunrise painted on the other. Both the rattle and prayer feather had been her maternal grandfather's.

Holding the prayer feather in one hand, she shook the rattle to the rhythm of an ancient peyote song. Humming to herself, she focused on the raven's message. The cawing had a discernible rhythmic pattern. An image formed in her mind: a horizon with the light of dawn spreading through the sky. It was the image of a new day, one of joy. The cawing in her awareness blended with the rattle becoming a different sound. It was the sound of a ceremonial drum voicing the heartbeat of mother earth. The drumming became louder sweeping away all clouds and darkness. A rainbow, Peyote Woman's symbol, joined her to the horizon glowing with dawn's light. Understanding flowed through her. A new day was coming, a time of joy and drumming. She would be prepared.

Chapter 7

Although Rainbow Inn was closed, lights shone through the windows. Fog had flowed in and enveloped Ocean Avenue and its denizens. Inside the Inn Mary, Od, and John were sitting around Mary's personal table, which always had a reserved sign on it. A pot of jasmine tea was in the middle of the table. John had doubled up with a side of dark chocolate mocha. He felt a desire to indulge himself. It was that kind of a night.

Since an exhibit at the California Academy of Sciences in Golden Gate Park had highlighted the history and virtues of cocoa and its many by-products, especially dark chocolate, Mary had crafted a variety of drinks using the indigenous American bean. Depending on the ingredients added to cocoa powder or syrup, the resultant mixture can be very nutritious and healthy or downright injurious. What many people considered chocolate was a mixture containing a large amount of sugar and dairy products, which of course were unhealthy.

Od was describing his new board game Archon Empire. "It's a pilgrimage from start to end. Archon tries to prevent a player from reaching the goal, the finish line. Archon sets up obstacles that can kill, maim, capture, or delay a player." Od radiated his pleasure at the game plan. "What do you think about it? Any suggestions?"

"What's the goal?" Mary inquired. "What rewards does a player receive?"

"It appears to be a pilgrimage through an arduous journey," John commented. "All those trials and tribulations happen to the player."

Od agreed, "Our life's journey from birth to death."

John drank some of his mocha before remarking, "That's not much of a reward, death I mean."

"It's a puzzle, a series of moves," Mary proposed. "Are there any chance elements like throwing dice or selecting cards at random?"

"I haven't got that far, but there could be," Od answered. "Randomness is part of reality."

Mary sipped her tea and then asked, "Do you think randomness exists or is it we just don't know and call our ignorance random or chance?"

Od declared with certainty, "Our ignorance of course."

"What about different options for choices, and we choose one rather than any of the others?" John posed.

"If we make the choice for any kind of reason, there's no randomness in our selection even if we flip a coin like flipism philosophy," Mary affirmed. "Our reasons may be faulty or foolish, but chance isn't involved in making the decision."

Agreeing, Od responded, "Yes, and our ignorance occurs because we don't know what the actual consequences are or will be."

Mary developed the thought. "There's always some uncertainty. It's like making moves in chess, thinking several moves ahead but not knowing the outcome because one doesn't know what the opponent will do. It's a best guess scenario."

"Yet life presents choices that aren't predetermined or destined, wouldn't you agree?" John offered. He sipped some tea, its flavor blending with the previous mocha taste.

Both Mary and Od nodded agreement.

John continued, "Well, is there an agency that presents particular choices? Why do these choices appear at this time? Why not other choices?"

Od's eyes shone. "Ahh, a basic cosmic dilemma."

Making her move quickly, Mary proclaimed, "To be or not to be, free will versus predestination. It's actually an unsolvable idea."

Od put down his cup. "Why so?"

"Because the issue can't be stated so it can be refuted or affirmed." Mary saw mate in two. "What type of experiment could be done?"

Perceiving the reality leak, John stated, "One of those basic assumptions we choose and take on faith. Okay, why choose one over the other? Some will choose free will and others predestination."

Mary acknowledged John's point and then declared, "There's a third possibility also. A combination of the two, a tendency toward one side or the other."

"Like a well-traveled path or a less-traveled one," Od suggested. "The well-traveled path has a large groove or channel that encourages a certain direction."

"Yes, like a river bed that becomes a canyon or gorge," John added.

"With less of a channel there's more potential for different options," Od affirmed.

"How does the discussion apply to the Archon game? Well, the game is obviously a mind game, at least if I were playing it. Like chess is." Mary brought the focus back. "Are there opponents or is it a single player against the board like so many computer games?"

John had an aha. "A single player or several can participate. And the goal at death is to have acquired advanced consciousness."

Mary looked at her two friends and smiled. "We're talking about a master mind, of course."

"Why it's the master game from John's vision we're now talking about," Od exclaimed.

Nodding, John said, "Yes. The fusion, the blending of both our games."

Mary was delighted. "It's a game of life from birth to death. Our goal is to increase our mind power or consciousness to the highest level, the master level, by the time we reach the end in death. Excellent. I'll play it."

Applauding, Od rejoined, "Aren't we all playing it now without realizing we are?"

John responded, "Perhaps a few individuals recognize the fact. Od, your game connects to some ideas I had recently about my vision and the master game based on it."

They both waited, sipping their tea, as John collected his thoughts. "The thesis underlying the master game," John paused momentarily and then continued, "involves psychic power like the Force in *Star Wars* or Tao in Chinese philosophy. It's definitely not the type of magic which uses spells, potions, wands," John chuckled, "broomsticks, animals, stone crystals. Now what would a mage do without them? Only mind power is available. Our goal is to raise our consciousness by applying mind power, but to do what? My basic concern is protecting and defending the environment. What other areas should we consider?"

"That's easy. Economic issues," Od replied.

Mary and John laughed.

"Of course, Od, we wouldn't have guessed you'd suggest economics. Actually, depending on one's view, all community issues are important," Mary remarked.

"I agree. I was thinking, though, about ecology and economics. They make a pair."

"In what way, John?" Od asked.

"Well, both words are derived from the Greek: *eco* means house; *logy*, from which the word 'logic' is derived, denotes order or arrangement; *nomy* implies management. So ecology designates the ordering or relationship of the parts to each other and to the whole house. And economy deals with household management."

"Yes. Oh my. The house is our environment, Mother Nature. John, that's a superb thought." Mary exuded delight.

"Indeed, if we're not managing our household properly, we'll soon be impoverished. The next stage is extinction." Od was adamant.

John shone with an inner light. "A sudden thought. Real, everyday models for our eco-twins are Hank and Helen."

The two seniors had lived in the neighborhood for years. Just as no one knew their last names, their past histories had been lost in the sands of time. They were Hank and Helen, unrelated to each other, living their own separate lives. They were guardians of the neighborhood.

"Of course," Od noted, "Hank is the economic side." Od had always admired Hank's street smarts and practical skills.

"Then Helen is the ecologic part," John replied.

Mary was laughing. "Do they know this or are we just laying a persona on them?"

"Definitely the latter. An image in our mind that gives energy to our game design," Od affirmed.

John remarked, "We could inspect their thoughts and feelings about the economic meltdown and the serious ecologic issues."

"Here are two people who are on the edge of the community looking inward toward the social power at the center and outward at the wilderness," Mary declared.

Od agreed. "They're definitely aware of the power structure and its operating system."

"No blindness there," John exclaimed. "Total clarity for both."

"They might be too cynical for most people who stick to their fantasyland view of reality," Mary proposed.

"People of total denial." Od was on a roll.

John was thoughtful. "Deniers create their own world, but that's what we all do, isn't it?"

Mary the realist commented, "Yes, but when confronted by the facts we should adjust our view to correspond to the world. One of the beauties of chess is players must always accept the given situation as it is. They can't fancify it or they lose. Chess is a reality-test game."

"For many people it's difficult, a challenge to make such an adjustment," John stated.

"What if they have reality leaks?" Od grinned at his friends.

"I'm available to help them," John offered.

They all laughed.

Mary stopped the discussion of the master game. "It's time to replenish the teapot. John, do you want another dark chocolate mocha?" John nodded in affirmative. She glanced at Od, "Anything more than tea?"

"No, tea's fine," he replied.

When Mary returned, having refilled everyone's cup, she brought the focus back to the blending of John and Od's games. They agreed the basic structure of the game was Od's Archon Empire. The Demiurge and its Archons ruled the cosmos. The game, however, would focus on the Earth since that was where they lived. Eventually they might extend their range of action and play into the solar system and perhaps through the galaxy into the remainder of the universe. It was John's vision and Od's game design, but Mary was conducting the event.

"Our journey through life isn't a straight path but has many twists and turns, yet we all end at death. The goal is to have as much consciousness as possible at the finish. It's not a competition where players seek to have a greater quantity than others but for each individual to gain as much as she can," Mary proposed.

"The Archons have placed obstacles on our path to prevent our gaining any more consciousness than the little we received at birth," Od asserted.

"Maybe the Archons are even trying to diminish that amount and turn us into robotic humans." At the moment John was perceiving the absolute depths of reality.

Mary picked up the teapot and topped off everyone's cup. Posing the issue of raising consciousness, the central goal of the master game, she queried their views. After sharing and critically examining their opinions, they agreed people have many choices and, depending on their talents, they should use the methods best suited to overcome an Archon challenge. Because all mental powers would be available–psychic, the Force, Tao–they would use these powers to perform particular actions while participating in current events.

They would support Gaia against their Archon opponents: they were Gaia's defenders. Accepting the eco-twins Helen and Hank as their guides, they would design an overall strategy for opposing the Demiurge and its minions. On specific issues they each would devise tactics fitting to their particular talents. Thus they would operate from consensus following their individual path.

As Mary picked up the teapot, Od raised his hand. "No more please."

"I'm finished too," John commented.

"Shall we adjourn for tonight then?" Mary suggested.

"Second, Od said.

"Make that unanimous," John affirmed.

Chapter 8

Sitting in South Park, Marilynn Raylon finished composing the new entry and pushed the send button. Putting the tablet on her lap, she leaned back against the park bench. She felt happy, invigorated by sharing in the Imaginative Journey Game on cosmiclefty.com. One of many participants, she had joined the game last year. All participants were involved in writing LC's novel. LC had supplied the basic structure, underlying themes, and central characters. And he maintained control of the story's overall direction. Its working name was Global, but near its completion they all would be involved in selecting an appropriate title.

She had never thought of herself as a writer, yet she was enjoying the new project and realizing a talent for imaginative thinking. Each contributor could add up to four characters to the story and narrate their journey through the many-layered reality of LC's fantasy world. So far she had entered two characters Fallyn and Roger. Today she had composed a new episode for Fallyn, describing her travel plans to Hawaii. Marilynn's creative endeavor was sent to the author who then inserted the new material into the story and updated the work-in-progress online.

The website also hosted a chat room where participants could exchange ideas and discuss their writing. She was considering introducing a third character to the story and had already presented the idea to other members. She was now awaiting their suggestions.

Marilynn glanced around South Park and observed people as they sat eating lunch or texting. Others were leisurely strolling around the park grounds. Placing her tablet into her purse, she stood and walked toward a highrise office building across the street from South Park. Lunch break was over, and she would be busy in the afternoon before quitting time arrived.

Clicking the save icon, Lefty Cosmos pushed back from the computer. He had been toiling on his novel for three hours and needed a break. His writing was the central project of his life, and he envisioned the novel as a global enterprise, involving the internet community. The story mirrored his creative project. Kindred souls were joining his online community and participating in writing his cyber novel.

He required time to develop the underlying role Marilynn Raylon, an important character in the story, was to play. He had already identified several characters who formed the story's nucleus. They were people the dominant themes revolved around and initiators of the main action.

Walking over to the loft's windows, he looked out at South Park below. He had a five year lease on the loft located in the upscale South of Market Area or SOMA of San Francisco, near downtown and the bay with its smart cafes, bistros, and boutiques. His employer Pacific Highloft Security was only two blocks away.

After the workday ended, he had hurried home to work on his literary creation. He was occupying a piece of real estate in cyberspace and terraforming it into his own landscape. People were learning to use their new Commons. Sharing and communal activities were gaining participants from all over the globe. Energy and enthusiasm were increasing among cyberspace residents. His creative actions were another ripple in the immense tidal wave that was occurring.

Shadows had darkened the park and street lamps were illuminating the neighborhood. An inner voice called, suggesting his favorite bistro was the next item on the evening's agenda. Pivoting, he strolled into the loft's central area, an open space circular in shape, and entered the bedroom, another of the twelve rooms radiating off the central hub. Once he had completed his grooming, Lefty put on his party jacket with its spacious pockets, checked his money supply, and joined the nightlife of South Park.

The sky was partly cloudy allowing a few stars to be visible. A warm breeze enhanced the pleasantness. He walked across the park, which had the same name as the neighborhood, to the other side where Bistro Royale was located. Royale served a fine variety of liqueur coffees that measured up to his high standards. Entering, he glided among the many patrons already enjoying Friday night's activities. He went directly to a table where his friend Charlotte was sitting with a male companion he didn't recognize. She leased a loft on the second floor of his residence building and was employed by the neighborhood's most popular boutique, Dorothy of South Park, offering the finest in ladies' apparel and accessories.

Charlotte saw him as he approached the table and waved. She nudged her companion, who also looked at Lefty. When he reached the table, Charlotte introduced him to her companion Bruce. Shaking hands with Bruce and touching fingers with Charlotte, Lefty seated himself.

"Lefty is employed at Pacific Highloft Security," Charlotte remarked to Bruce.

"What's your job description, Lefty?" Bruce asked.

"I'm a programmer and systems analyst. My specialty is cyber security, developing shields against the menaces lurking in cyberspace."

"You've prevented several hacking attempts, haven't you?" Charlotte was encouraging him to tell one of his exciting security tales.

"Tell us about them in all their gory details," Bruce requested. "I'm a software developer and we can share stories."

The waitress arrived and took orders. They all chose liqueur coffee, but each selected a different liqueur. Baileys Irish Cream was Lefty's choice. Tonight he would indulge and enjoy the weekend's start. He had the next two days to spend on his literary project.

Chapter 9

Shasta sat at her round table in the living room. A bright fire in the wood-burning stove insert in the hearth was warming. The stove was set into the old fireplace, which never worked well, producing more smoke than fire. The wood stove was ideal and very efficient too. She had studied her journal entries for the past week. Ideas for her new story were there hidden among the chatter and noise of her thoughts. She was seeking a seed that would grow into a new adventure for the investigative firm of Peaches Peoples.

Lucy was napping on the far edge of the table next to a pile of magazines. Karma entered the living room with Ralph following. Jumping onto the couch, Karma curled up and watched the activities. Carrying two glasses filled with martinis, he put one on Shasta's table and the other on a small table beside the couch.

Shasta picked up the glass and sipped the martini. "Yes, extra dry. Very tasty. Thank you, dear."

"At your service." He smiled at her.

"How was the first day of your psi project?" she inquired.

After the Friday evening interview and guided tour of the Institute, Ralph began his participation the following Tuesday.

"Well, the hours are good, two to three pm two days a week, Tuesdays and Thursdays, but the pay is nonexistent."

"From what little I've read about psychics, they normally give their service free for the public welfare."

"Like assisting the police. Yes, I've read that too. So I'm doing my pro bono service. Yet I think I'll gain some benefits."

"Such as."

"Ideas and thematic material for the new magic show I'm designing."

Shasta peered into the fire, watching the moving fiery forms. "Perhaps I can benefit too if you'll share ideas and experiences. I'm at a closed door. Nothing is coming through at the moment."

"I'm delighted. That would be great. You know, I feel like a lab mouse, and although I do share my responses with Philip and the twins, it's not the same as opening up and talking about my experiences in an intimate way with you."

"Like sharing our dreams."

"Definitely. Let's treat my project as a set of strange and perhaps surreal dreams."

"A parallel universe or alternate reality."

"Indeed."

"And what kind of tests are you doing?"

"At the moment basic ESP prediction tests. I guess what the next ESP symbol will be."

"You've known Philip for quite a long time. When did you meet?"

"Back in the late 1960s. He's a few years younger. It was at a workshop on consciousness and techniques to expand it."

"Ah, the spirit of the times. Everything was so alive then."

"And the energy flowed between extremes."

"Yes, love and brutality. Often the social events were excruciating yet at times tender and touching."

"Philip had completed his doctorate in psychology at Stanford. He had a strong interest in consciousness and its potential applications, especially in the field of psychic research."

"Weren't scientists studying brains waves and their beneficial uses?"

"In fact, the principal speaker at the workshop was Charles Tart, a pioneer in brain wave research using bio-feedback devices. Later he branched out into psychic research."

"The alpha wave was found to enhance meditation."

"We stayed in contact. I was deeply involved in philosophic issues of the mind. The ideas available then sustained my search for a way to express them in magical form, routines that purport to be real psychic actions. And Philip was enchanted by my view of the field and wanted to learn about the magician's role and the mentalist's act."

"I remember. You were performing some mentalism at the Magic Cellar for awhile."

"The times were alive with magic. New and imaginative realities beckoned." Ralph smiled, an inner awareness shone forth. "But I discovered it wasn't the most popular act for a mage. Spectators wanted more of the traditional approach. I think the setting at the Cellar also encouraged such an attitude."

"It had many props that belonged to Carter the Great, didn't it. I also felt I was at an old time vaudeville performance."

"Philip had gained employment with the Stanford Research Institute (SRI) and worked in psychic investigation. Many of SRI's projects were contracted by the federal government. Some were super secret at the time, such as research in what was then called ESP areas—remote viewing and other unusual mental activities. The federal government finally stopped funding the projects when word leaked public money was being used for unscientific new age inquiries.

"Of course, supposedly Russia was involved in psychic studies, and the US didn't want to lag in the superiority race, as we had done with sputnik.

"That recent film *The Men Who Stare at Goats* about the military attempt to use psychic forces—that was a comedic takeoff on those projects that began in 1970s." Ralph rose from the couch and went over to the hearth. He put a wood log into the stove. After he had returned to the couch, Lucy leaped down from the table and jumped into his lap. He began petting her as he resumed the narrative.

"During his tenure with SRI Philip attended a lecture by Edgar Mitchell, the Apollo 14 astronaut. Mitchell's psychic experiences, including telepathic experiments on the spaceship, deeply influenced Philip, who had a type of epiphany. He spoke with Mitchell after the lecture and was so completely impressed with him he became involved with the Institute of Noetic Sciences (IONS). Mitchell had founded IONS in 1973. It's still doing challenging work on the edge of scientific thought."

"I've heard of it but have never paid it much attention. What exactly does 'noetic' mean?"

"It's derived from the Greek word 'nous' and IONS uses it to mean 'intuitive mind' or 'inner knowing.' They occupy a central part of contemporary psychic research."

"Let's pause here. I need to check on dinner. And you might refresh our martinis."

Ralph got off the couch and followed her into the kitchen. The kitties were leading the parade, hoping for treats.

The aroma from the oven was tantalizing. "What's for dinner?"

"Curry lamb casserole."

Once they had resettled in the living room, Shasta asked, "The twins, I'm curious about them. They seem so different, strange."

"I don't know too much. They're unusual, I agree. But I don't quite know the reason for their oddness."

"When I first met them, I thought they were a married couple. Their features are so dissimilar. I was surprised when we learned they're twins."

"Blond Geri and brunette Jerry."

"But the eye colors, so totally unexpected. Geri's gray and Jerry's blue."

"And their facial features, a rather oval shape compared to a longish narrow shape."

The ashes in the stove glowed. Ralph rose and put another log in. "What's most remarkable is their background story. According to Philip, they were born in northern California and grew up in a tiny town called Likely near Alturas. They studied at Stanford, completing their degree, worked at SRI for awhile, and then did volunteer work at IONS where Philip met them. He was so fascinated by them and their interest in his field of research he gave them a temporary position at the Institute. They've done so well they now have a five year contract for the project."

"Okay, sounds good, so what's the issue?"

"Philip doesn't completely believe their story. All the information he has checked is accurate, but he has some doubts. And he doesn't understand what their goal is."

"If they're performing well, good at their job, what more can he expect. I can understand that situation."

"The twins have developed several refinements for the energy exchange process and are very excited about their work. Philip has a fine team whatever secrets lie hidden in their past."

Shasta glanced at her watch. "It's time to fix the veggies. We can continue the discussion later."

Chapter 10

Philip stopped reading. Bookmarking the volume, he put it on the table beside him. He rubbed his eyes. Stretching his arms in the air, he yawned. Getting up from the chair, he went into the kitchen and made coffee with his coffee maker. He should go to bed. It was midnight, and he had to be at the Institute early. But his mind was restless. Sheldrake's book stimulated his thoughts. Ideas were clustering and generating links. Placing the mug on the table, he sat down at the computer and stared at the screensaver depicting a series of waterfall images.

Rupert Sheldrake's recently published *Morphic Resonance* offered researchers in many disciplines innovative ideas and a conceptual framework that could assist in explaining the many scientific findings of the last fifty years or more. When his first book, *A New Science of Life*, had come out in 1981, it had created an intense controversy. An editorial in *Nature* had stated emphatically the book was "the best candidate for burning there has been for many years." Sheldrake's investigations continued to be unsettling to many. He still had his name-calling critics and his supporters.

As a participant in the twenty-first century scientific movement toward a better and more accurate theoretical support of the evidence, Sheldrake was in the forefront. Philip had attended Toward a Science of Consciousness Conference in 2008. Sheldrake's paper "The Evolution of Telepathy" was a cogent and impressive stone in the new foundation of science.

His hypothesis of formative causation, which has frightened many in the scientific community who constantly stay within their conditioned, habitual patterns of thought, proposes that "nature is habitual. All animals and plants draw upon and contribute to a collective memory of their species."

Philip opened the document that contained his conceptual framework. He had added morphic fields to his ongoing theoretical development. A primary concept in contemporary thought proposes nature and its laws are in process, constantly evolving. In a sense nature 'learns' with time and experience. Humans as a part of nature are a prime example. When quantum physics began to emphasize fields as a model of explanation, other disciplines acknowledged the concept as important. The radical change in cosmology had, of course, destroyed any hope for a revival of nineteenth century materialism.

For years Philip had thought a field theory with its wave frequencies is the foundation for all psychic phenomena. Consciousness equals resonance. Consciousness requires a specific personal form to leave its precise imprint in a field. Sheldrake's concepts of morphic fields and formative causation had the rigor and depth to provide the model.

Actually, the true problem was psychological. Human nature, like its parent, was habitual. Most of the time habits were beneficial and led to survival, until the environment changed. And then–Philip started writing.

As a researcher he had basic ideas, assumptions, that were the foundation for his work and search for knowledge. They were intuitive and as yet unconfirmed. The primary idea implied psychic power was an exact mode of natural energy existing throughout the universe. Its domain and proper scale were yet to be determined. But it was there. Once the energy's place along the cosmic scale was fixed, rules and laws of its domain would be accessible. Natural laws were related to the scale of the domain they were governing. When the scale changed, the rules could change too. His project was to disclose the process of psychic power and study it.

The project's results so far confirmed the morphic field idea. Ralph's excellent performances had directed Philip's thinking in an alternate direction, one that could be the potential for another stage in evolutionary consciousness. If psi power had morphic fields for different species, then learning to apply the energy would become easier as more individuals practiced and performed. It was the Hundredth Monkey Story pure and simple. Many skeptics called it an exception and others just repressed the data, forgot it, a psychological escape mechanism humans apply too often. Definitely Ralph was an exception. His results stood out like a beacon in the fog. Philip smiled at the metaphor.

He stopped writing and stood up. Curiosity touched him. What was the night like anyway? He walked over to the window in his study and pulled back the curtains. Hey, it was foggy, a heavy wet fog. Perhaps he was resonating with a morphic field. He listened for the foghorns mounted on Golden

Gate Bridge. Ahh, he heard one. Good, he thought, all is well. He returned to the computer.

Ralph is an individual, he began writing, who has a hidden talent that can be developed. No doubt, there are many individuals like him, waiting to be discovered and assisted in fulfilling their potential. Ralph's paranormal performances were a first step in establishing a morphic field for his personal psi waveform that would reside within the general psi field. The twins had suggested more challenging experiments for Ralph, and he had liked the idea immediately. Ralph's psi waveform would have the opportunity to increase its presence in the general field. The twins, they were something else. He was curious about them but didn't pursue his questions. After the project ended, he could go further in his findings.

He thought of Ralph's participation in the energy exchange tests. The evidence confirmed Ralph had an unconscious influence on the pressure balance between positive and negative pressure flow. When Ralph had heard the results, he had acted surprised and amazed, yet, Philip felt, Ralph had suspected some type of active involvement in the event.

Even Shasta and the kitties had been active, though unconscious, participants during the original happening at their home. Smiling, he recognized Lucy and Karma's roles as familiars. Cats had a legendary history as being able to amplify and resonate psychic energy fields. And dogs too, as Jerry would insist. No doubt, they had a link to morphic fields that tied into human fields, an overlapping of sorts.

Does Ralph have any other psychic gifts, he wondered? And does Shasta? He thought about her, so warm and charming. A good chance she does. Perhaps the twins could coax her into a few trial runs. I'll ask them to encourage her.

He stopped and rubbed his eyes. Glancing at his watch, he decided it was time to sleep. A good dream would be helpful, he thought. He would prepare his mind for dreaming.

Chapter 11

Rainbow Inn was quiet, and the stillness gave Mary a feeling of serenity. Business had been brisk, and now she could relax. She was in a pensive mood. Sipping a cup of seven herb tea, she reflected on the events of the past week. Both John and Od were in high spirits, bursting with enthusiastic energy and ready to begin a new chapter in their lives. Their energy, especially combined, warmed her. The serendipity was amazing. Both were inspired at the same time as if some cosmic button had been pushed, igniting a change in vision. And that's what it was, a transformation in their worldviews. Well, not really a fundamental change but a new direction and apparently a new quest. After all these years she had gained basic insights into her two closest friends. They were similar in many ways. Both had a strong sense of purpose and a determination to match. Both were willing to take risks if they thought benefits would accrue. And both had a sharp, penetrating intelligence although they applied it in their own way.

Emotionally, they were completely different. John expressed his emotions and feelings freely without restraint. His emotions were varied, complex, and often intense. Not a simple emotional display for him but a mixing, a blend of feelings finely tuned. Od, on the other hand, was reserved, and although deep down his feelings were intense and strong, he controlled their energy flow. An emotional display was not Od's style. A subtle and clever manner was most appropriate for him.

Mary smiled inwardly. She was more similar to Od in this respect. John was a rainbow of many feelings. His emotional indulgence glued the bond among them.

They were all approaching their senior years. She was definitely uncertain of her attitude about the end game. What would be her strategy? And more importantly what would be her long range purpose? Her mind required an integrated plan, one offering choices and branching paths. Both Od and John were indicating their vision was for the long range and would maintain them until they left earthly life. But would it? Would they soon find a new vision and go chasing after that?

She paused, thinking about the image: "a chasing after." Was that the truth of their quest? Only another journey seeking a hidden and undefined treasure? Perhaps the essence of life's journey was only one quest after another. Well, if so, what quest should she choose? She had enjoyed their discussions about the master game. Their bonding was primarily on the mind level although they both attracted her in a sensual and physical manner.

Her quest—yes, she stood on the edge of the horizon peering in all directions. She turned and looked back over her past life and the many quests she had undertaken. Most were successful, some total failures, and others soon lost their attraction. After winning the world chess championship by beating Sam Runner, she had held her title for four years before retiring undefeated. She had gone up against the world's best players, all masters at the game, and deftly retained her title.

Chess was now less important in her life. She still hosted chess tournaments at the Inn for Bay Area chess clubs. She enjoyed giving lessons to bright and devoted students. And Thursday evenings the Inn stayed open until ten pm for serious chess players. Besides the drama of chess, the Inn's stage had seen numerous dramatic performances. The Players, a neighborhood drama club, continued to entertain with their Saturday night shows. Music remained a source of joy and gave her solace when a dark cloud hovered over her. More down moods seemed to beckon now than when she was younger. Aha, she smiled, the golden years might be only glittering fool's gold. Well, she was here and choices were available. It was time to view her options.

Traveling offers exciting experiences. I haven't done much, she thought. Those tour companies have many choices. I could meet new people, enlarge my group of acquaintances. Okay, traveling is a plus.

I could write my memoirs and do I have a lot to say. Yes. And a book or two on chess. My favorite games. A book about winning the world championship—that of course could be in my memoirs.

Oh my, I can see myself sitting in my rocking chair, twittering my friends. Ha! Not yet by any chance.

Surely, there are other opportunities. I'll let the thought settle in the back of my mind and sprout.

Sensing a presence, she glanced down and saw her orange tabby cat staring at her. "Shalom, how's my sweet kitty?" When she reached down, he got up and walked over to her and rubbed against her hand. "Do you have any thoughts for me?" She picked him up and cuddled him. "Well, Shalom, it's time we lock up and go home." She kissed him on top of the head, put him down, and they walked to the entrance and left.

She was restless and had awoken around 4:30. Her mind was busy, endlessly routing thoughts from one topic to another. She dressed and went to the front door. Her calico kitty Cresy was sitting there waiting to go out. Mary bent down and petted her. "Ready for the new day? Well, let's journey forth." Mary opened the door and Cresy bounded into the cool morning. Early light was breaking above the horizon. Mary's home was next to the Inn, and she entered the back door into the kitchen.

Moving quickly, she strode to the stage area and picked up her saxophone from its holder. She blew a few riffs and stopped. No, not the sax but a different sound, she thought. Replacing the instrument, she walked over to the drum kit. She tapped on one of the tom-toms for a few moments, but again the tonalities weren't what she wanted. Picking up the pair of bongo drums nearby, she sat down at a table and tapped out a rhythm. Not quite right yet, but close. The formless thought she had awoken with was taking shape. It grew from a desire deep inside, close to her soul and elemental feelings. A set of harmonic tonalities resonating together echoed in her mind. If she could find the instruments to make her soul music, she would be happy. She stopped playing the bongos and was silent.

Her goal, her quest, was clarifying. She knew in her being music was the source of her power in the master game. A composition, a theme-song–yes, she would perform and vibrate with music. The bongos were okay but not the sound she heard in her soul. A drum or percussion of some sort must form the basic tonality for the rhythm. Hearing the back door open, she placed the drums on the table and, getting up, walked into the kitchen.

Harriet, the Inn's chef, was hanging up her coat. "Good morning, Mary."

"Morning, Harriet. What a pleasant day so far."

"I'll wait until noon before saying. Morning is when most problems suddenly appear." Harriet filled the hot water heater and then started making coffee.

Mary smiled at her. "I'll leave you to it. I'll check supplies for our weekly order." She went into her office. Booting the computer, she thought about her quest and then put the vision on hold as she opened the inventory spreadsheet.

Later that evening while a few remaining customers finished their meals, Mary sat in her favorite spot and surveyed the room. Her chair, unlike the restaurant's regular chairs, had special seat and back cushions. The table was small and suitable for her personal use, yet was large enough for her friends to sit at. No frustrations today. By noon Harriet was in a jolly mood, and the food delivery system was operating smoothly.

Now she released the hold on her vision. Relaxing, she heard the sounds that vibrated her body and mind. A feeling of sharp alertness surged through her. Her imagination projected a picture of several people seated around a large circular drum, a Native American drum group. Yes, she remembered the powwow last spring at San Francisco State University. The drums were large and produced a deep, vibrant sound. And the singing. Yes, with singing, often high-pitched, the combination was very close to her vision.

"Yes!" Her abrupt and rather loud shout startled the two remaining customers. She waved at them. "Would you like some music with your meal?"

When they both agreed, she picked up her sax and played a soft melody for the evening hour. She quit after the customers had left. Now to the drum kit and some rolls, she thought. As she warmed up on the tom toms, she envisioned a small Native American hand drum. She would check the internet for Native American drum sources. Members of the Native American Student Organization at SFSU could certainly give her advice on selecting a drum. Yes, a hand drum for personal use and–of course a large drum, powwow style for a group of drummers, the San Francisco Drum Group. Because the drum would be her magic wand to raise consciousness, the goal of the master game, she would call it San Francisco Consciousness Drum. They could hold sessions at the Inn. Perhaps someone from one of the Native American drum groups in the Bay Area could tutor them. She paused and then stashed the drumsticks.

Closing time was here, and her staff would be finishing up. When she returned home, she would begin making preparations for the next generation of consciousness drummers.

Chapter 12

Reaching over and turning off the alarm, Lefty Cosmos tugged the covers around himself for another hour or so of sleep. He had stayed at Bistro Royale until last drinks were called and dropped into bed soon after arriving home. Sleep with pleasant dreams was his wish, and he wasn't disappointed. It was close to noon when he did wake up and slowly got out of bed. He first turned on the coffee brewer before heading for the bathroom and a shower.

Dressed, refreshed, and ready to move, he filled his portable mug with a special brew made from Jamaican beans and set off for an afternoon of outdoor activities. The day's weather was warmer than normal and dry, the same it had been for more than a week. The global weather changes were causing a crazy winter. Normally it was the season for most of San Francisco's precipitation to occur. Drought, however, was on the horizon, and if the Sierra Mountains didn't receive sufficient snow, water rationing would be required in the summer.

The morning fog had disappeared. A gentle breeze from the bay flowed through South Park. People were enjoying the afternoon in the park. Lefty strolled about until he found an empty bench. Sitting down, he relaxed, sipping his coffee and allowing his mind to drift.

Thoughts flowed by, all linked to his novel. He decided to focus on the writing project. His website was gaining popularity. The increasing number of people commenting on his working novel was encouraging. Devoted fans and enemies alike were fueling his creative juices. He blended as many of the opinions as possible into the story. The chat room allowed surfers to express their thoughts and feelings, bringing to the work a diversity of views and talents that would produce a masterpiece. He closely monitored the chat room and had expelled a few persons for abusive behavior. Being an e-book and residing in the cyber zone, the novel would be comprehensive, unlimited by physical size or the creative ability of one individual and grow into a communal enterprise on a global scale. The basic framework and underlying themes would accumulate creative imaginings from many viewers.

He thought about the character Marilynn Raylon, a typical young woman in today's corporate society. Her attitude, views, and opinions were all shaped by the dominant corporate culture. She and her colleagues in the corporate world populated the novel. They were the new middle class, the managers for the corporate elite, the one percent. They were the nine percent, devoted to their social, economic set and overseeing the activities of the remaining ninety percent of society.

Marilynn had a major role in the story because she would be involved in discovering the secret about the rulers and their agenda. She was a composite of several women acquaintances who held middle and top level managerial positions.

Lefty sipped on the straw in the coffee container and heard gurgling of emptiness. He decided time was at hand for food. Leaving the park, he walked to Crepes Cantata. He especially liked the crepes, and the coffee was decent.

Noticing several empty tables, he selected one by the windows. He could people-watch while he enjoyed a late afternoon repast. The waitress had taken his order when he saw Kathy Hamilton enter. She stood glancing about and then observed him waving and proceeded to his table. When she reached it, he stood and they hugged gently.

As Kathy was sitting down, he gestured for the server to return and then sat. Once Kathy had placed her order, he asked her, "What's been happening? I haven't heard from you for a couple days."

"Ha. No one has. I've been immersed in my music. Phone's off, door's locked and my food supply's enough for several days. I came out now because I've the basic structure for my new piece written and my Muse has taken a holiday."

He smiled at her. "I've been quite involved in my novel so I haven't tried to contact you. It's serendipitous. We emerged from our cells at the same time."

She laughed. "Actually, I thought I might find you here. My intuition is fired up. So much creative energy."

The waitress brought their orders of crepes and coffee. They were silent as they ate. They had known each other for over a year and had formed an intimate bond. Lovers, yes, but more importantly close friends. They enjoyed each other's presence without the need for chatting.

After their meal they sat, lingering, watching the activities in the park. Kathy touched his hand. "I've a new CD I'd like you to hear."

Lefty liked most kinds of music, but his favorite style was jazz, especially fusion. "Whose music?"

Kathy composed in the modern classical style. Her pieces were usually for small ensembles. She considered her musical tastes to be global and fused melodies and rhythms from other cultures into her work. "It's Kronos Quartet's latest recording. It's fantastic."

Lefty beamed. "I'm ready for a holiday from my novel. Is tonight okay?"

"Definitely. We can listen all night. I've still got food for tomorrow."

"Let's stop by my place first. I've some wine I'd like you to sample. It'll be great for an all night session."

Chapter 13

The man leaned back in his executive chair. The data were troubling and indicated a potential security breach, which, if not contained, could develop into a major opening in the defensive wall. His global empire could easily be destroyed. Research at the Institute was on the verge of a breakthrough. He should have stopped the project at its inception. Now too many people were involved. His only choice was a risky venture. He would go in and disable the research, corrupt it so it wouldn't be acceptable to the scientific community.

His strategic idea was similar to entering and exiting a highly secure computer system without leaving any traces of his presence. Several of the subjects in Philip Austen's project were showing strong psychic abilities. If Austen and his team gave these individuals good training, they could tune into the Cosmic Psi Spectrum. The individual displaying the most promise was Ralph Garland, who had progressed quickly and surpassed anyone's expectations. The focus would be on Garland, at the moment the central figure in the project. Disrupt his behavior, throw his goals into doubt, weaken his confidence, and lead him onto a different path, one ending in failure.

He went online to his private account hosted at an invisible IP at one of his clouds and logged on. A virtual machine he had developed operated all his clouds which were located in different parts of the world. His primary site was in Cayman Islands, a renowned outsource for secret affairs.

He had specially designed the firewall to prevent ninety-nine percent of would-be attackers. The remaining one percent was the uncertainty principle, which couldn't be eliminated. The account was the gateway to the electromagnetic spectrum. His name for it was Ethereal Net. He liked the word 'ethereal' because of its ambiguity. A historical meaning was celestial, the upper regions of space, the invisible dimension. With modern technology a more apropos usage referred to a protocol analyzer. By surfing the Ethereal Net, he could capture and retrieve any and all signal and data traffic he wanted. All data were now available if located in the electromagnetic spectrum. With his cleverly crafted decoder he could break coded data. All information was at his fingertips. His empire was rooted in data, which fed and nourished his many businesses.

He entered a command onto the touch screen. Complete data on Ralph Garland started to gather. While he waited, inwardly pleased, he surveyed three monitors exhibiting his view of the world. Directly in front of him in the center of the workstation was a 55-inch monitor and on either side was a 46-inch monitor. Normally each side monitor displayed ten windows linked to specific channels. When a particular event caught his attention, he switched the affair to the central monitor.

The light indicating data retrieval was finished blinked. He logged off with his private signature—Tau, a name of diverse meanings as was his character.

He sat, silent, a vibrant energy surging through his spine. The sensation was exhilarating. He rose from the executive chair and, leaving the command bridge, descended five steps to the main area, which was sectioned into functional units located along its circumference. All the furnishings were those of a well-endowed CEO's office.

Tau ambled to the kitchen unit and removed a bottle of mountain spring water from the refrigerator. Opening the bottle, he swigged some water and strolled to the game station, which contained seven consoles. Tau was a techno-guy and had always loved technology. As a child he had delved into the operations of the electromagnetic field and played with many gadgets and mechanisms using its energy.

He sat down and turned on one of the consoles. He would play a game of his own design. It was programmed to increase its level of difficulty every time he won.

Chapter 14

John walked down Ocean Avenue feeling quite sprightly. A bounce was noticeable in his movements. He was headed to The Empty Hand, San Francisco's foremost magic store. Several other magic shops did business in the city, but Alice Moore's shop was the best, well-known among professional magicians and hobbyists. And it was one of the neighborhood stores.

The trio had decided they required equipment for their master game, tools to enhance their performance, things people would recognize and view as necessary for their craft. Mary had her musical instruments and chess pieces while Od could utilize anything in his Trading Shop. What can I use, John had wondered? His garden tools were available but that didn't feel right. Focusing on his vision, he had seen the answer. He was a magician and of course would need magician's equipment. So he was going to Alice's to outfit himself. And what a fine day to start an adventure. The fog was melting back toward the ocean allowing the sun to brighten the neighborhood.

Entering the magic emporium, John was beguiled by the sight of so many items, the working tools of the magician's trade. Glass cases were filled with strange and no doubt wondrous props. Alice Moore was talking to a customer so John browsed, letting the atmosphere soak in. He could learn much by sensing the different flavors of energy flowing around him. He went over to the book and magazine section and leafed through several books. He had thought carefully about his request and was prepared when Alice had finished serving her customer.

"Hi, Ms. Moore," he greeted the slender redhead, "I'm John Ocean. I'm interested in purchasing some magical routines and props."

Smiling brightly, Alice inquired, "What are you looking for?"

"That's it. I don't know because I've never performed magic before. I've only watched performances."

"Well, well, a newcomer and potential initiate."

He wondered about the meaning of that–an initiate. He answered, "Yes, I'm a beginner. What are some basic routines and props? I know about wands of course and definitely want one."

She replied, "The basics it will be. We have magic sets, but they're more for young beginners. I think you should start at the adult hobbyist level. Let's see what your interests are. What would you like to do? There are so many areas in magic: stage, close-up, mentalism, story-telling–these are some broad categories."

Laughing, John said, "I don't think I'm ready for the big stage yet, nor TV. I would like to entertain my friends. You know, vanish and produce things."

Alice looked at him intently. "Some sleight-of-hand routines then. Perhaps cards, coins, balls, things of that nature."

John nodded in agreement. "What does mentalism involve? Is it mind-reading and making predictions?"

With a flowing hand movement Alice responded, "Yes, those effects but, hey, a lot of others too. Hmm. Here's my suggestion. DVDs are available that present different types of magic. Magicians give performances and then demonstrate the workings of the routines. It's a teaching device. I would also suggest, actually more of a recommendation, you seek professional instruction. Take lessons from a knowledgeable pro."

A strong feeling of aha flooded John. "Yes, of course. I'll want assistance besides the DVDs. A teacher who can answer my questions."

A fiery sparkle in her eyes, she replied, "I know just the person, Ralph Garland. He's been in the business for years and has just released a DVD of his most recent performance, The Alchemical Light Show."

John was intrigued. "I'm definitely interested. Okay then, I would like a wand–that seems to be a badge of magic–several DVDs including Garland's, and his phone number.

When John left The Empty Hand, he was elated and felt as if he were levitating, yes a feeling of lighter than air.

Chapter 15

Sitting at the desk in my test chamber, I was caught up in a reverie, flowing fragments of thoughts, mainly memories. The morning had been rather chaotic and normal routines had been broken. Shasta was busy working on her novel when I climbed out of bed. She had gotten up at three am. The portal of her imagination had opened its floodgates and torrents of creativity filled her. I was distracted several times during my morning physical exercises and was doing a bad job of coping with the day. A dream I had shortly before waking seemed to be the source of mental disturbance.

And here I sat supposedly ready to start another remote viewing session. To gain my focus and enter my still point of the turning world, I went back to my first test at the Institute. If random memories were the culprit, series of linked memories should be the hero slaying the monster of distraction.

My first group of tests was a guessing game of predicting the forthcoming ESP card. A physical card wasn't used, but a keyboard and monitor were the equipment. Every ten seconds a green light lit, and I pressed one of five keys. Each had one of the ESP icons on it. When my response had been recorded, a predetermined ESP icon appeared on the monitor providing reinforcement, both positive and negative. This group lasted four one hour sessions. In the next group of tests I advanced to the stage where no feedback was given. For an hour with break time I punch every twenty seconds. Only later did I learn the results. And so my participation in Philip's project slowly developed.

More challenging tests were offered, and I became adept at taking psychic exams. Positive-negative energy pressure experiments followed the ESP sessions. I was given specific tasks to do. They all generated emotions. Some were frustrating, others pleasant. The most upsetting occurred when Jerry hurried into the lab and told me we had to get out of the building because it was on fire. He was excited and babbling about the fire department being called. I was caught by excitement and fear. As we hastened to the staircase,

I discovered an inner nexus that was calm. I dispersed the negative emotions and began exuding positive energy. By the time we had reached the first floor, the pressure was balanced. Jerry and I went into Philip's office, and I learned the event had been a test I passed successfully.

My scores on the different tests were quite good. Usually above chance, indicating a talent for this type of work. I vividly remember the afternoon Philip talked to me in his office about a new psychic adventure.

"Ralph," Philip was displaying a wry grin, "you have a definite gift for psi activities. The results of your tests are superior to most of our subjects. Congratulations."

"Thank you, Philip. I don't presume to know the reason for the gift, as you call it. I only respond on an intuitive level. I don't think I can take any credit." Inwardly I was elated. Some of my old and seemingly lost self-assurance was back.

"We have a rare treat for you. A delightful reward for your success. We've decided you're an excellent candidate for remote viewing. I've spoken about it before."

"Yes, I'm familiar with the activity. In fact, Shasta and I have seen the movie *The Men Who Stare at Goats*."

"It was the project the federal government contracted which brought the sky down on them when certain public leaders learned about it. And they shall be nameless."

"And it actually works, you're suggesting."

"The rumors, quite reliable ones, are certain federal agencies are still gathering data by remote viewing. Private industry in data collection has blossomed as much as the security industry. Really, the two go together."

"So my reward for good results is to become a remote viewer. I'm willing to try." My soul was overjoyed. Down deep I knew here was the journey that would change my life, the one leading me to the philosopher's stone.

"Wonderful." Philip exuded pleasure. "I'll contact the twins. They'll show you the techniques."

My practice sessions took place in the Institute's meditation room, located on the second floor at the back of the building. It was a corner room with windows on the two exterior sides facing Sutro Heights Park and the ocean. The window curtains could be closed darkening the room completely. And I did close the curtains thinking the fewer distractions the better. Later I left the curtains open and achieved better results in my meditation. I discovered a visible contact with nature gave me a feeling of serenity and allowed me to reach the meditative state more quickly. Once I learned to flow into my still point and merge into silence, I was ready to learn the choreography of distant viewing.

I tried several of the recommended procedures, but none was satisfactory. Early in the project Philip had given me a list of books in the Institute's library that might be helpful. The previous week I had read Joseph McMoneagle's *The Stargate Chronicles*, which describes his life and adventures performing psychic activities for federal agencies. He was particularly adept at remote viewing. And of course, I found his methods useful. His biting and rather bitter criticism of the federal government when it started its denial of the effectiveness of these activities and destroyed his career and smeared his character was eye-opening and confirmed other data I had read about the use and misuse and abuse of people with psi abilities. It made me think strongly about keeping such gifts secret.

Yet something similar occurred to Edgar Mitchell after he had returned from Apollo 14 voyage and published the results of his experiments. Mean-spirited critics and deniers arose and tried to discredit Mitchell. Such detractors have always been around. These bullies and terrorists seek to hide data, observations, and ideas they disagree with and often are frightened by. The truth, however, will eventually shine through.

My mental guide appeared in a dream. After Shasta and I had discussed the dream in detail, I realized its significance. Its main purpose was to reveal my remote viewing procedure. Besides my alchemical studies I had researched the craft of astrology.

Here I digress. At the basis of all knowledge that has been, is, and will be called science is craft. From this source all human knowledge has arisen and ultimately returns to. It is the human practice of making and doing that constitutes craft.

The natal chart contains twelve houses based on the twelve zodiac constellations. An individual's life can be seen as a journey through the twelve houses in twenty-eight year cycles. The idea of a passage through the houses was the illuminating lamp.

The design, which I developed and has given me success, constructs a mental mansion with twelve houses or rooms. Each room has its own furnishings which I have learned. I start the remote viewing session by getting into a meditative state and emerging into silence. When I am ready, I walk through the rooms, beginning with the first one. The natal chart has the houses in their sequence formed into a circle. I continue my journey until I reach a room that has a bright light, the illuminating icon. It is the house that links to the distant viewing site. In the room I find an object to focus on. Then I perceive the remote viewing site and its contents. It's like I'm there, totally there, seeing it from all directions in the round. When I'm satisfied, I leave the mind mansion and return to the test chamber, write my report and send it in.

It's easy and it's fun. Or has been until the last trip, the principal reason I'm so disturbed today. Philip wants me to return to the same site. Of course we're not performing the usual activity where I don't know in advance the site's location. Normally, viewing the chosen site confirms a certain paranormal phenomenon. Today, I'm to go back so I can overcome any fear or difficulty I might have acquired from last time's failing performance.

Having processed the memories of his past sessions through the last one, which he has placed into a hermetically sealed container as if it were a deadly virus, Ralph was now ready to enter the still point where silence reigns. He emerged into the first room and strolled through his mental mansion. Each room he went through was dimly lit indicating it wasn't the site room. The illumination was sufficient, though, to prevent him from bumping into any of the furnishings. He disregarded the suggestion of danger lurking in the darkness. He knew there was none. Yet the potential was always there, a ghostly presence deeply imprinted into his memories. The darkness could hide danger and threatening perils.

He paused at the portal of the twelfth house. It was the brightly lit place and where the monster hid waiting to destroy him as it nearly did last time. When the monster had appeared from nowhere, he had been so frightened he shrieked. He couldn't locate the focus object. If he could have, the peril would have vanished. The dreadful creature, as it came closer, slowing crawling across the floor, gained visible appearance. He recognized the fiend. It was a Gorgon, directly culled from ancient legends. Without thinking, he turned and ran out of the room into room eleven, fleeing back to his starting point. The Gorgon's voice howling, "Ralph Garland, we're waiting for you, Ralph Garland," echoed through the corridors of his mind.

The Gorgon was only a figment of his imagination, rather wild at times, but still he believed he could handle it. After debriefing with Philip and the twins, he felt better. Philip told him he must revisit the site again or he would live in fear the remainder of his life. Shasta was very understanding and at the intuitive level supportive. Even the kitties gave him support. Shasta offered the best advice: treat fear as a holographic image and pass through it without harm. She had reminded him of the great Italian poet Dante. In the second book of *The Divine Comedy* Dante comes to a ring of fire he must pass through to continue his journey to the top of Mount Purgatory. He is frightened, remembering the destruction savage fires had caused throughout the world. He is encouraged by the thought of his beloved whom he desires to meet at the top of the mountain. Steadying himself, he walks through the ring of fire without harm and continues his journey to the top.

Girding himself as if he were a knight of olde, Ralph walked just inside the doorway of the twelfth room, house of mystery and secrets. Carefully observing with all his senses, he couldn't detect any presence, whether dreadful or benign. The room filled with light, all of its space open to view. The memory of his failure made him uneasy. Then the room had seemed to be dark or at least it had shadows and dark corners. But that scene should be impossible. He inspected the memory and the thinking threaded through it. His rational processes proposed the Gorgon was hidden in the darkness somewhere in the room before it suddenly appeared. It couldn't just appear in the totally lit space, could it, so his reason stated flatly.

Ralph laughed. What a fool. He had fallen for the oldest trick in the bag, the production of objects. The mage inside asserted himself. He knew several methods for the production routine. It all depended on the object produced, its size and shape.

He was familiar with the room's furnishings. He glanced about. They were all in their proper places. The closet had caught his attention when he entered. He immediately went over and opened the closet door. Inside were clothes from the earlier part of his life. Turning, he saw a large chest on the floor beside a table with a small reading lamp that was brightly illuminating the room. Going to the chest, he opened it and surveyed its contents, a variety of small objects, many he was acquainted with and others he had never seen before. A mirror was on the wall beside a large photograph of San Francisco shortly after the 1906 earthquake and fire. On the other side of the mirror was a bookcase. On the top self were magician's props. The wand glittered. He smiled remembering his youth when he had become charmed by magic. The wand always stood for the mage's power.

He walked up to the mirror. It was his focal point for viewing. He breathed deeply, calming himself as he always did before viewing. He focused on the image in the mirror.

He gasped. He felt faint and had a strong urge to turn and flee. He steadied himself and calmed his breathing. Clearing his mind of all internal noise, he recorded the image before his eyes.

"Oh, my God," I exclaimed. "That's me in the test chamber. Sitting so still, almost like I'm sleeping." I increased my focus. The me was breathing softly. Eyes were closed. "I'm having an out-of-body experience (OBE). It's the first time I've knowingly had such an experience."

An aha emotion jolted me, and I realized a truth so secret and so wondrous I giggled like an adolescent. A new energy surged through my body. "Well, my Gorgon, where are you and your sisters today? I must thank you, though, for upsetting my well-grooved mental processes and ejecting me out of my habitual worldview." I left the twelfth house in my mind mansion and found myself back in the test chamber.

The air was clear and the sky light blue. Philip and Ralph were enjoying the late afternoon at Cliffside Cafe. They were seated at a table in front of one of the large windows Cliffside was noted for. The windows provided a 260 degree view.

The Farallon Islands, lying over twenty-eight miles west of San Francisco, were visible as was Point Reyes to the north of the city.

The cafe offered the usual fare for a beachside location: seafood dishes and chowders, sandwiches, and a variety of desserts. Philip was treating Ralph to refreshments after his successful venture earlier in the afternoon.

"What an amazing happening. I still don't really believe it." Ralph felt an inner excitement.

"Of course, some people will say you were hallucinating or, even more mean-spirited, you're lying." Philip nodded knowingly. "Now you understand the secrecy we maintain. When the results are published, we'll have plenty of criticism along those lines. But there's no need to be hassled during the project."

"I can tell Shasta, can't I? I'm sure she'll be discrete."

"Oh, yes. Only be certain she realizes the issue."

"The OBE event is a transformation in my being and my worldview. I'm on a new path."

"Another metaphor is an alternate reality or parallel universe."

"I can see it as a theme for a magical act, after the project is finished of course."

"Actually, Ralph, you don't have to wait for the project's conclusion. In a dramatic theater setting or an imaginative novel the theme can be used anytime. It has already been done. And you aren't suggesting our project is involved."

During the evening's happy hour Ralph told Shasta about his session at the Institute.

"Oh, goodness. I–I don't know what to say." Shasta picked up a tissue and wiped her eyes.

"Dear, are you okay?" Ralph was very concerned about Shasta's emotional expression.

"I'm fine. Let me gather my thoughts." She paused and blew her nose. "I'm happy and yet sad. I'm not sure why."

"I feel buoyant. I could dance all night–I've so much excitement."

"Oh, I don't know. I hope it doesn't change us, our bonding."

Ralph got up from the couch and went over and hugged her. "My experience can only make our love stronger," he whispered. "I've a new view of life. I feel like an adolescent ready to conquer the world."

"I don't know if I can keep up with you. I haven't had your experience, and so I don't have the same feelings and energy."

"You could join the project and start the testing process and eventually have the same happening."

"I suppose so. But I'm not that interested, especially now with my book. And perhaps I wouldn't have an OBE. Then I would be disappointed." Shasta was in a down state of mind. "I'm having some difficulties with the book, a type of writer's block. I get stuck and go in circles."

"Yeah, that's it. Use OBE or at least remote viewing as a theme in the story. Then you could imagine the experience."

Shasta glanced at her empty glass. "Dear, please get me another martini. And make it very very dry."

Ralph took their glasses into the kitchen for a refill. Shasta recognized the symptom: she was in a creative depression. She often fell into such an emotional trough while working on a book. Normally, gardening was a healing activity, but with the silly changeable weather, either warm and dry or cold and damp, she had the weeds under control and there wasn't much else to do. Enjoying their repast at Ocean Delights was another venue for raising her spirits. This time she felt helpless. She could try Ralph's suggestion and find out if it helped her.

Returning with the refill and giving Shasta her glass, Ralph said, "I make a toast to a fun and happy change in our lifestyle." He extended his glass toward her.

She paused and then extended hers until they touched. "Yes, I toast to that too."

"We have very few have-to commitments in our life. We have work and our household and that's it."

"It's a very big commitment, I think." Shasta stopped and listened inwardly. What was she doing? Was she frustrated because Ralph was so damned happy? Her mind cleared, and she recognized the nexus of the feeling. They hadn't shared the OBE other than Ralph describing it to her. Oh, dear, she thought, my mood's been terrible. I shouldn't project my frustrations, mainly coming from my writing block, onto our bond.

"Dear, I've had an aha." She smiled sweetly.

Ralph relaxed and accepted the wellbeing his sweetheart was expressing. "What is it?" he inquired.

"I realized I was mixing my writing problems up with your adventures at the Institute. I definitely need a break. Can you take time off? Certainly after such a momentous event in your participation, Philip will let you."

"A short trip out of the city. I'm enthused. Where?"

"A few days up north at Smith River would be delightful."

"I'll phone the motel this evening. If accommodations are available, we can leave tomorrow."

"Wonderful. I already feel better." Shasta got up. "I'll check on dinner."

Chapter 16

Opening the Ideas and Themes document for the new work, Shasta read through it. Sitting back in her chair, a smile graced her face. Her secret being was happy. She surveyed the orchids while inner silence spread. A vivid memory of the dream from two nights ago appeared before her. The dream was no doubt inspired by their recent trip to Smith River in the redwood country of northern California. The journey had been refreshing, and she had returned invigorated.

Early morning, she was in a redwood grove. The loggers had arrived and were preparing their tree-cutting equipment. She called to her friends who came running from their campsite where they had spent the night. Each had chosen a tree to stand by, to protect, to hug. The loggers, guarded by sheriff deputies with their menacing clubs and pepper spray canisters, marched forward, a mean look in their eyes, chain saws ready.

She stood before them hands out, a gesture to halt. Then she spoke, a voice filled with authority, "Stop there. Do not come into the forest any further. You cannot cut any trees here in the grove. They are sacred. Now turn around and return to your vehicles. Leave here in peace."

As if magic had enchanted the loggers and deputies, they stopped, turned around, and returned to their trucks and vans. Soon they left the grove. The tree-huggers cheered and danced to the beat of a hand drum. The dream had ended there. A satisfied and calm feeling had enveloped her when she awoke. She had accomplished a very important victory.

Shasta was puzzled by the dream. Loggers definitely don't act like that nor do sheriff deputies. She knew from personal experience. She had been a participant in the great northern California logging wars, defending the redwoods from clear-cutting and preventing the ravishing of the earth. Normally, deputies would proceed forward to the forest defenders, clubbing and pepper spraying them whether they were tied to a tree or gone limp on the ground. The deputies would then drag the earth defenders to waiting vans and haul them off to county jail. The loggers could now clear-cut without challenge.

Another unreal part was her stance. Rooted to the earth, she was secure in her goal and undaunted, facing the evil empire's earth destroyers. Her voice had power. Shasta paused. Yes, her voice–the dream centered on her use of voice. Oh my, she thought, a whole new vista opened up for her viewing.

Images of singing and drum playing inspired her. A variety of voices, tones, and timbres sounded in her mind. Thoughts clustered and moved by. A woman and mother's voice is the first voice to imprint on an infant's mind. A mother speaks to her child more than any other person for the first few months of a child's life. A mother's emotional range of voice has power and influences her child. A mother's voice is the foundation for a child's voice-sound memory.

Ideas embedded in stories she had read over the years flashed by. Frank Herbert's famous use of voice in the *Dune* series. The Bene Gesserits manipulated the power of voice for controlling others and attaining their goals. Voice was their primary tool and weapon. Religious groups have always used musical instruments and singing for their ceremonies and spiritual activities. The 'om' or 'aum' sound of the Hindu religion was also well-known. In the modern visually oriented world sound was definitely a hidden power–its secret exploited only by initiates. Sound and voice would be a theme, perhaps the dominant one, in her novel.

Well, now, she wondered, a quirky grin appearing on her face, how would Peaches, Aeneas, and Virgil respond to voices and sounds? Super-computer Virgil would analyze the sounds and report on them as physical waveforms. Peaches and Aeneas would add other levels of meaning, especially an emotional dimension.

Ralph's involvement with Philip's project birthed another thematic idea. Ralph was happy with the role of subject in psychic experiments–a new game for him.

Peaches and company can investigate some occurrence connected to a role-playing game, a threat or crime or something. Inspiration built to a roaring fire. She began typing.

Peaches Peoples was reading the morning edition of the *Berkeley Barb* when Aeneas spoke over the intercom. "Ms. Smith is here to see you. She has a concern that we might help with."

Peaches put down the newspaper and waited. The office door opened and Aeneas ushered Ms. Smith into the office.

"Hi, I'm Gloria Smith." She extended her hand to Peaches, who gave it a firm yet gentle grip. Peaches indicated a chair next to her desk.

"Please be seated, Ms. Smith."

"Oh, just Gloria is fine. I'm not pretentious."

"And I'm Peaches. How can we help you?"

Oh, I don't know if you can. If it's the type of investigation you do." A troubled look flashed over her face.

"Tell me the situation and I'll decide if we are able to help." Peaches gave her an encouraging smile.

"Friends in my support group recommended you and— Well, my cat is missing."

"We usually don't take missing persons or cats cases."

Gloria laughed in embarrassment. "No, it isn't a real cat. It's a figurine, a porcelain cat. It's about this big." She spread her hands apart about seven or eight inches.

"Yes, we often take cases of missing objects. I presume it's valuable."

"Well, not so much in monetary value but more sentimental. It was my grandmother's. I inherited it from her."

"And when did you miss it?"

"Last week. I had gotten home from work, oh, around six pm or so. I heated some water for tea as I always do. When it was ready, I went into the living room, kicked my shoes off, and sat in a big chair that was my grandfather's favorite. Relaxing, sipping my tea. Strange, but I happened to glance at the end table by the entertainment center. That's where my TV and music system are." She paused. A look of panic showed and vanished. "I noticed the empty space. At first I didn't realize what was wrong. Then I sprang up and crossed to the table. I just couldn't believe what I was seeing. I should say what I wasn't seeing. The cat was gone." She pulled a tissue from her sweater pocket and dabbed her eyes.

Peaches studied her closely, detecting a very troubled person. The cat was obviously quite important to her, to her very existence. No less than if it were a real cat, a member of her family.

"I'm so sorry. It's just my cat has such a deep emotional attachment. It was my grandmother's wish I should take care of the cat for her. And now

I've lost it. I just don't know–" She broke off again and dabbed her eyes with the tissue.

"Gloria, let's pause here. Would you like a cup of tea? We have green, chai, and jasmine."

"Oh, yes, jasmine would be fine."

Peaches pushed the intercom button notifying Aeneas, who answered immediately. "Please brew a cup of jasmine tea for Gloria."

"In a jiffy," he replied.

Peaches smiled at Gloria. "Where do you work?"

"I'm assistant editor for the *Berkeley Barb*. My reporters cover the local political scene, especially the more activist groups."

Aeneas' voice came over the intercom. "Tea's ready. I'll bring it in." The door opened and Aeneas served Gloria her tea. After he had left, Peaches asked, "I imagine a lot of people have visited your home. Is there anyone in particular who might take the cat?"

"Oh, yes, everyone at the office has been there. Last year I hosted the winter solstice party. And of course friends from other parts of my life. Why, all of my support group. I don't know if I can give a number, only many people have been there." She sipped some tea.

Peaches thought, the situation is quite complicated. Too many people knew about the cat. And she didn't mention if she had any suspicions. "What day last week did you notice it missing?"

"It was Thursday. We had a breaking story about Occupy Berkeley and the police action against them. We had to rush to make the evening deadline for the morning edition. We did it. I was stressed and wanted to have a quiet evening at home alone. When I realized the cat was missing, I was frantic. I phoned Sonya, my closest friend, and she came over. It was a comfort for the moment. Then the next day Jackie from my support group called and I told her. She was the one who suggested you."

"We'll take the case, Gloria, and try our best, but I can't guarantee we'll find your cat."

"Oh, yes. It must be found. I know it might be lost forever, but I don't want to think about that now."

"Aeneas is my assistant and is quite an able investigator. We work closely together. We'll require a great deal of information. Do you have any photos of the cat? We'll need as much data about it as possible. Also your friends, anyone who has been at your home recently. Aeneas will visit your residence, if that's okay, and inspect the doors and windows, any possible entry point. We'll need the information as soon as possible to begin our investigation. Perhaps Aeneas can visit sometime today?"

Gloria nodded. "Of course. All the details. Just the facts." She forced a grin. "I'll get right on it. Certainly, Aeneas can come over later this afternoon. I'm leaving the office early. Say about four pm. Here's my card with the pertinent facts."

"Thank you, Gloria. Aeneas will have our standard contract ready for you to sign when you leave. There's an advance of two hundred dollars. If you don't have your checkbook with you, Aeneas can get the check this afternoon."

Gloria smiled. "Thank you so much. I know you'll find my cat." She shook Peaches' hand, turned and left the office.

"The new case has been labeled Mystery of the Missing Cat," Virgil's voice boomed through the room.

"Well, Virg, any first impressions?"

Aeneas entered the room as Virgil replied, "We should have refused to accept the case. We do not have any data to start with other than the porcelain statue is missing."

Peaches chuckled. "Virg, don't panic. Your empty hard drive will be filled soon enough."

"I cannot panic. It is not in my nature." Virgil sounded indignant.

"It's certainly the hoots," Aeneas remarked. "Virg, the case is the type I enjoy. Nothing to start with. The potential is exciting."

"Okay. Here's the schedule. Virg, you'll get background data on all the actors in our little drama as soon as Gloria gives us her list. And Virg while you're waiting, you can make a list of possible motives for the disappearance of the statue. Aeneas, this afternoon inspect her home carefully. You know what to do."

"And what will you be doing, dear leader?"

"Virg, you're becoming insufferable. I'm about ready to ask Aeneas to reprogram you. Okay. I'm paying a visit to the *Berkeley Barb*. Does that satisfy you?"

As Aeneas left, Peaches sat down at her desk and picked up the *Barb*. She turned to the page where the masthead was located and examined the names of the staff and their positions. An underlying feeling told her the *Barb* was involved in some fashion. Then she leafed through the paper, checking for any news article that might be connected with the case. Gloria was editor for the reporters on the local political scene. Perhaps something was printed that might have a bearing on the case. She got up and went to a box in the corner. Rummaging through old newspapers, she culled all the *Barb*s and carried them to her desk. Now for a little research into the past.

At three o'clock sharp Aeneas arrived at Gloria's residence. His investigator's tools included a tablet and a briefcase containing items he thought necessary for the location. Data entered into his tablet was simultaneously transmitted to Virgil. The super-computer assessed the data immediately.

Gloria lived in an early twentieth century mansion that had been restructured into four apartments. Her apartment had four rooms: a fairly large living room, a kitchen-dining room and two bedrooms, one being used for her office. Both front and back doors were secure and hadn't been tampered with. The windows were also secure, and Aeneas couldn't find any evidence of entry or attempt at it. He studied the end table where the statue had stood. With his client's permission he snapped photos of the living room and kitchen. Along the path from the front to back doors the culprit had probably traveled. The back door opened onto a small porch with stairs leading down to the backyard that was enclosed by a fence. He also photographed the backyard.

Gloria gave him a large manila envelope containing a list of staff at the newspaper and her friends, three photos of the statue and details of its size and construction. Driving back to the office, Aeneas gnawed on an idea about the method used to vanish the cat. He wouldn't tell Peaches or Virgil until he was more certain.

Chapter 17

A new experience filled with enchantment was in the making. Many marvels lay in store for him. John rang the doorbell and waited.

Shortly the door opened, and a warm and rather sensuous middle-aged woman smiled at him. "John Ocean?"

"Yes, I am."

"I'm Shasta Garland. Please come in."

Ushered into the living room, John peered about, noticing a comfortable place that felt cozy and inviting. Ralph entered and greeted him.

Graciously, John remarked, "You have a very nice home."

Shasta smiled. "Why thank you."

Ralph, the proud homeowner, commented, "We've been living here for thirty-seven years and we've bonded with it."

Just then two kitties paraded in and walked over to John, giving him the once-over. Lucy rubbed against his leg, and Karma sat down and began cleaning her front paws.

John's attention was captured by the kitties. Smiling, he spoke to them. "My. My. Such cute kitties." Looking at one and then the other, he asked, "What are your names?"

"They're fond of greeting guests," Shasta remarked, "but don't let them bother you."

"Oh, I like cats very much," John responded. "My friend Mary Rainbow has two and I'm very fond of them."

Ralph was enjoying the reception the kitties were giving. "The yellow tiger is Lucy and the torbie is Karma."

Reaching down and petting each kitty, John said, "Karma and Lucy, I'm very delighted to meet you." They both purred affectionately and rubbed against him.

"Mary Rainbow, she owns Rainbow Inn, doesn't she?" Shasta asked.

"Yes," John answered. "I live across the street from her."

A sudden awareness touched Shasta. "That's your lovely garden there on the corner next to Trading Shop."

"Yes," John replied. "The shop's owner, Od Tinker, is a good friend. Actually he, Mary and I have become a trio."

Smiling knowingly, Ralph commented, "The trinity of Ocean Avenue. I've heard stories of strange events occurring at Rainbow Inn."

"I've been in Trading Shop," Shasta remarked. "Oh, my, what a strange man Od is. I was quite surprised when I asked the price of a basket, and he replied by asking what I had to trade for it. Then he explained his business practice. Since I wasn't prepared for a trade, I was able to 'trade' cash for the basket."

"We seldom visit the Inn," Ralph mentioned. "I'm afraid our favorite place is Ocean Delights down the street."

"That's a neat spot too," John acknowledged. "My loyalty to Mary though is too strong for me to go there often. One time you–looking directly at Ralph–were doing some magic. I enjoyed it immensely, but Mary has her own style of magic too."

"I'll bet she does." Shasta beamed at John. "Speaking of refreshments, would anyone like coffee or tea?"

John inquired, "What type of tea do you have?"

"How about some chai?" Shasta responded.

"Great. Thank you."

"I'll have coffee, please," Ralph remarked.

Shasta left for the kitchen.

Ralph spoke first. "So you'd like lessons. Are you serious in your interest, do you want to perform professionally or will it be a hobby?"

Ah, John thought, the grand question, and yes and no is the correct answer. "A hobby. At the present point in my life I'm seeking new and challenging projects."

Ralph nodded. "Fine then. The magic business is difficult and in today's economy business is slow. A hobby it is. Do you have a particular type of magic you would like to perform?"

Shasta returned with tea, coffee and a plate of cookies. After they both thanked her, she retired to her upstairs study to work on her novel.

John selected a chocolate chip cookie and tasted it. "Excellent," he said and quickly finished it.

After munching on a ginger cookie, Ralph replied, "We always serve cookies at our Assembly 2 magic meetings. I'd be happy to bring you as a guest some month."

"Assembly 2? What group is that?"

"It's a local group of The Society of American Magicians, the oldest community of magicians in the U.S. One doesn't need to be a member to attend although if you come frequently you'll be asked to join."

"Sounds like fun. Yes I would like to attend a meeting. Do I have to perform a magic routine?"

"No, you don't, but when you feel ready you can."

"Back to your question. That's one of the things I would like to discuss. I watched the DVD of your show and was completely impressed. If I didn't have much interest before, I certainly do now."

"That's very kind. I'm glad if I can strengthen your involvement in the magical arts."

"We could start with some basic routines. And I'd like to explore mentalism also. I haven't bought any props only several DVDs and a wand."

"A wand? What do you want to use it for?"

John laughed in embarrassment. "The wand seems to be an icon for magicians and their craft."

"It certainly does. Okay then, some wand waving practice. You can try out some of the effects I have to find any you wish to perform. And some lessons in various types of mentalism. How often do you want a session?"

"Let's say two days a week, if you can spare the time."

"Two days it is. Any particular ones?"

"What's best for you?"

"Monday and Wednesday."

"A deal. Can we start today?"

Smiling, Ralph stood up and beckoned, "Let's go to my studio."

Chapter 18

Marilynn Raylon had joined the chat room and was hoping someone had responded to her plan for sending Fallyn to Hawaii for a short vacation. Yes. Sedna Waters had answered and was presently online. She liked Sedna and they were having fun chat sessions.

She opened Sedna's message: "So Fallyn's traveling to Hawaii. Floyd's planning a business trip there. Perhaps they could meet."

Marilynn answered, "Oh, that's exciting. Yes, of course. Let's have them get together."

"They're staying at the same hotel and they meet—where?" Sedna replied.

Marilynn wrote, "At the pool or on the hotel's beach. Fallyn loves to swim but doesn't have much chance in San Francisco."

Sedna responded, "Ok. The pool would be better. Floyd isn't much into swimming. He can go to the hotel's pool to relax and notice her and sit down beside her. They can strike up a conversation, and then he can offer her a drink. What does she like to drink?"

Marilynn wrote back, "One of the Hawaiian nonalcoholic beverages, tall and sweet with lemon. What are Floyd's interests? What kind of business is he involved in?"

Sedna replied, "He works for Charybdis, LLC, a surveillance company that sells equipment and software to businesses and governments. He likes tennis and sci-fi films and books. How about Fallyn?"

Marilynn answered, "Oh she likes sci-fi stories and also detective mysteries. Water sports are her favorite. She's employed by Scylla Investments, an assets management firm."

"I'm signing off now and will start working on the first meeting. Let's talk tomorrow," Sedna texted.

Marilynn signed out of the website and turned off the tablet, placing it into her purse. Early evening in South Park was so delightful. Now though the fog was rolling in bringing with it a cool breeze. She buttoned her jacket, rose, and walked toward Crepes Cantata, her favorite supper place. She was happy about a joint adventure with Sedna and looked forward to the Hawaiian excursion.

After she had ordered, she thought about Hawaii and the trip she had taken with her younger sister Lori four years ago. With her sister tagging along, she didn't have any opportunity for a romantic involvement. On the next visit, she had resolved, she would be alert and ready for an enchanted affair. Three months ago she had been promoted to assistant supervisor, and the new assignment had kept her busy, so she had decided to save money, especially now with an increase in her pay, for an extravagant second visit to Hawaii.

Creating a journey for Fallyn, Marilynn could envision potential engagements and their complications. The creative imagination was an avenue for her to gain a better understanding of herself. She knew sharing the adventure with Sedna and her character Floyd would deepen the experience.

Stretching his arms, Lefty Cosmos stood and entered the central area of his loft. He did a series of movement exercises to release the tension built up from working at the computer. Glancing at the large wall clock, he realized it was 8:30. Saturday night had begun, but he still had plenty of time to groove with his friends. Grabbing his jacket, he departed for Bistro Royale.

Chapter 19

Shasta sat down at her table in the living room. Ralph was already ensconced on the couch with Lucy lying on his lap and Karma curled up beside him.

"Well, how did the first session go?" she inquired.

Ralph sipped his extra dry martini and then replied, "Very well. John has good concentration and a strong desire to learn. After the social chit-chat during refreshments, he opened up, and I got to know some of his background."

"Oh." Shasta perked up. "Like what?" Picking up her martini, she tasted it and smiled, pleased.

"Performing and demonstrating are excellent vehicles for sharing stories. My story leads to his and it keeps going." A wry grin graced Ralph's face.

"Ralph," Shasta implored, "don't keep me in suspense. Tell all."

"I thought magicians were a weird group. He's an investigator."

"An investigator. What's so strange about that profession?"

"His type of investigation is inspecting reality of different people, groups, things. I guess any and everything."

"Reality inspection. Whatever is that?"

"My question exactly."

"Ralph, please. The misdirection is excruciating. Tell now or I'll hide the martini mix."

"You won't believe this. Let's say it's a dream I'm describing."

"I'm listening."

"These are his exact words. I quote, 'My profession is a fusion of detective, psychologist, and shaman. But the fusion—the proper mixing—is the important part, not the three components. Other ingredients, more subtle, are also needed.' And then he proposed a compelling comparison to gardening. 'When I make the proper soil for my delphiniums, nitrogen, phosphorus, and potassium are necessary; but without the correct amount of trace minerals like calcium, zinc, and magnesium the delphiniums would not blossom properly.'"

"Yes. I can understand the analogy, but I still don't understand what exactly he does. I mean what if he were a character in my novel, how would I describe his special service and behavior?"

"Indeed. Perhaps you should watch, observe and inspect his reality."

They both cracked up laughing.

"Hmm. We need Harold Magian here. Can you get in touch with him?"

"I doubt it. I haven't seen him for a long time."

A fellow mage, Harold had arrived from New York to assist Ralph with his Alchemical Light Show and, when the performances were concluded, had left.

"John stated he began his inspection by pinpointing the energy leaks first. He thought that was easy. He called it only a matter of proper perception. Normally, he could rely primarily upon his vision, but he had learned early in his career the other senses could discover hidden problems too. So he always conducted a complete exam of his client. The main challenge, he remarked, was prognosis; could he prescribe a cure? That was often difficult because the client might not wish to make the healing changes, might believe the cure was worse than the disease."

"Well, that is making more sense. Hmm. The whole psychic energy phenomena are coming to center stage. You got involved with Philip's energy experiments. The positive-negative pressure idea. Then ESP tests. And now remote viewing-OBE adventures."

"You're right. The new focus is on psychic energy. There's probably a connection. I'll explore that with him."

"Who, John or Philip?"

"Ha, maybe both but definitely Philip."

Ralph noticed his glass was empty. He stood up and grinned. "Another round?" he asked.

"Yes, but I should go and start dinner. You can do the honors with the drinks."

The kitties led the way into the kitchen.

Chapter 20

Geri Meadows arrived home a little after eight pm. Setting the bag of takeout on the kitchen table, she removed her jacket. "Sorry, I'm late. Another Muni bus delay."

"I wish the city would establish a decent management for the public transportation system. It would be a real benefit to the people," Jerry responded. He walked over to the front window and observed the night sky. The twins rented a top flat of a six unit building on Potrero Hill in the eastern part of San Francisco. It was ideal for their purpose. Each had sufficient work space and privacy. The kitchen, dining area and social room were the commons.

"I've finished my report on Ralph. Have you got yours done yet?" Geri took the food containers from the bag and placed them on the table. "Tonight's meal is veggie, created by the chef at Organic Feasts."

Jerry entered the kitchen. "No. I'm about done though. I need to analyze his last test." He grabbed a plate and started loading food on it.

"I've been thinking. We need to determine his understanding of the golden path. Where he's at intellectually." Geri watched her brother take a sample from each container.

Jerry moved into the dining area and sat at the table. "A lot is still at the intuitive level, way down in his unconscious. But yes, we must make a definite verification of the stage he's at." He pointed at the string bean salad. "This is good."

Geri was too involved in her thoughts to notice. "So far the work at the Institute portrays his talent for paranormal activities. We require tests that diagnose his cognitive ability as it pertains to our study."

"Perhaps we should schedule a social hour with him and talk about his profession as a magician. Then we can move the topic to the Alchemical Light Show. With clever questions we could ferret out his ideas and their clarity on Hermes' craft." Jerry tasted the tofu beef casserole. "This is okay. Not a favorite though."

"Hmm. Let's devise some experiments that are fun and challenging. It's obvious he's getting bored. I certainly would be by now." Geri went to the kitchen table and helped herself to a plate of food and walked into the dining area and sat down opposite her brother.

Jerry paused from eating. "The OBE revitalized him. As he gets back to the more routine tasks, he'll lose interest."

"Yes, he'll wonder about Philip's purpose. With such an exciting happening he'll want more." Geri was picking at the food on her plate. Her thoughts were controlling her attention.

"It's up to us to do that. Philip can get into a tedious loop. We'll charm Philip with our proposal, something very imaginative. He'll love that." Finishing eating, Jerry got up and took his plate and fork to the kitchen sink and washed them.

"Let's each construct several tests on our own and then get together and merge them."

"Yeah, they should be fitting for a magician, a very imaginative one."

"One who has psychic gifts."

"I've finished programming Ralph's personal psi channel. It's linked to the path. When I've concluded my report, we can input the data."

"I'm very curious to discover if he has any influence on other links."

"Ralph's use of his mind mansion should be the basis for any psychic activities."

"For some, okay, but we need to seek his full potential, so morphing is required."

"We'll structure a dialectic of morphing for Ralph's field."

"Yes, movement between opposites will generate a multilayered resonating waveform."

"And he'll have an expanded horizon of gateways with branching paths through psychic space."

"Yes, a psychic logic that will provide the key to the Greater Mysteries."

"It should increase his consciousness of the golden path and the archetypes hidden within his mind."

Having eaten very little, Geri carried her plate into the kitchen and placed it in the refrigerator along with the containers of remaining food. "Tomorrow we can mix the leftovers together into one big dish." She smiled at her brother.

She returned to the social area and picked up her purse. "I'm going to my room and begin developing the fun tests. I'll see you in the morning."

"I'll listen to music for awhile. In the morning then."

Geri was up at six am, showered and made coffee before her sleepyhead brother even stirred. She had a fruitful session last night designing several projects for Ralph. They had the required charm to enthrall a magician. The mental activities should evoke some type of magic in the psychic realm. His most recent magic act indicated a fascination for storytelling. Her designs all had a story with magical, alchemical symbols embedded in them.

Chapter 21

Shasta entered the kitchen and fixed a cup of coffee. Ideas for Peaches' new case were waiting to be birthed. Taking the coffee, she went upstairs to her study on the second floor.

The house had three bedrooms, all on the second floor. One room was her study and the other two were master bedroom and guest room, which also doubled for storage.

Placing the cup on the desk, she studied the orchards. She touched the soil's surface in each pot and decided they didn't require watering. Now she would get back to the adventures of Peaches and her friends.

After reviewing ideas filling her mind, Shasta sat quietly at the computer. Words began to flow. Her fingers moved across the keyboard.

The empty pizza box rested on the desk in Peaches' office. Aeneas licked his fingers, having finished the last piece of the extra large with-everything-on-it pizza. Peaches sipped the last drop of coffee. Now with full stomachs, they could rehash the day's activities and digest all they had learned about Gloria and her missing cat.

"It's time for reports. Aeneas, please go first."

"Gloria's apartment is quite secure. I didn't find any attempts at entry. The material she gave me, I've delivered to Virgil. I'm definitely puzzled by the situation. Because of its size, about seven inches high, I can't believe a guest walked out with it and she didn't notice. It's a vanishing act a magician might perform."

"Okay then. No theories however improbable?"

"Not at the moment. I'll think about it." He did have an idea about a possible method for removing the cat without detection, but he'd wait until the idea had developed before presenting it for discussion.

"I've printed out copies of my background search for your perusal," Virgil declared. "And I'll give you both a summary of my findings."

"Yes, we'd like to hear that," Peaches remarked.

"First is a short bio of Gloria's life. Our client grew up in Southern California in the hip Venice area. Her dad was a surfer and her mom was a part-time waitress and made horoscopes for extra money. They were poor and lived on the edge of poverty. Gloria liked to write and kept a journal that helped her remain sane. She took journalism courses at the local community college. And as soon as she had enough funds, she moved to Berkeley and got a job with the *Barb*. She proved her ability and moved up to her present editorial position."

"Her sanity? Has she a medical history of mental illness?" Aeneas was very curious.

"No medical history of mental problems. I surmised given her life as a youth she could easily have fallen over the edge."

"It's your interpretation, then?" asked Aeneas.

"Yes it is. If I may continue, Gloria once in Berkeley participated in the new age hippy scene, including the use of drugs. There is no record of any arrests or hospitalization for drug use. I've only been able to track a few of her many acquaintances from that period. Her life was too messy for finding all the links. Her former roommate and, I presume, lover, Sean, died several years ago."

This time Peaches broke the monologue. "You have evidence Sean and Gloria were lovers?"

"Again inference from the data."

Both Peaches and Aeneas chuckled.

"Is there something wrong?" Virgil inquired, not understanding the reason for the hilarity.

"No. Please continue Virgil. You're doing fine," Peaches replied.

"Yes, to continue. The background checks on her friends and business associates did not uncover any peculiarities that stood out for further investigation. Until we have more data, it would be a waste of time to go further into their backgrounds."

"So we need to focus on any anomalies," Aeneas remarked.

"Were there any unusual bits of data that raised your eyebrows, Virgil?" Peaches asked.

"Yes. One item in Gloria's background was troubling. All her grandparents had died before she was born. Her missing cat was not given to her directly by a grandmother. It probably passed down to her from her mother."

"Well, that's something to begin with. Virgil, find as much data as possible about this type of figurine. Let's put on our thinking caps, get a good night's sleep, and see what we come up with in the morning." Peaches was ready to relax and stretch out with a fun movie. She loved oldies, especially noir mysteries.

Shasta leaned back in her chair—enough for Peaches and friends for the moment. The bad guys come next. She had been giving the culprits serious consideration. They had recently watched the last and final Harry Potter film. Magic and sorcery were in her mind. Her Muse held up the torch of imagination, and she followed the shining path. She began typing.

"That was Wanda from the *Berkeley Barb*. The situation has changed." Merlin rubbed his forehead and then pinched the bridge of his nose.

"What happened?" Morgan asked. She picked up negative vibes from Merlin's worried countenance.

"The cat was stolen from Gloria's apartment. She has hired a private detective firm to investigate and recover the cat." He shook his head in utter frustration.

"How in the world did that happen? Who else knew about the cat and its hidden secret?" Morgan was displeased with the news.

"Nothing's certain. All that's definite is the cat is missing. Maybe Gloria hid it."

"A possibility of course. If she did, that would imply she knows about the charm concealed inside the cat. Do we have any information she knows?"

"None I'm familiar with."

"If we don't get the charm, our plans will be ruined."

"Yes. And we might as well close down Sorcerer's Landscape. As it is, we're on the edge with the economic downturn, and our adversaries Forseti the Wilde and Glitnir the Shining are ready to pounce on us if we show any weakness."

"What firm did Gloria hire? Did Wanda say?" Morgan inquired.

"Yes. Peoples Investigations. It's some two-bit company located in Albany. Wanda checked it out. Two investigators. Peaches Peoples the owner and her partner Aeneas—no last name."

"They can either help or hinder us. We need to learn as much as possible about the firm and their personal background. I'll phone Jed Beers and request a check."

"Curse it. Without the charm we're not able to tap into the psychic voice channel."

"And we don't have time to increase the power of our throat chakras to avert disaster."

"More importantly to challenge the liege master of Tower Mansion. What can we do? We've designed such a wonderful plan. To think it'll all be for nothing if we don't obtain the charm."

"Moaning isn't going to help. We must make plans to use those detectives to assist us. Too bad they aren't a large company, and we could buy information from one of their employees."

"We can do something similar. We ask Jed to hack into their computer system and set up a link to us. Then we'll obtain all their data without their knowing."

"Superb. Have Jed get started, both the check and the hack job."

While Morgan was on the phone with Jed, Merlin ruminated over their earlier struggles.

They had lived in Kansas City. Morgan had grown up on the Missouri side and Merlin on the Kansas side. They had met at Cafe Intersection on the Kansas side adjacent to the state line. They both had graduated from high school and were at loose ends. Merlin was considering college. Morgan was totally uncertain of her future.

In 1980 destiny had brought them together, and they formed a bond immediately. They both had participated in the role-playing fantasy game Dungeons and Dragons. They felt more alive and real while involved in the game than in their everyday lives.

They joined forces and established a store that sold Dungeons and Dragons accessories, equipment, games and books. In the early 1980s their business was extremely successful, but the 1980s recession took its toll, sales slowed, and then the 1987 stock market crash ruined them. They lost their investment in their money market account, which defaulted. They had overextended themselves, believing in the market optimism spawned by President Reagan and his economic team. The bank demanded its loan be paid. They went into bankruptcy.

In 1989 they heard San Francisco calling them. They arrived, settling in Oakland in the East Bay, and became involved with the remnant of the Dungeons and Dragons set, which was fast evolving into Sorcerers and

Wizards. The new fantasy encompassed the idea or belief in real magic. Warfare was no longer fought with traditional weapons whether ancient, medieval, or modern but only with magical tools. The new style appeared before the Harry Potter stories and continued to move parallel with them.

They had hidden away emergency funds their bank didn't know about. When they left Kansas City, they used those funds to set up a business in Oakland. They bought remainders from many small fantasy game outlets as the recession destroyed them. They had rented a small apartment and a secure storage space. At first they just collected goods. Eventually they leased a small storefront for a retail outlet and business address. But their main interest had been caught by the growing belief in real sorcery. So they searched for material of all kinds dealing with real magic: books, pamphlets, incense, crystals, wands, and other accessories used in the magical craft.

They had bought into Reaganomics and its voodoo economic policy, paying for their blind faith with their innocence. The bitter experience had became the fiery coals of fury burning brightly in the furnace of their souls. They rejected their station among the ninety-nine percenters and now selected the dark path of power. Anakin Skywalker was their hero. They were preparing themselves to transform into the Darth Vader mode. That was the path winners, the one percenters, chose. The peace-loving, tree-hugging nerds were the losers, always. History was their proof and affirmation.

"Jed is on it. We should be linked into Peoples Investigations' computer system by midnight," Morgan relayed.

A smile crawled over Merlin's face. "We can't wait on them to find the cat. We need to locate it first. Is the night propitious for water mirror scrying?"

She examined the week's horoscope. "Yes, tonight is good. I'll set up the water basin."

Shasta was startled when Lucy jumped into her lap and rubbed her head against Shasta's arm. Ah, Shasta thought, I was so involved with the Muse I lost track of time. She peered over at the study's door. Karma sat patiently waiting.

"Okay, sweeties," she said to them, "let's go fix dinner." She put Lucy on the floor and stood up. The kitties were already trotting down the stairs as she left the study.

Chapter 22

Saturday afternoon was delightful in South Park. She glanced at her watch. Sedna should be arriving soon. While waiting, Marilynn thought about Fallyn and Floyd's time together in Hawaii. They had enjoyed their affair immensely, romping on the beach, dining at fashionable restaurants, dancing at nearby clubs, romantic late night strolls along the palm-lined boulevard, and greeting the morning together.

They planned to stay in contact–Fallyn in San Francisco and Floyd in Seattle. But something Floyd had said triggered off an uncertainty in Fallyn. The conversation they had at the airport before going to their flight gates rolled through Marilynn's mind.

Fallyn was beaming with happiness. "I really enjoyed our time together."

Floyd smiled. "It was enchanting. Let's keep in touch."

"Oh, definitely. You're so sweet."

"You're more than wonderful. But I might not be what you think I am."

Fallyn was startled. "What do you mean?"

Floyd looked at her searchingly. "We had a fun time together, but we don't know each other that well."

"Oh, of course. I do want to know you better–a lot better." Reassurance bolstered Fallyn.

"I'll be in San Francisco in a couple of months. We can see each other then." Floyd stepped forward and embraced her. They kissed.

"Have a safe journey home–and don't be fooled by glamour." Floyd turned and walked toward his flight gate.

Fallyn smiled and waved and then walked into her flight waiting area. During her trip home she had fun replaying fond memories. When she was back in her apartment, though, she remembered Floyd's final remark: "don't be fooled by glamour." What did he mean?

Marilynn had been troubled by the parting and had quickly engaged Sedna in a chat room session. Sedna's reply increased her concern: Sedna had asked to meet her in person and tell her the import of Floyd's final comment.

Then Marilynn remembered Floyd's statement they didn't really know each other. Marilynn had taken it to suggest strangers meeting and enjoying each other's company for a short time on a vacation weren't able to have an in-depth sharing. Both Fallyn and Floyd were on their best behavior, wanting to please and enjoy and romance. The way he had looked at her before turning and walking away–a strangeness shrouded the action. Stop worrying, Fallyn had told herself, and hold onto fun memories.

Marilynn paused her reverie of the Hawaiian episode when she saw Sedna approach. After their greeting, Marilynn suggested a snack at Crepes Cantata and Sedna agreed. During lunch they learned more about each other, sharing stories of their youth.

After lunch they strolled through South Park. Sedna halted, causing Marilynn to stop. Sedna looked at her. "Can we go to a quiet and private place where I can tell you my story?"

"Why of course. Come, we'll go to my apartment."

Once they were settled in Marilynn's social room, they sipped chamomile tea, chatting about trivia. Sedna commented on the comfortable furnishings, then turned and scrutinized Marilynn.

Sedna spoke with intent, "What I have to say is a secret between us. You'll think I'm being paranoid, but I must ask if I can check for electronic spying devices in your apartment."

Marilynn was startled. "What? Why of course you can."

Soon Sedna returned, satisfied the apartment was secure. Sitting down, she began revealing her secret.

"Most humans don't know the truth about our world. We believe in a superficial surface we sense. Beyond that surface is a secret reality, a strange and fantastic world. The real global leaders, hidden from us, aren't the one percenters we think are the rulers. Many artists have caught glimpses of the true structure and conveyed their visions in their works."

Marilynn was bewildered. "I'm totally confused. So many questions are popping into my mind. First, how do you know this? What is your evidence? I mean, it's a fantastic story."

"All I ask is you discover the truth of what I'm saying. Experience it directly. Will you?"

Marilynn was silent. A disturbing energy rumbled deep within her. She didn't want to know, but she had to. Her voice was strong. "Yes. What should I do?"

Sedna leaned close to Marilynn and described the verification plan that would demonstrate the world's reality. When she had finished, she grasped Marilynn's hands. "If you agree with my view, let me know in the chat room. Tell me Fallyn's looking forward to visiting with Floyd while she's in Seattle on a business trip."

"And if I don't find any evidence–"

"Tell me Fallyn is unable to make the business trip."

"Fair enough."

"I must catch the airport shuttle bus leaving in thirty minutes. So good-bye for now."

They hugged each other. Sedna lifted her finger to her lips. "Remember, silence."

After Sedna had left, Marilynn sat down, deeply troubled. The strange theory revolved in her mind, looping back upon itself. Wanting to shut it off, she retrieved her tablet and began composing an adventure for Roger whom she hadn't followed recently. Fallyn's adventures had erupted, smashing her view of reality. At the moment Roger's life was quite ordinary and uncomplicated. She wanted to keep it that way.

Chapter 23

John Ocean stood on the brink of enchantment. His life had always been surreal, at least as far as he could remember. Even when he was young, inexplicable events occurred. His dreams were often weird. Drama seemed to be inherent in his life. He frequently desired calm and serenity, but seldom had it. Now he was on the threshold of an exciting change in his career and worldview. He was going to be a magician, a wizard of the psyche.

Od and he with some assistance from Hank had redecorated his second bedroom. It had been a guest room for infrequent overnight visitors. It was now his magic studio modeled after Ralph's. He admired Ralph greatly and found him to be a fine teacher of magical techniques. A large, full length mirror was hung on one wall. New lighting fixtures were installed to facilitate practice sessions with the mirror. Bookshelves and storage containers were placed along another wall. Eventually he would hang some posters of famous magicians.

Strolling over to the mirror, he turned around viewing himself from all angles. He went to the desk next to the door and picked up the wand, his badge of magic's brotherhood. Ralph had shown him several gestures and maneuvers. The exact movement actually depended on its use in the routine. Ralph had emphasized a primary principle: the wand has two purposes. First is the dramatic gesture enhancing the effect. More importantly though is the second purpose: misdirection. The wand captures the audience's attention while the magician performs 'invisible' moves. He would conduct his own feats of wonder. He waved the wand and, revolving toward his right, watched his movements carefully. Ralph had a camcorder for recording practice sessions. A good idea, he thought. Mary did the same for musical and drama practice.

He had his first challenge. Ralph asked him to design a four or five minute act involving several routines. He had learned the best act had a theme weaving it together. The theme was the first choice. He decided to start playing the master game, so a theme from the game would do nicely. He picked up his mobile and phoned Od, who agreed to a master game session that evening at Rainbow Inn.

"That was great." Mary was enthused.

"Do it again," Od requested.

John performed a simple coin vanish and reappearance a second time. He sat back in his chair feeling gratified.

"So John will play the mage in the master game. Od, what's your role? Have you decided?" Mary inquired.

"I'll be an itinerant, a traveler who seeks the truth with his Diogenes lamp. I'll have many disguises, appear differently to different people. I'll carry a bag of fertile thoughts and wares to barter." He beamed.

"Wonderful. A mage and a traveling truth-seeker. And I'll be an impersonator. All three of us have a common theme: mages are also known as shape changers, the traveler with his many disguises like Sherlock Holmes, and the musician impersonator displaying a variety of personas."

"Not a chess player?" John asked.

"I've been giving my part serious thought. At first chess player seemed most appropriate and most clichéd. Music touches my soul in a way chess never did.

Od and John stared in amazement.

"I was a musician before I ever played chess. It's a more basic language than chess. The seed evolved and grew and here's the conclusion. My instrument is the Native American drum. For personal use a hand drum but for public performance a large round drum that's played at powwows. And I'm starting San Francisco Consciousness Drum Group. Everyone who wants to perform can join. I'm lining up some Native Americans who will tutor us." Mary sat back in her chair, radiating a glow of pleasure.

"Fantastic," John exclaimed.

"Ahh, we've had an epiphany," Od declared. "The image is clear: We're the patchwork trio."

"The quilt of many images," John added. "We have a wand, a drum, and a lamp of truth. From them all things shall arise."

"Okay. Next on the agenda is selecting our first action." Mary surged with energy.

"It should be dramatic, a big splash on the cosmic stage," John proposed.

"No, something small and rather insignificant would be a lot better." Od looked at Mary for agreement.

"Let it be both, a very fine paradox. John likes paradoxes, so—" She faced John with an inquiring demeanor.

"Thanks." An ironic tone was conveyed by his reply. "Okay, on the spur of the moment, not deliberating too long, I'd suggest a set of performances that oppose the Archon's activities.

"Where?" Od asked.

"Here at Rainbow Inn, of course." Mary was delighted with the idea. "That's brilliant, John."

"Which activities?" Od queried.

"Our eco-twins will choose," John responded.

"Of course. Who better than Helen and Hank." Od was delighted.

"Well, it's about time we told them of their involvement. I hope they agree." John was concerned.

"Helen's fixing soup tomorrow, and Hank usually shows up for that. I'll talk to them both then." Mary was glowing, filled with high spirits.

With a knowing smile, John looked at his friends and asked, "How about another viewing of Ralph's magic show?"

"When?" Od inquired.

"Tomorrow night at my place."

Mary removed a tablet from her bag and checked the calendar. "Fine," she remarked.

"I'll be there," Od responded.

Mary brightened. "I'll ask Helen and Hank if they would be interested."

"Nine, tomorrow night, then." John replied.

Chapter 24

Alice Moore checked off items on the inventory list for the morning's shipment. When she had finished, she began shelving the products. The front door opened, triggering a four tone chime. She glanced toward the door and spied Ralph entering her magic emporium, The Empty Hand.

"Hey, Ralph, what's up this morning?"

"Morning, Alice. A new shipment of magical goodies, I see."

"Where have you been? I haven't seen you for awhile."

"We've been up at Smith River for some leisure time."

"The Ship Ashore resort you like so much?"

"Yes, at the river's mouth where it empties into the ocean. It's a fun place. Wildlife watching is fantastic. So how have you been?"

"Business has been slow what with the recession we're in. This is the first shipment of new and replacement products in several months."

"Anything come in I might like? I'm seeking material involving mentalism and psychic phenomena."

"Changing your focus, are you? Did you lose interest in alchemy?"

"I'm branching into another area of the occult–a parallel path."

"Hey, kiddo, let me show you some exceptional ESP cards. They're top of the line." Alice's eyes sparkled.

Ralph was startled, revealing his surprise. "Where did you hear that word?" he asked.

"Something from your past, kiddo?" Alice was amused, enjoying Ralph's discomfort.

"Very definitely. During the 1960s, my journey to the east."

"Your stay-over in Chicago, correct. I'm reading the recent biography of Frances Ireland Marshall. What an amazing lady and her story contains so much important history of the magic scene in Chicago."

Ralph's memory clicked on, flooding his mind with the adventures of his youth. First his stay in Chicago and then on to New York. "Frances was wonderful. She helped budding unemployed magicians, offering them jobs at Magic, Inc."

"Yes. She had a regular magic industry operating. The Magic Shop with her first husband Laurie Ireland and when he died, marrying Jay Marshall, New York's magic icon."

"They also had a printing and publishing business and hosted a stage for performances."

"I love all the background of the magicians of that period and the venues they performed at. Places like Matt Schulien's restaurant where magicians, including Matt, performed. But hey, kiddo, enough memories for now. I've copies for sale. Let me show you a great ESP deck." The red haired wizard took a deck from the shelf behind her. "Here's a special deck; it has super power."

"Really. I thought all ESP decks were the same."

"Okay, kiddo, I can't fool you today. So I'll demonstrate a simple yet elegant routine."

Alice removed the cards from the case. Shuffling the deck, she offered it to Ralph to cut. He cut the deck several times. Alice picked it up and spread the deck face down. "Ralph, please take a card, anyone you want and place it face down on the counter. Don't look at it."

Ralph followed instructions. Alice then dealt twelve cards face down into a pile. Afterwards she placed the remaining twelve cards face down beside the first pile. "I'm going to turn the top card of each pile over simultaneously. Like this." She turned over the top card of each pile. "Let's watch for matching pairs."

She continued turning over the top cards until a pair of circles came up. "We'll place these circles to the left of the selected card."

After several more cards were turned up, another pair of circles appeared. Alice put them to the right of the chosen card. She finished turning over cards. No more pairs of the same symbol came up.

"Here are four circles. Let's see what the selected card is." She flipped over the chosen card: a circle. "Well, Ralph, five circles produced from a shuffled and cut deck. Is this psychic power or what?"

Ralph stared at the cards. "Excellent. It has the feel of real magic."

"The effect is a classic by Howard Adams, called Cidentaquin. I've several DVDs of ESP routines. Check them out." Alice pointed to the DVD section of the store. "So what initiated the branching path into other occult regions?"

"Do you know Philip Austen at the Institute?"

"I've heard about him and his work, yes, but never met him."

"Well, I'm a participant in his latest project investigating certain types of psychic phenomena."

"Hey, that's rather serendipitous. I've started traveling on that path too. Here–" Alice picked up a pamphlet from the counter and handed it to Ralph. "I'm giving a presentation at the Toward a Science of Consciousness Conference. It'll be hosted by the University of Arizona's Center for Consciousness Studies."

Ralph read the pamphlet. "Actually, that's the direction Philip is heading. Occult investigators are now applying the rigor of scientific method with its theoretical underpinnings."

"It's marvelous. The occult is no longer hidden but is now out in the open where we can all view it."

"So what will you offer?"

"I'm inspired by Jeff McBride and his presentations at the International Alchemy Conference."

"Of course. His Mystery School is acclaimed. Eugene Burger and other mages of kindred spirit are involved in the school. McBride's routine with masks is fantastic."

"It's super, according to one of Percy Juska's protégés, Kim Lowe."

Percy Juska was one of several Bay Area magicians who gave free performances Saturday afternoons. A small area at the back of the shop was reserved for wondrous journeys into magic land. Normally a devoted group of young women and men gathered to watch and observe the enchanted offerings. Percy, like many other magicians, gave lessons in the techniques and maneuvers of the conjuring craft. The youth were the future of the craft and live presentations were more captivating than video.

"Kim, with Percy's encouragement and assistance, attended a workshop at the Mystery School. She was awed. And more importantly she is now totally dedicated to the art.

"Anyway, back to the Consciousness Conference. I'll demonstrate a selected group of routines to display psychic phenomena. I've been researching and have made a list of the primary significant effects in the field. And

I've been adding to my own collection. In fact, I decided to start a new section in the shop especially for material centering on the occult."

"A fine opportunity for you. Well, originally Philip offered me a consultant position at the Institute. His idea is similar to the thesis of your conference presentation. I'm to show the techniques a magician uses to simulate psychic power in all its varieties. He thinks the essence of the mage's act is similar to the method, at least on the surface, a psychic would employ. He was disappointed when I told him most magicians who perform some sort of mentalism don't really act as if they have power at all. So it's difficult for them to give a convincing performance. In fact, many in the field don't want members of the audience to believe they have power. Of course, some people will believe because they want to, and there's no way to dissuade them."

"Yes, indeed. The famous example is Harry Houdini and Arthur Conan Doyle, the father of Sherlock Holmes. Doyle was a true believer and refused to accept Houdini's word he was only applying the conjurer's art."

"So I told Philip I'd be delighted to consult and exhibit some of our craft but without pay. The exercise would be mutually beneficial."

"Definitely. I'm with you on that. I've been getting antsy to be in the center ring again. I can continue to manage the shop and also do some performing. A conference presentation is the answer. I'll close the store for a few days and bounce around the country at apropos moments enchanting the scientific crowd."

"A great image. Let's turn on scientists to our art and display where their craft dovetails with ours. A rare but much needed blending of the two disciplines."

"The magical art is grounded on science, on knowledge. We test new props and methods, a real hands-on experimental model. When the results are good, we exhibit them to an audience, perhaps at first our colleagues and later the general public. Our audiences are as critical, if not more so, than scientists are."

"Alice, here's the big news. It's exciting and downright mind-expanding."

"You've turned lead into gold."

"Not quite but just as improbable."

Alice fixed her gaze on Ralph with an attentiveness that proclaimed 'I'm listening to all you say and I'm examining it critically. And I'll catch any sleights or misdirections you offer. So go on, I'm waiting and ready.'

Ralph started at the beginning: the strange event Shasta and he had experienced and his discussion with Philip about it. The recordings that were made at the house. His joining Philip's team to participate in the project. The experiments focusing on psychic power and his most recent mind-shattering experience, the OBE.

For several moments Alice was silent, digesting the data. Then a smile began to grow on her mouth, and suddenly she erupted into loud explosive laughter. "An out-of-body experience. Ralph, that boggles the mind. I can't believe it. I mean I can believe you had should an experience and you weren't hallucinating but— I'm flabbergasted. Talk about synchronicity, OBEs are where I'm now in my research. Oh boy, your report is too good to be true." She laughed again.

"Alice, you should get involved with Philip. I know he'd be interested in your consultation and participation in the project."

The door chimes sang. They looked over there as Alan Dove entered.

"Greetings, Alan," she said, "I haven't seen you for awhile. How have you been?" She pushed a pen and notepad across the counter toward Ralph. "Please write down Philip's phone number. I'm intrigued." She then turned her attention to Alan Dove, a magic hobbyist who had been devoted to the art since childhood.

After writing down the number, Ralph walked over to the special section on psychic matters. Almost immediately he found items that ignited his imagination. Immersed in the enchanted realm, Ralph lost all sense of time, and it was no more, not until he had found a sufficient collection of magical goods to keep him happy. Gathering up the items, he moved toward the counter. Alan had left, and two young women were watching Alice demonstrate a flower bouquet effect. The two women observed silently in amazement as the original bouquet multiplied into several more. They applauded when Alice had finished and bowed. They bought the effect and left the store playfully debating which one would perform the routine first.

"Alice, your section on psychic phenomena is a delight. Here's all I can afford at the moment." He placed several books and DVDs on the counter.

"I can order things for you if you have a special need. The collection is only a beginning of what's available."

Ralph was happy and his hands were full when he left Alice's enchanted realm.

Chapter 25

His supervisor was saying, "No, you can't do that. It's against the law. It's forbidden."

Lefty was upset. He only wanted to use his natural gift, his special talent for what he could do best. But his supervisor was adamant. Lefty was prohibited from applying his mind power. Anger built within, and he wanted to yell and strike back at the supervisor. But he couldn't. Frustrated, he stalked away.

Waking up moaning and grumbling from the weird dream, Lefty was in a fog and slowly got out of bed, staggered through the central hub to the kitchen and started some coffee, and then went to the bathroom to piss. He splash water on his face and moved slowly back to the kitchen. Pouring coffee into a mug, he went into the living room and sat.

What a bad dream he had woken from. His asshole supervisor, always on him for stupid silly things, didn't know shit. Now in the dream the supervisor was telling him to stop using his intelligence and mind power. What the fuck was going on? Was the dream a sign for work today or tomorrow or soon? Would he be laid off?

He looked at the clock. It was still early. The dream woke him too soon.

After getting dressed, he filled his portable mug with coffee and went out into the park. The morning was pleasant. He sat down on an empty bench and mulled over the dream and the feelings triggered by it. He had learned some things about dreams and their meaning from Kathy, who was in a dream workshop. All the characters were different parts of his personality. But messages from the outer world could creep in, like the trickster, a part of his personality but still channeling outside influences.

The smell of salt in the air was refreshing. A gentle breeze was coming from the bay, and the sun was warming the park. Finishing his coffee, he decided to go to Crepes Cantata for a small breakfast before going to the office. The dream was a vivid memory and would reside in the background while he worked. He realized it had alerted him to potential threats from his supervisor.

He had decreased the heat of his anger, allowing it to warm his soul without igniting it. Upon entering his loft, his first thought was the family album, a treasury of family history, lore and legends. He hadn't read the book in years. A powerful yearning gripped him, a desire to explore his roots. Straightway he went to the bookcase containing seldom read works and from its dusty location took the album, carrying it over to his reading chair. He decided to spend the evening reviewing his background. Placing the book on the side table, he walked into the kitchen and brewed a mug of coffee and then returned to the night's project.

So much he had forgotten about his family's history. Some of the legends he had never actually understood. And the lore concerning the inherited mental traits–these he had pushed into the back chambers of his mind when he was a child, a repression that had grown stronger with time. Now, reading about these special talents, he had memory flashes of events during his youth when he had exhibited unusual skills. His sharp intellect, which he had honed over the years into a brilliant mental tool, was the one skill he had accepted and utilized as far as possible. But those other talents, natural gifts his parents had called them, were of another kind altogether. They were in the paranormal zone, psychic skills that were considered unnatural or downright superstitious, figments of his imagination. If he displayed them, he was liable to be punished or at least ridiculed. The family history recited many cases of relatives who had been harmed, tortured, or murder if they revealed nature's gifts. A dam burst in his mind, and he was flooded with memories of how he had struggled to control and hide his dangerous talents.

Overcome with exhaustion caused by the all-consuming anger he had been experiencing, Lefty fell asleep in his chair, the family album resting in his lap.

He woke up puzzled. Weird dreams two nights in a round. This one was the opposite emotionally. It was upbeat. He was holding a lamp resembling an electric lantern. Its light was spreading around him dispersing the darkness. What was surreal centered on shadowy figures hidden in the darkness. They were human shaped but vanished when the light struck them. The meaning here was much clearer than in the previous night's dream about his supervisor. The shadowy human figures exuded emotions of fear and evil, meanness and cruelty. The positive power was destroying the negative force. A classic example of good overcoming evil. He nodded to himself–perhaps a positive outcome was in his future.

Lefty Cosmos had begun a series of strange dreams that would bring confusion and distress to his life. The dreams would fuse together his inner and outer experiences, pushing him toward self-understanding.

The third night's dream was even stranger. It involved Marilynn Raylon, a major character in his novel. She was being chased by sinister, creepy men who wanted to capture and torture and kill her. She ran into a dead end alley. She turned toward the attackers, took out a flashlight and shone it at them, wanting to see who were threatening her before they did her in. It was a small penlight with a tiny LED bulb, but when she switched it on, the beam became brighter than normal and illuminated the alley several feet in front of her. When the men ran into the circle of brightness, they dissolved into nothingness. He awoke at this point relieved she was safe and had eliminated the threat.

Yet he was puzzled again because the dream centered on an important character from his novel. In that sense she was part of his personality, certainly, as all the characters were. The creative process was involved in dreams and wakening state artistic works. It didn't make any difference whether the outcome was a physical crafted artifact or inner mental drama embedded in his memory database.

The dream of the fourth night brought the pieces together and cemented a solid conceptual and underlying theme. Fortunately it occurred early Saturday morning, and he had two full days to work on his global novel. The fourth dream was something of a reprise of the first one. His supervisor, who now was appearing more like a monster from some ancient legend or fable, was threatening him with torture and death if he didn't stop his creative activities. He was told on penalty of death to remove the character Marilynn from the story and never ever use the theme of light and illumination. A conventional story of romance and adventure would be acceptable.

The whole affair was crazy. He fixed a small breakfast of sesame bagel and coffee. While he was thinking about the meanings of his dreams and novel, the phone chimed. He glanced at the caller-ID. Kathy was calling and so early too. She was a night owl and seldom got up before noon. He answered the call.

Kathy spoke with urgency, "Lefty, are you okay?"

"Yea, I'm fine, just not awake, but sure I'm okay. What's up?"

"I had a strange dream and woke up with my heart beating fast. It was frightening."

"Oh, what was it about?"

Her voice trembled. "You were being murdered, tortured actually. Dying from a hideous maiming. My god. I literally shrieked aloud."

"Really! Listen, let's get together. I've had strange dreams too."

"Yes, let's talk. Come on over. Give me half an hour. Okay?"

"Right. I'll be there. And say, I've picked up several sesame bagels I'll bring along."

"Wonderful. I'll see you shortly."

Too much weirdness is happening, he thought. Now Kathy's involved. I don't believe it.

He had met Kathy two summers ago and first noticed her in South Park enjoying nature and feeling its freedom. He didn't have the opportunity to introduce himself until he saw her sitting at a table outside Crepes Cantata. She was by herself, and he decided on the spur of the moment to ask if he could share the table with her. Smiling, she agreed. It was an auspicious beginning. Their acquaintance blossomed into a deep, intimate friendship.

When she opened the door, Lefty noticed her face was etched with worry and her usually bright gray eyes, now filled with suspicion, were darting around the hallway searching for hidden dangers. He stepped into her apartment and moved quickly into the social area where they had spent many pleasant evenings together. He started to ask about her dream, but she hushed him with a finger to her lips. She pointed to the couch, not the chair he usually sat in, and then turned on the sound system at higher than normal volume, producing a mellow musical background. She sat close to him and spoke.

"I know I'm being apprehensive, but I've reason to be scared. Last evening I heard loud footsteps in the hall. When I peeked out, I didn't see anyone.

Then preparing for bed, I heard voices in the hall and your name was mentioned. I was too frightened to check this time. I did look through the spy hole in the door. Again I didn't see anyone. I had gotten into bed when I heard voices in the living room, rather soft so I wouldn't be disturbed by them. I turned on all the lights in the apartment with the remote master control I have on my bedside table. I yelled out, 'Who's there?' After several minutes of silence, my mobile in hand ready to press 911, I gained enough courage to venture into the front of the apartment. My fear gave way to relief as I checked all the rooms."

Lefty put his arm around her shoulder and hugged gently, kissing her on the cheek. "We'll deal with the situation together." She leaned against him, sighing deeply, and then straightened up and said, "You better hear about the dream."

He breathed in deeply and exhaled. "I'm ready," he replied.

"You're imprisoned in a room that has only one entrance. I'm above looking into the room through a window and watching the unfolding events of your torture. I'm frightened, totally scared out of my mind. Several men in black suits act like guards and a couple brown-suited men seem to be supervising the activities. The leader, the CEO of operations, is well-dressed in expensive attire, even wearing a power tie. He's sitting in an expensive executive chair. The torturing device seems to be electrical. Wires are connected to different parts of your body. You are naked except for your shorts. A crown-like device is on your head. It seems to provide the greatest electrical shock."

Kathy paused, closing her eyes and rubbing her temples gently. She glanced at Lefty. "I need a short break. Let's fix some tea."

When they had returned with cups of tea, Kathy continued. "The next is most gruesome. The monstrous CEO directs the guards to dismember you, cut you into small pieces and scatter them around the landscape. I freak out totally. I scream and wake at the moment they start to cut you."

She leaned into Lefty and hugged him. "Oh, my dear, the vision is so awful." She kissed him and told him she had an enlightened awareness after the fear had subsided. "I guess the thought is some sort of message or symbolic meaning conveyed through the dream. I was completely lucid. The CEO's motivation for his crime stood out, was clearly delineated, as if I were mentally linked to him.

"Lefty, he believes you have been eliminating his people, his servants and workers, with your lamp of light. The light awakens the life principle in them, causing them to vanish. The illumination dissolves the bond between soul and body. When the soul leaves and evaporates into air, the body collapses into a shell that disintegrates."

She paused and sipped some tea. She smiled at Lefty, who remained very quiet and attentive, and resumed her story.

"The second reason the CEO hates you, the primary one, is you hold in your mind the image of a bonded soul-spirit. The image has symbolic and craft levels of meaning."

"Awesome!" Lefty leaped from the couch and pranced around the room, shouting, "Yes. Yes. Yes." He stopped, realizing Kathy was frowning, a puzzled look on her face. He sat down again and hugged her.

"A moment of illumination for me. The frightening experiences and nightmare you had tie in with what's been happening to me. I've had four weird dreams in four nights, the last one today before you phoned. I'll describe them. You'll understand better. For some reason our lives are linked on a mental level, perhaps even in psi zone. But first, let's refill our cups."

As they returned to the living room, Lefty commented, "You know, Kathy, our adventures are making sense to me, not completely, but I've a feeling our creativity is involved."

Seating themselves on the couch, they sipped tea. The music had ended, allowing silence to pervade the room. Kathy broke the quietness. "I think something positive is occurring here. But what?"

"I'll describe my dreams," Lefty replied. He peered inward gathering his thoughts and then proceeded to relate the four dreams he had experienced over the past four nights. Kathy listened, nodding at times, and began to sense a positive change occur in her mind.

"Lefty, I agree your writing project is connected in some way. Also, my experiences of hearing noises–footsteps and voices–are somehow enmeshed in our relationship. The phenomena were happening in psi zone, and I didn't realize until now."

"I've an unformed thought waiting to be birthed. Two major characters in the novel, Marilynn Raylon and Sedna Waters, are involved in a secret, a mystery about us humans and our society. For some reason my creative imagination is stuck. Nothing is flowing at the moment."

"Your Muse is quiet?"

"Probably on vacation."

"When my Muse is silent, not singing to me, I turn my attention to other activities–things I enjoy without any connection to my music. Normally, after clearing my mental space, musical ideas start popping into my head. And then I'm off and composing. Once the gate opens, I'm flooded with thoughts, often too many to write down."

"Good suggestion. I've been planning to visit all the art museums. That's a project unrelated to my novel. Would you like to join me?"

"I'd be delighted. I've another thought. Marilynn was in your dream so she should be the character who assists in solving the puzzle. Work out the implications of the dreams through her."

"Yes. Brilliant. I'll do that." Lefty stretched and stood up. "I should be going."

"My day has become bright and I'm famished. Let's fix some grub and then go museum-hopping." She got up from the couch and kissed him. "Yum. My appetite is stimulated. Quick, let's start food preparation now." She grabbed his hand and hurried into the kitchen.

Chapter 26

Leila Lubec glanced at her watch—9:45 am. Her client would arrive at ten. She put down the book she was reading, a humorous and gritty tale with comedic twists and turns about two guys who meet in prison and their life after release. The feminine lead is a psychic swindler who speaks a pseudo jargon of astrology and spirit world. The comic character touched her deeply, softening some of the sharpness of her own career as therapist. Her calling involved what is commonly considered the occult. Yet within the ancient secrets dwell hidden treasures of healing, both mind and body. She applied the traditional tools in her practice to diagnose and cure. Although official science still denied the existence of psychic energy, Leila knew the power as a guide and assistant.

The morning's client, Doris Clayton, was retuning for the third time. Today Leila would give her an I Ching reading. Having studied Carl Jung's psychological ideas, Doris had undertaken an inner search to weave a new Self-Ego combination. Leila was assisting in Doris' self-analysis and transformation. During the first meeting they had discussed Doris' concerns and scheduled a series of sessions. At the second appointment Leila did a tarot card reading. Doris was so pleased with the surprising revelation she left buoyed by refreshed vigor.

Leila had majored in clinical psychology at Stanford and, after completing her degree, took graduate level studies at the C. G. Jung Institute of San Francisco. Of all the twentieth century psychologists she had discovered Jung was a kindred spirit. Not only were his ideas more profound and enlightening but his personal life experiences were closer to hers. Jung knew the inner world as she did. Her visionary experiences were on a par with his. Although she would never write and publish her red book, her journals substantiated the greater consciousness Jung had proposed.

Her therapy often required entrance to the psychic world through meditation. Over the years she had learned a variety of techniques for forays into the spiritual realm where she could more easily communicate with her spirit guide and gain insights. She always chose the procedure best suited to her client's situation.

Hearing the front door chimes announcing her client's arrival, Leila got up from her desk and went into the outer waiting room where Doris was sitting on the couch. Doris displayed heightened anticipation for forthcoming revelations.

After the office had closed for the day at five pm, Leila reflected on her last client Fred Baxter. The encounter was indeed an amusing adventure. Fred was a drop-in. When she entered the waiting room, he was standing in front of the watercolor landscape painting hanging on the wall behind the couch. Upon first greeting she detected a hidden secret. She thus supposed he was here to learn more about the secret and its meaning.

Ushering Fred into her inner sanctum, the middle room of her workspace, the back room being the office, she noticed his aura was strangely titillating. Once they were sitting, she started the interview to find out what his needs were. It was then she recognized the jokester hidden beneath his silly grin and his real agenda was to reveal her as a fake.

Fred had requested a palm-reading, something she seldom performed. His question centered on a business proposal he was considering. He wanted to know if he should make the deal or not. He held out his hands palms up as requested, and she grasped his hands in hers. Studying his aura, she sensed a disappointment in his life that still pained him. It concerned an earlier business situation. He had gone into business with a partner he had trusted. The partner later had cheated Fred of his share of the business. She also had the feeling the business proposal he wanted to know about was a tall tale he had invented to test her.

She remembered her words clearly: "Fred, you have been cheated before by a dubious business partner. The deal you have described sounds too close to the earlier disaster you still suffer from. I recommend you reject the proposal. And the person who offered the deal is someone you should be very wary of."

Fred had been shocked, a look of astonishment on his face. With a small amount of encouragement he had confessed his attempt to reveal her as a swindler. His friends had dared him, and he had accepted.

Leila laughed and told him now he had a much better adventure to report. Fred's countenance brightened. Amused at the situation, he thanked her and said he might come back for a real reading. Fred was a refreshing respite from her normally serious counseling.

Leila placed the grocery bag on the kitchen table. As she was sorting and storing the goods, she thought about her dream of the night before. Filled with symbols, it beckoned for unfoldment. When the chores were done, she would meditate on the dream.

The four room apartment on Miramar Avenue was her center for personal growth and transformation. When she left her office on Ocean Avenue for the day, she put all concerns about her clients in a special place in her mind. Back at the office she would retrieve them. Here was her intimate world. The small second bedroom was her quiet space where she could meditate and explore her inner being. If she needed to journey all the way to the source of her existence, she would do it here. The room was her inner sanctum while the living room was designed for leisure activities and socializing with friends.

Opening her journal, Leila read the dream entry, fixing it in her mind.

A rainbow image. She is sleeping and awoken by drumming. She gets out of bed and goes to the window. Looking out, she sees a rainbow. The drumming becomes louder. The rhythmic pattern begins to take on meaning as if words were being spoken. Voices arise fused with the drum beats. Singing and drumming energize her. Her mind is alert. She is sharply aware of her surroundings. An inner glow flows outward. Peace reigns within her soul. Her spirit guide whispers, "Walk in beauty, Leila."

The dream had ended with the words of her spirit guide. She recognized the import of the words. She was now ready for a meditative session that would reveal the dream's full meaning.

Leila selected her meditative position and method from several she had retained and refined over the years. The form must match the quest. For this dream she chose a variant of the Cholula diviner position. Leila sat on a low stool. Her right hand grasped the right leg below the knee while the left hand gripped the left knee. She shut her eyes and allowed her tongue to protrude slightly from her lips. She begin humming softly. Her mind emptied. At her center point she opened to the inner source.

The dream bud blossoms. The flower unfolds, revealing its inner secrets. She is looking down on the street and sees people dancing. Drumming and singing are in the background. Ocean Avenue is undulating. Wave after wave of ripples pulsate along Ocean Avenue. All the earth is moving. She sees a drum group. The drum is growing from the earth. Her focus changes and scenes flow by. She views different musical ensembles playing different instruments. People are dancing in front of a building on the avenue. A drum goes into the building. The building brightens, shining, illuminating the darkness. Shadows vanish. She is invited in. She goes in. The interior is brightly lit. People are dancing. The drum and its players are on stage–the center of activity. Food is being served. She exclaims, "There's the Ocean Avenue trio." Mary's in the middle. A rainbow glows overhead. Leila joins the dancing, pulsating to the rhythms of the drum. She feels light-headed. Alert, she beams her own light. Gracefully she glides around the room almost as if she were floating.

The images stopped. She sensed the touch of her guide. Focusing on her surroundings, Leila resumed a normal sitting position and then stood up and walked over to her desk. Sitting down, she wrote her meditative experience into her journal.

Leila paused. Breathing deeply into her pelvic region and down into her feet, she started writing, allowing the words to flow unimpeded.

The dream-vision is definitely set in the neighborhood. Ocean Avenue is the axis along which all the events happen. The drum is the center of activity. The drum brings forth light, a form of spiritual light involving consciousness. Now the building. Aah. The images rainbow, food, drum-playing on a stage, and dancing can only refer to Rainbow Inn. The proprietor, Mary Rainbow, is noted for hosting many varied events at her Inn. And the image of the Ocean Avenue trio is the clincher.

Something very big, very important is on the horizon, she thought. I'd better find out. Tomorrow I'll walk over to the Inn and investigate. At the top of the dream entry she wrote 'Drum of Consciousness' as the heading.

Chapter 27

Pleasant aromas filled the kitchen. Shasta paused and observed the work-table. The casserole was prepared to bake, and the salad ingredients were at hand, ready for cutting and mixing with dressing. Ah, the wine, she remembered. She went into a small pantry off the kitchen and selected two bottles of chardonnay and stored them in the refrigerator to be chilled. Ralph could deal with red wine later. She surveyed the list on the worktable and began checking off items. Feeling a warm delight, she was looking forward to the dinner party. It had been awhile since their last party. She was definitely excited. They would celebrate winter solstice with John Ocean, who was fast becoming a fixture in their lives, and his friends Mary Rainbow and Od Tinker, the Ocean Avenue trinity as Ralph called them. Rafé was also attending. Their arrival time was two hours away.

The food preparations were completed, and Ralph was finishing the dining room décor. Now she could prepare herself. Removing her apron, she left the kitchen and ascended the stairs to their bedroom. After laying out the evening's attire, she went into the bathroom and showered.

Lucy and Karma toured the living room, inspecting each arrival before settling beside the fireplace. A warm glow emanated from the stove insert. The hum of polite conversation filled the room. The Garlands and their guests offered background stories, creating a bond of friendship. A collective agreement, unconsciously given, governed conversation and storytelling.

Mary commenced with a short recital of important aspects of her life. Rainbow Inn had become a successful business. It attracted people from around the Bay Area, not only for its delicious vegetarian cuisine but also for its appealing atmosphere. A variety of activities were hosted at the Inn. Besides chess matches, Saturday night theater was performed by The Players, a neighborhood drama club. Music concerts were often held, allowing local ensembles the opportunity to perform. The peak of her life occurred when she beat Sam Runner for the world chess championship. The match was held at the Cow Palace in Daly City on the southern border of San Francisco. The strong support of her friends and chess-playing colleagues definitely assisted her victory. The positive energy had buoyed her during the down moments, especially after losing a game with Sam. She had retired as undefeated world champion after reigning for four years. Now she was involved in a new quest, the master game.

"The master game? What is it about?" Shasta inquired.

"I'll let Od and John describe it. It's their idea."

"Actually, it's a blend of John's and my ideas," Od acknowledged.

Lucy raised her head and observed Od with a quizzical stare. The timbre of his bass voice resonated, stimulating her curiosity.

Od told the Garlands and Rafé about his Trading Store, which he had opened about the same time as Rainbow Inn. Perhaps, he suggested, they were twins, situated across the street from each other. He expounded on his philosophy and religion, his basic economic ideas. Barter and trading were the underpinnings of human society. It was a game humans had learned at the beginning of their species, whenever that might be. He wasn't concerned with dating procedures and arguments over specific dates. He believed humans had always bartered in some form or another. When he arrived at his criticism of the use of money or currency as a barter exchange system, he became outspoken and incisive. The requirement currency with a fixed value be used for human commerce was the weakness in the economic system.

Ralph was caught up with Od's thoughts. Economics, other than daily living, had never been of much interest to him. When Od mentioned he had received his BA with a minor in philosophy at SFSU, Ralph realized he had another intellectual companion to toss around ideas.

Od narrated inventing Archon Empire, originally conceived as a board game with a digital version. But now—and he pointed at John—adding the vision of his friend the master game was birthed. Od paused. "It's your turn now, John."

"It was a dream vision of a game centering on consciousness. A drama expressed outwardly but also performed in the mind. A blending of the two—inner and outer. I told Od and Mary about my thoughts. When Od added his, we had the master game. It's goal is to increase our consciousness. Individuals don't necessarily compete against each other. They measure themselves according to an ideal."

Shasta was fascinated. "What do you do? What are the activities?"

"Each of us has chosen a performance style and the appropriate props," John replied. "Mine involves magical routines." He nodded at Ralph. Taking a wand from his pocket, he gestured, waving it. Suddenly, it transformed into a multi-colored silk cloth. He acknowledged the applause and stuck the silk into his pocket.

"With Ralph's assistance I'm developing a variety of routines for my act. I'm impressed with his premise magic can teach and display ideas. Mary and Od can describe their styles." He glanced at them.

Od smiled at Mary. "Okay," she said, "I've selected music, which has been a very important part of my life since I was a child. My instruments are saxophone and percussion. For the master game I've selected the Native American drum as the model. For most occasions I'll use a small hand drum. I've ordered a custom-made large drum, the size of a powwow drum, for a drum group which I'm starting—San Francisco Consciousness Drum Group. We'll practice at the Inn. Also I've got tutors for drumming lessons open to anyone."

"That's awesome, Mary. I'd loved to participate." Rafé was excited. She had remained in the background and had been listening without much input. But the announcement touched her deeply.

"Oh, yes, Rafé. I'd be delighted if you joined. And please tell anyone at SF State who might be interested."

"I'm sure some members of the Native American Student Organization would participate. We've discussed having a drum, and your offer would be a wonderful opportunity for us to improve our drumming and singing."

Directing her attention toward Od, Mary declared, "You're on stage."

Od stood up. "Proclaiming the virtue of bartering, I play the role of itinerate, journeying through life offering my wares for barter. I, Odysseus Tinker, am at your service. A minstrel show, we'll have. Here on drums is Mary of Rainbow. The famous magician, John, Count of Ocean, will mystify and enchant with his wizardry." Bowing to the chuckles, Od continued, "After the performance I will offer you goods that will raise your consciousness and delight your mind. May the force be with you." He sat down to a round of clapping.

"Od is addicted to *Star Wars*. Old Ben Kenobi is his super hero," John commented.

"Actually, John, since I'm no longer in exile, but have returned to battle the evil Archon Empire, it should be Obi-Wan Kenobi. I'll let you in on a secret. My true hero is Yoda, the great Jedi master."

Mary spoke up quickly, "We've hogged the limelight for too long. I'd like to hear Rafé's story."

Rafé blushed. "Well, I'm taking my MA in theater out at State. For my thesis project I'm creating the role of Native American storyteller who employs magic craft to assist the narration. I'm designing routines to match the story. Ralph's view of magic presentation has influenced me. It's awesome." She looked over at John and smiled. "I've been Ralph's assistant for nearly two years. I'm performing some magic at Ocean Delights. Actually, Mary, I've been wondering if the Inn could use my act occasionally? But I wouldn't want to interfere with John."

"Why, yes. That sounds fine." Mary replied. "John's not doing much at the moment."

"Rafé, we could put a show together. Each perform some routines." John paused and then turned to Ralph. "What about the three of us, Ralph?"

"Could you link with the master game?" Shasta asked. She was intrigued by a game that raised consciousness. If they could get involved–

"And so it grows." Od clapped his hands. "The six of us can form the nucleus. What a combination of talents."

"Shasta can write the scenarios. Mysteries are her line," John suggested.

"I'm in. Maybe Peaches and Aeneas can play too," Shasta responded.

"Ralph, I enjoyed watching the DVD of your magic show. I think we all did." Od paused, gathering his thoughts. "That scene toward the end where the mage transforms the model he's making into the real princess. That was stunning. Truly magical. I'll never forget it."

"And the finale with the two large eggs. You used an egg effect frequently, but this scene was astounding. Perhaps when I reach an advanced state, you can teach me the routine." John was enthused.

"I've several questions but now's not the time to ask them. The show was very moving on an intuitive level. I've always enjoyed magic acts. Yours, though, had substance. It left me thinking, just like a good chess game."

Ralph was in a mellow mood. The wine, a merlot Mary had brought, was very tasty. The fire in the fireplace was a warming light that enhanced the conversation. He smiled, listening to Mary's praise of the Alchemical

Light Show. All three were in agreement it was a fine and enlightening performance. Karma was curled up on his lap. Petting her, he focused on the dancing flames in the stove. He decided to act as if he were involved in a remote viewing session.

Ralph had refined his distant viewing techniques since the original journey. Instead of starting in the first room and continuing through them until he reached the room with the illuminating icon, he placed himself at the still point, which in his mental mansion was a circular room in the center of the twelve houses. Ralph was able to view all twelve doors. As his intuitive sense sharpened, he became aware of the exact room that had the illuminating icon. He entered the room immediately.

He was standing in the still point of his turning world. Circling him were the twelve doors. He walked immediately toward the door of the fifth house and, opening it, stepped in. He noticed the wood-burning stove was illuminating the entire room. Quickly he went over to the chair facing the stove and sat down. He allowed his imagination to transform the flames and burning wood into recognizable figures. My goodness, he thought, that form looks like Geri and the other one Jerry. Hah, they're in the fiery furnace probably planning some new adventure. It was easy to sharpen the focus and enlarge the image.

The twins were in their apartment on Potrero Hill. Geri was standing, looking out the window, while Jerry was sitting in an upholstered armchair. Ralph thought he heard them speaking. He let the viewing happen.

"How far has Ralph progressed, do you think?"

"It's time to move him to the next stage."

"We'll have Philip approve the next set of tests. He's anxious to proceed."

"But we must be extremely careful from now on he doesn't suspect our agenda. We can't allow our feelings to show when we tell him the results, whether positive or negative."

"Yes, we've come too far to goof up and give away our goal."

"The sequence of activities must be fine-tuned so each one increases his comprehension enough without shattering his focus."

"Here's the sequence list I believe is best." Jerry stood up and walked over to his sister.

She took the paper from him and studied the list. "Only one difference of opinion. Here, the third one should be last. Okay?"

Jerry took the paper and thought for a few moments. "Yes, I see what you're thinking. All right, that's the path. Let's hope Ralph is able to accomplish the task."

"If he fails, we'll introduce another set that will move in a different direction."

"Yes, we don't want him to realize the undertaking and what we're seeking to learn."

"Definitely not. His mind might collapse causing the loss of his psychic skills."

"The path is narrow and perilous."

"And something else. It's only peripheral to the project, but I've often wondered about the inner workings of his mind. He leaps over obstacles and lands safely."

"I have too. His guardian spirit must be very loving and devoted."

"And he, at least unconsciously, must be fully open to the guidance."

"Ralph, dear. Ralph."

He felt a touch on his shoulder, a slight vibrating touch. He came out of his reverie and saw Shasta standing in front of him, bending toward him with her hand on his shoulder.

"What? Huh?"

"Ralph, dear, where were you?"

"Ralph, you seemed to be watching some scene or event, a film," John remarked.

Ralph looked around the room. Everyone was staring at him with concern and bewilderment. Smiling sheepishly, he said, "I guess I was at that. What a strange experience. Similar to remote viewing I do at the Institute."

John was quick on the uptake. He had become alert and was watching Ralph, noticing changes in his aura. He had known Ralph for several months and become acquainted with his normal behavior, but he had never seen Ralph act so peculiar. John carefully inspected Ralph's vibratory waves. At the moment all were regular. Yet earlier his aura conveyed a cluster of varying colors.

Karma jumped down from Ralph's lap and strolled over to the dining room door where Lucy was sitting patiently. Shasta noticed the kitties and laughed. "We're being told dinner is ready. I'll go and check on everything first. Ralph, please come and help."

Ralph stood and followed Shasta through the dining room into the kitch-
en, the kitties leading the way.

A few minutes later, Ralph reappeared in the dining room doorway and
beckoned. "Food is being served. Please come in and be seated, wherever
you wish. We don't assign chairs."

The guests entered and quickly found a placed they liked and sat down.

Rafé was the focus of dinner conversation. The Ocean trio listened intently to Rafé's description of life on the reservation. And they had many
questions about her people, the Citizen Potawatomi Nation. Each of them
had a personal set of inquires. Od desired information about the nation's
history and relationship with other Algonquin nations. Mary was most curious about the life of women, both in the past and today. John asked about
the religious and spiritual beliefs and practices.

Rafé provided detailed answers that satisfied them. She didn't, however,
speak about the Grand Medicine Lodge and the Midewiwin ceremonies.
Although she did mention some were members of the Native American
Church, she didn't offer details of the ceremony and practices. She had told
Ralph about the Medicine Lodge and her membership in the Native American Church, but John Ocean was only an acquaintance. If and when they
became friends, she might speak about this part of her life.

Dessert and a choice of tea or coffee were served, and the conversation
centered on stories revolving around the denizens of Ocean Avenue. The
party concluded with one of Ralph's raven stories. Mary, John, and Od took
their leave with gracious compliments paid to the Garlands for a fine and
delicious dinner party. Rafé left a little later after asking Ralph's advice about
a new routine she was working on.

Neither of the Garlands was sleepy. The dinner dishes washed and in the
drainer, the living room tidied–their minds were too active and they needed
to unwind. They kissed each other, a reward for the successful party and
went to indulge in late night activities. Shasta went upstairs to her study and
started thinking about her work-in-progress. Ralph walked into his studio
across the hall from the kitchen and sat in his rocking chair where he did
much of his thinking.

He settled in, rocking back-and-forth and allowing his thoughts to glide
through his mind. The disturbing experience seeing the twins in their apartment, he needed to digest. Was it an actual remote viewing event or only

his imagination creating a vivid fantasy? What criteria could he apply to evaluate it? He definitely wasn't going to share the happening with the twins or Philip, at least not until he understood the meaning of the scene. What kind of agenda did they have that was a secret? What was that about possible damage to his mind? The notion was scary. He wasn't certain whether he should even discuss it with Shasta. She would probably be frightened too. Perhaps even ask him to stop participating in the project. He would examine the event carefully, inside and out, before he told anyone.

Lucy jumped into his lap and curled up, giving him her knowing smile. He gently scratched behind her ears. Purring, she put her head on her paws. Rocking in the chair was relaxing and allowed his thoughts to flow without impediment. He would treat the experience as a dream and apply dream analysis. It was a definite advantage because he wouldn't need to decide the viewing's reality quotient. Understand its meaning first and then worry about whether it's fantasy or not, he decided.

Is there a reason or meaning for seeing the twins, he wondered: is it some sort of sign and what or who initiated it? Perhaps more than the twins' agenda and their secret was involved. Why, for example, should he learn they have a secret goal?

Perhaps some part of his mind intuits potential danger, a precognitive skill, and so the viewing is a warning to be on guard and protect himself. Appearances are deceiving, and he, a mage, should know. He'll observe and detect any misdirection and hidden actions. Look below the surface. If the event is precognition, he's learned unconsciously he has the skill, which can help him. Ah, the still small voice, another confirmation given. He'll act normal also and not give away his feelings, his knowing about them. Perhaps he should use his remote viewing skills for his own benefit. Of course, the idea is certainly one important conclusion from the experience. The event was unconsciously triggered, but at the Institute he can consciously go into distant viewing mode. He never thought about doing it on his own, for his own purpose. But now it is a must. He will practice at home and select his targets, especially the twins and Philip. If the twins have a hidden goal, why not Philip. Nothing is what it seems–basic premise for magicians. He can play the game. He will be a magician at all times and places, awake and asleep. "Call me Mage," he said aloud. Lucy perked her ears, alert. He stroked her and, gliding back and forth, returned to his thoughts.

Another aha moved him. He had discovered his role in the master game. He was the mage with Harold as role model. He wondered about Harold Magian. He hadn't heard from him since his return to New York City, at least his supposed return. But where does a being like Harold go back to? It was an intriguing question but very speculative and a digression from the issue at hand. Probably the trickster was at work diverting his focus. The books on Carl Jung's ideas about human nature he had borrowed from the Institute's library and was now in the process of reading offered illuminating concepts that dovetailed with his views. Certainly the archetypes in the collective unconscious, like the trickster and king and queen, were powerful conceptual tools. But back to the strange happening.

Ralph remembered when Philip had indicated a sense of uncertainty about the twins' background. So they possessed a secret, one or more, known only to themselves. Captivating to speculate about–he would let the thought grow in the darkness of his inner being.

Really, how much had his skills developed? The twins had implied he had advanced but still had further learning and growth. He would scrutinize his activities in the project and identify the sequence of the experiments and their results, his successes and failures. Of course if the twins were playing a deceptive game, he could be given the wrong appraisal of the results. He didn't interpret them or see the raw data. He was only told whether he had succeeded or not.

Chapter 28

Private-eyes on the low end of the monetary scale always had lousy coffee in their offices. Peaches was proud she had good tasting coffee available—nothing but the best. The aroma from her cup tingled her desire, and she sipped the hot brown liquid, a Colombian roast. She was amused when she had read Virgil's report, announcing a hacking attack late last night. The supercomputer had tracked the attacker to its address and then onto a link that had been established to another computer.

Aeneas, the master techno-genius, had installed a firewall that had two prime functions: to prevent intrusion and generate a mirror wall that reflected an image of a computer system operating in a standard fashion. The hacker would receive only garbage data, a make-believe detective business.

She pushed the intercom button. "Have you read Virgil's report?" she inquired.

"I have. Quite interesting," Aeneas replied.

"Come in. We should discuss the event."

Aeneas entered the small office and sat down in the chair closest to the desk. He studied his boss and partner, who continued to maintain her robust six foot one, one hundred eighty-nine pound physique. He marveled that she exuded such a femininity many men lost sight of her intellectual and physical skills. Her well-chewed and unlit Cuban cigar rested in an ashtray on her left. She was sipping her morning coffee. When she put the cup down, she asked, "What's your take on the new development?"

He grinned like the cat that caught the mouse. "Another fish hooked. We have a definite adversary who's obviously seeking the cat too. They don't have it and want to keep track of our investigation. They probably have a paid informer at the *Barb*. And they have a computer geek who can hack well enough for the average system."

"Of course, he didn't know about our supercomputer." Peaches was also amused.

When Aeneas had joined Peaches Peoples, forming the present investigative agency, he had brought with him his computer Virgil. He had designed and built the computer to his personal specifications. Virgil was more powerful than the famous HAL and its descendants. Virgil was the third and hidden partner of Peoples Investigations. It could see, hear, and speak. Camera eyes, miniature microphones, and speakers were placed in strategic areas of both their offices and living quarters. Virgil could speak thirteen languages with different voice registers and understand those languages in their spoken and written forms; it was a veritable language wizard. Peaches and Aeneas always spoke to and treated Virgil as a person. During most interviews, though, Virgil was silent so as not to scare clients or give away his powers.

"Virgil, you performed admirably." Peaches liked to praise him. Aeneas had programmed a simple male personality in the supercomputer. Virgil had the ability to learn from experience–an advanced form of artificial intelligence.

"Thank you. I highly appreciate your praise," Virgil responded.

"How do you interpret the hacking attack, Virgil?" she asked.

"I would agree with Aeneas' analysis with two minor additions. First, they knew the secret of the cat's importance, and we should obtain as much data as we can about the secret. Secondly, since they didn't steal the cat, either a third party purloined it or Gloria hid it. My surmise is Gloria has put it in a safe place because she's afraid of losing it."

"Yesterday you indicated the grandmother story was false, at least the way Gloria told us. So she refused to tell us the true nature of the cat and the reason it is so precious," Aeneas commented.

"I'll perform an in-depth search of Gloria's life," Virgil announced.

"Check out her former partner Sean. The clue might be there," Peaches added.

Shasta stretched her arms, stood up and crossed over to the window overlooking the garden. The strange and abnormal weather patterns were confusing the plants. One day above average temperature, the next below average–the plants and animals living around them were caught in fluctuating process. She went down to the kitchen, fixed herself a cup of fresh coffee, and returned to her novel.

She directed her focus toward Merlin and Morgan to learn what they were doing.

Morgan handed Merlin a printout. "Here's the first report on the activities of Peoples Investigations. Business as usual. They've been performing standard background searches. Nothing important has turned up."

Merlin read the report. Finishing it, he stared into the distance. "Last night's scrying was a bust."

"Oh, I don't know," Morgan replied. "Gloria was acting strange."

"She's worried that's all. I now believe she knows the secret. So she wants it back for her agenda."

"I agree she recognizes the charm's power to tap into the psychic channels. She probably has used it. Living with Sean that long, she should have absorbed some of his knowledge."

"I examined the report on Peaches and Aeneas. Their background doesn't indicate any great potential to stand in our way."

"Peaches Peoples, a country girl who came to the big city to find success and ends up running a low end detective agency in Albany. And this Aeneas. A dropout from the word go. Personally, I sympathize with his parents. He was a privileged youth growing up in an upper class family. He rejected his social class and status, so of course the family threw him out."

"There's one thing that bothers me about Walter Edison Blenford III aka Aeneas. The data indicate a dedication to computer technology and possibly an advanced ability in the field."

"A typical bohemian, dabbling in the latest fad, computer and digital games." Merlin's sarcasm was brittle.

"Well, if I remember correctly, we were bohemians too dabbling in games and such."

"Yes, but we tried to better ourselves. And we weren't born with silver spoons and nannies. If it weren't for the cursed Reaganomics, we'd be well off now."

His bitterness was too tiresome. Morgan had accepted their destiny and was working now for a brighter future. Merlin's anger always generated negative energy in her, and she didn't like it. "Okay. All I'm saying is we should be alert to potential threats from that direction."

He nodded and then sank back in his personal reverie.

She studied her long-time partner. Aging was not fun, but it was part of life and a stage to travel through as best they could. Her vital source always bounced back, shoving her into the fray once again. When San Francisco beckoned, she was enthralled, ready to leave behind what might-have-been and discover their fortune in the golden land. And by goddess they had accomplished much.

They had finally located Sean Everday's book and deciphered his notes written in a crabbed style. He had stashed the charm inside the cat figurine and given it to Gloria as a token of his love. Whether he had told her about the charm and its purpose, they didn't know. Whatever, they would possess the charm and gain control of Tower Mansion, the loftiest channel in the cosmos, the only frequency the Destroyer couldn't manipulate. Morgan, Queen of Isle of Apples, was a famous and powerful mage–her namesake and mentor. She, the new Morgan, would reinstate the long line of women magi into the highest level of the cosmos, the Space beyond space.

Chapter 29

The Garlands left their house in Ingleside Terraces and strolled to Ocean Avenue. Turning east, they leisurely walked to Ocean Delights, a favorite place for a pleasant outing. Ben Said the owner was at the counter taking orders. The menu listed a variety of coffees, teas, pasties, and sandwiches. The most popular item in the sandwich category was the pita falafel. Customers could choose from several different fillings. The Garlands, though, came for coffee and pastry and, most important, socializing with their gang, a group of friends who had bonded together years earlier.

Gordon Russell, a stalwart of the group, was in heated conversation with Dale Pepper, another long-time member. Gordon was a retired City College of San Francisco English instructor. Dale taught music at SF State. Shasta went over to the table while Ralph placed their order with Ben.

"Well, what's the big debate about? I sensed the heat of argument as soon we entered."

"Debate? Argument? I was expressing some thoughts about San Francisco's resident coyotes, and Gordon was displaying his fiery wit."

"I was explaining to Dale the holes in his thinking." Gordon grinned. "And I believe I was succeeding."

Shasta laughed. "You were inspecting his reality for leaks, was that it?" She kept a straight face.

Gordon was momentarily confused. Dale howled and, slapping the table, remarked, "That's it, Shasta. I'm leaking thoughts and Gordon is attempting to plug the holes."

A scowl transformed into a wry grin on Gordon's face. "There. You see, Shasta. What a hodgepodge of metaphors. No wonder your thoughts are so confused." He directed the last statement to Dale.

"If you have reality leaks, Dale, you require the services of a reality inspector," Ralph suggested as he deposited two bear claws and coffees on the table.

Peering quizzically at Ralph, uncertain whether he was being ironic or not, Gordon responded, "Pray tell, who might that be?"

Shasta jumped back into the fray. "Our Ocean Avenue neighbor John Ocean."

Dale beamed. "Of course. I've met him. He's a friend of Mary Rainbow. When I was starting my ensemble, we played a few gigs at Rainbow Inn."

"Yes. Tea and vegetarian cuisine. Excellent food for those who forsake meat," Gordon acknowledged. "The Ocean Avenue trio: Mary, John, and Odysseus Tinker. What an odd group they are. I've been in Trading Shop a few times. Remarkable collection of items."

"Greetings. What's on the canvas today?"

They all turned toward the voice as Merle Leong approached the table. Dale and Ralph moved to open a space as Merle pulled up a chair. A visual artist, Merle had very definite ideas about art, the creative imagination, and the path an artist should take. He was an outspoken Taoist and often sprinkled spiritual ironies into his conversation.

"I can tell you're in a serious debate over a trivial matter. Let me offer the solution," Merle announced.

"Where's Emma?" Shasta inquired.

"At the moment she's busy earning a nice living so her freeloading husband can continue his artistic path undisturbed by worldly concerns."

Everyone chuckled. "Merle, come off the literary garble. It's unseemly for a Taoist," Gordon pronounced. Once a teacher, always a teacher–was one of Gordon's favorite maxims. Even in retirement he was unable to drop his role as an authority figure.

Laughter ensued again.

"Ho," Merle declared, "I'll paint your faces and transform them into masks for Ralph's next magic show. It'll be titled Magical Masks."

"Such exuberance. Your Muse must be singing to you," Shasta said.

"Ah, dear Shasta, you're the true Taoist, perceiving beyond appearances. Yes. Your surmise is totally correct. My Muse is currently guiding my brush, creating a great work, deep and revealing."

"Can you reveal something about it now?" Gordon asked.

"Once it's finished, I'll have a studio showing and you'll be invited. But now only silence." Merle placed a finger on his lips.

"Ralph, are you still involved with the Institute project?" Dale inquired.

All eyes focused on Ralph. "Yes, I am. We've had some excellent results."

"Philip and his team have praised Ralph's skills." Shasta beamed, proud of her husband.

"Still guessing the next ESP card in the random sequence?" Gordon's cynical edge was bared.

All eyes continued staring at Ralph. He was on stage and ready for a performance.

"Actually, Gordon, my tests have increased in difficulty and strangeness." He paused, allowing his audience to anticipate his new activities. "I'm now remote viewing and have become quite good it." Ralph permitted silence to spread. He noticed Merle nodding approvingly. Dale was grinning.

Gordon took the bait. "I remember reading about those psychic experiments in the 1980s or so. The government was involved, I believe."

"Yes. Actually, the experiments began in the 1970s after we learned the Soviets were doing such research. Our government certainly didn't want to be left behind again," Ralph replied.

Shasta sensed a quiet presence behind her and turned. "Hi, Rafé, please join us." She made room for her at the table.

"Rafé, how are your classes doing?" Dale asked.

"Very good. My adviser and master's committee have accepted my proposal to create and perform a magic show for my thesis. They'll of course ask me questions about it for the orals." Rafé's happiness radiated out from her soul.

Ralph smiled like a proud uncle, having encouraged her and devoted himself to teaching her methods and operations of the magical world.

"Will your performance be open to the public?" Gordon was enchanted with the idea. His attitude toward magic and the occult in general had changed since his participation in Ralph's Alchemical Light Show. Gordon had written the narrative script and acted as the narrator in a speaking role. Learn by doing as someone once proposed.

"The theatre department has applied for funding from the university. It's uncertain at the moment. The chairwoman has stated she would seek funding elsewhere if necessary." Rafé displayed her worry.

"The whole campus is clamping down because of budget problems in this recession. The music department has had to take a large cut in its budget by cancelling classes," Dale responded. He was very unhappy.

"Education, especially for the arts, has always taken the brunt of budget-slashing," Gordon, the knowledgeable cynic, proclaimed.

Ralph sensed negative energy permeate their space. He applied his skill at energy exchange. He emitted positive vibes that bonded with the negative, transforming it into positive. The change was apparent when Shasta brightened and proposed a solution.

"I've a thought. Ralph and I have become friends with Mary Rainbow. We'll talk to her about using Rainbow Inn."

Ralph added, "In fact, I'm giving magic lessons to John Ocean."

The others looked surprised yet optimistic.

Merle was the first to respond. "Beautiful. A joining of Ocean Delights gang with Ocean Avenue trio. I love it."

"How did you start giving lessons to John?" Dale was intrigued.

"Oh, no. Not another sleight-of-hand artist on the block. I don't think I can take any more," Gordon moaned.

"Gordon, I believe you have some serious reality leaks. You should contact John for his services as reality inspector." Dale was delighted with possessing the upper hand.

"Surprisingly, he phoned and requested the lessons. I invited him over and, after appraising his interest and purpose, I agreed. Alice Moore had made the recommendation. He had visited her store and bought some magic props and said he wanted lessons." Ralph paused remembering John's desire to learn about the wand. "He stated directly he wanted to learn the movements for the wand. He took his out and started waving it." Ralph gestured awkwardly.

"Oh, my god, another wand-waving magician." Gordon couldn't help himself as he laughed.

"It's getting more and more brilliant and fits into my present canvas. Here's my suggestion. We invite the trio to join our social gatherings."

"Yes," Shasta exclaimed, "and we rotate our meetings from here to the Inn, back and forth."

"I second," Dale answered.

"All agreed?" Shasta inquired.

They all nodded in accord.

Ralph was pleased the energy exchange had worked so smoothly. He must be more alert to situations and transmute energy when required.

Shasta was feeling good and exhibited her happiness. "Here's some gossip from down the street. Do you know what the trio are planning in their hideaway, the Inn?" She exuded a feeling of let's share some secrets.

Everyone at the table waited impatiently to hear the latest story.

"They're designing a game that blends ideas of John and Od. It's called Master Game."

"A variation on Nietzsche's ideas?" Gordon wondered.

Ever the mage Ralph picked up the thread. "Last week I visited Od's store, and we traded ideas. He has a sharp mind that discerns the basics, the inherent premises. I enjoyed our conversation; I believe he did also. Business is slow at the moment, and he has a lot of time to speculate and play with ideas. While I was there, I surveyed his used book collection. He has some fascinating books. Anyway, he's put together a cluster of ideas derived from various sources. These ideas provide the conceptual structure for his game, Archon Empire."

"Archon? What's that?" Merle inquired.

"The influence is from some Gnostic Christians and Plato. Archon is the name for the Demiurge's chief administrators, who often number seven depending on whose story we read. The Demiurge is the ruling deity of the universe–what most people would call God. Little does the Demiurge realize, but it is overshadowed by an unknown spiritual transcendent divine being, who is the actual source of the universe and its laws."

"Wow. A heavy intellectual system." Dale was impressed.

"The Gnostic religious approach is called gnosis, direct experience of the divine," Ralph continued.

"Awesome." Rafé was spellbound.

"Od recognized the multi-layers of the structure. He's placing a political, social interpretation on it. He does believe knowledgeable Gnostics did the same thing. A group of symbols like the Gnostic ones can have several levels of meaning."

"Just like alchemy," Rafé added.

"Any symbolic system for that matter. The ancients always applied four levels of interpretation to any text," Gordon asserted.

"That's the synopsis of Od's Archon Empire game. John dreamed he was a magician performing some routines, including waving a wand. Probably the basis for his desire to learn wand maneuvers. The dream underlies his vision of a master game. Its goal is to raise consciousness of the participants. They don't compete against each other but seek their own advanced consciousness."

Ralph waited for responses. He began to speak again, but when Shasta held up her hand, he closed his mouth.

"Okay. You got a summary of the game. Each participant selects tools to play the game. John is a magician with magical props. Od is an itinerant tradesman with wares to barter. Mary has a challenge. She is a world chess champion and an excellent musician."

Shasta noticed Dale silently applauding. "Mary decided music would be her source. She chose percussion. Not any percussive instrument but Native American drums. She has a hand drum and–here's her big vision–has ordered a large round drum, the type used at powwows. She plans to set up San Francisco Consciousness Drum Group."

Dale erupted. "Wonderful. I'm ready to participate."

"My career is centered on consciousness-raising. I'm already participating," Merle commented.

Gordon smiled, not ironically but gently. "I see excellent potential. Count me in."

Rafé was delighted. When she realized the gang was watching her, she announced, "I'm involved too." She didn't mention since hearing about the drum project at the Garlands' dinner party, she had spoken to several members of State's Native American Student Organization. They were positively enthralled.

Ralph stood up and spoke with a sense of mystery, "I'd like to give a demonstration of psychic power." He removed a packet of cards from his jacket pocket. He spread the cards face out to his audience, indicating that they were different. He closed the packet and dealt two cards at a time face down into two alternate piles, showing each pair to the group and saying, "These two cards are of different value and color." Once the cards had been dealt, Ralph placed one pile on top of the other and picked up the packet.

"Now comes the crucial part, the time when psychic power can be applied." He removed a card from the packet, asking, "Whose hands have power?"

He looked around at the group. "Gordon, do you have power hands?" Gordon stared at his hands uncertain what to answer.

Ralph walked over to him. "Gordon, I believe you do. Shall we find out? Please touch the card and send your psychic energy into it." Gordon placed his right hand on the card and concentrated.

"That should suffice, Gordon. I can definitely feel energy in it." As Ralph removed the card from Gordon's grasp, the card began to vibrate.

"Ah, see the psychic power is moving the card." Ralph put the vibrating card on the packet and gripped it tightly.

"Now to discover if Gordon's hand power has made a change in the cards." He dealt pairs of cards face up onto the table. Each pair was now the same value and color.

Ralph shook Gordon's hand. "Gordon, you do have excellent psychic power. You should consider talking to Philip, maybe participating in our project. We can use more volunteers."

Gordon studied his hands, smiling, "A very fine demonstration, Ralph. I've certainly discovered new powers in myself."

Cheers and applause erupted from the audience, now including other fascinated patrons.

Chapter 30

When the doorbell chimed, I started for the front door but stopped. Shasta's voice rang out, "Hi, John. Come in. Ralph's in the studio."

John Ocean strolled into the studio, energy bouncing before him. "Ralph, guess what?" he exclaimed.

"It's good to see you so enthusiastic," I replied. "I give up. What's your secret?"

"I had a wonderful inspiration. I watched the film of your show again last night. And I woke this morning with a vision."

I studied him, deliberately taking my time, forcing him to wait in silence. Nodding my head as if to indicate full attention, I said, "Please tell me."

He walked over to the mirror, then turned around facing me. "Well, the vision had fused the floating ball with the talking head. A blending of two routines–what do you think? Say, the floating head rattles or the mage can rattle it in his hands."

Excellent, I thought. "Yes, it can be done. We can float just about anything with the proper equipment. Do you have a story for the effect?"

"That's what we can discuss. I only had the image."

"Do you have any feelings associated with it?"

"Mmm. Yes, I do. On the scary side. Not so much fear as an uneasiness. Like some danger is lurking, and I don't know what or where."

"Excellent. John, your assignment for the coming week is composing a story for the prop. I'll draw some sketches and consider materials for construction. When we have a story, and it doesn't need to be in finished form, I'll show you the workings of the floating ball."

"Okay. A fun assignment. And I'm ready for today's lesson."

"First, you'll perform the routines you've been practicing, which will be recorded. Afterwards, we'll review the session."

I positioned my rocking chair to watch John's performance. When he was ready, I turned on the video camera and sat down. Observing his sleights, gestures, and overall movements closely, I noted several places for improvements. His handling of coins, balls, and silks was excellent. His production, vanishing, and manipulation techniques displayed skill and finesse. John was a fine learner and devoted to the craft. I was delighted to be assisting in his growth and development. Rafé had given me the taste and desire for my new role as teacher and mentor, initiating newcomers into the ancient art of mystery.

My most recent mentor Harold Magian had taught me much, not only techniques but, more importantly, ideas and underlying philosophy. His lessons conveyed the metaphysics of magic. His compassion and encouragement were healing salve I required at the time. I realized, when he left, he could show up unexpectedly any moment.

When John finished, he turned and bowed to my clapping. We then watched the recording of the session. His unerring talent at finding leaks, as he called them, was finely tune. I was impressed. He identified most of the weaknesses I had noticed, so I had very few suggestions for improvement. I focused on his main challenge, one of personality rather than technique.

"Bravo, John. Well done indeed. I would recommend you take a closer look at your attitude while performing. You exude too much 'everyone look at me' energy. The presence of master mages is pure being or existing. The audience is totally aware of the mage who has full contact with them. The bonding is accomplished without grandstanding. Your presence still has a touch of uncertainty, a lack of self-assurance. The audience will sense the weakness. You don't need to lose focus by checking to see if the audience is watching. When your presence is strong, the audience will be glued to every action and happening on stage. Except of course for the movements you don't want them to know about."

We both laughed, sharing a moment of awareness.

"Yes. I do, don't I, waste energy wondering what the audience is doing. Excellent advice. I'll start working on that this afternoon with the new routine." John grinned with self-confidence.

The new routine was the linking rings, a classic that requires the best handling skills and mastery of misdirection. All beginners should learn the effect. Masters will inspire awe in their audience. After retrieving the rings from the box they were stored in, I held them up. "These rings are the props for today's routine. I'll perform and then demonstrate. Please have a seat."

Chapter 31

Rafé beamed. "Oh, yes," she told the handsome young man and fellow student, sitting beside her in Chavez Student Center. "It sounds like a lot of fun."

Jeffrey Brooke smiled broadly, his longish black hair framing his face. "I'll write down my address." Taking a pen and notepad from his bag, he wrote out the information and gave it to her. "We'll start greeting guests around seven pm."

"How many people will be attending?" she inquired.

"It'll be a smallish party. We've agreed to invite no more than four apiece. I'm only asking you." His eyes were tender and happy.

"I'm honored." Rafé touched his hand with hers.

Jeff grinned and rose from the chair. "Until tomorrow." He gestured and then walked away.

Her life was blossoming. New, exciting opportunities were popping up. Glancing at her watch, she got up and hurried to her theater workshop class. Jeff was a member of State's Native American Student Organization. They had met at a meeting three months earlier and began getting together for refreshments at the student center several times a week. They had some similar interests and cultural differences that excited her curiosity. Jeff was a member of the Pawnee Nation of Oklahoma. Traditionally, Pawnees had inhabited the rolling grassland plains, specifically what is now the state of Nebraska. Her roots were in the woodlands around the Great Lakes. He was warm and soft-spoken, two qualities she admired. One common interest was their equal desire to find a means of expressing their culture through the performing arts. Jeff was working on his masters in Broadcast and Electronic Communication Arts. And he had a deep knowledge of his traditional roots–a very big plus in her eyes.

Since she had arrived in San Francisco, Rafé had dated but hadn't developed a serious romantic relationship with anyone. She had been too busy with her studies and part-time job performing magic to get deeply involved. She thought of herself as a modern young woman, a set of values that conflicted with those of the more conservative members of her family. She didn't feel a conflict between her strong desire for an understanding of her people's tradition and living a contemporary lifestyle. Her career came first and raising a family was of secondary importance. Men were able to have both a career and family so women could do the same.

A slender young man, wearing small earrings, opened the door and beckoned Rafé in.

"Hi, Art. How have you been?" she greeted him.

Art Allen grinned. "Very well, thank you. How about yourself?"

"Very good," Rafé replied as they entered the living room. She glanced around the room, recognizing those present. She caught sight of Jeff just as Art whispered, "He's over there." She moved to the small group he was involved with as Art strolled to the dining area, his ponytail bouncing high on his shoulders.

Jeff noticed her and turned to greet her. He was conversing with Tim Hill and Kim Shakeena. After the mutual greetings, Jeff mentioned Rafé and he had similar ideas for their masters' projects.

"Yes, I'm designing a magic act that will portray many Native American stories. Dramatic magic is an excellent format for conveying cultural themes."

Kim gently clapped her hands. "That's wonderful, Rafé. And what's your project about, Jeff?"

"My magic is a different sort. I'll stitch together music and film clips. My idea is to present some of my peoples' cosmic beliefs, a blending of the three worlds."

Art returned bearing a drink. "Rafé, would you like this glass of apple-cranberry blend? We don't have much to offer other than plain apple or grape juice."

She took the glass. "This is fine. It's a favorite beverage of mine." She smiled at him. Art was cute and, she thought, possessed an elfin-like personality. He was a member of the Pinoleville Pomo Nation, which had its main reservation and headquarters in Ukiah, a small town north of San Francisco.

Stepping forward to gain her attention, Tim asked, "Rafé, what's this I hear about a drum group forming at a cafe on Ocean Avenue?"

Rafé laughed. "It's official. Mary Rainbow, owner of Rainbow Inn, is forming a drum group. All are invited to join." She had mentioned Mary's project at a recent NASO meeting to a few people, knowing the power of the drum.

"Both men and women?" Kim wanted to know.

"Yes. She's purchased a powwow style drum and has asked members of several Bay Area drum groups to give lessons."

"What's the purpose?" Tim inquired. He was often skeptical of the dominant society's exploitation of Native American culture. A member of Seneca Nation, one of the original five nations of Haudenosaunee or People of the Longhouse, Tim was working on his MA in political science and law. His sharp eagle-eyes sought for any hidden agendas the Anglo society might have or be planning.

"Now comes the weird part," Rafé replied. "Mary along with the other two members of the Ocean Avenue trio are planning a happening they're calling the Master Game, a game of raising consciousness."

They were all giggling now, trying to stifle their hoots and guffaws. Other party-goers looked at them wondering what the hilarity was all about.

"What's involved in the Master Game?" Kim asked.

"Who else is participating in the game?" Tim threw out.

"I've heard strange and sometimes magical things happen along Ocean Avenue." Art was losing control. Suddenly he let loose a loud "Ho."

He lifted his arms in the air waving his hands. "I've an announcement to make. Quiet please. The residents along Ocean Avenue are planning a Big Time to raise everyone's consciousness and heal the earth. They're forming a drum group to express mother earth's heartbeat. All are invited. Application forms are available." He paused and pointed at Rafé.

"Yes, sign up at Rainbow Inn on Ocean Avenue. See Mary Rainbow for details."

The hum of voices increased, and a wave of enthusiasm flowed among the young people.

Standing tall at six foot four, Jason Capture Bear Bailey sang out, "Heyokas are back again."

Jimmy Mike joined in, "Return of the heyokas, ho."

Laurel Powers yelled, "The people, yes."

More laughter resounded among the partiers as they separated into small groups.

Rafé and Jeff glided off to a quiet corner of the living room. "I've a request and I'm hoping you can help," she said.

"Yes. What is it?"

"I'd like to draw on stories from different nations and not rely only on those from my people."

"I'd be happy to give you some Pawnee stories. Any particular kind?"

"Yes. Origin and trickster stories. I thought I might make a link to your project."

Jeff beamed, his delight shining forth. "Oh, yes, yes. A great idea. Perhaps we could find some thematic parallels."

"Definitely. They wouldn't have to be similar. They could be different variations of the theme, perhaps even opposite views."

"Even better. We'll have more to work with."

An intense buzzing of voices attracted their attention. A small noisy group had gathered around the front door. Art was standing there with his arm around the shoulders of an older lady. People were taking her hand in a gentle clasp. Art strode forward into the middle of the living room guiding the lady beside him. They stopped. "Ho, Ho," Art called in a deep bass voice. The room quieted and everyone looked at the couple.

In the silence Art spoke softly, "I'm honored to introduce my Aunt Mabel Billy who's visiting San Francisco for a few days. She's here for the California Basket Weavers Conference. Many of you are familiar with her work. If you want to become more acquainted with her baskets and those of other California weavers, please visit the exhibit now on display at Caesar Chavez Student Center."

Students gathered around the couple to talk with the well-known basket weaver.

"She's a dreamer too, you know." The voice startled Rafé and Jeff. Ed Sumatzkuku was smiling at them. A member of Hopi Nation, Ed had a talent of remaining so still and silent he was invisible for many people.

"She is? A medicine woman?" Rafé was amazed and filled with awe.

Jeff nodded in agreement. "Art's been telling many stories about her, getting us ready for her visit."

"Tomorrow we're hosting a special luncheon for her and a few of her close friends. We hope to learn more from them," Ed commented.

A sly smile crossed Jeff's face. "Rafé, I'll tell you what transpires at the luncheon, especially if it's magical."

Rafé felt at home with Jeff and his three roommates–Ed, Art, and Tim. Warm, positive energy permeated the house. If any negative forces had existed, they had been dispelled. Jeff had mentioned to her the four roommates had performed a cleansing ceremony with sage before they had moved in.

Tim was the most serious of the four and could become quite intense about social and political issues concerning the federal and state governments' relationships with Indian Nations. He was tall and muscular, an avid sports fan of ice hockey and lacrosse. He had played both sports while in high school back home.

Like Art, Ed was medium height. Ed, though, was more supple and vigorous in his physical movements. His only sports interest was table tennis, which he excelled at. Like Jeff, he was enrolled in Broadcast and Electronic Communication Arts MA program. Unlike Jeff, Ed planned to work in the production end of radio and TV. Ed seemed to have an inherent skill with electronic media, a knowledge that may have evolved with him from the earlier worlds his people had traveled through.

Art was the different one. He walked the less traveled path. His life goal had been set at an early age. He wanted to be an herbalist and dreamer, a medicine man moving along the spiritual path. College courses offered only limited knowledge for his chosen career and degrees were of no benefit unless he wanted a state certified position as counselor or therapist. He had finished his BA and received the degree, but now he was uncertain. Should he continue on for his MA or go back home and become a student of one of the few remaining Pomo dreamers like Aunt Mabel? She had told him she would be delighted to mentor his apprenticeship or she would talk to some other medicine people for him. Perhaps with her presence at the moment a sign would appear and show him the way.

Art's dilemma was rather common among the younger generation of Native Americans, especially those who had a deep respect for their cultural traditions and didn't want to forsake them, yet wanted to participate as fully as possible in the contemporary world and its latest technology. It was a struggle and at times painful conflict between differing views and values.

Rafé felt a fierce struggle of competing values deep within her own being. Since childhood she had sought a path of harmony and beauty, the road her Native American Church now directed her toward. She was fortunate to be guided by the loving hand of her spirit guide. Her quest was to fulfill the role Peyote Woman had set for her.

The hug and kiss at the door before she left was tender, a heart-warming embrace. Rafé sensed a growing bond between them. Her mind focused on Jeff as she walked to the bus stop, her soul flowing with affection for him.

Chapter 32

Her cell phone chimed. Peaches picked it up and looked at the caller ID. It was Virgil. Aeneas was the other person who knew her unlisted number. The film had ended, a lightweight Japanese anime production. She enjoyed their images of superheroes. She pressed answer button.

"Hello, Peaches. This is Gloria. I–hmmm–I lost my cat. I'm scared. Please call me ASAP."

Weird, Peaches thought, she's hired us to find it. The fear was noticeable. No wonder Virgil relayed the call.

Peaches dialed Gloria's number. It rang twice and was picked up.

"Hello." Gloria's voice was trembling.

"Gloria, this is Peaches. What's happened? You sound scared."

"I'm frightened. Please come over. My cat has been stolen."

"I don't understand," Peaches replied. Her voice conveyed puzzlement. "You hired us to find it."

"It's really stolen this time. I lied to you. I fear for my life. I believe I'm in danger."

The fear was real, Peaches decided. "I'm on my way."

"Oh, ask Aeneas to come also. Yes, the two of you. Ring twice, pause and ring once. That's the signal. Bye."

Peaches dialed Aeneas and told him to hurry over to Gloria's. She was on the way and would meet him there outside. They would check the premises first before visiting Gloria.

Aeneas was waiting for Peaches when she arrived. After getting out of their cars, they walked around the perimeter of the apartment house. Lights were on in Gloria's first floor apartment. The only other apartment with a light on was on the second floor opposite hers.

"All clear. Let's go in and hear her story," Peaches said.

The door opened on an anxious appearing Gloria, who led them into the living room.

"I'm so stressed out," she complained. "Please sit. I can fix coffee or tea if you want."

"We could use some coffee," Peaches replied.

Aeneas jumped up when Gloria started for the kitchen. "I can help," he suggested and followed her.

Peaches surveyed the room, noting its décor and function. It wasn't her office or workspace. More likely a social and relaxing place. She noted the TV-audio system, the reading chair, table with magazines and newspapers, and a bookcase.

Gloria returned, Aeneas–carrying a tray with coffee, sugar, and milk– walking behind her. Placing the tray on an end table next to the couch, Aeneas served the coffee and then sat down facing Peaches, who was on the couch, and Gloria, who was sitting in the reading chair. He removed a tablet from his jacket and turned it on. Aeneas had installed a miniature audio recorder-transmitter in the device. Their conversation would be sent back to Virgil for analysis and storing.

Peaches studied her client. "Well, on the phone you said you had lied to us about the cat and now it's actually missing. Will you please explain. We'd like the truth this time. We can't help you otherwise."

"I hid the cat because of threats to steal it. This morning I went to retrieve it, and it was gone. Now I don't know what to do. I'm frightened."

"Okay, the basic facts are laid out. Now we want the whole story from beginning to present. Where did the cat come from? We know it wasn't your grandmother's. What's so important about the cat? And who might want to steal it? We'll ask questions along the way." Peaches stared at her intently.

Gloria breathed deeply a couple times. "It's like this. Sean–I've mentioned him–and I lived together for about six years. Sean was a genius but never could get his trip together. At the end he lost it and unraveled. He died of cancer." She paused and wiped tears from her eyes.

"Sean was a role-player and participated in a number of different games. I was only a little bit, just enough to stay with Sean. At the start of our relationship I was madly in love with him and would do anything for him. But during our time together we gradually grew apart. Our interests changing and moving in separate directions. During the last two years of his life he was totally engrossed in the Sorcerers-Wizards game. I'm sure you're familiar with it." She glanced at her audience.

"The basic premise of the game is grounded on the idea of real magic. To play with dedication one must believe in real magic. Total belief, no doubts, acting like magicians of olden days. It was freaky. I was frightened by the seriousness and complete commitment. It was an either-or situation. You're with me against the evil wizard and his gang or you're on their side against me. I mean I couldn't be that serious, a true believer. So as I mentioned, Sean and I drifted apart. We still lived together, and I maintained a semblance of partnership, like performing the domestic chores, which he expected from his woman. He did call me his queen, his first woman. But it was too old-fashioned. I'm just there for his benefit—no life of my own."

Silence reigned as Gloria sank into her memories. "I'm sorry. I did see a therapist after Sean died. And she helped me greatly. Okay, the cat is what it's all about now. Yes, the cat was Sean's, and he gave it to me for safe-keeping and my personal use. A month before he passed on, he performed a ceremony during which he gave me the cat and showed its secret and function. It was magic—holy serious stuff. I didn't realize the cat's true nature and significance until later, after I was feeling better. Then I disposed of his belongings and inspected the things he left for me. He finally had his life organized, right at the end. This stuff for Goodwill, this for trash, and this for Gloria. That's how he had marked the groups." Pausing, she blew her nose.

"The cat. It's hard for me to talk about. I'm sorry." She started crying.

Peaches spoke softly with tenderness. "Gloria, take your time. We can stop for awhile and return later when you're more up to it." Peaches smiled at her.

"No, it's better to finish now. We must find the cat. We can't let it get into the wrong hands. That would be a disaster."

Peaches and Aeneas exchanged wondering glances. Their curiosity was alert.

"The cat has a hidden chamber in its chest. Inside the chamber Sean keep his charm which he wore around his neck like a necklace. Not all the time but only when he was using the charm. Otherwise the charm remained in the cat."

"The charm is the significant item, not the cat containing it?" Peaches inquired.

"Yes, definitely. It's magic. I never realized how magical it is until much later. And then I became worried someone might learn about it and steal it, perhaps harming or killing me in the process." Gloria stopped and looked at her empty coffee cup. "I'd like more coffee, anyone else?" She started to rise, but Aeneas was up first. "I'll get refills, Gloria," he announced.

The two women sat in silence, Gloria deep in her memories, and Peaches quietly watching her, evaluating the story so far.

Aeneas returned and served coffee.

Gloria brightened a little. She sipped coffee, feeling refreshed. Then she spoke, "I don't know how much background you both have in occult and magic and various esoteric fields of knowledge. Sean was brilliant. He immersed himself in it all. No boundaries for him. Well, the charm is linked to the throat chakra. Are you familiar with the chakra system of energy. The kundalini root and lotus blossom crown?"

A little bit," Peaches informed her.

"Not much," Aeneas acknowledged.

"I'm not the expert Sean was. But I picked up bits and pieces from him. The chakras are part of Hindu Sanskrit tradition and flow over into Buddhism. The human body has a subtle energy system, more on the psychic level. Chinese acupuncture is similar."

Peaches nodded understanding. She was familiar with acupuncture and acupressure techniques and their basic assumptions about the body.

"There are seven main chakras, energy centers, from the base of the spine to the top of the head."

Gloria began sobbing, and Peaches stood up and went over to her. She rested her hand on Gloria's shoulder. Speaking quietly to her, Peaches said, "Gloria, we're your friends and we'll help in any way we can. If you wish, we can take a break."

Peaches placed both hands on Gloria's shoulders and massaged them gently. Gloria relaxed and moved her head in a circle several times. "Thank you. That feels good. Where did you learn the technique?"

"When I was young, growing up in Indiana, I learned the best method to milk cows. Gentle massaging is the basis for milking. Then I just applied it to humans." Peaches maintained her hands on Gloria's shoulders.

"I suddenly had this memory of Sean on his deathbed telling me his cancer was caused by his archenemy, the evil sorcerer Vortigern, who had cast a spell on him. His fate was destined, and he couldn't prevent it. I was so upset. I mean I couldn't believe in the magic spell, but Sean's faith in its reality was too much. I think that was the main reason I cracked up after his death. My therapist thought so also." Gloria began crying again.

Peaches gently massaged Gloria's shoulders and neck until the tension was released.

"Oh, thank you. What wonderful healing hands you have. If the detective business bottoms out, you can always offer massage service. The charm was an aid in Sean's battle against his opponents. He applied its magic and usually won any conflict." Gloria stopped and glanced at Peaches and then at Aeneas.

"You don't have to believe the reality of the game to understand the charm's significance. And it does work regardless of one's belief." She glanced again at Peaches and Aeneas. They both nodded their agreement.

"The throat chakra is one of seven main chakras. Sean called it Vishuddha. It's involved with communication, intuition, creativity. Sean said it's a link to the astral and psychic voice channels. It's considered the first level of advanced consciousness. It's a healing vortex because it's associated with the thyroid gland." She paused, waiting for questions or comments. When none was asked, she continued, "The most important part, its real magical use by people like Sean–it's a link to the astral level. Sean was able to leave his body and travel in the astral belt or channel."

"Whoa," Aeneas exclaimed. "Please walk me through that bit about astral travel again."

Gloria smiled. Peaches smiled back. It was the first time Gloria had smiled in their presence.

"Okay. The out-of-body-experience or OBE is the primary method of traveling for magicians. The witch with her broomstick is a metaphor and child's version of the actual procedure. One's double or spirit or soul–I've heard all those names and many others–is the part of ourselves that leaves the body. Sean called it his double. The battles magicians wage are fought in the astral plane. The physical representation of this reality, like in the Harry Potter films, is a popular version for most people who can't see the astral world. The charm, which is a miniature replica of the big cat, linked to the throat chakra. Sean wore it around his neck as a necklace. He said he could perceive the astral level and communicate on the voice channel. When he left his body, he would lie down wearing the charm. I've watched him while he was out there. His body was so quiet, his eyes closed, not much of a facial expression. His breathing slowed down so it seemed unnoticeable to me. At first I was scared, thinking maybe he had died. I don't know. I didn't really understand much of it. Certainly not the ideas and beliefs." She stopped. "You understand what I'm saying?"

Peaches, still massaging Gloria's shoulders, replied, "I follow the story although like you I don't understand how it all can work."

Aeneas grunted his agreement. He wondered what Virgil would make of it all.

"I eventually tried the charm, following Sean's instructions. It was weird. I can't really describe it. I don't believe I had any OBEs, but I don't know. I'm not sure what it's like. I did have the voice communication experiences. Oh, my. How strange. Voices I couldn't identify. Gradually I identified certain voices and kept track of them. Some were friendly, others mean or hostile sounding. Then about a month ago I heard two voices I had never heard before. They were near. By this time I was able to discern distances and emotional vibes. I was able to hear them clearly. So they were close by, somewhere in the Bay Area. They were usually together and they called each other by name: Merlin and Morgan."

"Wait," Peaches said. "Merlin and Morgan have come up in our investigation recently. Does the Sorcerer's Landscape mean anything to you?"

"Yes. Merlin and Morgan talk about Sorcerer's Landscape. I've presumed it's the name for a company, perhaps theirs."

"Of course. Good. We're finally located one of the adversaries. Please continue," Peaches replied.

"Well, they talked about Sean and a book of his with notes in it they had deciphered. The notes were about the charm and its function. They wanted it badly. They talked about Tower Mansion and its master. They could use the voice channel for gaining control. More war game strategy. Later they learned about my relationship with Sean and thought I might have the cat or know what happened to it, so they discussed plans to steal the cat or threaten me. That's when I decided to hide it. At least they wouldn't find it unless they tortured me so much I told them. I thought I was being clever to hire you and make public the report of the cat's disappearance. And now it's gone."

The tension had disappeared from Gloria's shoulders. Peaches returned to the couch. "Well, we have a real case now. I don't think Merlin and Morgan were the culprits. We've been watching them." She wasn't going to tell Gloria about Virgil, their super secret.

Aeneas laughed inwardly. The astral plane is as wild as the digital internet world. Both are unbelievable to most people. The internet can be accepted because it's the physical representation of the invisible electromagnetic field with its waveforms.

"Obviously there's a third party involved. Who could that be? Some of Sean's old friends who knew about the charm? Another wizard who can link to the voice channel and follow your movements? Let's assume the reality if only for solving the puzzle. We've a thought problem. A let's pretend situation." Aeneas offered his proposal for consideration.

Gloria stood up. "Now my confession is finished, I'm actually hungry. I'll make some snacks and fresh coffee." She went into the kitchen.

Peaches declared, "What a tale. I'm just a little country girl. It boggles my mind. So, Aeneas, what are your hidden thoughts on the subject?"

"Only one conclusion, however improbable. A magician of advanced degree was listening and detected Gloria and figured out she had a powerful charm. Since we don't know all the players in the game or their number, let's pretend it's the master of Tower Mansion."

"All right, we'll pretend. But why first consider the master and not someone else?"

"Because the wizard has so much power, he–I'm using the term to mean both genders–controls Tower Mansion. He certainly doesn't want to lose his position as king of the mountain. Assume also he has assistants who can watch the underlings for any attempt at overthrow of his rule. A veritable security state–he has eyes and ears everywhere in the astral world. Okay?"

Peaches smiled. "Go on. I'm enjoying your tale."

"Next, assume anyone entering the astral plane is spotted, identified, and tracked as federal agencies like NSA do on the internet and broadcast frequencies. Gloria appears in their sights and she is followed. They may even be able to detect the device she is using. It may have a signature. Gloria is small-time and they just watch.

"Now Merlin and Morgan learn Gloria possesses the charm. Their knowing troubles the master because these two want to remove him and gain control–the ancient power ploy. What does the master do?" Aeneas grinned at Peaches, delighted at the puzzle he had served to her.

"Why, of course. He employs them without their knowledge of his manipulation to threaten Gloria. He encourages them to steal the charm and that threat forces Gloria into action. She hides it, a natural response, which the master probably predicted."

Gloria came in bearing a variety of tiny sandwiches and coffee on a tray, which she placed on the table. "Please, help yourself," she said.

Peaches gave Aeneas the sign of 'we'll continue later' and reached for a sandwich. Aeneas got up and retrieved a couple of them.

Shasta paused and listened. A feeling of being watched touched her. She swiveled and gazed at the doorway. A surprise expression marked her face. Then she chuckled. Lucy and Karma were sitting patiently at the doorway, focusing their total attention on her. She glanced at the computer clock. Aha, the kitties' sense of time was precise. It was five pm. She got up and headed downstairs with the kitties leading the way.

Chapter 33

I was in the third room and saw the illuminator. The room was brightly lit, yet something was wrong. I could sense an anomaly. I inspected the room carefully. All the furnishings were present and in their proper location. But what? I moved around the room examining the walls for anything missing or new. Then I went over to the window. Streetlights glowed, shining on several parked cars. No pedestrians. All was silent.

I turned and walked toward the middle of the room. An aha struck me. That was it. An eerie silence pervaded the room. But why not? The rooms never had any sounds. Silence always presided. A difference I couldn't explain was noticeable now.

Another thought caught my attention. Why am I here? I don't remember being at the Institute nor given an assignment.

I moved back to the window. The scene hadn't changed. Suddenly, a brilliant flash of lightning illuminated the street. I waited. The thunder's roar—where was it? Again another flash and another, yet silence remained. Dumbfounded, I turned. The door into the central room was closed. As I walked toward it, I glanced to my right and stopped, startled. The wall had an open archway leading into another room. Automatically, I climbed to the archway. Pausing, I looked back, noticing the floor sloped downward. Room three was receding from view. I felt slightly faint. I stepped through the archway into the room, which should be room four, but it wasn't. Or room four had changed completely. The room wasn't illuminated by its focal point. A central area was lit, and the remainder in darkness.

I quickly strode into the center of light, sensing a strangeness. Glancing around, attempting to penetrate the darkness for lurking danger, I stood in the light. I felt an emptiness. Stepping to the edge of the light, I peered into the darkness, letting my eyes adjust to the gloom. Revolving in a full circle, I realized the room was bare of furnishings. No furniture, no wall hangings, no decorations of any kind. It was empty.

I looked up at the light source but was blinded by its brightness. So the room had one fixture, a light overhead. I felt something touch the back of my neck. I jumped. Panicked. Seeing the end of a rope, I pulled it and a ladder descended. Without thinking, I ascended the ladder. At the top was clear sky, a deep blue night sky. I climbed to a platform under the night sky. Creeping close to the edge, I looked down. Nothing was below and only sky above. The platform was floating in space. I was puzzled. I could stay here, perhaps indefinitely, or jump into unknown darkness. An aha brought a grin to my face. I would fly and travel, seeking adventures in new worlds.

Blinded by a brilliant lightning bolt, I nearly fell off but clung to the edge, as a loud thunder-roar shook the platform. Another light followed by a roar. I thought of Thunderbird, a very special spirit being for many Native Americans. And its opposite, Underwater Serpent.

Gnosis flooded my soul. I leaped from the platform and flew. An immense sensation of calm guided my maneuvers. I soared and dipped and glided into the beams of a waxing gibbous moon.

With eagle's sight I spied below a pond reflecting dancing moonbeams. I dove toward it and deftly landed beside tranquil waters. An ancient wood bench was at the water's edge. I sat and breathed in fresh invigorating air. Bliss sat beside me and we embraced.

Hearing a rustling, rattling sound, I looked for the source. A small house, its door ajar, was nearby. Curious, I walked over to the building. Opening the door, I viewed the interior. A lamp sitting on a table lit the room. I entered. My life changed that night. I marveled that my quest succeeded. I discovered myself, a truer part than I had ever known as far back as I could remember. Seated at the table was my double, a happy, gracious Ralph Garland. We talked that night until the rosy fingers of dawn crept over the horizon. He knew all I remembered and all I had forgotten. He knew what I kept repressed and behind the doors of denial. He knew it all. He was my truth and I desired to be him. We arose and embraced.

Morning sunlight shone through the window, warming my body. I opened my eyes and smiled at the light. I felt Shasta beside me, cuddled close. I lay still so as not to disturb her. I lay silent and glad.

I felt as if I were in my twenties and had difficulty containing my emotions until tonight's happy hour when I would describe my dream to Shasta. John was coming over for his lesson in the afternoon. On the phone he mentioned he had composed a story outline for the dancing skull effect. This morning I was at loose ends. Shasta was working on her novel. At breakfast she had said her Muse was still singing to her and her imagination flowing.

Relax, I thought. What would my double tell me? Enter the still point. Of course, I've been compartmentalizing. The circular room is available all the time, not just for remote viewing. When I awake in the morning, I should enter it if I'm not already there. It should be my permanent place, my inner home, unless I desire to go somewhere else.

As I stepped into my studio, I sensed a tranquility. Here was my physical space and the circular room was my mental. I glanced at the mirror, wondering if I would see my double. What a strange experience even if it was only a dream. How often do we meet our true selves? Today was a special occasion, a celebratory moment.

Smiling at my mirror image, I decided to show John the technique and fundamental concepts for levitating small objects. I'd prepare the floating globe and make some sketches of a lightweight skull to levitate. Going to the shelves storing magical equipment, I removed the talking-skull and set it on the work counter where I serviced and repaired my props. The skull was made from a synthetic material and wasn't too heavy. If it would levitate and maneuver without difficulty, I wouldn't require a new skull. For the rattle part, a small container of beads hidden in the skull would be perfect. I retrieved the levitating apparatus and set up the skull for a few trial runs. If it operated easily, I would be prepared for the afternoon's lesson.

Pausing, I peered at the mirror. Moving closer to it, I examined my features. My double looked like me, like the mirror image but something was different, something I didn't possess at least at the moment. My quest was to discover the difference, the special trait my double had. He knew everything about me, everything I knew and more. I lacked his quality of–of perfection. That's it. He was perfect. The template of what I should and could be. My role model and mentor, my teacher. From him I take lessons to become my true, perfect self. Yes, it felt right, a seamless fit. Easy to say. Performance is the challenge. But my goal is clear and attainable. A dare I will take whatever the risk. If the quest interferes with my work at the Institute, so be it. But I'm thinking now it'll dovetail nicely. In fact, the work there is an enhancement to my quest.

Chapter 34

His mind was afire, buzzing with thoughts as it always did after watching the film *The Matrix*. Today's viewing was unique. He felt personally involved in the drama, one of the characters caught in the net of Great Machine Society. He now had an understanding that touched his soul. His intellect was lucid. An intuitive awareness dissolved mental confusion.

Lefty's experience was on the level of gnosis. In the background he heard the Muse singing. The song was conveying details about Eduardo Guchol and Henry Gorman, two characters in his novel. He sucked on the straw in the coffee container and realized the coffee was about gone. Focusing on the outer scene in the park, Lefty allowed his thoughts to recede into the background. The sun was peering out from behind clouds and a slight breeze was blowing off the bay. He stretched his arms upward, releasing tension. He would return to his loft and begin recording the Muse's song.

Mug filled with steaming coffee, Lefty sat at the keyboard, waiting for thoughts to flow. He would visit Henry, who was more like himself. In his present lucid state Lefty recognized Henry as a close double to his own personality.

Henry pushed the off button on the remote and the TV screen went blank. Having watched *The Matrix* every year since it was released, he was still impressed. Its power remained strong and it spoke more clearly to him with each viewing. He owned the complete trilogy, part of his treasured film collection.

He had his own personal battle with the Machine, the governing corporate complex. Without thinking, he dipped a chip into the salsa and put it into his mouth. He had been accumulating data for the past six months that clearly demonstrated the truth about the country's supposed democracy and constitutional government. Within the week he would post his blog detailing the true state of affairs with links to the cloud storing the actual data. As a founding member of Ever-And-Anon, he was ready to light the fuse that

would start the revolution. The quantity of data was enough to raise awareness and lead seekers to further knowledge and understanding of political
and social reality. The evidence confirmed the existence of the ruling elite
and robot-like humans who managed the Corporate Machine for them.
Ignorance and delusion were primary weapons managers used on people.
Since the data were published in cyberspace, all who wanted to know would
learn the truth. He was unconcerned about those who wished to hide behind their ignorance and remain in their prisons.

The next stage was gathering data to show the process and method the
elite used to control the managerial class. He had several ideas, but without
evidence there would be no posting. His ferret probes were now searching
throughout cyberspace and culling evidence from all databases. Very few
had firewalls that could withstand his lock-picking, especially backdoors,
the treasure gate for all cyberpunks.

His hand dropped to the chip bowl and found nothing. Henry paused
his mental processes. He looked into the bowl. It was best he stopped his
munching–a good way to add more pounds he didn't need. He pushed
himself up from the old, tattered armchair and walked around the room,
stretching his arms and swinging them in circles. Feeling relaxed, he started
off for the kitchen when he noticed the message flag blinking on the 42-inch
TV screen hooked to the computer system. The screen was large enough to
monitor the operations on his four computers simultaneously. The flag indicated a chat room conversation was happening at Ever-And-Anon website.
He logged in and read the ongoing session.

Tau was perplexed. Too many strange occurrences had intersected his affairs. He rose from the command desk and left the bridge. He went to the
elevator and descended to the ground level, the main area of his residence.
He walked down the corridor to the swimming pool. Invigorating exercise
was a fine healer. Later he would examine the situation and devise a plan of
action.

Refreshed, his mind clear, Tau reclined in a cushioned armchair. He was
in the library, a room for leisure activities and informal socializing, and enjoying a tall glass of iced chai latte. A Mozart composition was playing quietly in the background. His mind drifted over the disturbing information.
A new troublemaker had emerged. Although the threat posed by the latest

adversary was different from that of Ralph Garland, the danger to his global hegemony was as great. Before leaving the bridge, he sent DOG to retrieve all available data on Lefty Cosmos. DOG was a sophisticated data gathering program, which made quick assessments by sorting data into broad categories for later detailed analysis.

He had a special watch folder for potential threats like Philip Austen and the Institute. Lefty Cosmos was now an inmate of the watch group. All data, however tenuously connected to Lefty, would be filed there. Any updates posing a serious risk would trigger an alert.

Tau changed directions and concentrated on current federal activities. He was delighted with the government's Total Information Awareness Surveillance Program, which now fed NSA's Utah Data Center. Located at Camp Williams near Bluffdale, Utah, part of Salt Lake City's outer metropolitan area, the Center was gathering and storing more information than any other facility. It was the finest source for data on the world's population.

No system was secure from the eyes of DOG, including the Utah Data Center. He had at his fingertips data from all over the globe–government, business, and individual. The US government might take over a corporation, as it did Megaupload, and confiscate all the company's data thus giving certain government employees insider information of work in progress of thousands of companies that had posted their files on the website. The knowledge would be worth millions of dollars to smart and clever individuals who would use and sell the data.

Data control equaled wealth and power. He had been exploiting the process for over a decade and now was reaching the pinnacle of success. His small team of techno-experts were masters in their chosen fields of software and hardware development. He was the brain who viewed the complete picture with all data available and made final decisions.

He picked up the tablet from the side table and pressed the master button keyed to the print of his forefinger. The screen showed Lefty Cosmos' file. He read it and then let his mind play with the information. Lefty was a knowledgeable programmer and security expert. Being employed by Pacific Highloft Security insured his skill and talent were excellent. His job performance wasn't the issue. In fact Lefty was a young man whom Tau would consider hiring if a position became available. No, it was Lefty's off-job, leisure-time activities. His global novel, an online work-in-progress involving others with similar ideas and attitudes. DOG had retrieved the recent additions to the story and chat room texting. Tau was very unhappy with Lefty's project because the young man had ideas and theories that were menacing to public order. And public order was what Tau relied on. It was his cover and external security for his empire.

Lefty was planning to destroy the façade of social-political decorum and broadcast ideas that were too close to the truth. Even though Lefty's work was a fantasy sci-fi tale, many people would certainly be influenced by the underlying themes and symbols. And such an affect on people's thinking was dangerous. The foundations of the political-economic pyramid would be shaken and perhaps disintegrate.

Tau placed Lefty in the security watch folder's red zone. He began devising a strategy for the eventual future when he must destroy the young novelist.

Chapter 35

John was bubbling with energy. "Ralph, I've had some insights," he remarked as he followed him into the studio. John had arrived earlier than usual for his afternoon lesson.

Ralph surveyed his student, noticing the bolo tie he was wearing. "The Thunderbird pendant is beautiful. Where did you find the bolo tie?"

"It was crafted by a Zuni artisan. I bought it from the Heard Museum in Phoenix. I researched the symbolic tradition of the Thunderbird after I purchased the bolo. I was amazed. So many First People have Thunderbird as an important spirit being."

Ralph smiled. "The cultural traditions of indigenous people are wonderful sources for insights and wisdom, especially for us moderns who have lost touch with our roots."

"Od has expressed a similar idea. We moderns have forgotten our cultural heritage and are off-balance. The political and economic scene today is a prime example. So many fools running around acting big and superior."

"I've been digging deeper in Native American culture. Rafé has inspired me. For a long time Shasta and I have collected Native American art. You may have noticed some pieces at the dinner party."

"I noticed several, but I didn't have time to examine them closely."

"Come, I'll show you a wood sculpture of Thunderbird and Underwater Serpent." Ralph led John out of the studio into the living room. He pointed to a wood sculpture, about a foot high, hanging on the wall. "Thunderbird has caught Underwater Serpent in its claws. The artist has represented Thunderbird as an eagle, a common image. Notice the human-like head arising from Thunderbird's back. The human feature denotes the soul or spirit. So the image isn't a regular eagle but a spirit manifesting as an eagle, which could only be Thunderbird."

"Such exquisite work. The carving is precise and detailed. My, the serpent has wings."

"The Ojibwa or Anishinaabe People also use the name Underwater Panther for the Serpent, who is the greatest power in the Lower World. Thunderbird is the great power in the Upper World."

"Really. It's quite intriguing. And where are we?"

"The Middle World, of course. The shaman or medicine healer is able to enter the other two worlds with assistance from spirit guides. A balance must be maintained between Thunderbird and Underwater Panther. There are special ceremonies for harmonizing the worlds."

As they walked back to the studio, John remarked, "Thunderbird—it's a spirit being, so does it interact with us through a physical manifestation."

"Yes, as an incarnation."

"The idea is the seed for my story. I've two queries though. Can a spirit handle physical objects as a spirit or must it be manifested? And can floating objects be moved by a spirit?"

"In séances yes. The spirit can move objects. You can apply psychic power to the story. Spirit doesn't have a body but can manipulate objects and influence human behavior. So the action must be accomplished on the psychic level or by using psychic force to operate on physical objects. If spirits can accomplish the feats, humans can too if they have the ability. The action, when humans perform it, is called telekinesis."

"I was thinking of a shaman or medicine healer. The healer may deal with the spirit that is causing the illness or perhaps a bad shaman who does evil. An assumption of a spirit level is present."

"Yes. The spirit plane and physical realm interact. The shaman has techniques for using the spirit world."

"Since the story and routine are for the master game and raising consciousness, the healing involved is of the mind. Exorcism is a traditional model. Assume something specific is preventing consciousness from increasing, so the healer must counteract that agent and its spirit power or psychic force."

"Okay. You have a conflict with potential dramatic development. What comes next?"

"I'll have a modern setting with three characters."

"And you'll be the healer. Which roles do Mary and Od play?"

John laughed. "You guessed. But actually I wasn't thinking of them. They have their games to play. The triad is an ancient symbol and often the foundation. No, the bad guy is more abstract, an adverse force that's latent in the cosmos. More in keeping with Od's archon game. It's a negative force but not evil."

"Like the trickster in Jungian psychology."

"Yes. It prevents growth of consciousness by misdirection or distraction rather than a face-to-face confrontation."

"So the shaman tries to heal the patient and must counteract the negative force."

"Yes. Let's call it a bad spirit. It lurks in the background and causes a person to succumb to its negative energy."

"Like falling asleep or into a stupor."

"The person behaves at a low level of awareness. Goes around in a daze. I was thinking the healer could use some floating objects in a ceremony which shocks and upsets and arouses the patient. Thus the rattling, levitating skull."

"We can employ the séance background which definitely shocked believers. Okay, good. Have you developed any more of the story?"

"No, that's it at the moment."

"Fine. I'll observe your lesson. Then we'll discuss the method for levitating. Also I've made some sketches for a rattling skull that floats. We can go from there."

John stood silently as an idea formed in his mind. Ralph watched, noticing the increasing brightness of John's aura. John faced the mirror. Retrieving his wand, he gestured as if he were conducting a musical ensemble. Stopping, he turned toward Ralph.

"I've been in aha-land. Oh, what a fool I've been. Suddenly an idea formed before my eyes. My patient is the audience. They're the ones I'll heal with my magic."

Ralph nodded. "I've a routine to show you. It fits with your proposal."

He walked over to his storage shelves and took a tarot deck from its cloth holder. Ever since his sweatlodge healing ceremony, he had started treating more everyday objects as sacred. It was a major change in his attitude, and his sensitivity had expanded. He had begun with his basket necklace and Zuni bear. Enlarging the sacred region of his life, he now gave many of his craft's tools the same treatment. He picked up a small stone and carried both to the performing table on stage in front of the mirror.

"The routine is an example of effects that may serve your purpose. I'll use fifteen cards of the major arcana."

Ralph picked up the tarot deck and dealt off fifteen cards, which he shuffled. He asked John to cut the packet and then dealt face down three piles with five cards each.

"John, please select one of the piles and look at its cards. Mentally chose one of the cards."

John viewed the cards and nodded. "Okay, I've selected a card."

"Please shuffle the packet. Then place it on top of one of the other piles."

After John had completed the task, Ralph said, "Now place the other pile on top."

Ralph picked up the cards and dealt them face down into five piles. "John, please look at each pile and indicate which pile has your card."

John viewed the packets. "This one," he remarked as he laid the packet face down.

Ralph removed the other four piles from the table. He spread the face down pile his assistant had indicated. Taking the stone, he commented, "The stone has power and receives and transmits psychic energy. Hold the stone and mentally project the image of the chosen card into the stone. You'll be increasing your mind power by doing so."

John took the stone and focused his attention on it.

Ralph waited for a few moments. "Have you projected the image?"

"Yes, I have."

"Please hand me the stone. Thank you. Now I'm going to use the stone to identify your chosen card. Please continue to project the card's image into the stone."

Ralph slowly moved the stone over each card. Suddenly the stone vibrated violently over one card.

"The stone says this is your card." He turned over the card. It was the Magician. "You chose the Magician card."

John applauded. "Bravo," he exclaimed. "Yes. I like the routine. You're correct. It is the sort of magic I'm interested in. It's empowering. The assistant does the magic."

"And so does the audience since the assistant is an audience member. Your patient-assistant represents the audience, the group that will be healed by raising its consciousness."

John's excitement overflowed. "Yes. All the disparate pieces fit together. Raising mental awareness by mind power magic. It's seamless."

Ralph smiled, expressing his encouragement. Solve et coagula, he thought. "You can go a step further by giving a reading of the chosen card. Consider the implications of the routine. Was your selection of the pile by chance or guided by an invisible force? What power motivated you to choose the Magician?"

"Of course. Basic cosmic questions. Actually, when I saw the Magician, I automatically selected it. I thought it was a sign for my new path. I don't even remember the other four cards. Because I was aware of my choice, I've no difficulty believing my picking that particular pile was guided by a power and not chance."

"You were presented with three alternatives. Do you remember your mental state while you were considering which to choose?"

John closed his eyes, peering inward. "No, I don't. I guess my memory is focused on seeing the Magician and thinking: Wow. A sign."

"Imagine the process involved as a weaving of different material as basket weavers do. The woven basket has its own design and any images on its surface also have a design. Thus the basic reality with its patterned covering."

John paced around the studio, reflecting on Ralph's comments. The basket metaphor depicted the structure of reality. Both Ralph and Shasta were creative individuals. Their imaginations were fertile and discerning. Metaphors were symbolic and often disclosed hidden parts of the world. Magic was expanding his sights. Storytelling and symbols were tools to convey wisdom. Ralph's philosophic leanings were contagious and inviting, often opening new paths.

"I'm exhilarated, Ralph; already my consciousness has expanded to include alternate portals for knowledge."

Ralph was delighted with his student. How fortunate he was to be able to guide someone as devoted and enthusiastic as John Ocean. "Well, let's see a performance of the routine you've been practicing. Afterwards I'll demonstrate the methods for floating objects." Ralph pushed the rocking chair into viewing position and sat down.

Chapter 36

DOG was traveling through ethereal net when J.S. Bach's "Air on G String" played through the music-in-the-round system. Tau became alert. The famous Bach composition was the musical motif Tau had given Ralph Garland and was keyed into Ralph's personal psi waveform frequency. DOG would continue retrieving data while Tau checked on Ralph.

He switched on the waveform channel in the main monitor, opened the database for waveform equations, and typed 'psi spectrum' on the touch screen. Psi bosons existed in the psi spectrum. Actually they were manifestations of the field. Like all bosons they could occupy the same quantum state, if they had the same energy.

He selected the set of equations appearing on the monitor. Waveforms of the psi field moved across the screen. He entered the GPS coordinates for Ralph's location. He now had a lock on Ralph's psi waveform's global positioning, an exact location.

Tau had gotten psi spectrum waveform equations from an eccentric mathematical genius many years ago during the heyday of mind-bending events when people yearned to go to the edge of the universe and risked their lives trying. He had dared and was enjoying the fruits of his endeavors.

Reading the decoded data from the incoming psi waveform, Tau realized Ralph was thinking about performing a distant viewing session. He knew he had to act before Ralph entered the central room of his inner mansion.

He retrieved the transmitter ring from its holder on the desktop and placed it on his right index finger. The ring was a techno-magical wi-fi device linked to the psi waveform generator-transmitter. The ring allowed him to surf psi field just as he could travel ethereal net with the virtual machine. The 'magic' ring suitable for psi traveling, he had purchased from another weird genius of the Oz variety.

Switching off inner noise, Tau thought one word, "Go." He launched into the cosmic psi spectrum, zooming in on his adversary's mental mansion, and slipped into the central room. He moved quickly around the room opening slightly each of the twelve doors. Tau vanished and reemerged in his office.

The strategy was simple. Whenever Ralph entered a room, a change would automatically occur in the room's furnishings. The alteration was undetermined until Ralph stepped into the room. Ralph would cause anomalies to grow in his psychic journeys, debilitating his mental power. A ripple effect would generate doubts and anxieties in Philip and his team. The demise of the Institute's project was inevitable.

After Ralph had completed today's remote viewing, Tau would examine the data, identifying the change and clarifying the significance of Ralph's experience.

Most people, especially among the scientific intelligentsia, would deny the existence of cosmic psi spectrum if they heard about it, calling it only a silly superstition. The fools were easily netted and rendered harmless. Those individuals open to the possibility of the impossible were the greatest danger and threat to his survival.

He left the bridge and walked down the stairs to the main room. Going to the refrigerator, he took a bottle of cold spring water, a refreshing treat for his adventure. He went to the game station and sat down at a console and began a game.

Memory of the OBE dream remained close to the surface of consciousness. My impulse was to explore the houses and learn what the dream encapsulated. I had nothing planned for the afternoon. Shasta was busy upstairs working on her novel. She was fortunate. Her Muse was singing to her. I closed the study door but opened it when I heard scratching. Karma was standing there. Our kitties don't like closed doors. So be it. No hidden recesses not even in the mind. It was a sign I told myself. All is open for my exploration. I thanked Karma for her assistance and sat down in my rocking chair. The movement relaxes me, and I can silence my mind easily.

I was in the inner chamber of my mental mansion. Revolving, I studied each of the twelve doors, which were all ajar. Well, I thought, that's unusual. Normally they're all closed. The central room is a full circle and lacks furnishings with one exception. A circular rug, seven feet in diameter, rests on the floor in the exact center. The room is lit without any apparent light fixtures. When I arrive there, I am standing on the rug. I can stand or sit or take whatever position I want to be in. I sat down and began slowly revolving from left to right around the circumference. The doors remained ajar. No strange or weird feeling was present.

My attention was drawn to room seven. I stood and walked over to the door, opened it completely, and entered. Glancing around the space, I didn't notice anything out of the ordinary, yet I felt a vague sense of wrongness.

I inspected the ceiling and upper part of the walls. Nothing. Everything seemed ordinary. I knelt, ready to sit, when I saw it. A spiral design was engraved in the hardwood floor. I didn't remember its presence from earlier visits to room seven. Sitting down on the spiral design, I closed my eyes, something I've never done while here.

A vivid image of a staircase spiraling upward appeared before me. I had a strong urge to climb the stairs. I stood up and walked to the stairs and ascended them. I was reminded of my dream—the room at the top of the stairs. Here was the room, whether of my dream or not I didn't know. The room was circular and the walls were glass—a 360 degree view. I moved close to the glass walls and peered out onto San Francisco's landscape. I saw Downtown, the Mission, the Castro, Mt. Davidson, Twin Peaks, and the Marina extending along the bay. Golden Gate Bridge was brilliantly lit by the afternoon sun. Directly below the room was Pacific Heights, where many of the city's wealthy reside.

My attention was drawn to a specific house. Focusing on it and zooming in, I watched an activity in one of the rooms. It was furnished as an office. The room was large and the furnishings were lavish. No surprise for the location. It was a corner room and a smaller room was adjacent with connecting doorway.

I scrutinized the people present. A rather tall man in a well-tailored suit was seated at a desk. A man and woman were sitting in chairs in front of the desk. My curiosity caught, I increased the audio and listened.

"Did you get the cat, Mr. Pew?" The tall man at the desk spoke with authority.

"I'm sorry Mr. Tamm, Sir. We did not." Mr. Pew was tense when he replied. The woman sat in a rigid position.

I was alerted. A missing cat. What's happening here, I wondered? I decided to watch for awhile.

The authority figure, Mr. Tamm, stared at the woman. Then he said, "Ms. Plum."

Ms. Plum spoke, "We went to the place she had hidden it, but someone else was there before us and took it, Mr. Tamm, Sir."

Mr. Pew quickly added, "Our surveillance indicates Gloria Smith doesn't have it. She has told her hired detectives the truth, Mr. Tamm, Sir."

"The truth?" Mr. Tamm scowled at his assistants. "She told them everything?"

"Most of the background but not all of it. The detectives don't know our agenda. They are focused on Merlin and Morgan, Mr. Tamm, Sir." Worry lines creased Mr. Pew's brow.

"Those two scallywags were a clever diversion. So another party has entered the game. Maintain surveillance on all parties. Those detectives may well aid us to secure the cat. They're dupes like Merlin and Morgan. Find that cat. I want a report tomorrow morning by eight, and remember, the cat's voice, its signature." With a wave of hand he dismissed them.

I was definitely intrigued by the drama that had been staged. I watched awhile longer. Mr. Tamm spent the time reviewing reports on his monitor. My inner voice, which doesn't rely on the five sense for data-gathering, told me Mr. Tamm was CEO of Tower Mansion, a limited liability private equity firm that held controlling interest in diverse corporate enterprises, and a powerful man. I didn't know if I would be able to come back in the morning, but I was going to return and soon. The happening was quite exciting.

I heard Lucy purring softly. I scratched behind her ears as my rocking motion continued. Glancing around the studio, I noticed Karma on the desk resting with ears perked up and then glanced at the clock suspended above the desk as if it were levitating. It was still early. A peaceful setting suitable for travelling to other realities.

Chapter 37

Ralph put another log on the fire. He stared at the flames encircling the logs in the stove. He had decided to tell Shasta about recent distant viewing experiences but hadn't selected the experience to relate first. Should he describe them in a chronological order or tell her about the latest one? He returned to the couch and sat down. Lucy immediately climbed onto his lap and began purring. Karma was resting on the circular table when Shasta entered the living room.

She placed her martini on the table and organized the items there. Karma looked up at her and then put her head back down on her paws. Shasta rubbed her behind the ears. "Well, all settled for the evening?"

After Shasta sat down, Ralph asked about the novel's progress. She beamed at him. "It's going quite well. I've added several complications and another set of villains. Peaches and her team have their job cut out for them. Guess what? The story is gathering ideas about psychic forces. The whole thing with Philip and his project has obviously inspired my imagination."

"Sounds wonderful. How are you fitting psychic energy into the story?"

"Well, I started with the theme of Dungeons and Dragons which morphed into Sorcerers and Wizards." She winked at him. "Now these role-playing characters use real magic. My Muse has suggested the magic is based on psi power. Also I had a dream that contained the seed idea."

His curiosity was heightened. "What was the dream idea?"

She related the dream about her voice and its ability to stop the loggers and then described the application so far of the seed idea.

"So voice and other sounds are involved in the psychic energy field?"

"Yes. The Bene Gesserit concept. I came up with the notion of voice channels."

Ralph's eyebrows raised. "Channels and channeling? Shasta, that's remarkably close to some ideas Philip has. He's told me about Rupert Sheldrake and his theory of morphic resonance."

"Oh, really. And what is morphic resonance?"

"I'm not sure I can explain it adequately. It's a possible solution to the issue of form. Where do the rules and principles and prototypes of form exist and what is the process that informs matter? For example, why does a diamond always have the same crystalline structure? Or a rose have the traits of its kind? More or less of course. If the chemical or atomic makeup of a diamond or rose is analyzed where is the formative cause?

"Perhaps a clearer example–cells in your body are very diversified–specific cells for the heart, liver, brain, bones, flesh, muscles, and so forth. These cells all contain the same DNA–yours. The DNA has been analyzed, but no explanation is forth coming for the diversity. How does the DNA in your heart cells, which is the same as in your brain cells or the rest of your body, generate the proper form and shape for a heart cell? And actually the heart itself has several different types of cells. Where in the chemical molecular structure does a specific molecule exist that causes the proper form?"

"I'm puzzled. Really, that's a marvelous question. I guess we just assume the formative principle is there somewhere because the materials are always grouped into the correct shape. An invisible cause or formative agency. I like it. Thank you, dear. I may use it in my story."

"So his theory of morphogenesis follows a less traveled path and has been roundly criticized for not adhering to the official line. Besides, he is also noted for his research in parapsychology, the field Philip is into. In Sheldrake's theory the existence of forms is separate from matter that is organized into structure. In other words, formative cause isn't in chemical molecules that make up the DNA nor in their arrangement. What he calls morphic fields contain specific formative causes for particular groups of entities whether living or not. The forms aren't static and eternal as in the Platonic system but evolving with changes in nature. His basic concept is that of ongoing process." Ralph stopped and peered at Shasta.

"That's a big conceptual load you put on the table. I'll think about it. I presume he's written books."

"Yes. The Institute library has several of them. I'll borrow one for you." He inspected his glass. "I'll get a refill for us. Then I can tell you about some of my experiences."

While he was in the kitchen, she considered the potential of the morphic field idea. It was similar to what she was calling channels. Hmm, she thought, 'field' sounds more scientific than 'channel,' especially with the term's common usage denoting channeling psi forces.

Placing the drinks down, Ralph gave her a knowing smile. "Pretend I'm describing a dream as we've done before." His still small voice as the guide, he narrated the most recent remote viewing activity, the Pacific Heights adventure. When he had finished, he sat back in the couch waiting for her lucid commentary. After a few moments of silence he realized Shasta was gazing at the fire, no doubt gathering her thoughts. He waited. Eventually, she stared at him intently.

"I must confess your tale upset me deeply. First, let me ask you if you've been reading my work-in-progress. If you have, that's okay. But I need to know." Her face exhibited uncertainty and queasiness.

Ralph was amazed by the question. "No, dear, I haven't read any of your new novel." He would never read her writings without her permission. And he realized she knew that, but for some reason had to ask him. He was now troubled also.

"Okay. Thank you. Some of the characters in your viewing event are similar to characters in my story. In fact, some of the names are identical. And more importantly the plot has the same basic theme."

He sat up sharply. He focused his attention and increased his alertness. The situation was too strange. "Please explain," he requested.

"Merlin and Morgan are two important characters in the story, the major villains in fact until recently. Now I have a more dominant villain who seems like your Mr. Tamm, Sir. I don't have a name for the character yet but only call him master of Tower Mansion."

Ralph did a double-take. "Really? Maybe we need to call John Ocean for his services as reality inspector, check out our reality." He was trying to bring a little levity into their discussion, decrease the negative energy. He chuckled.

Shasta picked up on the humor and laughed lightly. "Here's a short synopsis. Peaches has been hired by Gloria Smith to find her lost cat figurine. The statue has a hidden chamber that contains a smaller version of the figurine. It is a charm that has magical powers. The charm enhances the throat chakra, which is a link to the astral plane and the voice channel of psychic energy. Merlin and Morgan are after the charm. Gloria has hidden the figurine because she has received threats. When she goes to the hiding spot, she discovers the cat is really missing. She now confesses to Peaches her ruse. Merlin and Morgan want the charm to increase their psi power so they can overthrow the master of Tower Mansion. The master is probably the one who has taken the charm, at least that is Peaches and Aeneas' theory at the moment. It's the point where I'm at now."

Ralph was flabbergasted. "The situation is much more mind-boggling than when Harold suddenly appeared in my studio, apparently stepping from the mirror. It seems I've entered the world of your novel. It's totally confusing."

They sat in silence. The known world they had accepted faithfully all their lives was now in tatters.

Shasta started giggling. Ralph wondered about her mental state. She quieted and said, "The absurdity is too much. We can use the happening to learn. Obviously some of our most cherished beliefs are no longer tenable. Remember all the beliefs we've had to give up since childhood. Your experience is true and during it you gained data about my novel. How? The explanation is beyond us at the moment. Perhaps someday–"

"Excellent. I hear Peaches speaking. We assume the mystery and start at our present point. I'll talk with Philip and probably let the twins in on the issue too. I've been leery of them for awhile but that's another story, one for later. Remote viewing is little understood, and our project is breaking new ground. Perhaps the fabric of reality has been morphed by the project. And maybe I really should discuss the anomalies with John Ocean."

"Ha!" Shasta exclaimed. "Query: do I make changes in my story to fit the data you've gleaned from the viewing? Also do I use the data in the story's development?"

"Allow your Muse to decide, that's my suggestion. We're now entangled with other realities. That can be another theme for you."

"Yes. Oh, my. What an adventure we're having. We both should let the experience and its meaning remain in the background. We'll do further research and thinking about it, but no decisions now." Rising, she walked with the kitties following into the kitchen to check on dinner.

Ralph had moved inward closer to his basic self, a puzzled expression on his face. His mind opened onto a sequence of scenes folding into themselves, morphing into surreal landscapes. Boundaries vanished and realities entangled. He could choose the portal to any of them.

The tantalizing aroma from the Spanish rice casserole baking in the oven whetted her appetite as she prepared the succotash. The salad was last to fix. She was multi-tasking. Her hands busy with dinner preparation and her intellect focused on the reality issue. Ralph had proposed he had entered into her imaginary world with remote viewing. But what if instead her imagination had unconsciously drawn on the everyday world? Dreams sometimes merge with daily life. The creative imagination might also select with precise accuracy from the waking state reality. The creative imagination had been a channel for gaining knowledge for centuries. Many famous artists and philosophers had availed themselves of its power.

Ah, she thought, that word 'channel' again. Well, whether 'channel' or 'path' or 'road' or whatever–the idea was the same. Whether the psychic dimension of reality existed or not, the ideas she had expressed in the story were acceptable for a work of fiction.

If she could increase her creativity by distant viewing, well– She allowed the thought to germinate.

Chapter 38

When Shasta had woken in the morning, sunlight streaming over the bed, Ralph gently snoring, her Muse was singing sweetly a recurring refrain: knowledge is power. The lyric stayed in her mental background through breakfast. Now ready to start a new chapter of Mystery of the Missing Cat, she realized the meaning of her Muse's message: all knowledge is available. Take what you want for your purpose. Ralph's experience was available for her use.

Gloria switched on the ceiling light. She went to a door of a fenced-off storage area in the basement of her apartment building. Unlocking the door, she entered followed by Peaches and Aeneas.

"I hid it over there." Gloria pointed to a wall covered with wood panels. "The basement area here was a family room when the building was a one family dwelling. The house was built in the 1920s, and the studs and beams are oversized compared to today's residential buildings." She tapped on the wood paneling. "The studs are two by six and there's plenty of empty space behind the these panels."

She strolled to a section of the wall and pushed on it. A part of the panel slid to one side. "Sean believed the hiding places down here were for liquor storage during Prohibition, you know, illegal contraband. There are secret hideouts all over the basement. As far as I've discovered, the only one in my storage area is here."

She reached her hand into a dark recess and quickly pulled it out. "See. Nothing is there. Here is where I placed the cat. Now the space is empty." Anxiety arose in her voice.

Aeneas removed a small flashlight from his jacket pocket and shone it into the dark recess. The powerful beam illuminated the space. He shook his head. "I don't see anything."

Peaches was about to turn away when she felt a strange sensation like a very quiet sound barely audible. She listened. Concentration registered on her face. She went to the opening and stuck her hand into the darkness. Reaching deep into black space, she felt a hard object. Grasping it, she pulled it out of its secret hideaway.

"Here, is this your cat?" She held up a porcelain figurine of a sitting cat.

"Oh my god! It's safe." Gloria took the cat, hugging it. "How can I ever thank you?"

Peaches smiled inwardly. Just pay our bill, she thought, but outwardly she said, "This caper isn't finished. We're back at the beginning. The threats still exist. Bad guys want to steal the charm and use it for their own malicious purposes. We do know two of the enemy, Merlin and Morgan, but not much about the leader of Tower Mansion and his purpose and agenda in the game."

"You're correct, of course. Let's retire to my apartment and share thoughts. I'll fix a little repast."

Once they were back in her apartment, Gloria went to the kitchen and prepared a tray of snacks and drinks. As they waited, Peaches inspected her experience. She had always followed her intuition, but the feeling was different from any she could remember. It was more like a voice that was present but barely audible. She had noticed a tingling of her throat around the area of her larynx. She had touched her throat and felt a slight vibration. She decided to tell Aeneas, but Gloria returned and she would wait until later.

"Here are some munchies and coffee for you two. I'm having tea." She placed the tray on the table and invited them to help themselves. "I'm sorry I forgot the napkins." She hurried back to the kitchen and just as quickly returned, handing them napkins.

The trio were silent as they enjoyed the food and beverages. Finally, Gloria, after wiping her lips, asked, "Well, what are our plans now?"

Peaches was prepared. A strategy had emerged from her intuition. "First, I'd like to see the charm. I've heard so much about it. It seems such a fabulous treasure even Indiana Jones would seek it."

Gloria picked up the cat, twisted its left ear, and when the chamber door in the back opened, she removed the charm, a tiny replica of the porcelain cat. She held it up by the attached necklace and extended her hand to Peaches.

"What a lovely pendant," Peaches remarked as she took it from Gloria. She sensed a warmness in the charm as she held it in her hand. Without thinking she placed the charm against her throat and felt a tiny vibration. "Do you mind if I put it on?" she inquired.

Gloria responded, "Oh, please do. Tell me what you hear."

With the charm resting against her larynx, Peaches listened. Aeneas watched and recorded the happening without Gloria's awareness. Virgil would observe simultaneously.

What a strange sensation, Peaches reflected. I'm hearing voices not in the normal way with my ears. The voices are in my mind though. The only difference between these and audible voices my ears pick up is volume. These inner sounds are softer but still distinct and clear.

Peaches glanced at Aeneas, who was watching intently, and then looked directly at Gloria. "I'm hearing voices, people talking. I'm calling them inner voices to distinguish them from our audible voices. Two people are conversing. One sounds like a woman and the other a man."

Gloria brightened. She felt more secure than she had in a long time. Peaches was definitely in her world. "They're probably Merlin and Morgan. The more you listen the better you'll recognize voices. What are they discussing?"

"They're talking about you and the charm. They believe Tamm has it."

"Tamm?" Gloria asked. "I haven't heard of him."

"He's the owner of Tower Mansion." Peaches swiveled toward Aeneas. "Do a background check on Tamm and his connection to Merlin and Morgan." Aeneas texted Virgil.

Listening to her inner voices, Peaches began to rock back and forth in a slow gentle rhythm. She stopped. "A break for us. Our culprits are planning to burgle Tower Mansion soon and search for the charm they believe is hidden there."

"Oh, what fools they are," Gloria declared. "Sean thought Tower Mansion was impregnable. It's surrounded by a powerful force-field. How will they enter without a magic tool like the charm?"

"That's what they're debating now. Morgan is suggesting a subtle maneuver and Merlin, his frustration at a bursting point, wants to storm the walls, so to speak. They're so far apart on strategy they'll never agree."

Suddenly Peaches with a thoughtful demeanor looked at Gloria and asked, "Will you give me permission to use the charm for the duration of our assistance?" Peaches intuited the charm held the solution.

Surprised by Peaches' request, Gloria exclaimed, "Of course, yes. That's a wonderful idea. The charm has always frightened me. I wore it for Sean's sake. Because he wanted me to be part of the game. Oh, I should teach you the secrets about its use."

Peaches was pleased. They now had a weapon to battle the enemy. A strategy would evolve once they understood the charm's secrets and operation.

While Gloria was demonstrating her knowledge about the charm's functioning, Aeneas conversed with Virgil, who was compiling a detailed report on Tamm and his Tower Mansion and the Merlin-Morgan connection.

Chapter 39

Eduardo Guchol was thinking about Marilynn Raylon, her face appearing more frequently the past several days. He hadn't seen her for awhile and they did have fun times together. He had been too busy preparing next week's gallery showing for visiting her in San Francisco. She had been sent an invitation to the opening night reception, so he hoped she would attend.

Some flowers in his backyard were starting to bloom. He enjoyed their colorful display. Many holograms which would be exhibited at the gallery portrayed flowers in his garden. With only a few days before opening, he had much to do, putting the finishing touches on his art pieces. Eduardo specialized in creating holographic vistas, a new type of performance art. The holograms or holos depicted nature's beauty or computer-generated surreal landscapes. He often added a layer of sound to the pieces, especially those that created walkabout settings, places where patrons could immerse themselves in imaginative landscapes.

Lefty had a difficult time maintaining his concentration on Eduardo and the up-coming art show. Alien thoughts were appearing and distracting him. He saved the Eduardo file and opened a new page, titling it Cosmic Game. At work yesterday Vance, one of his colleagues, was showing a book of visually perplexing images: moiré patterns, mazes, and optical illusions. He was fascinated by the great variety of mazes.

Walking home after work, his visual imagination produced a series of mazes morphing into each other. What a great digital game it could be, he speculated. Mazes were now spiraling through his mind, suggesting a game designed for the website where people could play or subscribe to and receive the latest maze game. The results would be sent to his website and a score given for correct responses. Developing the basic architecture of the game program would keep him busy all night. He got up and walked to the kitchen and brewed a large supply of coffee.

Returning to the computer, Lefty decided to devise a simple game with a series of four mazes, each one more difficult than the previous. He designed a maze-solving filter that would put a player into one of five categories. The bottom or category one is a player who can't solve any maze. Category two is for solving one maze; three for solving two mazes; four for solving three mazes; and five for solving all four mazes. He envisioned a prize for the top maze-solver.

He typed code and the game architecture started to grow. He was completed focused on the exciting project and didn't notice the dawning light.

When he had finished writing the program, he turned off the computer and got up. He needed a few hours of sleep before venturing out for an afternoon of weekend activities. Perhaps he could connect with Kathy.

Chapter 40

Karma was napping on the round table when Shasta entered the living room. She placed her martini on the table and sat down. She gently rubbed Karma behind the ears. Karma sighed and purred. Ralph arrived and sat on the couch. Lucy jumped onto the couch and snuggled against his thigh.

After sipping her drink, Shasta spoke, "Dear, I've thoughts I'd like to explore with you. You have a fine talent for presenting ideas with clarity. I'm more on the intuitive level and express them the way they come to me."

Ralph laughed. "I still have a secret from you."

"Oh, really. And pray tell what is that secret?"

"It wouldn't be a secret if I told you."

"Oh come on Ralph. Share it."

"My thoughts, unformed when they birth, take a long time growing into clear ideas. When they're ready for the world, I bring them forth."

"So they sit on the back burner for awhile."

"Yep. I'll often inspect them closely before I decide to share them with others."

"I've a set of questions all linked together. The primary one is whether I've the ability to perform remote viewing? I would like to learn the procedure for my creative activities."

Ralph was indeed surprised. But he shouldn't be, he realized, if he had been more aware of her recent imaginative work. "I think you'd do well. I may not be the best teacher for the project though. I'll talk with Philip. I'm certain he would be interested."

"Yes. The Garland team operating in the astral plane. Actually it's for my own use. However, if the only way I can learn is at the Institute, I suppose– Like that saying 'quid pro quo.'"

"I don't believe Philip would have an issue here. What exactly do you want to do?"

"Here's the cluster of thoughts, not too well formed. Help me untangle them. I'd like to look in on my characters as you did when you remote viewed Tower Mansion. You learned something I didn't know yet. Of course I'd love to do the same thing." She paused, searching Ralph for a sign.

Ralph smiled. "That would be quite beneficial."

"Now these notions popped into my mind. They all concern creative process and artistic role. The philosophy of art—so Mr. Philosopher assist me with your analytic skills."

"I'll try."

"I'd like to use distant viewing techniques for my creative imagination so I could observe my characters early. Let me explain. As the process operates now, I listen to the characters and watch their daily activities. Data flow from the creative imagination into my awareness, and I write down the thoughts. The first question—can I go a step further and actually peek into my imagination and view different parts of it as the story develops before it moves from there to my consciousness? Further consideration leads to the notion of an imagination or creativity channel which I can view while my mind is working before it transmits the results which are what I receive."

Ralph's eyes sparkled. "How delightful. You've certainly presented some exciting ideas. The concept that touches me immediately is the creativity channel. And it links to Jung's collective unconscious and Sheldrake's morphic fields. Are these ideas growing in an area of the mind that is closed to our awareness or are they in a meta-level? Or perhaps they start in a meta-level and then move into our own unconscious. Some very important philosophers have argued artists channel, like mediums, ideas which are put into their art works. Plato is renowned for the view. In his *Apology*, Socrates' great defense at his trial, the idea is expressed poets channel and don't actually understand the beautiful ideas embedded in their works. Plato isn't talking about the craft part, which is learned. He is alluding to the inspirational meaning that conveys truth and beauty."

"So where do these beautiful ideas reside?"

"Plato posits a realm beyond our everyday world, which he describes as a reality of appearances, a constant stream of coming and going. Nothing is permanent. All is changing."

"Oh, like that Greek philosopher—what was his name?—who said we can't step into the same river twice."

"That was Heraclitus. From the few remaining fragments of his writings he apparently argued reality is in a constant flux, more a process of transformation. For Plato Heraclitus' view is correct for our everyday world of appearances but a more real and permanent reality is that of the Forms or Ideas, a meta-realm of perfection and eternity."

"Of course, theologians have argued certain ideas are in God's mind and so are eternal and permanent. Are the collective unconscious and morphic fields like that?"

"No, I don't believe so. Sheldrake specifically proposes these groups exist in everyday space and time and can change. His basic premise rests on process as the foundation of the cosmos. Jung also appears to think in a similar fashion. I'm not an expert in the works of either, so I can't definitely say."

"Humans aren't the only creatures with a collective unconscious," she remarked with an ironic edge.

Ralph was puzzled. "Oh, who else?"

"I presume many species do. Certainly ants. Colonies around our house have learned and collectively remember our kitchen and its location. Even after we've destroyed most, if not all, of a colony, new members know. And about the ant bait too. There must be a collective memory about its danger. Perhaps nothing specific, but still they recognize it as a threat."

"Oh, yes. You're right. All species learn and their collective memories evolve over the centuries. Migrating animals have a group memory."

"With its GPS navigation system too. My mind is bubbling. Ideas overflowing. Okay. Here's a thought. What's commonly called Zeitgeist, the spirit of the age. Is it like the collective unconscious or morphic fields?"

"Yes, Zeitgeist might well refer to those two concepts. They all might be talking about the same thing. Cultural paradigms shaft; new viewpoints arise, and old ones disappear from the scene. The notion of a perennial philosophy implies a changing scene which has an underlying substratum. Using the river metaphor—when the river is low the bedrock is visible while during the rainy season turbulent water flows over the bottom and only the surface is apparent."

"Yes, the idea of continuity and change. Next, what is the poet's relationship to the cultural river. Does she ride the surface, crafting what most other poets are making? Or does she plumb the bottom for deep insights which are revealed in her works?"

"Some artists go too deep and never return."

"Hidden knowledge is a dare to some and an off-limits to others. So are we poets actually leaving our bodies and going into an alternate reality like indigenous medicine workers do or are we only delving into the unconscious of our minds?"

"Shasta, that's brilliant. Who knows? Only the shadow does, or the trickster. Based on my recent experiences I would propose OBE. And my reading of traditional practices indicates the same conclusion. Philip's project may clarify the issue. A scientific research program to study paranormal psychology is a serious and courageous undertaking. You mentioned the dare. Well, Philip has accepted the dare, and it may be the death of his scientific career. The paradigm may be changing, but the official position is still diametrically opposed to 'dabbling in the occult.' Few research funds are available and fewer still venues for presenting and publishing the results."

"Excellent. We seem to be on the same wavelength. Channeling from the same source." She laughed with a giggle. "More. By whatever way we artists gather imaginative materials, what can we do while we're there? Do we only collect ideas or can we actually manipulate the system, make changes in the material contained in the repository? How close to the source and birth of ideas can we artists go?"

Ralph was silent. A quizzical look on his face, he suggested, "The answer isn't in. Only those who have tried have any data. It's a matter of gnosis, of direct experience. No lab experiment can verify the outcome unless it focuses on an individual's experience."

"Such as you're performing at the Institute."

"Yes, exactly. So, based only on my personal gnosis, OBE is the real thing and explains much. My viewing of Tamm breaks the paradigm. I had entered into the domain of the creative imagination. My thinking, rooted in what I've learned so far, implies I had inadvertently produced minor changes in reality's fabric and these changes had a multiplying effect. Eventually, my viewing has jumped into alternate realities that run parallel with each other. Philip and the twins have mentioned string theory which, I guess, is on the leading edge of quantum field theory. String theory proposes a multidimensional universe. But the concepts were beyond me, and I didn't pay much attention. I'll broach the issue with Philip."

"Multi-dimensional? How many more?"

"A specific number hasn't been agreed on, but several more than our space-time four dimensional reality has."

"So, why is a multi-dimensional world important?"

"Psi energy would be more easily explained."

"I think we should ask John Ocean for his views. He's a reality inspector, isn't he. You know, I really enjoyed our visit with the Ocean trinity at our dinner party. Let's visit Rainbow Inn and become more involved with them. I don't see them coming to Ocean Delights very often. We should make the move, invade their territory. What say?"

Ralph beamed. He loved the sparkle in her eyes. She was so inspired and charmed him completely. "Yes, let's do and soon."

"Okay, I'll remind us in the morning."

Chapter 41

Remote viewing has certainly stretched, if not transformed, my notions of reality. After our discussion and sharing last night, Shasta and I agreed to give serious thought to the questions raised. The theory of entanglement is fine for subatomic particles, but does it apply to our world ruled by Newtonian physics? When I arrived at the Institute for my afternoon distant viewing session, I considered talking to Philip about the strange anomaly of my Tower Mansion experience. I decided not to say anything at the moment. My inner voice counseled patience, so I would wait.

I sat quietly in my lab, focusing my concentration into a point of light.

Slowly I inspected all twelve doors, which were closed. A sense of normalcy pervaded the inner chamber. I didn't feel any weirdness. Breathing deeply and without hesitation, I walked to the sixth door. The door opened before me as if it knew my intention. Entering the room, I looked around for any incongruities.

Something there is that loves change. Surveying the room for the illuminating icon, which should be brightly lighting the space, I realized the fish trophy hanging on the wall was no longer the icon. In the past the fish's eye had been the focal point for viewing. Inspecting all the furnishings carefully, I detected a soft glow radiating from a table beneath the fish trophy. I walked over to the table. Its top was inlaid with a chess board and pieces were placed on the squares ready for a game. I studied the pieces. Noticing the white queen was brighter than the other pieces, I picked her up and focused on the crown.

I was observing a room where several chess games were being played. I watched each game for a few minutes until my attention centered on a specific board.

Chess is not my forte although I do play the game. It has never attracted my whole being. A fun diversion at various times in my life–I have played little in the past few years. Shasta and I used to play opposite each other, an enjoyable evening's entertainment. We now have other forms of entertainment besides active endeavors in our chosen fields.

The game was about half over and was proceeding in a predictable manner. Unless one side made a stupid blunder, the game would continue for awhile. Because strange mental trips have happened to me recently, I wasn't too surprised when a series of images moved through my mind showing all the previous moves from the opening to now. Thus, I was allowed the privilege of having witnessed the game without having been present. I was certain the twins had incorporated into my guidelines the request to write up an analysis of the game. So I decided to study the board carefully and be prepared for the task.

I was beginning to feel a tug, a sign my viewing time was winding down. Before I did leave, a series of images flashed before me, the board positions through checkmate.

Back in my cell at the Institute, I began writing my report. The game analysis was nearly complete when I remembered a detail I had forgotten. A large photograph of Mary Rainbow receiving the world chess championship trophy hung on the wall behind the game I was observing. I inserted the data and finished the game analysis.

Geri laid Ralph's report of his Mechanics Institute viewing on the desk. Facing her brother, she asked, "Have read his report yet?"

Her troubled countenance was reflected by Jerry's stress-lined face. "I did." His voice trembled.

"We must verify the presence of Mary Rainbow's photograph. It wasn't there when you took the pictures of the room."

"I did. I phoned this morning. The photograph has been on the wall since the championship match several years ago."

"How could you have missed it? It's so large."

"Sis, I didn't miss it. It just wasn't there. That's all. I can't explain it."

Jerry was in a daze. He rubbed his face. Standing up, he stretched. He directed a frown at his sister and shook his head in disbelief.

"Okay. It's a new object in the room and its presence is inexplicable. First we'll double check. We'll visit the chess club and talk to the president and any other members there. Then we must carefully review all of Ralph's reports seeking the slightest clue, especially incongruities. He has been in room six before, and the previous viewing is the one to focus on. We'll start by comparing the two reports down to the minutest detail."

"Agreed. Then we'll inspect all the other reports in chronological order," Jerry proposed.

Geri was upset by the uncertainty. The precise and clever plan they had so painstakingly designed was destroyed. A weakness had developed, and they were ignorant of the cause. Until they had sufficient knowledge, they couldn't prevent total failure. She pushed back a beginning panic attack and concentrated on Ralph's earlier reports.

Chapter 42

It was a lovely afternoon. The sun brightened Ocean Avenue. The Garlands strolled along the business corridor, inspecting shops. Several storefronts that had been empty for months now sprouted businesses. One hosted a bicycle shop. An acupuncture-acupressure clinic was adjacent. Contemporary Fashions, a clothing store, had opened a few doors down the street. Activities were bustling. The Garlands were on their way to Rainbow Inn. Shasta had phoned in the morning and told Mary they planned an afternoon visit.

Pleasant aromas, emitted by herbal sachets hanging from ceiling rafters, greeted them when they entered. Flowers were everywhere, on windowsills and tables. They both felt the Inn's warm and inviting ambience. Od saw them and waved, beckoning them over. They pulled up chairs and sat down at a table with Od and John.

Ralph noticed the reserved sign and inquired, "I see you have a special table."

John responded, "Actually, it's Mary's private table. But we're allowed to sit here."

"As long as we behave ourselves," Od added.

Amused, Shasta asked, "What kind of mischief do you cause?"

"Hang around long enough and you'll witness some outrageous antics," John quipped.

"If you're easily upset, this isn't the place for you," Od retorted.

Mary arrived at the table, setting down a platter of cookies. "Hi. Welcome to my humble abode. What beverages would you like?" After taking their orders, two coffees and two teas, she retired to the kitchen. Casual conversation flowed easily around the group. Ralph noticed the banter between John and Od sometimes conveyed sharp ironies. Mary returned and placed a tray with five mugs on the table. Once she had served her four guests, she sat down and took the remaining mug.

"Here's to our good health," she proposed. They touched mugs and voiced their agreement.

"How's the master game progressing?" Ralph wondered.

"Do you have many recruits for the consciousness drum?" Shasta inquired.

The trio glanced at each other and then Mary spoke, "Over twenty people have signed up. I'm amazed at the response."

Shasta smiled. "Student texting has been busy." Her eyes sparkled, catching everyone's attention. "Rafé has told her friends at State, specifically the Native American Student Organization."

"Oh, no wonder." Mary clapped her hands silently. "I was surprised many applicants knew drumming and asked about tutors. I was curious about their source of information."

"Indeed. Getting students involved in the game is a plus. They're the ones who inherit the future and the forecast isn't very good." Od was adamant.

"It's horrid," John interjected.

"But the future is yet unformed, so let's raise consciousness." Mary decisively changed the direction of conversation.

"We can create new, better options with our imagination." Shasta was in accord.

"Ralph, what exciting remote viewing adventures have you had recently?" John turned from Ralph and faced Mary and Od. "Ralph's been telling me about his weird experiences with distant viewing."

Ralph was silent waiting for his inner voice. He sensed an opening of a portal and gazed back and forth at his audience. "Actually, the latest developments have shattered our notion of reality. My story is totally unbelievable so listen to it as if I were relating a dream."

He paused giving everyone the opportunity to grok his statement. He would assist them on their path of gnosis. The moment was at hand. "A recent viewing activity involved me in an abnormal situation. I entered into another form of reality. I observed the imaginative world of Shasta's latest story." He glanced at her and gently clasped her hand.

"Not realizing where I had been viewing, I told her about my experience. She was shocked, completely nonplussed."

Shasta broke in. "I think my heart stopped for a second when Ralph was describing the scene he had viewed. How could it be?"

"Of course, she wondered if I had been reading her manuscript, which would be the most likely, and sanest, explanation, but I hadn't. I had peered into the future of the story at least as far as she had gone. I heard information she hadn't expressed."

John was close to levitating. "Are you saying you were in Shasta's creative world, in her mind?"

"How fantastic," Mary declared.

"Please, continue, Ralph. I'm fascinated." Od had an appreciative mien.

"We've agreed to accept my experience and leave any explanation until later."

"An excellent idea," John remarked. "Many of my experiences have been too weird to explain, at least from the dominant viewpoint."

Ralph squeezed Shasta's hand, giving her the sign. "I accepted Ralph's information and incorporated it into the story. More importantly, I decided to participate in the distant viewing project at the Institute. Philip was very gracious and enlisted me in the program. I'll be performing for my own purpose: I want to observe the characters in my story before my Muse communicates the latest news about them. Philip thought my goal fit into a subdivision of his project, investigating artistic creativity."

For once the Ocean Avenue trio was quiet, absorbing the strangeness and its potential meaning.

Ralph gave them time to evaluate the information. Then he continued, "Based on all my remote viewing experiences, I've become entangled in other realities and parallel worlds. No one at the Institute has an adequate explanation. Philip has surmises and potential theoretical concepts that fit into his working hypothesis. He and his team have discussed conceptual tools like parallel universes and string theory. They have mathematical equations beyond my ken. Their basic thinking assumes I've somehow transformed reality by causing minor changes."

"Here we go down the rabbit hole." Od was ready for the ride.

"Yes. Down and out through the other side and upward." Mary was enthusiastic.

"That's Dante's clue." Gnosis shone on Ralph's countenance.

"Dante's clue?"

"Meaning what?"

"What's the secret?"

"We mages are honor bound to keep our secrets to ourselves," Ralph stated.

"You can tell me, Ralph. I'm a magician now," John announced.

"Oh, Ralph, don't play Mr. Mystery Magician. We'll all take the oath of silence, won't we?" Shasta looked questioningly at the others.

"Actually, it's more the mystic and alchemist's secret than the magician's. And magicians were put down in hell," Ralph replied.

"Weren't alchemists too?" Od asked. His copy of *La Commedia* was well-worn from frequent readings.

"Yes, so that leaves the mystic. Certainly Dante's journey simulated that of a mystic, even concluding with a vision of the Divine."

"Okay. Now what's the clue?" Mary was forcing the issue.

"Like all mystics who seek gnosis or direct experience, Dante first journeyed down into hell before ascending the spiral staircase to the heavens. Of course he climbed to the top of the spiritual mountain and then he and his significant other, his Eve, levitated skyward traveling through all the then-known levels of heaven."

"Of course. The path is so obvious it's invisible to most of us." Od felt the firm foundation.

"Nineteenth century romantics recognized, if only unconsciously, the psychological truth revealed by Dante's journey," Shasta offered.

Quiet followed the storm of ideas. After a few moments Mary announced, "I'll refresh the drinks." She gathered the mugs, placing them on the tray, and marched off to the kitchen.

"I've been telling Od and Mary about my thoughts for a magic act with the floating, rattling skull," John commented.

"I'm definitely impressed," Od declared.

"What will you be doing with your role, the itinerant salesman?" Shasta inquired.

"I'm thinking of adding some musicians, a traveling minstrel ensemble. I guess Mary's musical enthusiasm has been an inspiration."

"You might contact Dale Pepper, a friend of ours. He has a group, the Meadowlarks. I'll give you his phone and email." As Shasta was writing the information on her notepad, Mary returned with the refilled mugs.

While they were sipping the drinks and chatting, Ralph heard his still voice and he liked the thought. He spoke to the group, "I've a routine I'd like to share with you, an entertaining interlude while you're enjoying your drinks. The effect channels psi power."

Ralph stood up. Taking a cloth bag and pair of dice from his pocket, he removed a tarot deck from the bag. He shuffled the deck and then put it on the table. Peering around the group, he focused on Od. "Od, would you assist me in this happening. Your aura is strong, indicating a high level of psychic power."

"Of course. I'd be delighted," Od responded.

"Please take the dice and roll them. Chance will rule."

Od threw the dice. The number was eight.

Ralph retrieved from his pocket a small green stone bear. He held it up, showing it to the group. "The bear is a powerful charm crafted by a Zuni artist. It has guided me for years. Od, please take the stone bear. Hold it gently." Ralph handed the bear to Od.

Ralph picked up the tarot deck and shuffled it again. "Chance has selected the number eight." He counted seven cards from the deck. He looked at Mary. "Mary, please take the top card on the deck, which is the eighth card. Show it to everyone but not to me. I'll turn my back for a moment."

She removed the top card and displayed it to the others. Ralph again faced the group. He had replaced the seven cards back on the deck. Spreading the cards, he asked Mary to insert the chosen card anywhere in the deck. She slid it into the middle. Closing the deck, Ralph put it on the table and asked John to cut it several times.

Then Ralph faced Od. "Od, please assist me by demonstrating your psychic power. Mentally project the image of the selected card into the bear charm you're holding." Ralph waited for a few moments and then asked, "Have you projected the image?"

"The image is embedded in the charm, Ralph," Od acknowledged.

"Fine. Please hand me the charm. I'll ask its help to identify the chosen card." Taking the bear, Ralph scanned the faces of the cards. Suddenly he stopped and studied a card. He waved the stone bear over the card. "Yes. Yes." He exclaimed. "The bear says this is it." He showed the card to the group. "Is the stone bear correct?"

Applause erupted, approving the result. Ralph held up his hand. "I believe Od deserves a round of applause for his psychic skill." As the group again applauded, Ralph shook Od's hand, giving him a personal thanks.

"Ralph, that was astonishing," Mary declared. "I would like you to stage a magic show here at the Inn. The posters will announce: See the Amazing Garland. Psychic energy blazes forth. Enchantment and spirit power abound."

"Ancient mysteries revealed," Od added.

Merriment played its tune and laughter engulfed them.

John had been pensive, considering Mary's idea of a magic show. He held up both hands, quieting them. "Now hear this. As part of the master game a magic performance will be given. Both Ralph and I will entertain. A double bill: The Amazing Garland and The Mystifying Ocean."

Giggles and laughter erupted.

"Oh, you guys. You're forgetting a marvelous magician who should be in the show too," Shasta proclaimed.

They all were taken aback, uncertain of Shasta's reference.

"Of course, how silly of me," Ralph stated. "Rafé will be the third mage on the billboard. She's designing an act for her master thesis, as you know."

"Yes," Od exclaimed. "A master thesis must be performed in the master game. With the acts of Shasta, Mary, and me included the show will have six productions."

"The Consciousness Fair with six rings and more to be announced." Mary pointed to the stage. "There sits the heart of the Fair, the Consciousness Drum. It'll be in the center ring." A large round drum was in the middle of the stage. Mary jumped up and hurried to the stage. She picked up a stick and began tapping the drum.

While Mary was tapping a rhythm on the drum, John got up from the table and walked over to the stage. He took his wand from his pocket and, with dance-like movements, waved it in tempo to the drumbeats. Slowly he released the wand. His audience gasped. The attention of everyone in the Inn was captured and directed toward the performance on stage.

The wand remained stationary. Then it floated away from the mage toward the drum. It made a circle coming back to him. He touched the wand and it leaped in the air and then lay still in front of him. He grasped the levitating wand and again gestured with it to the drumbeats.

Applause resounded through the Inn pulsating with the drum. Consciousness reigned as Queen of the Day.

Chapter 43

The traffic light turned green. As Marilynn started across the street, she sensed a mental alarm and paused. A car sped toward her, veering around the corner and nearly hitting her. She gasped. Crazy goon. She gave him the finger as the car sped away. Pedestrians behind her were pressing forward, and she moved with them, reaching the other side safely.

It was the second time today she had a near accident. Earlier in the afternoon she went to the office lunchroom for coffee. The coffee pot was empty. As she reached for the pot to start a fresh batch, a small voice caused her to stop and inspect the pot carefully. Then she noticed the handle appeared hot. She barely touched it before yanking her hand away. The coffee machine was set at high, and the pot had become a heat hazard. She turned the machine off and waited for the pot to cool before picking it up and filling it with water to brew more coffee.

After arriving home, she decided to record the strange events that had been occurring the past several days. Actually, the weird stuff started after she initiated her experiments at the office. She had developed her own version of Sedna's instructions. After six weeks of investigation, the findings confirmed Sedna's premise: people at the top of society's hierarchy–business, government, education and religion–weren't the real rulers. They were only the top administrative level of the global corporate state, the managers for the elite who actually control the world. Who these elite were she hadn't the slightest clue. But her tests had demonstrated the corporate administrators were different from most humans, the workers. Sedna had called the corporate mangers 'robo-humans.' Marilynn' s personal term was 'robo.'

Based on data Sedna had given her, she had performed six tests. They were done without anyone's awareness, a secret survey she had accomplished. She had gathered evidence a robo's thinking ran in loops guided by conventional patterns and associations, a composite of buzz words, clichés, and stereotypes. Robos were literalists. They had learned verbal expressions by rote and didn't always 'know' what they were saying other than reciting the words in the proper context.

The humor test was the most amusing and cool. Robos had a limited sense of humor. They liked gross bumbling pratfalls, stupid blunders, and childish jokes that humiliated others. Their playfulness was immature, no more than adolescent at the most. Usually they didn't understand wry or subtle humor or double entendres. Irony was especially lost on them.

They were often quite intelligent with exceptional mental skills, for example, memory retention of data and mathematical calculations. They could feint the proper behavior for the situation and so seemed normal.

A couple weeks ago her small voice, as she called it, suggested she play a mental game with people, especially at the office. At times she knew she could be 'on the same wave length' as someone else, like they were communicating mentally. Sedna was a good example, like they knew what the other was thinking or feeling. She wouldn't call it telepathy but–

She decided to use some psi power and send thoughts to various members of the company when she was in their presence or nearby. The experiment was simple. She mentally called their names, seeking their attention and notice. If they seemed to 'hear' her, she asked them a simple question. A few of her follow colleagues responded, but no supervisor ever did.

The confirmation was clinched by two situations Marilynn had experienced last week within three days of each other. The first case involved her recently hired supervisor Ms. Deidre Darkson. Marilynn had applied for the position, a definite advancement, and believed she would get it. She had the experience, the intelligence, and great personnel reports. As assistant supervisor she got on well with all the staff. She saw herself climbing up the ladder of success. So when Ms. Darkson was hired from another company, Marilynn was dazed and then angry. But she contained resentment and welcomed Ms. Darkson and spoke well of her to the staff.

The second event tied it altogether. As assistant supervisor of Product Enhancement Department, she attended the official welcoming ceremony for four new employees, all hired for upper managerial positions. CEO Clive Scampman presided at the ceremony. Listening to him and observing his behavior, she realized the truth behind Sedna's thesis. The firm's CEO, whom she had always admired and respected, having only nice words of praise for him, now stood before her naked. His faults were so obvious she wondered how she could have been deceived for so long. He definitely fit the type: he was a robo. Now she realized, as she sat stunned and enlightened at the same moment, Ms. Darkson and the other three new supervisors were all hired because they too were robos and would quickly marched up the corporate ladder to the top floor.

Marilynn smiled inwardly. Yes, everything made sense. The basic links were joined. She had gained gnosis.

She stopped writing, saved the file and closed the tablet. A hungry feeling arose. A shrimp salad, she thought, would be delicious. I've the ingredients. And a slice of sourdough. Yum. She entered the kitchen and began preparations.

Fixing the salad allowed her mind to clear. She realized her own consciousness was growing because of the experiments. Now she was alert to other people's 'psi potential.' Was it high, low, or normal. She learned to sense the potential through an inner feeling. She was able to detect psi potential in some of her fellow staff members but not in the supervisors.

After dinner she signed in to the chat room and sent Sedna a message: Fallyn was traveling to Seattle and she was looking forward to seeing Floyd.

Chapter 44

I was excited as I sat in the small lab room at the Institute. Ralph and the twins were present for formal launching. Philip was back in his office viewing the proceedings on a monitor. For a week I had been practicing a set of meditative exercises Geri had shown me. She and her brother were very helpful and encouraging. I tried all the recommended techniques, selecting those I found most advantageous. One in particular I enjoyed: focusing on the tip of my nose. I use the focus now when I prepare to write. It's relaxing and dispels mental noise.

And Philip, he was a perfect gentleman. I had expected him to require a signed contract with all sorts of forbidding limitations attached. But to my surprise, he was happy to provide me an opportunity to learn remote viewing and apply it to my creative activities. The only stipulation was allowing him to record all the experiments done at the Institute. Fair enough. I accepted.

I smiled at Ralph who acted somewhat anxious. The twins smiled back obviously delighted to participate in my first distant viewing. I stepped into my silent zone as I had been taught. Quiet and peaceful. When I first began meditation, I worried I would fall asleep. The state of mind was so restful and relaxing. I surprised myself when I remained awake and alert.

Ralph had described his mansion of twelve houses and his method for utilizing it. I had decided on my own visualization. I had designed a landscape based on my namesake Mt. Shasta. I had been born and raised in Dunsmuir, California, nestled in the side of the 14,162 foot mountain. I had selected areas of the mountain that held importance for my life. My favorite place was Panther Meadows about 7800 feet up the mountain slope. As a child I had discovered its special power. It was a sacred place, and I always felt comfortable and secure there. So Panther Meadows had been my choice for the portal to my creative imagination. If I couldn't enter here, I probably would be unable to perform remote viewing at any other location.

Well, gee whiz, I exclaimed. Oh golly be. I haven't said those words since I was a child. And here I am now viewing Panther Meadows. A regular bird's-eye view. It doesn't seem to have changed much since I last saw it two years ago. Wow. I feel lightweight and lucid, very very lucid, more so than in my lucid dreaming. My little girl pokes her head out and asks to spend the whole time just being here, enjoying the presence. But I am on a quest to find the portal to my creative imagination. She'll have to wait for another time. I must find the focal point and from there go forward. Ah, I recognize it. The rock the streamlets flow around on their way down the slope. It actually attracted my attention. Unbelievable. The stone has a reflective surface. Okay. Now what do I see.

Peaches was leaning back in her chair, chewing on an unlit cigar, a rather expensive Cuban brand, and reviewing Virgil's extensive report on Mr. Tamm, owner of Tower Mansion, a private equity firm that held controlling interest in diverse corporate enterprises. She studied the detailed biography of Mr. Tammuz Dumuzi, called by his fawning servants, Mr. Tamm, Sir. The family name, Dumuzi, reached far back into history extending further than written records existed. A regular dynasty. His family nickname was Tammy.

The family's corporation had undergone several name changes and proliferation over the centuries. Tower Mansion was the holding company and maintained controlling interest in several thousand companies.

Peaches smiled. Virgil had portrayed the corporate structure as a highrise building with many floors. The holding company was on the top floor. Below was an equity firm covering several floors. It utilized different strategies: corporate takeovers; leveraged buyouts; venture capital investments; and growth capital offerings. The next section downward was the financial market players buying and selling currencies, bonds, and derivatives such as credit default swaps. Tower Mansion held huge amounts of sovereign debt, more than any sovereign nation did. The ground floor contained the lobby and several offices. The lobby, more like a small plaza, covered sixty percent of the floor space. A high vaulted ceiling rose above the floor. A fountain was the central display and art works graced the walls. A mezzanine overlooked the lobby-plaza and provided offices for the security team. The lowest section located in the basement contracted the exchange of weapons, drugs, and other controlled goods.

Being the center of the global corporate oligarchy, Tamm was above the law of nations and outside their control and regulation. Tamm was the true rule of the planet.

Hmm, she wondered, what's going on in Merlin and Morgan's collective mind that they believe they can beat Tamm and take over his enterprise? It's crazy. Virgil's data indicate Tamm sees them as insects without much of a bite. But he's a control freak and is upset by any sign of disorder. So goodbye Merlin-Morgan duo. And more importantly for our side he's also a need-to-know addict. He must know everything and limits data to those below him, who, he believes, is everyone else. Bloated with pride, he views himself as a god ruling his little domain. I wonder if he ever dreams of launching a conquest on the remainder of the solar system.

Aeneas' voice flowed through the intercom: "It's finished and ready for performance."

"Please, bring it in," she replied.

Exuding enthusiasm, Aeneas strode into the office and gave Peaches a tiny microchip. "Here it is. Attach it to the charm and you'll have increased power."

Peaches took the chip and placed it on the base of the charm. It attached immediately as if it were magnetized. "So, what happens?"

"Whatever is sent or received by the charm is automatically transmitted to Virgil. And Virgil can send through the charm. Thus, his language skill with its many voices and sound effects is at your disposal."

"I'm impressed. Thank you both. We can now challenge Tamm if it's necessary. I would as soon not if we can solve the situation without doing it."

Understanding the wisdom of her words, Aeneas agreed. "Too much chaos would cause unpredictable events. We've stepped into a game we know little about. Perhaps we can contact Tamm and negotiate a deal?"

"A fine idea. Let's work on a strategy."

I was back in the lab room. Wow, a fantastic experience. I'm going to enjoy these happenings. I proceeded to write the promised report for Philip. When finished, I left the lab and rode the elevator to the first floor. Strolling to Philip's office, I noticed the sprightly bounce to my movement. Knocking on his office door, I entered when he gave me a come-in gesture.

"The report's been sent. What a delightful experience. I appreciate your assistance and encouragement."

Philip downloaded the report, scanned it and then smiled. "You've accomplished your goal. Wonderful. Ralph's upstairs at his desk. The twins have given him another challenge."

"I'll go on up. I'll phone for another session, perhaps next week. Thanks again." I left and headed for the stairs.

When the Garlands arrived home, Shasta announced she was going to her study and write out all the information she had gleaned from the viewing session and would give Ralph a full description at happy hour. She hurried upstairs and soon was typing on the keyboard. She had been forewarned many details she was unaware of during the viewing were in her memory and would be mentioned in her description. The report she had given Philip described her experience up to observing Peaches and Aeneas. Philip only wanted to know her procedure and its success. He had a notion artists might develop the procedure to enhance their creativity.

She heard Karma meowing. She glanced toward the door. Both kitties were sitting there waiting for their supper. Oh my goodness, she thought, time has fled. She completed the episode and saved the file.

"Okay, kitties, let's get some food." They bounded down the stairs leading the way.

Chapter 45

The doorbell chimed. Lefty glanced around the central hub, wondering if the place looked good enough. It was too late now to do any more tidying. Kathy had arrived. He went to the front door and let her in.

As she entered the central room, she smiled and remarked, "You've really made some changes. It looks fantastic."

He beamed. "Thank you. Yes, you view my very latest vision. It reflects the new me."

She laughed. "The new you? Well let me immerse into the ambiance and get to know you." She kissed him on the cheek.

He started to pull her close for another kiss, but she playfully pushed away. "Not now. Later. Tell me about your adventures, your dreams and imaginative writing."

"Please be seated, guru. I'll serve the wine first." He strode into the kitchen off the central hub and shortly returned with a bottle of white wine and two glasses. He poured the wine and handed her a glass.

She sipped. Her eyes brightened. "Where's the wine from? It's delicious."

He tipped his glass to her and sipped. "It is good, isn't it. It's Basa from southern Spain."

"A fine white wine. Yes. I hope you have more than one bottle." They both laughed.

"So, you said you had something exciting and special to show me. A mystery treasure, you called it."

"It's my family album. I've told you about some stuff in it. Now I want to show some of it, the family legends and lore."

"Show it? Is it a family film?"

"It's text and images, but in digital format so we can watch on TV."

"Okay. Just be sure the Basa is close by. I'm ready."

Lefty turned the lights off and the TV on. The family crest was shown on the screen followed by the heading: "Elwell Family Album." A table of contents came next. Lefty scrolled down the contents until he reached "Legends, Part IV."

"We're not going to see the first three parts of your legends?" Kathy inquired.

"No, not now. Part IV is where the mystery tour begins. You don't have to believe any of what follows. Just pretend it's a sci-fi or fantasy story."

"Okay." She sipped more wine and leaned back against the couch.

For thirty minutes Kathy was immersed in an amazing story of aliens—their use and perhaps misuse of humans, a tale calculated to astonish and dissolve conventional beliefs. Her first reaction was an entertaining script for a grade B sci-fi film. Yet Lefty had introduced the story as part of his family's history, the legendary part but still—

Lefty watched her closely and then grinned. "Okay. What do you think about it?"

She laughed. "It would make a fun film. Seriously, though, I'm not clear about certain parts of the story. Can you give a short synopsis?"

"Of course. Then afterwards ask your questions. But first I'll open the other bottle of Basa." He jumped up and hurried to the kitchen, soon returning with the wine.

She held up her glass, her eyes twinkling. "This is very good. I'll buy some soon."

Lefty peered into his inner space and then began. "Aldes are an advanced species of intelligent creatures and inhabit a planet circling the star Aldebaran. The name for the home planet, their earth, is Alde. They've searched the galaxy for planets that possess life forms conducive to bearing their children. Our earth is such a planet, one of many planets that host the sprouting of consciousness-seeds, individuals with soul-spirit vessels who can become enlightened.

"We humans were chosen from all the other life forms here because we have traits that provide the best opportunity for the development of Alde children. Humans are two legged animals standing upright. Our prehensile hands and the architecture of our brains are also important traits.

"The Alde seed is planted in the fetus after it is developed and ready to be birthed. So the baby has an Alde consciousness-seed. In the most nurturing environment the Alde seed grows into a soul- or light-seed. Many seeds never reach maturity."

Lefty stopped, observing Kathy sitting relaxed on the couch. "Are you getting bored?" He glanced at her wine glass. "Need more wine?"

"Heavens no, I'm fascinated with the story. I'm letting it soak into my imagination. And I've plenty of wine. Please continue."

He smiled. "Okay, then. The Aldes view life as spiritual. The physical body is only a vessel for life-spirit to use for a limited time, to grow and develop in, but the body has no other purpose and is disposable and recycled by the planet. The animal body is a container for a specific time and purpose. Aldes have four stages of growth. Living in the animal body is the first stage, the childhood period. The second stage uses an astral body while the third utilizes a vessel unknown to us. The final state is full maturity."

Kathy leaned forward and gestured with her hand. "Why, the stages are similar to metamorphosis many creatures on earth undergo. Do we know anything about the final mature state?"

"No, we don't. Now at death the light-seed is released, and if its vessel is strong enough, it is able to pass through psi-field and emerge into the galaxy ready for the second stage, which we could call adolescence. Creating a vessel to move through psi-field is a major task soul-seeds must achieve. Many don't possess a strong enough vessel and are prevented from leaving earth. They eventually become part of the life-debris. Often their consciousness is so powerful it dominates the psychic level of earth's psi-field. It's like they're a ghostly presence. Their mental voices remain active in the psychic realm."

"What is a psi-field?" Kathy inquired.

"All planets with life forms have a psi-field that prevents life-debris from floating off into space and thus polluting the galaxy, a natural anti-pollution system. Aldes modify psi-field on planets where they plant consciousness seeds by embedding a filter in psi-field that allows light-seeds with a specific degree of illumination to emerge and develop through their adolescent period and beyond."

"Let's pause here," Kathy suggested. "The story is quite exciting, and I need more wine to stimulate my imagination."

Lefty ceased the narrative and refilled the glasses. They both sipped wine, savoring its flavor. She nodded her head and said, "Please continue."

"A seed cloud hovers above earth's psi-field. The cloud releases Alde seeds which then pass through psi-field and enter the fetus at birth. The seeds are attracted by the fetus and enter easily. The fetus' physical soul, the animator of its body, has an attractor that draws the seed to it."

With a dramatic tone he asked, "Are you ready for the battle between good and evil on a galactic level? A glorious space saga?"

Kathy laughed. "Yes, a thrilling struggle with the good guys winning."

"Aldes have a galactic adversary who opposes them and attempts to destroy them. Aldes call the enemy Moleks, another intelligent species from the constellation Musca in the southern hemisphere. The name of their planet is Molek. They try to kill Alde children when they emerge into the galaxy from the hosting planets. Fortunately the seed-cloud is invisible to Moleks, who can only perceive individual soul-seeds and these they can harm and destroy."

"Wow, it's an awesome tale," Kathy declared.

"Well, after emerging from earth, light-seeds are weak because energy has been consumed to pass through the planet's psi-field. Aldes must hide the location of the hosting planets and veil the emergence of their children. Moleks search the galaxy for Alde hiding places. Moleks have seekers and destroyers who can enter a planet's psi-field and seek out Alde children living there. So these Alde children must be aware of potential killers and protect themselves. The children learn Molek warriors are also ready to devour them when they emerge."

"You mean they eat the Alde children or are you being metaphoric?"

"The children are caught for food. They are considered a delicacy by Moleks, believe it or not."

"So it's not like an ancient feud of vengeance?"

Lefty chuckled. "No, Moleks eat many different kinds of life forms. They especially enjoy intelligent species."

"So, in terms of galactic struggle of good and evil, the evil ones see the good guys as delicious food and catch them for dinner. Oh, my god! What an astonishing idea."

"There's more to galactic life than you've ever thought. Yes, the good guys, Alde children, are only food in the Moleks' mind."

"Okay, I've another question. Tell me more about the children's lives and the reason many don't emerge at death."

"During childhood on earth Alde children care for each other and learn to apply their gifts to situations on earth–environmental, political-social, and spiritual activities. Childhood is a learning process and also a weeding out. Some children atrophy because they don't cultivate their skills and thus enhance their spiritual light.

"Individuals perceive the enlightenment as increased consciousness and spiritual power. The light-seed encourages people to overcome the body's hold and physical desires and explore and enhance mental and psychic talents and skills. The arts of course are an area where people can improve their spiritual gifts. Artists work within the culture of their times using materials and techniques available."

Kathy commented, "Yes, the arts provide great opportunity for individuals to find and improve their talents."

"These natural gifts make Alde children quite sensitive to their future. The hardest fact for Alde children to accept is only a few light-seeds will be strong enough to exit psi field and most will remain as life-debris. Many upsetting questions flow through their young minds. Why can't we all go to the next stage, that is, what we call paradise in our infant fantasy? Is this a just universe? What kind of creator would create such a world? Why are more seeds planted than will sprout and fruit? Why are physical bodies, animal bodies, required to host the light-seeds? These are a few questions that disturb them."

"Those questions are disturbing. I've been bothered by questions like that for years. Do you think I'm an Alde?" She appeared puzzled.

"You may well be," he replied with assurance in his voice. Then he continued, "One sign a light-seed is absent, dead, or undeveloped is a display of frequent violent behavior or advocating violence. As children grow and the light-seed increases, violent behavior will disappear or at least be minimized." He gave her a wondering look. "How often do you exhibit violent behavior?"

She laughed. "Not too often but when I was younger–oh boy, did I ever. I would throw things, not at anybody, but just throw stuff on the floor or at the wall. Whenever I had difficulty with a music composition I was working on. Bingo! My frustration fired up, and I'd throw pencils, pens, paper, notebooks, whatever. I still have frustrating days, but now I turn my attention to something totally unrelated and, wow, the anger disappears."

"That's cool. I've learned to do that also. Just change my focus."

"What happens after the children emerge?" She was intrigued.

"Well, soul-seeds after leaving earth find a safe haven in the astral field to develop their adult forms. They must stay alert to the threat posed by Moleks."

Kathy held up her hand. "I wasn't clear about words and symbols embedded in our language. What was that all about?"

Lefty sipped some wine and was silent for a few moments. "It's an important point. I hope I can explain it. Embedded in human language are key ideas revealing the truth and purpose of light-seed existence and the Aldes' galactic role. These ideas are expressed in the arts as symbols and images. Once displayed in the arts, ideas gain power and influence human lives and will assist in developing light-seeds. Cultures with ideas fully available have the most power to enhance enlightenment. Cultures repressing ideas will have little enlightenment, and so few light-seeds will become strong enough to emerge from the planet.

"The name 'human' designating our primate species is a linguistic derivative from the Aldes' language. They apply the name to the host species on all planets used for developing light-seeds. Thus the host species calls itself by this name."

He sat back on the couch and grinned. "Well, any comments or critiques? I thought you'd be giggling my now."

Kathy giggled, releasing her tension. "Oh, Lefty. What a strange, awesome story. Before I make comments, I've a final question."

He looked at her quizzically. "Okay, what is it?"

"When you were growing up, what was your take on these legends? Actually on the whole of your family history?"

"A fair question. I've always enjoyed fantasy and sci-fi stories. So when I reached my critical age, calling everything, or so I thought, into doubt, I relegated this part of the family history to the imaginative fiction genre. My family history extends back into the past thousands of years, beyond the written record. These tales are considered part of our oral tradition, conveying truths but not necessarily describing historical events. So I went from a state of childish belief to total doubt and onto my mental state today–the arts express important truths. For example, some family lore depicts natural gifts involving psychic talents. Recently I've come back to my childhood state but at an advanced level and accept paranormal phenomena, which are often difficult to prove."

"Really. That's cool. I've a few things to say about psychic gifts. But please continue. Why have you changed your attitude?"

"I've recognized my own gifts. I've inspected memories spotlighting events in the past when my talents were exhibited. And now I've been resurrecting them for the present."

"What talents are these?" Kathy inquired.

"I seem to intuit things either before the event or during it. I sense things about people that aren't obvious, like their hidden secrets."

"With my music I've developed some special skills I believe are more psychic than physical. And the insight has lead me to recognize other gifts."

"Like what?" he asked.

"Many visual artists see images in their mind. I hear sounds in my mind, clusters of sounds with certain rhythms. Often noises around me will trigger a group of sounds and I'll play with them, allowing them to develop. Most of my music is quite traditional with a tonal center and classical harmony, not the atonality of much contemporary music.

"Several years ago I had a strange experience. I heard mentally a weird grouping of notes. When I wrote them down, I realized I had an atonal composition, a fragment actually. Later at a concert of early 20th century music I heard the exact piece, composed by Anton Webern. After hearing it, I thought it was similar to one of my pieces. So when I got home, I looked at the score, and it was identical to Webern's work performed at the concert. I have a very strong memory for sounds. It could be called eidetic or photographic for sound clusters. So I know I had never heard Webern's composition before nor am I that familiar with his music."

She paused and sipped some wine. "Now the following event is where it gets really weird. A few weeks later I had another remarkable yet unsettling experience. I was singing aloud to myself and heard another voice joining in like a duet. The voice wasn't in my mind but right next to me as if another person was present. Well, that was shocking, to say the least. When I stopped, the other voice stopped and then started after I had begun again. Like you, I was into fantasies–spirit beings–when I was young and then outgrew them. So I wondered–spirit beings or hallucinations? Am I going mad or do I have a spirit guide?"

She raised her eyebrows showing her wonderment. "I did some research and came to the conclusion I have a special gift, one that allows me to hear the astral zone involving sounds. I learned the throat chakra is involved and so decided some of the sound clusters I've always heard were from the astral plane. Sounds crazy, doesn't it?"

"Yes, it does, as crazy as my talents."

"How can we explain the gifts?"

"The family's legends provided an explanation even if it's couched as a sci-fi tale."

"At least the Alde story relieves tension and offers support by referring to these talents as natural and good."

"Children growing up with the tale are encouraged to develop their talents but also be wary about potential threats from others who don't understand. Like most children's stories they give guidance."

"You said you could intuit secrets. Were you good at finding lost or missed placed things?" Kathy asked.

"Most of the time, yes I was. Really, family members often came to me for help finding things for them. What about you?"

"I learned. As a child I frequently panicked when I couldn't find something. You know, 'My god, where is it?' One time though I didn't freak out. I was silent and just sat in my chair, waiting. I'm not sure for what, but I did. I felt so peaceful, so different from my normal behavior. Then a small voice suggested I look under a pile of clothes beside my bed. Behold, my composition book was there. Ever afterwards I wait for my small voice, even if I want advice about something."

Chapter 46

J.S. Bach's *Goldberg Variations* was playing through the surround sound system. Carlyle Quincebury was reading a cyberspace spy thriller while enjoying the harpsichord performing in the background. A red light began blinking on the control panel installed in the arm of his chair. He pressed 'enter' and a red alert icon appeared on the screen. Below the icon 'Lefty Cosmos' was printed. He clicked on the link and read the latest data. Damn, he thought. Lefty's novel has progressed too far. If it continues, especially with the character Marilynn Raylon ready to divulge secrets about human society, the underlying truth would damage his business empire.

His security firm, Madrone Advanced Systems, LLC, wouldn't be harmed. In fact, business would increase with new threats posed by Lefty's ideas. His company was well-known in the field as an expert in total security and protection from cyber activities. But Lefty was on the edge of revealing the existence of psi spectrum. Ralph and his work with the Institute were serious enough. The scientific approach, however, was slow and its results didn't filter down to the populace quickly. Lefty's online novel could be the fuse, triggering a widespread investigation of psi field. Most people wouldn't be bothered by scientific skepticism. If Lefty's ideas became popular, more people would explore the psychic zone. A further, more critical peril was Lefty's natural gifts. Now he was being encouraged by his friend Kathy Hamilton, who also seemed to have special talents.

The source of his power and wealth was utilizing the data he gathered from both ethereal net and psi spectrum. The more people involved, the greater the opportunity for his ruin.

The electro-magnetic field required equipment for its minimal use. Exploiting the field at an advanced level, Carlyle relied on sophisticated technology and superior knowledge, which most people lacked. But utilizing psi spectrum was an altogether different situation. Many people had potential to tap into psychic energy but were either unaware of its existence or untrained in its operation. And more importantly the human mind supplied the technology. At the foundation of his philosophy knowledge equaled power. Sharing knowledge was equivalent to sharing power.

Carlyle rode the elevator to the bridge. When he sat down at the command center, he became Tau, a ruthless adversary to those who stood in his way. Rapidly touching the control screen positioned in front of him, Tau wrote two new episodes for Lefty's novel, one for Marilynn and the other for Henry. Tau had an invisible ploy for updating the novel with the new chapters.

Returning to the library and intriguing spy thriller he had been reading, he smiled. Lefty was going to be devastated.

Chapter 47

The Occupiers and violent police action against them was still top news. The corporate media tried to ridicule the Occupiers and deny police brutality, but the events wouldn't go away. Shasta had taken a break from her writing and was viewing online news at her favorite websites. Even campus police at many colleges and universities were now caught in the terrorist groove attacking peacefully demonstrating students. The police's favorite weapon was pepper spray applied to victims at close range.

Vivid memories of her youth were triggered by the news reports. Defending the forests, redwoods in particular, had been her political activism. She still remembered the pepper spray, the clubbing, and the dragging to the holding wagon.

Occupying had been a form of protest for a long time. No doubt the abolitionists protesting slavery and the women fighting for their political, social rights, especially suffrage, had used the tactic. No doubt police violence had been directed against them. The Civil Rights Movement had utilized the practice to great effect. Of course the anti-war demonstrators were next. Both these citizen outrages against a corrupt government brought down deadly penalties. Deaths of civil rights workers in the South. The massacre of students at Kent State University in Ohio by the Ohio National Guard. Public anger grew and not even the corporate media could quench it. Those heady days–so much love and innocence, so much anger and fear, so much government spawned violence and terror. She was nearing her seventieth birthday and although she didn't consider herself a source of wisdom, she had observed and learned a lot about human nature–the good, the bad, and the mediocre. A human population contained decent and kind people, mean-spirited creeps, and the fools who blindly followed.

She was constantly amazed at the path her memory took. Her imagination exhibited the movie *Snow White* before her eyes. She had seen the film as a youngster, and many of the scenes were still vivid. When Snow White was left in the forest to die, Shasta was frightened by the anger of the trees who seemed to threaten Snow White. Once the trees realized Snow White wasn't there to harm them, they quieted. And the animals assisted by be-friending Snow White.

Maurice Maeterlinck's *The Blue Bird*, a 1908 drama, was an earlier liter-ary work portraying the trees and animals' anger at human destruction of their nest. She had read Georgette Leblanc's *The Children's Blue Bird* in her youth and was chilled by the dreadful proposal to kill the humans. The film version she had seen was frightening but didn't express the same intense anger. Later in college she had read the drama. She was now old enough to understand the underlying critique of human hubris and greed Maeterlinck was revealing.

Talking of denial, I've been very adept at it, she remarked to herself. I haven't chosen my master game role yet. Well, I've been busy with the novel. Shasta suddenly laughed aloud. How silly I am, she reprimanded herself.

She rose and walked over to the window overlooking the garden. She watched Ms. Anna Hummingbird, who was busy gathering material for her small, cup-shaped nest. She envisioned Ms. Anna twining the materials together with threads from spider or cocoon webs. Yes, she thought, nature weaves an immense web of life from tiny one cell creatures to large multi-cellular ones. Hmm, an aha was forming and then it hatched. Of course, my master game role is grounded in my basic self. All things in nature, organic and inorganic alike, participate in nature's song. I'll be nature's singer and sing her song. It has many voices and forms, a cosmic symphony with choir. Beethoven roll over and join us. The Consciousness Fair will arise from the creative imagination.

Since starting her remote viewing sessions at the Institute, she had noticed a transformation in her creative processes. She sensed she had a more direct access to her imagination, as if she were observing from a different view, a meta-position. She could zoom in and out at her command. And inter-estingly the imaginative reality appeared more three-dimensional. Weird. Although she continued to perform sessions at the Institute for Philip's benefit, adding more data to the research, she did distant viewing at home for the purpose of her writing. And surprisingly she no longer felt rushed, frustrated, nor harassed by the creative process. She was definitely at leisure and proceeded accordingly. The experience was more god-like: she could perceive the past, the present, and the future of her characters. An enthralling feeling, and a pleasure too.

She felt an interior tug. Her inner voice, calm and quiet, was speaking. She went back to her desk and sat down. Soil was the foundation, the voice said. Opening the folder on soils, she selected the document on cryptobiotic soils. Here was an example of nature's process to build a living nest for all creatures. She read the document, sensing the basis for her song. Nature is the great alchemist, transforming barren rock, the lead, into a living habitat, the gold. Her magic power is awesome and beautiful. If humans would be guided by her, they would be a happier and less destructive species. Some scientists were trying to create life in a laboratory cauldron, a fool's errand. They should be learning the process that turns rock into a viable soil, a more fruitful and beneficial venture. She would establish her own microcosm in the garden, a small patch of land where she would place rocks that grow into a nest for plants and animals. Her small voice told her Ms. Anna would approve.

Shasta was at the workbench in the garage assembling tools for collecting mosses and lichens. One wall of the garage was set aside as a workspace for gardening tools and supplies. Next to the workbench were storage shelves and on the wall were hooks for large tools. Between the two wicker baskets she selected one with a handle. Inside she placed an old cookie pan she used for gardening. Then she added a trowel, a tableware knife and spoon, pruners and gloves. She put on her gardening hat and left.

She had prepared a site beneath the redwood tree in the backyard. Medium size rocks were set in a circle, the pattern a redwood grove has. She had inspected their property and had found some crustose lichen, which is the best for growing on rocks. A small patch of moss she had discovered under the fuchsias. The moss and lichen were now growing on separate rocks. Ready to search the neighborhood, Ingleside Terraces, she set out on her journey. She noticed some moss growing on the next door neighbor's roof, but wanted easy accessibility.

A fire was burning brightly in the stove, warming the living room. The Garlands were ensconced in their favorite places: Ralph on the couch with both kitties beside him and Shasta sitting at her round table, covered with items she might need. They were enjoying their evening extra dry martinis while sharing their daily activities.

"Today I was very ambitious and got involved designing routines for my magic show. Totally lost track of time. Karma came in and told me it was getting close to happy hour." Ralph sighed and petted Karma, who was sitting closest to him.

"The kitties are excellent timekeepers. Lucy gave me the old stare."

"What were you doing today?" Ralph asked.

"I've started a small rock garden. It's living rocks; it's very alchemical."

Curiosity gripped Ralph. "Living rocks and alchemy. That's amazing. And where is your laboratory?"

"Out in the backyard under the redwood tree."

"Ah, fitting site. Our redwood is sacred. What is your secret method to transform a rock into a living organism?"

"Nature's way. As an alchemist, I'm helping nature perform her work."

"And what is that?"

"Well, all alchemists know nature's goal, her personal agenda, is to turn all inorganic entities into living conscious beings."

"Yes, the light in the darkness, transforming the cosmos into enlightened consciousness. Dear, you've become a master mage."

"Thank you. I owe it to my friends, their help and encouragement."

They laughed. Ralph jumped up suddenly, forcing Karma to leap to the floor, and strode over to Shasta and hugged her. They kissed lovingly.

"Ah, the kiss of awaking. My sleep is over. My handsome prince has revived me." Delight danced from her heart.

"So, my beloved princess, pray tell the secrets of your heart."

"Sooth, my liege, for all these years unbeknownst to you, I've been performing alchemy in the laboratory of my soul. My method is nature's way and I've been following her path since birth."

"Such knowledge is overwhelming. I'm faint at heart."

"Shall I seek the smelling salts?"

"No, just another martini."

They both laughed, Shasta with a giggling trill. Lucy and Karma were quite alert and they smiled broadly like Cheshire kitties.

After Ralph returned with refills, he asked, "Okay, my dear, will you fess up? What is this living rock project?"

"I've attached several pieces of moss and crustose lichen on four rocks. Over time with a little help from their friends, they'll develop viable soil on the rocks' surfaces. The soil will sustain seeds and growing plants will attract insects and their predators. Such is my alchemical microcosm."

Ralph's inner spirit shone forth. He radiated happiness. "Can I assist? Be your helpmeet?"

"Oh, yes. Please. Guess what? Developing the project has increased my knowledge of microbiology."

"Share with me." Ralph was hungry for ideas.

"Several years ago on our Southwest trip we visited parks that had cryptobiotic soil crusts. We were fascinated by the phenomenon and did some research on the subject when we returned home. Well, I delved into the information and even added to it. I had an epiphany of sorts. At least a huge Aha. My new line of thinking led to the theory of endosymbiosis."

"I've heard the name, but it means little to me. Please elucidate."

"The theory rests on Lynn Margulis' thesis, which has been accepted, that certain organelles that now reside in eukaryotic cells form a symbiotic relationship. Originally, these organelles lived as separate organisms outside eukaryotic cells. During the evolutionary process, they were taken in and have developed a mutually beneficial partnership."

"I think you should explain the technical biological terms. I'm not too steady with their meaning," Ralph requested.

She smiled. "Okay. Nature has divided life into three types of one cell organisms: bacteria, archaea, and eukaryotes. The difference is that eukaryotic cells have their DNA contained within a walled membrane, that is, a nucleus. Often these cells have other structures also enclosed by membranes."

"Ah, nature's mysteries. Please continue."

"Bacteria and archaea don't have a nucleus. Multi-celled organisms have evolved from eukaryotes, so their body cells have a nucleus."

She paused, stretching her arms upward. Ralph stood up taking advantage of the silence. "I'll fix another round." He picked up their glasses and retreated to the kitchen. Shasta let her mind quiet, finding her inner space. When Ralph came back, she was ready for another presentation.

"The eukaryotic cells contain at least one organelle in a symbiotic relationship. Mitochondria and chloroplasts are two primary examples. They are both powerhouses, fuel factories. Chloroplasts operate photosynthesis processes in cells performing that operation while mitochondria generate the cell's energy.

"Now we come to lichens. They are a fine example of symbiotic relationship. The two normal partners are fungi and algae. The algae provide the energy and fuel with their chloroplasts. The fungi guarantee a more endurable structure, water-acquiring skills, and water retention ability. Together they survive very well, indeed."

"And when did they agree on joining together for their mutual benefit?"

"One of nature's mysteries. Early on in the evolutionary process."

"Do you think they squabble?"

They both laughed. The kitties smiled indulgently.

"Perhaps, if they misbehave, cyanobacteria join the couple. The third party would change the mix, establish different dynamics." She giggled.

"Ah, yes, the old adage of three's a crowd. Really, cyanobacteria are a component of lichens?"

"In some cases, yes. Cyanobacteria were the main constituent of cryptobiotic soil crusts. Lichens, mosses, and similar organisms can join too. I don't have any cyanobacteria handy, so I'm relying on lichens and mosses to build a viable soil. We'll discover what else is attracted and joins in."

Ralph remained quiet, peering at his queen. What an amazing mind she has—so nimble and quick.

Her eyes twinkling, she remarked in a hush-hush manner, "That's not my secret. It's only what I've been doing." She waited.

It took a few seconds for Ralph to register the import of her words. "Not your secret. You mean there's more?" His demeanor was questioning.

"My purpose for the living rock site is the foundation for my role in master game." She peevishly glanced at him.

He waited, then spoke, "What have you decided to play?" He was now more alert.

"I'm Gaia's singer. I'll compose songs to sing at Consciousness Fair."

A thrill vibrated Ralph's inner core. What more apropos could that be? The first time he had met her, he had recognized her earth roots. She was one of Gaia's guardians and not to be thwarted easily. Nature had nurtured an exceptional defender. He removed Lucy from his lap, putting her down on the couch, and rose. He walked over to Shasta and hugged her. This time the kiss was more yummy.

Chapter 48

Spending quality time with Kathy had buoyed his spirits. His mind was alert and ready to initiate creative activity. Lefty opened the novel and went to the last chapter where Marilynn had concluded her experiments and learned the truth. The next chapter would bring Marilynn and Sedna together again for a strategy meeting.

Startled, Lefty read the first paragraph of the last chapter and quickly scrolled backward to the previous chapter. His mind was conflicted, and he panicked. Taking several deep breaths, he rubbed his forehead and then stood and stretched. What the fuck had happened?

He scrolled back to the last chapter and read it carefully. After he had finished, he felt numb. He didn't remember writing the chapter. In fact he couldn't have, never in his life would he have written the chapter, which narrated in great detail Marilynn's kidnapping by villains unknown. She had left her apartment and strolled through South Park on her way to Caffe Park for dinner. The fog had rolled in early and visibility was low. Four men had appeared while she was in the park, grabbed her, and then vanished. She had never made it to the restaurant. The next day her employer had a phone call, supposedly from her, saying she was ill and would stay home that day.

Lefty was dazed. His security had been violated. Who could have entered his loft without his knowledge and added the new chapter? He got up and searched his home for clues. The activity released his tension and brought his thinking back to normal. The enemy had executed a perfect hack—no traces or evidence of his presence.

Standing in the kitchen waiting for coffee to brew, he was jolted by the idea the enemy had breached his computer system by crawling through cyberspace and coming in via a backdoor.

He copied the alien chapter into a new file, which was saved in a separate computer functioning as an archive vault. The writing style could assist in identifying the culprit. Then he deleted the chapter from the novel.

Vengeance sprang forth, and a powerful desire to locate and punish the hacker surged through him. While a security program with its anti-virus and malware searching tools was scanning his computer system, he went online to his website. He downloaded the chat room log data and would peruse it for possible threats. Next he opened the online edition of the novel and checked the table of contents. First numbness, then rage poured forth. He had expected the chapter of Marilynn's kidnapping to have been uploaded and listed, but another chapter also had been added.

He went to the latest concluding chapter and began reading. After finishing the chapter, he sat quietly performing his relaxation ritual, emptying his mind, loosening his muscles, and moving into a super awareness state. He was now relying on his natural gifts and gave himself over to his inner self. The word 'rage' blazing in capital letters flashed before him, followed by 'revenge.' He smiled. Yes, his whole purpose focused on those images.

His enemy, the evil one, had murdered Henry Gorman in his apartment. Again four men had sneaked into Henry's residence while he slept. They had easily bypassed Henry's security system. After they had tortured him, eliciting as much information as they could, they gave him a lethal injection of pure heroin and left evidence Henry was a heavy user and had overdosed. The police, closing the case, would easily find evidence of his hacking activities and membership in Ever-And-Anon that had been planted. The FBI would also be happy. The evil one would be safe and could continue to commit more crimes.

Lefty determined to stop him. He emptied himself of fear and trembling and became an adversary worthy of his opponent. His plan of action lay before him. He left the online edition as it was after copying and downloading the new chapters. The surface would stay the same. His actions would be invisible. He signed off and walked around the central room, his mind quiet. He went into the kitchen and brewed a full pot of Jamaican coffee beans. Filling his mug, he went back into the central room and sat in his thinking chair. The chair's back and lower part could be tilted allowing for a more reclining position. He adjusted the chair so he was semi-reclining.

Pieces of the cosmic puzzle were fitting together. Parts of his family's history, especially from the legend and lore sections, were illuminating his intellect. It was the moment he had been waiting for all those years, wondering what his purpose was. If the Alde tale had any truth, now was the time for him learn and live it. The word 'gnosis' stared directly at him and was replaced by 'consciousness' and then a field of light.

He moved to the computer and brought up Cosmic Game, the maze game he was designing for the novel. Well, it would still be part of the story and now much more–his weapon directed against the evil one. He began revamping the design. The game would search the cyber zone and point to the enemy.

Raising the mug to his lips, he realized it was empty. Time to rest and stretch anyway. He glanced at the computer clock: one am. He was nearly finished with his project. Another hour or so and he could upload the program to the internet. Refilling his mug with hot coffee, he returned to his work feeling pleased with the architecture of the game. He had a name for it–cosmic pod, a game of astonishing ingenuity.

The software would send millions of pods, each an individual entity capable of amazing deeds, through the internet. Any digital device connected to the internet would receive a pod, which would enter by a backdoor without leaving a trace and embed itself as a rootkit in the device. In its 'dormant' state the pod is designed to perform specific activities in the background.

First, it discovers the administrative password using a password cracking app. Then it copies the device's email address, addresses of frequent recipients, and the port(s) assigned to online service. The data is sent to a website set up to collect the information. When Lefty deems the moment is auspicious, the cosmic game will begin.

Daily, the pod sends a query to find a webpage Lefty will post as a signal to activate the pod. When the pod is activated, its program takes control of administrative functions and operates the device. The game design appears and announces the human operator must play the maze game before any other device use is permitted.

The game is a series of four mazes, each one more difficult than the previous. The maze-solving will put a player into one of five different categories. Bottom or category one is a player who can't solve any maze. Category two is solving one maze; three is solving two mazes; four is solving three mazes; five is solving all four mazes. The results, sent to Lefty's cloud collection center, affect the device. Letter grades are assigned for each category: F, D, C, B, A. The device receiving an F is shut down and can't be used. Device with a D has its power and capabilities limited to 25%; with a C to 50%; with a B to 75%; an A has no limitations but 100% capabilities. A timing mechanism has been set so the limitations will last for twelve hours, and then the device returns to normal operating capacity.

When the game is completed, the program shuts down, and any other program can now be run. The device operates at its grade level. The pod sends results and all data it has collected to Lefty's cloud collection center. Once a pod sends back the results and limits the device, the pod self-destructs and vanishes, removing all traces of its presence.

Lefty clicked upload and the program was online. Cosmic pod resided in a cloud with a virtual machine Lefty had especially crafted for secret cyber activities. Millions of games were flowing through cyberspace. He smiled, happy and at peace with himself. Finally he had accepted the challenge. Win or lose, he was fully alive.

Chapter 49

Peaches inspected her living room where she had decided to launch her journey into the astral plane via the voice channel. She had redecorated the room to make it suitable for psychic activities. The walls and ceiling were painted an off-white. A comfortable cushioned armchair was set against an inner wall. The chair was a recliner type for easy changing of the body's position. A small table was set next to the chair. On the table were a lamp, clock, and the cat figurine.

She rented a four room duplex in Albany about a mile from her office. Like the office her residence contained a computerized system linked to Virgil. All rooms were monitored. Without utilizing a handheld device, she could speak with Virgil and Aeneas at any time.

Gloria had impressed upon her the necessity for a secure and comfortable launching area so she could completely relax. During practice sessions Peaches had experimented with various chair positions until she found one best suited for her journey. The ambience of the room was important, and she had tried diverse light settings.

Arriving at eight pm, Aeneas would observe her first extended travel into psi dimension, visiting Tower Mansion. With Virgil's assistance he had designed and constructed a device, tiny in scale, that would enhance the charm. He had created electronic magic, fitting for the brave new world she was entering. Until now, based on Gloria's instructions, she had communicated on voice channels. Like wizards of olde, she would execute an OBE. Her double was journeying to Neverland of psychic energy and home of Tamm and his empire.

According to Gloria, she required a role-playing character for the game, a special identity. Peaches chose Athena, an ancient goddess figure. Peaches' everyday life now would be separated and shielded from the game. To prevent intrusion and maintain the privacy of her daily life, an elaborate biographical background had been constructed for her character Athena. The biography had been inserted into the game's history. Athena had been a player since the beginning.

Virgil's in-depth investigation of Tamm had identified important assistants and advisers. Tamm had a mentat, an alter ego, named Betel, a brilliant intellect with high speed computing skills. Betel, although in a separate physical body, was mentally controlled by Tamm. Anything Tamm believed and accepted, Betel would also, no questions or doubts.

Virgil had compared Betel to himself. Even though Virgil resided in a metal container, he was actually an ethereal spirit. Aeneas was his vassal, his incarnate servant who interacted in the physical world, the hands that performed tasks.

Of course, Aeneas had fits of laughter at the idea. Peaches had noticed a change in Virgil's behavior. He emitted sounds that could be considered laughter. Was Virgil learning humor, she wondered?

Aeneas' arrival halted her reverie. They discussed strategy and reached a mutual agreement. During her first trip she would view Tamm without visible contact. She would communicate on the voice channel at a very deep subliminal level and direct her voice to his insular cortex. Located within the cerebral cortex, it is a region where awareness of body states, especially a subjective sense of inner body, interfaces with emotions and sensations, like pain, warmth, and sounds. It influences a person's self-image and interactions with other people.

She planned to embed in the insular cortex several voice frequencies that would give her control over Tamm at the unconscious level. If she were successful, she would make future journeys to negotiate with Tamm and encourage him to agree with their proposals.

When she was seated, she positioned the chair so her back was slightly lowered and her legs were raised a little. The charm with its two tiny microchips attached hung around her neck against the throat chakra. Sinking into herself and allowing silence to fill her, she centered her attention on a visual image of Tamm Virgil had discovered searching the game's history. She felt her mind drifting and yet still focused on Tamm.

Wow, she thought. I'm looking down at him, an eagle's view. He's sitting in a lounge chair beside a swimming pool. Betel is seated next to him. Hmm. There's a third person. Ms. Plum, no doubt. She's holding a tablet ready for dictation. I'll increase the receiver's volume so I can listen in.

"Mr. Lart. What are the latest figures on the arms shipments to the Republic of Geuse?"

Peaches peered around the pool seeking the fourth person. He walked onto the pool terrace and approached Tamm. "President Geuse V is extremely pleased with the recent shipment of drone missiles. He has placed a new order for 500 more, Mr. Tamm, Sir."

"And the National Liberty Party, have we heard from them?"

"Leader Libr III has requested 5,000 automatic rifles, Mr. Tamm, Sir."

"Fulfill the orders, Mr. Lart."

Lart quickly tapped on his tablet. "The shipments will go out tomorrow, Mr. Tamm, Sir." He left the terrace and entered the residence.

Well, Peaches thought, Tamm conducts business as usual. I'm not interested in his many business activities, so I'll perform my psi surgery. Following Aeneas' instructions, she directed four different voice frequencies toward Tamm's head. Each frequency stimulated a memory voice channel, embedding a sound waveform in his insular cortex. Once accomplished, she activated one of the imprints with her Virgil tones.

Peaches uttered a soothing motherly sound, reminiscent of a lullaby, that guided Tamm back to his infancy. She hoped he would have a positive response. The first test was initiated since they lacked evidence for their predictions. Watching him closely, she noticed he relaxed, tension dissipating from his body. Betel glanced at his master and asked, "Shall I leave, Sire? Would you like Venusian to attend? Perhaps a massage?"

Tamm smiled. "Yes, do that, Betel. I'm in a very tranquil mood. And fetch Euphrosa to sing her mellow songs."

Very good, Peaches told herself. I'll leave and return later for more tests.

Aeneas saw Peaches move slightly. Her breathing increased to normal rate. Her eyes opened and glanced around the room, stopping at him.

"An awesome experience. I highly recommend it, Aeneas." She moved the chair to a sitting position. "I'm thirsty."

Aeneas jumped up. "I'll fix some drinks. What would you like?"

"Is there any orange juice in the frig? If not, coffee will be fine."

Shasta stopped writing. She suddenly realized she was thirsty too. Was Peaches' actions an imaginative reflection of her own state of mind? She had raised her awareness of the interface between Peaches and herself. Yes, a cool glass of orange juice would be delightful, she thought as she left the study.

Chapter 50

Philip and Ralph were drinking coffee at Cliffside Cafe. They were seated at a table in front of one of the large windows Cliffside was noted for. The picturesque view of the beach and rocky cliff below and the ocean, quiet today, was pleasant. Visibility was good, about ten miles out toward the horizon, but not clear enough to see the Farallon Islands twenty-eight miles west of the coast. The Marin Headlands to the north was lit by the morning sun shining through the Golden Gate.

Their meeting, twice postponed at Philip's request, was to examine anomalies occurring during Ralph's remote viewing sessions. Ralph had described details of his experiences that weren't recorded during the viewing nor in his reports. He had offered his thoughts, doubts, and questions. For him the puzzle was both exciting, stimulating his curiosity, and disturbing, shaking his notion of reality.

Ralph had developed a philosophical leaning early in his life. He began asking questions about Native Americans who had resided in San Francisco before Europeans had arrived. The Yelamu people, a branch of the Ohlone language group, had created an efficient and practical culture based on their knowledge of the land. Ralph's desire to learn as much as possible about the Yelamu soon branched into cultures of other Native Californians or First People. Comparing indigenous societies with his own initiated a series of queries that resulted in meaningful philosophic issues. His mind delighted in a play of ideas, and he discovered researching the subject satisfying.

Ralph's analytic skills had been honed sharp by his chosen field, the craft of magic, and his deep interest in alchemy, Hermes' art. Both disciplines brought into play the opposite sides of his intellect. Magic provided insights into human psychology and skills of coordinating mind and hand. Alchemy, more esoteric, challenged his abstract thinking and intuitive understanding of symbols. Both were served by an inherent skepticism strengthened over the years. Because of his romantic soul, Ralph had never lost contact with his inner self. His magic profession required a balance between the inner and outer, a gnosis bonded in the fiery furnace of performance.

The two men had similar mental traits that found delight pursuing intriguing ideas. Philip's intellectual strength was rooted in biology, and later he moved into the area of human consciousness. In his study of the exotic regions of human behavior, he was rigorous with his conceptual tool kit, always seeking to ground the evidence in a rational framework. Ralph was the ideal opposite with his intuitive approach to ideas and life in general. Early he had immersed himself in mystery of nature and human culture and the art of magic with its implied enchantment.

"Ralph, after a careful review of the viewing tests and a lengthy discussion with the twins, I admit I'm totally puzzled. And so are Geri and Jerry. However–" Philip paused and looked quizzically at Ralph and then smiled. "I'm extremely happy. Your experiences are too abnormal and weird to be passed over as the same results of thousands of tests. They will be challenged and that's a plus. It's a wakeup call. The deniers will find all sorts of excuses, but the open-minded will seek to find a rational explanation. And we'll provide them with a theory that ties in with the thinking of contemporary science from quantum field theory to cosmology."

"Philip, I'm delighted to be part of the project. Actually, my ego is enjoying all the rational, conceptual irritants that puzzle and provoke. I don't care whether my name is mentioned in the published papers. I'm bubbling with enthusiasm to be engaged in ruffling the feathers of those whose heads are buried in sand."

Philip laughed. "If Shasta has strange things happen in her tests, I'll be mighty pleased."

"Be careful of your wish, Philip. If she does, the anomalies will be weirder than mine. Her creative imagination is quite powerful. I should tell you she is able to perform lucid dreaming."

Philip was alert, staring at Ralph. "I didn't realize that. The talent might be applicable to remote viewing and perhaps other directions the project can take. I'll consider the potential."

They sat silently viewing the waves lapping the beach with gentle rolls. The tide was going out, baring more sand. Pelicans flew by and then plopped onto the water's surface. Thoughts tumbled about in Ralph's mind. He needed some firm structure to quiet the restlessness.

"Philip, if you have an explanation, however far out, I'd like to hear it."

"Well, first, let's say my conceptual foundation upon which my scientific studies are grounded allows for such anomalies and other strange happenings. It can potentially account for paranormal phenomena. Process is a key idea. The cosmos is a continuously evolving process. The future is undecided and uncertain. Predictions can be made, but they don't imply determinism or a fixed end result. Even though contemporary science has put into our tool kit such concepts as indeterminacy principle, uncertainty principle, superposition principle, entanglement, Higgs field, and other weird ideas, humans, even the most brilliant, have a difficult time applying the ideas as part of their normal thinking. Something there is in the human mind that dislikes, if not rejects, these strange notions. How much is cultural and how much genetic, I don't know.

"Of course, in our everyday life we make certain assumptions that guide our behavior at the unconscious level. We call it common sense because we all act the same way. A reciprocal relationship exists between ideas we create and influence the ideas have on us.

"So, the reality that is now forming doesn't require all the ingredients of the past. Take for example the case of Mary Rainbow's photograph hanging on the wall at Mechanics Institute's chess club. The twins were in a frenzy. I've never seen them in a such turmoil. Personally, I found the situation quite intriguing. A challenging puzzle. I realized then that my worldview differs from theirs."

"That's amazing–about the twins' reaction, I mean. When I heard about the issue, I wasn't upset. I thought it a mystery which I might never understand. Perhaps, it's my background in magic and alchemical studies."

"Yes, I've noticed your fluidity, your willingness to accept the inexplicable. The stone wall doesn't stop you."

Ralph chuckled. "Why should it? As a magician I've walked through walls and other solid barriers. A solid penetrating another solid is a classic routine. When I come upon a barrier, I immediately seek the portal, the gateway to the other side."

"A fine attitude, Ralph. I wish we had more like you working with the project. But back to theory. Let's assume a finite number of possible futures. An infinite number is another consideration that has been proposed, but a large number is sufficient for my explanation. We are constantly creating our future by our actions. I mean 'creating' in the sense certain actions will lead toward a specific possible future. For example, if we have another cup of coffee, that action will move us toward one possibility, and if we don't then another."

"And of course, if one has a fresh cup and the other doesn't, that's a third option."

"Very good, Yes, that's the idea. Our common sense says such a notion is weird and doesn't fit reality. But the weirdness is common sense at the quantum level of reality and may be so for all levels of the cosmos."

"What is an example at the quantum level?"

"Okay. The photon makes a choice at various times whether it will manifest as particle or wave. Another is Shrödinger's cat puzzle. Erwin Schrödinger designed it in 1935. The logic paradox illustrates the superposition principle. Imagine a scenario where a cat is locked in a steel container. Also in the container are a very small amount of radioactive substance, so tiny that an atom might or might not decay within an hour, and a device that can be triggered by one atom of radioactive material. If the device is activated, it will break a vial of hydrocyanic acid which will kill the cat. At any given moment we the observers don't know whether the substance has given off an atom that has triggered the mechanism. Only when we open the container will we know whether the cat is alive or not. Now here's the stinger. The act of opening the container and observing the situation determines the cat's fate. Our observation or measurement is the causative agent that selects one potential future over all the others."

Ralph widened his eyes in surprise. "You're saying it isn't a matter of our knowing but one of our action."

"Yes. The superposition principle proposes the cat's life is in a set of potential states simultaneously. Let's say at least two: alive or dead. Our observing the cat by looking into the container forces the selection of one of those two states. And we don't know which state until we observe the cat. We can't predict with any certainty. It's basically the 50-50 chance we have when flipping a coin."

"That is mind-boggling and consciousness-raising."

"Many physicists believe they have proprietary rights to concepts in quantum mechanics. When scientists in other disciplines, like myself, borrow any of the ideas, a great hue and cry of outrage bursts from the community of physicists. They claim the borrowing is a misappropriation because the concepts apply only at quantum scale. Evidence doesn't exist as yet indicating the ideas will be applicable at any other scale."

"And how do scientists like you respond?"

"I would propose the evidence for paranormal phenomena is on a par with evidence for quarks, bosons, gluons, and other subatomic particles. I'm open-minded about their research, so shouldn't they be the same?"

"Agreed."

"Ideas are common human property and not licensed to any particular intellectual domain. The issue is whether the idea assists in the explanation and is consistent with other concepts."

"So, if the superposition principle applies to the human scale, my noticing and reporting Mary's photograph on the wall at Mechanics Institute fixed a possible future and made it true."

"Yes. Of all potential futures, your action caused that possibility to become reality or at least one with Mary's photo in it. Again, a number of potential realities with Mary's photo exist."

"Thus, other elements of my activity are also involved in generating a specific future."

"Exactly. Now we can add the theory of morphic resonance. Many different formative possibilities exist. Our action expresses several forms or fields which have their own elements or traits."

"I think of styles or genera in a literary sense. The history of magic has recorded changing styles of magical presentation and effects. Magicians borrow from certain styles that appeal to their personality. Actually, the notion of style and personal signature can apply to all arts and crafts."

"Indeed. Fashions change according to our whims and tastes. But now we reach the great mystery. What is the causative agent involved in our choice at each and every turn, unconsciously or consciously?"

"Oh, I guess only the shadow knows. And perhaps the trickster too."

"For example, when you deviated from normal routine and took an alternate action, what was the causative agent? You told me you wanted to change the procedure. So you did. But why did you want to? And why did you take that particular action and not something else?"

Ralph laughed. A moment of enlightenment shone upon him. "Magicians often tell audience members who assist they have a free choice. For example, you could've selected a different card or stopped at a different moment. Statements like that are part of magicians' box of misdirections."

"More evidence to support my hypothesis magicians intuitively understand real magic. Their attraction to real magic is so strong at the unconscious level they spend their lives involved with it but at a safe distance. Under the guise of professional magic, earning a living or as a hobby, they pretend to be real magicians, who of course are pleased to entertain."

"And what happens when a mage goes too far and tries to conjure by applying real magic? Probably no one will believe it's actually happening."

"Yes. The deniers will fake him out with their knowledge of sleight-of-hand. But if anyone accepts the fact, the mage will be declared psychic freak. Perhaps a government agency will assert the mage is a national treasure and for the purpose of national security take control of the mage's life."

"So, you're researching the field of real magic." Ralph suddenly recognized Philip's secret agenda.

"Yes. Paranormal or psychic phenomena—the gateway to magic and cosmic mysteries."

Chapter 51

Carlyle Quincebury set his briefcase on the desk. The afternoon course on computer game design he taught at SF State was always fun. Students who enrolled in the class showed an aptitude and devotion for writing game programs. As a professor in the Computer Science Department, Carlyle taught three advanced courses each semester: two were on internet design and security. The advanced course on game architecture was his favorite and always attracted the best students. When he discovered very talented people, he offered them a position with his firm and so maintained top caliber personnel.

A chime played Mozart's variations of "Ah! vous dirai-je, Maman," indicating someone was in the hall wanting entrance. Carlyle pressed a button on the desk. A green light outside the door would blink, signaling permission to enter.

A young woman entered. "Good afternoon, Carlyle," she said. "How was class today?"

"It went very well, thank you, Bertha." He smiled at her. "The afternoon beverage is an iced chai latte."

"It'll be ready in a few minutes." She smiled back and retired from the library.

Bertha and her husband Don were excellent choices, he remarked to himself. But they'll be graduating at the end of the school year, and I should start looking for replacements.

Carlyle employed couples who were enrolled at State for housekeeping and other domestic chores. They had their own suite of rooms with a private entrance. He believed they should lead their own lives on their free time. Carlyle resided in a large house located in St. Francis Wood, an upscale neighborhood in the southwestern part of San Francisco. He was in walking distance to State, and Muni public transit service was available. The house was quite large, built in the 1920s, and he had added features, including a swimming pool and the command bridge on the top floor where he governed his commercial empire.

He was perusing his business accounts when Bertha brought his drink. "What are your plans for the weekend?" he asked.

"Study and study," She answered. "Midterms for both of us next week. Then the following weekend we decided to take a day trip to Sonoma and Napa and visit some of the wineries."

"Sounds fun," he replied.

After Bertha had gone, he thought about them—decent young people, good students, should do well after graduation, settle down and raise a family. And they weren't like Lefty Cosmos, prone to rock the boat. Bertha and Don walked the well-traveled path, he realized, like they should.

He departed from the library and took the elevator to the top floor, his command center. Entering the common room, he walked up the five steps to the bridge and sat down at the command console. Opening a financial spreadsheet, he examined accounts of his corporations scattered throughout the world. His global enterprise of linked firms was officially headquartered in Cayman Islands. The corporate web collected and sold data, which was securely stored in a chain of clouds. The security firm Madrone Advanced Systems, LLC, had its headquarters in downtown San Francisco. Madrone was an above board, visible company, following all legal requirements faithfully.

He heard Bach's "Air on G String" and glanced at the alert panel. The red light was blinking. Fixing on Ralph's psi waveform, he switched on the generator-transmitter's voice mode and listened carefully to Ralph and Philip discuss the anomalies arising from the reality changes occurring during remote viewing sessions. He had been tracking each session and was pleased with the complications caused by his entrance into the process. Yet as he followed the conversation Philip and Ralph were having, he became annoyed and finally angry. They were untroubled, actually finding the strangeness intriguing and full of potential for research. Only the twins were upset. The twins—the time was propitious to learn all there was about the them. Immediately he dispatched DOG to collect the twins' data.

The conclusion of the discussion was also troubling. Ralph mentioned Shasta's ability to perform lucid dreaming. A person with an aptitude to execute lucid dreaming had a gift many seekers of psi spectrum would do anything to possess and command. If she did become more involved in the Institute's project and learn techniques to harness her psi power, uncertainty would dominate.

His personal success was rooted in a well-regulated and predictable social and political order. Activities that destabilized society awakened the sleeping giant, the global corporate oligarchy, and increased difficulties for his business empire to operate.

Carlyle nodded to himself. The second act starts now. I'll immerse myself into their daily lives, he decided. Their Ocean Avenue environs is only a few blocks from my residence and from State–a pleasant stop on my way.

Chapter 52

An unlit candle in an ancient holder stood on a purple cloth. Behind it was a portrait of a saintly-looking man, who had a nimbus surrounding his head. Gordon Russell turned and peered into the other window. He saw an enlarged tarot card depicting the fool. He studied the card, noticing the carefree attitude of a young man, who seemed to be on the edge of disaster. A wry grin glided over his face as he opened the door and stepped into Leila Lubec's mystic realm.

The door chimes pealed three distinct tones. He studied the room as he waited. A couch occupied one wall, and two upholstered chairs were placed against the other. An oil painting of an older woman hung between the two chairs. Over the couch was a landscape watercolor. As he was inspecting the painting, the curtains suspended at the back of the room separated.

Leila contained her surprise. "Gordon, it's so very good to see you. Please come in."

Gordon uttered a slight laugh. "Bet you're wondering what I'm doing here?" He grinned broadly.

"Not for a reading I presume. Let's go into my private chamber where the spirits abound." Leila chuckled and went through the curtained doorway.

In the center of the room was a table and around it were two chairs set across from each other. Several chairs were placed against a wall. Opposite them was a cabinet with shelves enclosed by glass doors and three drawers below. At the back of the room was another pair of curtains.

The inner room was illuminated by a single, shaded light bulb hanging from the ceiling, creating a shadowy ambience as very little light entered from the outer area. The fragrance of incense touched his awareness. A feeling of peace and serenity permeated the surroundings.

"Please be seated, Gordon." She studied him, noticing a glow to his aura and a happiness emanating from his eyes. Gordon has a secret to tell, she thought. "Well, how can I help you?"

"Leila, you've probably heard news about events that will take place at Rainbow Inn soon."

"Consciousness Fair and Mary's round drum–yes, I have. I spent an afternoon at the Inn recently. All the excitement and positive energy along Ocean Avenue–it's wonderful."

"Yes, isn't it. You mentioned a reading, perhaps someday, but I'm here to ask if you'll join us in a happening at the fair?"

Another surprise, Leila thought. She scrutinized his countenance and then recognized Gordon's secret: he's in love. "I'd be delighted. What are you planning?"

"Well, we've just started and wanted you in at the beginning. Most of the group will be involved though Ralph and Shasta have much bigger roles. Merle and Emma, Dale and Margaret, and Charles Freeman, my partner, and me."

She laughed. "When I came through the curtains and saw you waiting, I was definitely surprised, not just because you were visiting but something else caught my attention. Then I realized you're in love. Wonderful. Tell me about him."

"In many ways we differ yet complement each other. Well, he's bigger than I am, more heavily built. He likes athletic pursuits. He works out at a gym and jogs. He watches major sports. I never cared for them and I'm not much of an exercise enthusiast. He must have the latest electronic device. I'm satisfied with what I've used for years. Now here's a major contrast. He has a fine intellect but uses it differently from my scholarly endeavors."

"What is his occupation?"

Gordon smiled, a slight arching of the eyebrows. "He's an architect, works for Human Spatial Designs. His mind centers on visual elements–geometric figures while I'm playing with words. I'm very attracted to his mindset and fantasy trips–all done up in spatial terms."

Leila sparkled. Her aura emanated a glowing warmth. "So your mind has words constantly running about, perhaps distracting you. And Charles visualizes two and three dimensional figures. Together you two form a higher language level, more akin to a rebus."

"Yes, like two dissimilar universes trying to communicate, two types of meaning. It's weird but engaging. We realize our contrasting modes and are fusing them into a meta-language."

Talking with Gordon was no longer a feisty sparring match. She was enjoying their conversation. "So paranormal experiences—you seem more open to them."

"Yes. Being with Charles has been a period of mutual understanding. At times we share intimate feelings and thoughts like we're in each other's minds."

"Like mind-reading or telepathy?"

"Ok. I've changed my opinions. I'm ready to explore new ideas, the unusual and extraordinary. During the 1960s I read all the books and smoked pot, wore beads and did everything else one was supposed to do, but I was totally critical of everything too. Like I was a puritan indulging in sin, enjoying myself but putting down the intellectual structure underneath the New Age philosophy. So I became a hardass cynic who nibbled brownies and drank nectar all in the name of the gods of pleasure. Now I've finally found the other half, my soul and inner self."

"Are you at peace?"

"Not quite yet. I'm in a serene and mellow mindset but haven't thrown away my intellectually honed sword."

"I'll be careful then. No sense in getting my head cut off."

They both laughed.

"Leila, to be honest I've always liked you even though my sardonic nature stood between us. I realize it was a defense mechanism. Charles has taught me to stand my ground as naked as I was born."

"That's wonderful. I'd be happy to join the gang's performances at Consciousness Fair. And I'm looking forward to meeting Charles."

"Some of us are meeting at Ocean Delights tomorrow and will discuss our consciousness-raising adventures then."

"I'll be there."

Chapter 53

Ben Said smiled at the customer who approached the counter. "Afternoon, Carlyle. Haven't seen you for awhile. How have you been?"

"Hello, Ben. Other than having a tall stack of papers to grade, I'm doing well, thank you."

"What's your drink today?"

"I'll have a chai latte." As Ben was preparing the beverage, Carlyle glanced around Ocean Delights. Ha, there sat the Garlands and their friends. And an empty table next to them. I'm in luck.

Taking the latte, he moved toward the empty table. He was placing the cup on the table when he heard Dale's voice call out, "Carlyle. Hey, come join us." He turned, smiling, and looked at Dale and his friends.

"Everyone, this is Carlyle Quincebury, a colleague of mine at State," Dale announced. Room was made and Carlyle joined the group after the introductions.

"What do you teach?" Gordon inquired.

"Nothing as fun and glamorous as music, I'm afraid," Carlyle replied.

"He instructs serious stuff. Computer programming and internet security," Dale remarked.

"I do have a few fun classes, though."

"Oh, such as?" Shasta asked.

"Game design."

"You mean like computer games for young people?" Merle wanted to know, thinking of his daughter Virginia, who had her own game station.

"Actually, the course provides students an opportunity to learn programming suited to game design. Students select the kind of game they'd like to develop, a personal choice."

Seated on Carlyle's right side, Ralph was sensing unusual energy flow. His activities with the Institute had sharpened his intuition. Perhaps his association with John Ocean had assisted his perceptive skills.

"We've been talking about the upcoming Consciousness Fair on Ocean Avenue. Have you heard about, Carlyle?" Merle wondered.

"I have, yes. Stories are fluttering around campus about it. It's attracted the attention of many students." He glanced at Dale.

"Yes, student communication has been working overtime," Dale commented. "NASO has posted flyers all over campus broadcasting the event."

"So, are any of you involved in the happening?" Carlyle asked.

"We all are," Ralph answered and turned to look directly at him.

"We all have a role to perform," Merle remarked.

Leila was detecting an underlying negative energy coming from Carlyle. Sipping her tea, she wondered about his presence at this moment—chance or planned? She decided to observe and say little more than a few pleasantries. "Anyone can participate," she mentioned.

"Join in and help raise consciousness," Gordon declared.

"I'd like to. Do I need to sign up somewhere?"

"At Rainbow Inn. Mary has a roster of participants. She's organizing the event," Dale suggested.

"Here come two of the biggest boosters of the consciousness drum," Ralph mentioned. He waved toward the door as Rafé and Jeff entered. They waved back and went to the counter to place their orders.

Rafé came over to the table while Jeff waited for the beverages. Ralph introduced her to Carlyle and prepared to make more room at the table.

"We'll sit here at the next table. We can still be involved in the conversation," Rafé said.

When Jeff put the drinks on the table, Rafé introduced him to Carlyle. Shasta glanced at Rafé's twinkling eyes and thought about the romance of youth. She looked over at Gordon, who was exuding his own love glow. Since Gordon had started sharing his life with Charles, he had become mellow. His sharp, often brittle, critical edges had softened, morphing into an inner warmth. The two made a fine couple, she thought.

Rafé nudged Jeff. "Don't look directly but what do you sense about Carlyle?" she asked.

Jeff sipped his coffee. "I've heard he's quite popular. Students line up for the game design class. What do you think?"

"I perceive mixed feelings from him. Like he's hiding something, maybe a secret agenda."

"Maybe it's the answers to his tests." They both laughed quietly.

"He seems to be attracted to Ralph. He's observing him without being obvious, a covert watching." She grasped Jeff's hand. "I'm a little nervous."

"You're right. A strong tension is present. And Ralph seems to be aware of it too."

"Strange, because I don't believe they know each other very well."

"Maybe it's one of those immediate aversions. Their inner energy conflicts. Something like that."

Now was the time for a magical feat, Ralph decided. The conversation had dwindled to repetitive loops. He stood, garnering everyone's attention.

Removing an ESP deck from his jacket pocket, Ralph peered around the table. His gaze fell on Carlyle. Smiling, he asked, "Carlyle, would you assist me with a psychic feat?"

"Yes, Ralph, I'd be happy to help," he answered.

Ralph put the deck on the table. "Please cut the deck more or less in half and place the packet you're holding face up on the table. Thank you. Now select the top card from either pile." After Carlyle had done as requested, Ralph asked, "Please hold the chosen card between your hands. I see they possess great psychic power. Project that energy into the card and then place it on the table."

Everyone watched Carlyle hold the card. When he had placed it down, Ralph said, "Now since the cards have ESP symbols, we'll use the three letters as the basis for further selection. For the letter 'E' select three cards from the piles. You can choose one or two cards from one pile and the remaining from the other or all three cards from one pile."

After Carlyle had made his choice, Ralph took the top card of each pile and put them on the table. The face down card remained face down. For the 'S' and 'P' Carlyle repeated the procedure and Ralph took the top card of each pile away.

"Here are three pairs of ESP cards. One card of each pair is face up and the other face down. What are the chances the first pair has the same symbol?" Ralph asked while looking at his assistant.

"Well, Ralph, I'd say one in five," Carlyle replied.

"Please turn over the face down card."

Carlyle held it up for all to see. It matched its partner, both circles.

"And if the second pair matched each other?" Ralph inquired.

"One in fifty," Merle commented.

"Please hold up the second down card, Carlyle," Ralph requested.

"Ahs," spring forth. Both cards were three wavy lines.

"And the third pair, what are the chances?" Ralph asked.

"Bravos" and applause rang forth when Carlyle held up the third pair, matching stars.

Ralph shook the assistant's hand. "Carlyle, you possess great psychic power. Have you performed any magic before?"

"Computer programming is the only magic I'm good at. Thanks, Ralph, for allowing me to assist." After a slight bow to the audience, Carlyle sat down.

Rafé and Jeff looked at each, sharing a moment of knowing.

Chapter 54

Sedna sat on a park bench across the street from Marilynn's apartment building. She was worried because she had lost contact with her friend. After she had received a chat room message saying Fallyn would visit Floyd during her business trip to Seattle, she had sent Marilynn a reply conveying her pleasure at the visit but asking to change the plans. Floyd had to come to the firm's headquarters in San Francisco for a very special meeting two days hence and they could meet then. Marilynn had agreed, and they had chosen a time. Sedna hadn't heard from Marilynn since. Repeated phone calls had gone unanswered. Her office had stated she was home on sick leave. Sedna had rung the apartment's bell several times over the last hour. No sign of Marilynn. So she had taken up watch across from the building's entrance, waiting for any encouraging sign. In another hour she would contact the building's management and talk with them.

Eduardo Guchol entered the apartment building and took the elevator to the fourth floor. He walked down the hall until he arrived at 409, Marilynn's apartment. He rang the bell and waited, intrigued by a surprise request from her to visit this afternoon. He rang the bell again and heard the chime sound. After a few more minutes he was puzzled. She had definitely stated three pm today for their meeting. He checked his phone in case she had made a change at the last moment. Nothing there. He turned around looking up and down the hall expecting someone to appear and explain the weird situation. Then he became worried. She was inside but had fallen and couldn't get up or had fainted or something even more serious. He required more information.

Thinking back over the past several months as their friendship had deepened, he remembered Adele Thorson, who lived across the hall in 412. They were close buddies and shared many interests. He walked to the apartment and rang her bell. Again he peered up and down the hall, and when he faced the door, it opened, and Adele was standing there. She recognized him and invited him into her home. Displaying anxiety, he told her the situation and expressed his concern and puzzlement.

"Eduardo, I haven't seen Marilynn in several days. And that's unusual. I've been working late and haven't felt like socializing but–you know, it's strange she hasn't been over to see me either."

"Should we call the building manager, do you think?"

"Better yet, I've a duplicate key. Let's go look."

They hurried to Marilynn's door and Adele unlocked it. The apartment appeared normal as they remembered it. Just like she had left for work in the morning and would be home later in the day.

"If she has gone on one of her business trips, it was very unexpected," Adele commented.

"We'll look around and see if she has taken personal items for a trip."

"Hello. Anyone home?" a voice called from the doorway and then the bell chimed.

Startled, Adele and Eduardo hurried to the door. They saw a woman standing there. She was frowning and surveying them with suspicion.

"Hi," Sedna announced, "is Marilynn here?"

"No, she isn't," Adele replied.

At the same moment Eduardo asked, "And who are you?"

"I'm Sedna Waters. Is something wrong? I was supposed to meet Marilynn here this afternoon." She glanced around the living room.

"Please come in, Sedna. I'm Adele, Marilynn's neighbor."

"And I'm Eduardo Guchol. Marilynn texted me several days ago to meet her at three pm today. When no one answered the door, I went to Adele's apartment across the hall."

"I have a spare key, and we decided to check in case Marilynn was here disabled."

Sedna felt an uneasy tingle run down her spine. "The situation is serious. I'm going to trust you. Actually, burden you with an unbelievable story."

"We were involved in checking to see if Marilynn had gone on a business trip when you arrived," Adele mentioned.

"Let's sit down and listen to Sedna's story," Eduardo suggested.

As she related the activities Marilynn and she were involved in, Sedna watched the expressions and behavior of her audience. Morphing from puzzlement to uncertainty to worry mixed with fear–their appearances changed with the narrative's development. When she was finished, they sat stunned. She realized they all were on the same wave length.

Eduardo spoke first, "Obviously, Marilynn is in grave trouble and needs our help."

"Oh, yes!" Adele jumped up. "Marilynn is never without her tablet and she keeps it in her purse."

"Of course. She uses it as a workstation and it's where her writing is," Sedna declared.

"Most importantly, it has GPS, one of the reasons she bought it."

Eduardo rose quickly. "If she has it, we can track her, discover her location, if we're lucky."

They began their search of the apartment. When they returned to the living room, they assured themselves both the purse and tablet were missing.

"We'll adjourn to my place," Adele announced, "and try to locate Marilynn's tablet."

When they were settled in the apartment, Adele picked up her tablet. "I've the same brand and model as Marilynn's. We bought them at the same time." She texted Marilynn's tablet and waited. Then she clicked on a GPS location app.

"Marilynn's tablet is located nearby. I'll map the coordinates."

Sedna and Eduardo sat quietly watching Adele.

"Well, this is weird. The tablet is located a block away at Garden Park Condos. It's the latest condo complex in the neighborhood and the most expensive." She went to the front window and stood gazing into the park. Both Sedna and Eduardo spoke simultaneously. "That's strange." "We'll devise a plan."

Having reached a conclusion, Adele turned and faced them. "My apartment will be our operational base. We'll reconnoiter Garden Park and locate the condo she is being held in."

Sedna quickly added, "We'll conceive a plan to release her either with or without the help of the police."

"In these times we can't trust the police."

"Let's get started. I'll fix drinks and snacks." Adele walked quickly into the kitchen.

Both Sedna and Eduardo opened their tablets. Each began jotting down methods to release Marilynn.

Chapter 55

The twins were in their flat. Worry plagued their countenances. "I don't understand the cause for the entanglements. The reports of Ralph's remote viewing indicate a sudden appearance of strange changes." Jerry was deeply puzzled.

"I'm concerned with our plan to steer him toward the golden path. If the plan fails, all is lost."

"The two are connected. We must identify the cause first; otherwise, we won't know the correct guidance that will resolve the anomalies."

"Can we agree the cause is located in his viewing sessions?"

"Definitely. And I believe I've found something, the divergence triggering the mixing of realities."

"Yes? What did you discover?"

"I think the incongruity occurred during a personal viewing. Remember, Philip asked him to write short summaries of any viewing he performed on his own time. After examining the reports, I discovered a minor variance when he visited Tower Mansion the first time. Entanglements began after that point. Quoting from Ralph's report: 'I was in the inner chamber of my mental mansion. Revolving, I studied each of the twelve doors, which were all ajar. Well, I thought, that's unusual.' A little later he said, 'The doors remained ajar. No strange or weird feeling was present.' Then when he entered the room, he felt 'a vague sense of wrongness.'"

"Yes. He noticed an alteration–the spiral design on the floor."

"Then the spiral staircase materialized and up he went into Shasta's imaginative reality."

"Excellent, Jerry. You've grasped the answer."

"I moved another logical step. An outside agent entered Ralph's inner room and altered the arrangement."

"Ah, a real mystery now. Let's focus on motivation. The agent's identity will follow."

"Two logical options: the agent wanted to assist Ralph or hinder him. I believe the probabilities indicate hindrance."

"Yes, of course. Assistance would be offered directly unless a trickster element is involved. But no, sneaky tactics imply an attempt to disrupt Ralph's psi activities, no doubt including the Institute's project."

"Someone who opposes Philip's research, perhaps."

"Who has the most to lose if the project succeeds?"

"Ah. A thought. The method reminds me of a hacker's attack, in and out without a trace."

"Okay. Through the backdoor or trapdoor. Trojan style."

"I've an intuitive sense the culprit isn't a scientific opponent. Why not wait until the results are published and then demolish them?"

"Yes. And crucify Philip at the same time. Besides deniers with their pathological disbeliefs could never accomplish a psi procedure. Obviously, the adversary is someone who wants to damage, even halt, the project and Ralph's experiments."

"I'm now of the opinion it's Ralph who's the nexus of the attack. Yes, it's an attack on psi behavior."

"Definitely. Who benefits then?"

"Someone with a cyber hacking mindset and an ability to surf psi field."

"Wealth and power are the ingredients for motivation."

"Okay, we'll begin our search."

"And when we glean anything, however trivial, we'll confer."

"Since he met his double, he has an excellent prospect to reach the portal to the self."

"With a strong adversary Ralph will require more direct assistance in his quest."

"We must devise a strategy to aid him."

Geri paused and allowed their thoughts to disperse. Quietness shrouded them. Then with a tenacious pose she spoke softly, "We must set up a psi shield around Ralph to protect him from the Destroyer."

"Definitely. Once he gains access to Psi Alpha, the loftiest channel in psi spectrum, he'll be safe and can journey to the Source Portal without peril."

Chapter 56

Shasta peered out her study window onto the backyard below. Another winter is nearly over, she thought. Like last year the weather alternated between cold and damp days and dry and warm ones. The plants were confused. Should they hibernate or begin a growth cycle. The animals were in the same situation. Even humans expressed uncertainty.

At happy hour last night they had discussed ethnic calendars different from the modern western or Gregorian calendar. Ralph had compared the Chinese twelve year cyclic calendar to European astrology of twelve houses or constellations. In the Chinese calendar each of the twelve years is symbolized by an animal. The one animal that stands out from all the others is the dragon. For Chinese people a dragon is a celestial creature, more akin to the heavens than to earth. It's the most spiritual and most freedom-loving and loves to dominate but hates to be bossed. Europeans, for the most part, have an opposing view of a dragon–an inferior beast linked to evil. Ralph had mentioned another view found in European tradition, that of an alchemical symbol. In the ancient art of alchemy a dragon had great significance. Its meaning depended upon what operation it was involved in. The discussion had birthed a seed idea for the finale of her story.

She walked over to the desk and seated herself. Focusing her eyes on the tip of her nose, she breathed in deeply, down to her pelvic region, and then exhaled slowly. She performed the activity several times before she was ready to write.

Peaches and her friends had worked diligently on the strategy they would apply to the negotiations with Tamm. Because of his great power, they must carefully balance their requirements with his goals. He must believe he was in control and would benefit from the agreement. Their plan was based on a weakness in the game reality. The total history of the game, all its events and participants, were duly recorded in its archives, which were available for all to view. Aeneas' inventive genius coupled with Virgil's superb computing skills created a scenario with complete video-audio fidelity that should seduce Tamm and his mentat Betel into believing the authenticity of Peaches' presentation.

Aeneas had designed and crafted a visionary device that would project a holographic image of a dragon into the game world's space. Peaches in her role as Athena had the ability to subdue and control the dragon, thus providing her with a leverage to negotiate a settlement with Tamm.

Betel hurried into the library where Tamm was reading. A bright fire blazed in the fireplace casting a warming glow throughout the room. Tamm looked up at his worried servant.

"Sire, a celestial dragon has entered the solar system and is fast approaching earth."

"What breed of dragon is it?"

"I've checked the archive database and compared its image with those in the record. It's a chaos dragon, Sire."

"First, we must protect our herd of dragons located at our moon base. Have them secured in the underground shielded campus."

"Very good, Sire. I'll also gather all the archival data on chaos dragons and their participation in our history."

"Yes, do that." Tamm returned to his reading.

Peaches was viewing the scene from her eagle's nest as she called her unique invisible place in psi zone. She noticed Tamm was reading a volume of Dumuzi family history which covered the colonization of the moon. Their plan was unfolding neatly. Betel should discover several historical events of chaos dragons attacking the earth and causing extreme damage. Virgil had embedded these scenarios into the archival database. The insertion procedure was accomplished without leaving any traces. Tamm and Betel would accept the fidelity of the historical record.

The present stakeout was much more comfortable and enjoyable than the normal ones she had done in the everyday world. She allowed her mind to absorbed all details of Tower Mansion. It was as if she could collect information without actually seeing or hearing anything. It was pure intuition.

Betel entered the library, his face a stone mask. "Sire, please view the historical record on chaos dragons. The file is ready."

Tamm pressed a button on the arm of the chair and a large screen on the wall over the fireplace brightened. A narrative voice related the four events when chaos dragons had penetrated the solar system and ravaged earth and its moon. The visual-audio presentations were terrifying. The dragon's deep bass voice howled and shrieked. From its mouth emerged fiery flames, dissolving everything touched. From its tail lightning bolts were emitted, fragmenting into tiny pieces all that was struck. Once chaos power was unleashed, disaster was guaranteed. The dragon had the ability to direct its horrendous force toward specific targets. Human weapons were unable to kill or stop the dragon. Eventually the dragon tired of its play and romped off into the galaxy leaving earth devastated.

The film ended. Tamm sat dazed. He lacked a plan. Because his ancestors were unable to prevent the attack, he felt defeated. Yet his pride and honor were at stake.

"Betel, devise a working strategy. We must have a defense in place before the dragon reaches the moon."

Betel was rigid. "Yes, Sire. I'll have a plan ready by then." He strode out of the room.

Peaches smiled. Now for the appearance of Athena, the savior.

The wall screen chimed and a voice announced a message had been received from Athena of Ithaca. Tamm spoke to the screen, which had a transmitter-receiver unit, "Play message."

The voice said, "Athena of Ithaca would like to discuss the issue of the chaos dragon now in the solar system. She has a plan to render the dragon harmless. If you are interested, please reply."

Tamm answered, "Yes, I'm interested. Can we converse now?"

Athena appeared on the screen. Aeneas had formed a holographic image from photographs of ancient Greek statues of the goddess.

Betel had arrived and was standing next to his master's chair.

Athena spoke, "One of my businesses is breeding and training dragons. I've a thorough knowledge of their behavior. Chaos dragons aren't indigenous to the solar system, but I have studied the breed. They originate from Thuban, a star in the constellation Draco, a notorious breeding soil for chaos dragons. I believe I can tame the dragon and send it home." Her tonality conveyed strength, decisiveness, and willingness to negotiate for their mutual benefit.

"What is your technique?" Tamm inquired.

"Before I describe my tactics, we should agree on the ground rules."

"And what are they?" Tamm's attitude was noncommittal.

"If I succeed, you will perform certain tasks."

"What are they?"

"I am Gloria Smith's friend and guardian. The agreement centers on her involvement in the Sorcerers-Wizards Game. You have taken an interest in her life and specifically the charm she owns."

"Ah." Tamm was now alert and aware of possible danger.

Peaches emitted a silent voice to Tamm's insular cortex, a soothing, accepting feeling that countered the anxious sensation. Peaches smiled, her countenance friendly. "Gloria wants to get out of the game. She never liked to participate but only did so for her partner Sean. So the first part is you will never harm in any way Gloria, her friends and associates as long as they don't participate in the game."

"What are the other parts?"

"The second part is you relinquish any claim to the charm and acknowledge Gloria's ownership. She may do what she wants with it. If the charm is used in the game, then and only then are you permitted to interfere."

"Any other parts?"

"Yes. The final section concerns Merlin and Morgan, who are Gloria's enemies and have threatened her with personal harm. She doesn't care what happens to them. You may take any action against them you wish."

"I see. Let me consider the proposal."

"Don't take too long. The dragon has sped past Jupiter and is closing in on Mars. Action must be taken before it reaches the moon. Call me when you have an answer." She signed off.

Tamm studied Betel and then asked, "What are your thoughts about the situation?"

Betel hesitated for a few seconds. Then he responded, "First, if she is successful, a grave danger is eliminated. And we have not lost anything. Second, Gloria Smith was never a challenge and only a minor player when she participated. No one associated with her, including the private detective agency she hired, are important to the game. They all are part of the great trivia of the world. If any should cause a serious problem, we can take action then. Third, Merlin and Morgan are also minor players who pose no real threat. Based on recent data, they are close to bankruptcy. I think we should encourage their financial demise. Fourth, the charm has power, but if it is not applied in the game, it is meaningless to us, just more trivia. My conclusion, Sire, is to accept the proposal."

"I'm inclined in that direction. My intuitive feeling is to trust Athena."

"I have one further consideration to mention, Sire."

"Yes?"

"Who will receive credit for terminating the dragon threat? I suggest you should receive the honor and praise. Since Athena is a goddess, we can have people honor her shrine. As world leader you must be recognized for your greatness."

"Very good idea. Yes, I'll proposed that."

Peaches smiled, watching their antics from her eagle's nest. Of course, she thought, you may have the honor. I'll be your inspiration. Good. So it was set. She didn't wait long before Tamm signaled her.

"I agree to the conditions you laid forth. I have one stipulation: I as master of Tower Mansion receive the honor and respect for ridding the solar system of the dragon threat. I'll announce you were my inspiration. Is that suitable?"

"Yes, it is. I'll begin the procedure to remove the dragon's presence from our world."

"Very good. Might I know what your technique is?"

"Dragons are quite sensitive to certain frequencies in the very high range. Chaos dragons are juveniles and exploit the solar system as a playground. When they tire of their sport, they go home. I employ a high frequency waveform that soothes and tranquilizes the dragon and causes it to seek its mother. The vibration touches its infantile memory formation and nature takes its course."

Tamm was surprised and also delighted. The solution was both ingenious and instinctive. "Excellent. I would enjoy watching the dragon removal operation."

"Here are the coordinates. The dragon will arrive in two minutes."

Tamm set the distant viewer and saw the dragon approaching. When it reached the specified location, it stopped, stood upright on its tail, then turned and sped back from whence it came.

Suddenly, unexpectedly, the chaos dragon twisted its body into a spiral and glided back toward the earth. It was moving at a leisurely speed but definitely aiming at earth's moon.

Tamm panicked. "Athena has failed," he shouted. "Betel, initiate the backup plan. Now!"

"Whoa!" Shasta yelled. She stopped typing. "What's happening?" she said aloud. "Whose ideas are being channeled through me?" Was Ralph somehow involved, she wondered? Well, I'll just delete the entry and start over. She selected Tamm's statement and pressed delete. Nothing happened. The line remained. Several more presses on the delete button convinced her another procedure was needed. She closed the document without saving it.

Realizing her nervousness, she breathed deeply several times and stood up. She walked to the window and stared into space. What happened is creepy, she thought, real weird. Obviously, I need a rest period.

She started for the door and halted. No, coffee isn't good at the moment. I'm already too stressed. Her reading chair beckoned and she sat down. I'll clear my mind and focus on my nose. Move into my inner room. Yes, use techniques I've learned.

Silence soothed her mind. She was observing Panther Meadows high up the slopes of Mt. Shasta. Her child, her younger self, was sitting on a stone gazing at flowers. Then hearing voices, Shasta looked toward the sounds. Two men were arguing, close to hitting each other. One man shook his finger at the other. "You're the evil one, Tau. And I'll trash you."

The other man laughed. "Lefty, you're outclassed. You'll never publish your silly ideas. I'll destroy you. You'll be nothing." Glaring, he turned and walked away.

Inflamed with anger, Lefty shouted, "My game-pods will find you. Then your empire is demolished." He stared at Tau for a long moment, before striding off in the opposite direction.

Shasta felt a wet tongue licking her face. She opened her eyes. Lucy was standing up on her lap washing her face. Shasta smiled. Petting Lucy on the head she whispered, "Thank you, Lucy. You're a sweetheart." She lifted her and placed her on the floor. Shasta rose. "Let's go fetch some munchies." Lucy was already romping down the stairs when Shasta reached the hall.

First things first, she thought as she filled the kitties' munchy bowl. Tea is the healing drink for me. Ah, a cup of green tea, yes, that will be the refreshment.

Taking her tea, she went out into the backyard and sat down beside the living rock garden. The afternoon had warmed to a pleasant sixty-five degrees. She felt her emotional roots sink into the earth, tapping its sustenance. She sat. Pure being.

She felt a presence. She knew. "Join me, Ralph. It's so pleasant in the garden."

He sat down next to her. "I saw you when I let the kitties out. They were at the backdoor waiting."

She took his hand. They watched the kitties. Lucy was rubbing against a catnip plant while Karma was observing ants.

Chapter 57

A wind chill was nipping him as he wandered north along King Street, passed the Giants' ballpark to where the name changed to The Embarcadero and further north until he reached South Beach Park overlooking the bay. The wind was invigorating, stimulating his brain cells and triggering his imagination.

Sitting on a bench, he watched the activity on the water. Several large container vessels were moving underneath the Bay Bridge, either going to port or heading for the Golden Gate and out to sea. If he had a bowl of hot clam chowder and a piece of sourdough, he would be in paradise. Later, he would eat, but now he must make some creative decisions.

His game plan was exceeding expectations. The game-pod had gathered data from millions of devices; many of them now had limited capacities. Collection clouds were analyzing the data seeking the winners, those players who had solved all five mazes. When they were identified and their locations mapped, he would be ready to attack.

He stood and turned toward The Embarcadero, leaving South Beach Park. He walked to Delancey Street and stopped. Somewhere in the area is Garden Park Condominiums. He had decided the residential building with upscale shops at street level should be fairly close to South Park but in an upper class neighborhood. He wanted the most desirable location and then put his building there, a building designed to suit his agenda. Marilynn would be rescued with a flair displaying his cleverness and natural gifts.

"Hey," he muttered, "wow, yes." He surveyed the site. An excellent location, he thought. He walked across the street and toured the surrounding environs. His imagination visualized Garden Park Condos with its open plaza situated in the center between two wings. Removing his tablet, he took photos of buildings in the block. Satisfied, he strolled toward South Park, a feeling of enthusiasm filling his soul. When he reached the park, he headed for Crepes Cantata for food.

After a pleasant and quiet meal, he walked through the park at a leisurely pace, feeling refreshed and exuberant. His mind was clear when he stepped into his loft. Peering about in case an intruder had broken in, he laughed to himself. The vibes were positive. Another all night session was on the agenda, so he brewed a pot of coffee.

He studied the list of game winners and their locations. His program had plotted the locations in a series of concentric circles. His loft was at the center and maze winners were spiraling outward. He would investigated those with addresses in San Francisco first, the most likely perps. A specially designed search-ware was collecting data from all available databases on winners located in San Francisco. While the program was operating, he decided to work on the novel. His trio of heroes—Sedna, Eduardo, and Adele—were planning their strategy to rescue Marilynn from the clutches of the evil one. His idea was to utilize the talents of all three heroes plus the talent of the prisoner Marilynn, whose gifts were at present hidden.

Relaxing in his lounge chair, Carlyle was amused. His office had provided a detailed report on game-raid, as the media had labeled it, which had caused the breakdown of the global computer system. Many online servers and personal devices had either shut down or operated at lower capacity. Then a miracle had occurred after twelve hours. The ethereal net was again working normally. Explanations and conspiracy theories were running rampant through the media. Talk show hosts were having a field day interviewing experts who babbled clichés and buzzwords. Blog writers were devouring each other, pointing fingers at their demonic opponents. Governments were discussing new anti-hacking laws and greater surveillance. The UN appointed a special commission to investigate.

He laughed to himself.

Madrone Advanced Systems had withstood the attack. He had personally designed the security system, which had a double-layered firewall. Embedded between the two layers was an architecture styled on a game model. If the winning solution wasn't given within two seconds, access was denied. Many personal devices of his employees had been affected by game-raid and the dolts were on a short list for early retirement.

Yes, his adversary was cleverer than he had expected. He was delighted. The challenge was greater and success would be sweeter.

DOG had gathered data pointing to Lefty Cosmos as game-raid initiator. The young man was escalating the conflict. Good. The idea to utilize a game as a hacking-malware tool was excellent. Carlyle's virtual machine, safely residing in a secure cloud, was able to identify and quarantine a game-pod as it was trying to enter. A forensic program did an autopsy on the pod, gleaning its architecture and secrets. The data were now stored in a cloud where he had given the pod a detailed inspection.

Game-pod was beautifully designed. Carlyle hadn't seen such elegant programming in years. Today's software was bloated with unnecessary lines of code. No wonder bugs were constantly cropping up and Trojans sneaking in and committing their dastardly deeds. If Lefty had turned in the pod as a project for one of his classes, Carlyle would have given him an A+. Such brilliancy. Too bad the young man had gone astray and lost his way, so to speak.

Mentally, he surveyed data collected from visiting Ocean Delights and Rainbow Inn. On the surface convention and regularity were controlling patterns. Consciousness Fair was a diversion and perhaps helpful to neighborhood businesses along Ocean Avenue. None of the players showed any indication of a hidden agenda. Their behavior was forthright. Such candidness was deceptive, though, causing a lowering of defenses. The danger inhered in unexpected twists and turns growing from their interactions. Ralph was known for his unpredictable actions, his I'll-do-my-own-thing whenever his voice called. He was the focal point and must be watched at all times. Most of his activities, including remote viewing, weren't threatening in themselves. But as Ralph's psychic skills improved, he would discover the portal in the psi spectrum, pathway to the Self, and if he succeeded in his goal, disaster would occur.

Carlyle knew deep within his being his business empire would falter and his own paranormal power would dissipate if Ralph fulfilled his quest. The other players weren't as close to discovering Celestial Source enfolded in psi field, although they could increase damage, especially if their actions prompted detours and distractions.

Shasta possessed hidden talents he couldn't discern clearly. He marked her with the latent danger label. The chief challenge was posed by the Garlands as a team acting in harmony. The degree of their inner entanglement was unknowable. Caution was the key.

John Ocean was totally impulsive, his behavior capricious. No doubt a regulating rationale guided John's moods and actions, yet it was incomprehensible to others.

Mary and Od were more predictable and less of a concern. Mary with her devotion to chess and music displayed creative talents suited to her imaginative disciplines. She could improvise and challenge preconceived notions of her audience. But she didn't take too many risks. She wasn't the type to accept a dare that led her to the edge of the abyss, unless extraordinary rewards were offered. Od, on the other hand, was quite predictable within his frame of reference. But if he changed, he would do it abruptly without warning. Sudden surprise was his forte.

Since Consciousness Fair offered an opportunity to watch and manipulate the participants, he would join the happening as a spectator. If he had to take action, he would be prepared.

Chapter 58

It was getting close to midnight, and they had been partying since nine pm—a Saturday night outing at Bistro Royale. The popular hangout was packed as always on weekend nights. High spirits, loud noises, shouts, laughter, talking—all blended into audio flood.

Lefty was enjoying the company of his South Park friends. They had been discussing the game-raid affair and its consequences. Lefty, smiling to himself, was laid back and letting the others talk.

Vance was complaining, "The name the media gave the malware lacks poetic quality."

"'Game-raid,' what a terrible metaphor," Anne said, "it's nothing but a media buzzword."

"It's not even accurate, either. A bunch of empty-heads babbling." Charlotte frowned and then sipped her drink.

"What I liked most was the way the whole system was brought down." Bruce was beaming.

"The plan was elegant. Philip K. Dick would definitely approve," Kathy commented.

Lefty wondered how his friends were affected. "Did any of you get way-laid by the malware?"

"It was simple to solve—no problem." Bruce was radiant. "I hope net gamester sends out more. Something to break the monotony."

"I've always liked maze puzzles," Anne commented, "and the excitement at the office was fun. I found out who the game players were."

Vance looked at Kathy and remarked, "You're lucky to be an artist, have your own business."

Before Kathy could reply, Charlotte responded, "Really, Kathy, being outside the corporate culture is heavenly."

Kathy chuckled. "But not totally outside. I'm dependent on funding and sales to pay my rent."

"Yes, but you don't have to kowtow to stupid rules and silly supervisors," Anne replied.

"Also," Kathy glanced around the table, "my music, whether it sells or not, is tied to the winds and whims of fashion and people's tastes."

Lefty decided to enter the conversation. "One thing you have, Kathy, and most don't is opportunity to indulge in your creativity. You compose for yourself besides pieces for pop consumption."

Her eyes sparkling, Kathy said, "Yes, I'm fortunate. I earn enough to spend most of my time creating music for my Muse and myself. But you all could do the same."

"Oh, not me," Vance complained. "I don't have artistic talents. Besides all I know is programming."

Anne turned to Lefty. "You're working on a novel, aren't you? And your specialty is security programming." She looked at Vance. "See, Vance, all's not lost."

"How's the novel going?" Charlotte asked.

Lefty glanced at Kathy, exchanging a knowing smile with her. Before he could respond, Bruce said, "The other day I came across a website hosting a novel in progress. It's run by an LC, whoever that is. And onliners can participate in writing the story."

"Oh, Bruce, that's Lefty's site." Charlotte nodded at Lefty seeking confirmation.

"Yes, I'm posting my novel online as it's being written and assisted by participants." Lefty was glowing with pride.

"It's amazing the number of onliners who are helping," Kathy remarked.

"How does it work? Can I join?" Bruce asked.

"All you do is open an account. An automatic response will be emailed and will state the regulations and procedures. The site has a downloadable policy file too."

Anne was delighted. "Lefty, that's wonderful. The whole globe can be authors. I like it. I'm going to open an account tomorrow."

Vance spoke in a hush-hush voice. "Why don't you use a theme of game malware in the story?"

"Yeah, the Jedi Knights strike back and bash the evil empire to smithereens. I'd like to be involved in writing that scenario. I'll join tomorrow too." Bruce was bubbling with enthusiasm.

"Who's ready for another round?" Vance inquired.

Kathy glanced at her watch. "I'm bowing out. Need to get up early in the morning."

"Me too," Lefty remarked. "I'll walk you home."

"Bunch of party-poopers," Vance announced.

Kathy and Lefty waved goodbye and emerged into wet fog hanging over South Park.

He pushed the blanket away and sat up on the edge of the bed. His mind was alert and he felt energetic. Smiling, he decided he had made the correct decision last night and limited his alcoholic intake, only four coffees with Bailey's Irish Cream. Going into the kitchen, he started brewing a large container of coffee with Jamaican beans, enough to last into the afternoon.

Sipping freshly made coffee, he stared out the front window onto the park. Last night with his friends was invigorating. He liked Vance's suggestion to include the game-pod theme in the novel. And he was delighted close friends would join the enterprise of an online, ongoing global story. He would get back to Adele, Sedna, and Eduardo and their plans to free Marilynn. But first he required a new character to introduce the game-pod theme. Faces and names glided before his inner vision like a slide show. He paused and then let the flow continue. A face froze and he studied it. His childhood friend Nick, tall and lean Nick Hampton. Played on the high school basketball team–a great forward with an excellent hook shot. Whatever happened to Nick? Well, I won't use his name, Lefty thought, just his appearance. Okay, what will be his name then?

He went into the kitchen and refilled the coffee mug. "Thomas," he said aloud. Thomas–Tom–a doubter. Defoe, yes. Again childhood memories sprang forth. How he had enjoyed the adventures Defoe wrote. Okay. I got it. Tom Defoe who has the appearance of old friend Nick.

He went to the computer and opened a new file. Basing the game-pod theme on his own experience, Lefty wrote for an hour before taking a break. With a fresh cup of coffee he stood at the window, watching the ships on the bay. A major decision loomed. What is Tom's motivation? Remembering Bruce's enthusiasm, aided and abetted by drinking, he intuited the answer. So many members of corporate culture were caught in an economic vise, struggling against the tyranny of trickle-down corporate management and at the same time committed to living their own lives and following their quest to journey's end. He was one and had discovered a way to subvert the system: the online novel. With Sedna communicating her wisdom and understanding about the world to Marilynn and the others, motivation was inherent in the story's foundation. Poor Henry was murdered because of the knowledge.

Time to visit the heroes planning their strategy in Adele's apartment. As he was reviewing the last part of the chapter, the green alert light flashed, and one of Kathy's songs played through the speakers. The tracker had results pinpointing the most likely suspects for the villain's role. The pod was unable to enter four computer systems located in San Francisco. His intuition selected one of the four—Madrone Advanced Systems, LLC. The CEO of the privately held security firm was Carlyle Quincebury. Data about him was still accumulating. The evidence was strong enough to assume Carlyle was his enemy. Since Carlyle lived in St. Francis Wood and taught at State besides administering his business empire, Lefty decided to place Tom Defoe in that part of the city, the southwestern section. Now he would return to his heroes.

Sedna was aghast. As she told Adele and Eduardo one of the others had been murdered, they became pale.

"That's horrible news. I didn't know Henry. Can it be connected to Marilynn's capture?" Eduardo asked.

"Yes, I was acquainted with Henry. He was a cyber-geek and was getting ready to host information online at various blogs about the true nature of society and the ruling elite," Sedna replied.

"Obviously, it all fits. I don't believe in coincidences," Adele declared.

"Who would want to commit such crimes—murder and kidnapping?" Eduardo asked.

"Let's contact other participants in the project," Sedna suggested.

"Of course. We should rally together and share our information. It's the best way to protect ourselves," Eduardo agreed.

"I'll sign into the chat room right now," Sedna announced.

Adele and Eduardo were waiting for her to send out the call when Sedna let out a "Wow!" The two stared at her, wondering.

"We have a fourth. While I was composing our message, a Tom Defoe posted a very intriguing statement. I'll read it. 'Hello, fellow authors. Something strange is happening to the project's participants. Henry Gorman was murdered and Marilynn Raylon kidnapped. I've a plan to protect ourselves against the predators. Email if you're interested–Tom Defoe.'"

"So do we know him?" Adele asked.

"I've had a few chat sessions with him. I like him and he's suggested several fascinating ideas for the story," Eduardo replied.

"Okay. Let's invite him to join us," Sedna recommended.

"Tell him we're gathering to discuss strategy here at my apartment," Adele responded.

"It's done," Sedna replied.

"I've an idea I've been developing the past hour. If we can create a diversion, we can get Marilynn out. I can utilize my holographic equipment for projecting holograms," Eduardo commented.

"Heads up. Tom replied. He's on his way on. He lives out near State so he should be here within an hour," Sedna reported.

"I'll fix some snacks and drinks. It will be an all-nighter." Adele rose and walked into the kitchen.

"Do you want any help?" Sedna asked.

"No. You two start discussing ideas. The food won't take long to fix."

"What's your idea about holograms, Eduardo?" Sedna asked.

Carlyle was furious. He had finished reading the latest data depicting Lefty's activities. Lefty was walking a highwire and must be stopped before bringing down the global system. Carlyle realized the only way to end the online writing project was to terminate the author himself. Murdering and kidnapping major characters in the story had only exacerbated the situation. Carlyle knew he had to act swiftly and without hesitation eliminate the threat posed by Lefty's newest character Tom Defoe. Obviously, Tom was cloned from the author's attack mode, but utilizing him to publish the game-raid idea in the ethereal net was disastrous. Imitators would exploit the strategy, and the repercussions would be ruinous. The elite and their managers couldn't cope with a massive disruption of communication channels. And the process would feed on itself, a domino effect. With corporate and governmental structures collapsing, Carlyle's power would vanish.

He rode the elevator up to the command center and strode up the five steps to the bridge.

Chapter 59

Participants in Consciousness Fair were gathering at Rainbow Inn. It was mid afternoon and the sky partly cloudy, temperature in the low sixties–typical weather for an unusual spring when nothing was normal. Today was the first of three rehearsals. All performers required time to become familiar with the Inn's small stage and its surroundings. Expectations were high for a large turnout. Mary had plotted the location for as many tables and chairs as the fire department would permit and allow her servers to fill orders without crowding.

The two musical ensembles would be situated on either side of the stage–Consciousness Drum on the left and Meadowlarks on the right. Od was the MC-Ringmaster. He and Mary were ensconced in her office designing the lineup of acts, from first to last. Several acts were still movable. Until they spoke with the performers, they couldn't fix the final positioning.

Shasta and Emma were huddled at a table discussing the poetry they were presenting, offering helpful hints for effective staging. They decided to interweave their readings because a common theme linked their poems.

Merle was surveying the interior of the Inn for the best locations to hang his paintings. The audience would be given an opportunity to view them during show time. When the stage was clear, he would inspect the scenery, which he had designed and executed. Much of the scenery was digitalized and would be projected onto a floor to ceiling screen covering the back of the stage. A small projector was suspended from the ceiling in front of the stage.

Margaret and Dale were seated at a table near the Meadowlarks' performing site. They were discussing the musical background Dale's ensemble would offer. Margaret taught chemistry at Lowell High School. Several years ago she had been inspired by Ralph who had suggested she utilize magical principles and routines for demonstrations in her chemistry classes. She soon discovered the practicality of applying magic: students loved it and the chemical operations were easily learned. Margaret's dramatic happening had evolved from the classroom to Consciousness Fair.

Rafé, John, and Ralph were seated together polishing and refining their acts. All three were involved in each other's performance. A central symbolic thread was woven through the acts entangling them in a multilayered drama. Each focused on personal interests linked to shared ideas. Storytelling and accompanying magical routines fit together as one artistic conception.

John decided to portray absurd traits of reality, perhaps inducing an expanded awareness in viewers. He was glad to paint—thanks to Merle's insight—a picture of reality's paradoxical nature, its hard edges and soft bumps.

Rafé took the opportunity to depict traditional Potawatomi characters and storytelling with contemporary features woven in. Blending her worldview with modern culture was a path chosen by Native Americans who desired to draw life-sustaining power from their cultural roots. She was pleased with the design of her act and happy Ralph, John, and Od were participating in it. The act was the middle, the bridge between John and Ralph's performances.

Ralph selected the quest as foundation for his act—an intimate journey through his inner self. The experiences at the Institute were fueling the athanor of his soul. Since the brief meeting with his double, Ralph was seeking total gnosis with his inner being and its link to a cosmic source. Philip's ideas enhanced by the twins had transformed his way of thinking, dissolving ingrained loops and decaying patterns of thought. He may again have an opportunity to venture far inward with assistance of friends. John's strange gifts and Rafé's grounding in her culture fused with her enthusiasm to give her life meaning in a contemporary setting afforded the psychic support he required. As a mage he understood the irony inherent in light-darkness and sound-silence. Those supposed opposites were enfolded in each other.

Gordon and Charles were on stage performing their dramatic readings from selected LGBT literature. Mary had set up her video recording system so all acts would have an opportunity to review their presentations.

Leila was seated at a table by herself practicing the routine she would perform. She and Ralph had discussed varying options for a mentalism act. He had described several routines that fell into the mentalism category. In the end she went back to her personal expertise as consultant and psychic. When he had jokingly mentioned the reading she had given at their first meeting, she knew immediately the course to take. She had given him a rather conventional tarot card reading that birthed a bond between them. So now they had discussed methods for such a reading to be given as an entertaining magical act. He had detailed some techniques and pointed out each allowed her to apply her talent as 'psychic' reader of the cards. No longer an old fashion fortune-teller but now a modern magician of psychic forces.

An inner glow resulted in a smile. She had marched along the road of clinical psychology winning academic honors, had gone underground to study occult disciplines, had grown a blossoming career as consultant and spiritual healer, and now was branching into a different path–magician and master of the Force. Her giggles caught the attention of Gordon and Charles, who had finished their rehearsal. They smiled at her as they walked to their table.

Chapter 60

Virgil responded to the situation in a nanosecond. A green dragon, its tail raised high, roared out from the dark side of the moon and hurtled toward chaos dragon. Peaches recovered quickly enough and sent a waveform into Tamm's insular cortex. The great man relaxed, panic-attack subsiding. At the same instant she caused Betel to pause before he initiated their defensive plan.

Green dragon charged at chaos dragon and halted before it entered chaos dragon's fire range. Green dragon stood on its hind legs and pirouetted. Then it turned the tip of its tail toward chaos dragon and emitted a large mist of amorous scent.

"Wait," Athena instructed, "let's watch the dragons dance." She applied a soft controlling voice.

Tamm commanded, "Betel, stop. We'll watch."

Green dragon rolled over on its back and then stood up. It glided with sensuous movement to chaos dragon who watched with extreme verve. They touched heads. Chaos dragon stood on its hind legs and roar what could only be a mating call. Green dragon pranced away, peering over its shoulder. Then it flew out toward Mars and chaos dragon followed closely behind. As they vanished over the horizon, Tamm spoke, "Well done, Athena. Victory is ours."

"Gloria, your situation is resolved. You have nothing to worry about." Peaches and Aeneas were seated in Gloria's living room.

Aeneas smiled at her. "Gloria, it has been an intriguing case. I'm so happy you can return to your daily lifestyle."

"What about future threats over the charm?"

"Tamm has promised he will not bother you and has taken steps to remove Merlin and Morgan's threat. As long as you don't participate in the game, you're in fine shape." Peaches gave her a friendly look.

"I'm so grateful. Peaches, here's the check for your services." She blushed and then said, "Also, I want you to have the charm. It has bad memories for me, and I would like to get on with my life. You used it so well. Please keep it as a memento of the case."

She handed the cat figurine to Peaches, who graciously accepted it.

Peaches and Aeneas, wishing Gloria the best, took their leave.

Sitting in the car while Aeneas drove back to the office, Peaches held the figurine gently and wondered if she would again explore the enchanted world of the astral zone. A dare had been offered–would she accept it?

Chapter 61

Lefty saved the document and decided to give his imagination a rest. Allow Tom Defoe time to join Marilynn's rescuing team–Adele, Eduardo, and Sedna–and establish a bonding. His mug was empty. Going to the kitchen, he brewed a fresh pot of coffee. Stretching, he walked into the central room and stood. He was in need of diversion, something the opposite of writing. He went back to the kitchen, filled his mug, and headed for the front door of the loft. Stepping into the hall and locking the door, he strolled to the stairwell and went up the stairs to the roof entrance.

The roof had an area designed for tenants. A small garden of plants in containers were scattered among a few chairs and recliners, a place for tenants to socialize and enjoy the city scenery.

Lefty liked the roof because he felt more aware and in a peculiar sense elevated mentally while there. He was enthused about the new character Tom Defoe, who possessed exceptional talents. His creative juices surged forth as he ambled around the roof garden. Tom was one of the psychic skilled people much like himself. An idea flashed before his mind. He was thrilled by its brilliancy. He stood, motionless, as he reviewed Tom's plan to liberate Marilynn from her kidnappers.

The helicopter hovered over head. Three men strapped in harnesses descended from the copter. Two grabbed Lefty before he was aware of their presence and the third injected him with a soporific drug. Lefty lost consciousness and was lifted to the craft, which vanished into the night sky.

His head throbbed when he opened his eyes. The room was dimly lighted. Sitting up, he glanced around, but his mind was too foggy to concentrate. He vaguely remembered standing in the roof garden and thinking about the story. Then nothing. And now here he was. He heard voices. Was he hallucinating?

The room became bright. The glare irritated his eyes and he shut them. The voices were real and now were in the room nearby. Gradually he opened his eyes and looked around. Four men stood facing him. Two approached and grabbed him by the arms, yanking him off the cot and shoving him to a chair next to the opposite wall. Once he was seated, the two black-suited men remained beside him. A third man, brown-suited, guarded the door. The fourth man strode to Lefty and glowered at him.

"So, Lefty Cosmos, we finally meet. You're a pathetic creature." The cruelty in his voice stabbed Lefty.

He started to rise, but the two bullies stopped him. "Who are you? Why am I here?"

"You're supposed to be very intelligent. Can't you figure it out?"

The haze began to dissipate, and the small circle of clarity enlarged. At first doubts prevailed, shutting out the truth. But reality grew in sharpness. A moment of gnosis and he grokked the situation. His nemesis now held him prisoner as he did Marilynn. Lefty had learned enough about his adversary to recognize the eminent danger he was in. The game-pod project had succeeded, pinpointing Madrone Advanced Systems as the center of attacks against him.

He waited, realizing Carlyle Quincebury was impatient and would soon assault with verbal abuse and eventually physical harm.

Tau's scorn spiced his words. "I let your childish games go on too long. That's my failure. I didn't recognize the depth of your stupidity."

Lefty's intuition, one of his gifts, gave him a word, Carlyle's nickname, the one he used for his cyberpunk role-playing. It was Tau.

"Remain silent if you wish. That's your prerogative. Take the fifth." Tau's laughter was devilish.

Awareness exploded in his mind. His great galactic novel had expanded and now included his daily life. Tau's existence was entangled with his and his with the novel, a multiverse of realities. He broke into giggles that transformed into rollicking laughter.

Tau was bewildered, his men alarmed. The black-suited men grasped Lefty's arms and restrained him. Regaining his composure, Tau's anger was penetrating. "You think it's a laughing matter? Ha, you're in for a treat. Yes, you'll be delighted with my new torture techniques." Tau's face was frozen with meanness. "And you can report in detail on the effectiveness of the methods."

"Tau, are you trying to terrify me with your Darth Vader act?"

"Have you forgotten who Darth Vader is and the reason for his transformation? But you'll soon learn the power of fear and terror." Tau studied Lefty. "Perhaps you're hoping I'll relent, find my better nature. It won't happen. We're not related." Tau smirked. "You'll taste my best nature, the one placing me at the pinnacle of power."

"Do your best, then, Tau."

Tau nodded to the brown-suited man by the door, who moved to the table and picked up a pair of gloves. He put the gloves on Lefty's hands.

"The first test is a slight stimulation to your nervous system. Turn your lights on before they go out." Tau pressed a button on the control pad he was holding.

Lefty jerked and then again. "I'll increase the stimulation until you dance for me." Tau pressed the button again. A tremor pulsated along Lefty's spinal column and a series of spasms rocked his body.

"Having fun? Well, I am." Tau held the button down for several seconds. Lefty convulsed, drool seeping from his mouth.

Tau gestured to the brown-suited man, who stuck a vial of smelling salts under Lefty's nose. Regaining consciousness, Lefty glanced about before fixing on his tormentor.

"Ready for more fun and games? Eventually the escalating energy surges will cause death but not until I decided. Darkness will close in, Lefty, and that's the end of your novel."

Tau sent another flood of energy coursing along Lefty's nerve pathways. The jolts hammered his body and mind. Smelling salts were again employed to revive his consciousness.

His mind was sluggish. Synapses weren't functioning as they should. Death finally became real. He had no escape plan and no friends on the outside to rescue him. No one even knew of his plight. Kathy appeared in his mind. He would never be with her again. Sorrow touched his soul. Then another scene seized control: Kathy's dream. His present situation was similar. An awakening flash–he had related his family's history and she had bonded with it. A kernel of preservation grew into a heightened focus. He inspected his surroundings and a plan formed.

The glee in Tau's eyes was tough and unrelenting. A few more surges would bring on death and the lights would go out for Lefty, his cosmos becoming a black hole.

His secure mobile vibrated, and Tau retrieved it from his pocket. He peered at the code. Startled, he reacted quickly. Ralph was now his greatest threat, Lefty only a minor hassle by comparison. Approaching the end of his quest, Ralph would soon climb the astral staircase. If Ralph entered the portal at the top, disaster would erupt. The fabric of reality would be ripped, torn, fragmented, and so changed Tau would lose his power and control, his empire dissolving into vapor. Tau had to prevent Ralph from finishing the journey.

Tau signaled his men. They departed the room. His three assistants stationed themselves at monitors to watch Lefty. Tau hurried to his residence in St. Francis Wood where he would gain access to psi spectrum. All depended on catching Ralph and stopping him.

Chapter 62

Vendor stands and social action groups' tables lined both sides of Ocean Avenue for several blocks. A beautiful day–the sun was shining, temperature around sixty-eight degrees and a slight breeze of two miles an hour. Many people were mingling along the avenue; others were entering the Inn, which was filling to capacity. At high noon the show would begin.

Inside the Inn servers were busy taking orders. The stage was empty and anticipation was immense. A soft drumbeat pulsated throughout the Inn, slowly increasing in volume. Attention was drawn to a large round drum circled by drummers who in unison were tapping a rhythmic pattern. Singers now interwove their song into the musical texture–song and drumbeat. The musical number ended with a crescendo. Applause was interspersed with shouts of approval.

Od Tinker walked on stage carrying an electric lantern glowing with light, which he attached to a rope hanging from the ceiling. Slowly the lantern moved upward until it was at shoulder height. When the audience quieted, Od announced, "Friends, neighbors, and visitors to Consciousness Fair, we welcome you to join us in Renewing the World, a ceremony for all ages and peoples. We offer a diversity of entertainment and awareness-expanding experiences. Our artists display a wide range of creative talents. Here on the consciousness stage all things are possible." Pointing to the suspended lantern, he declared, "This lantern is Diogenes' Lamp shining the light of truth upon us today." The lantern rose until it was overhead. "Please join us then for an afternoon of fun, enchantment, and wonder." He paused before continuing, "The opening musical number was performed by San Francisco Consciousness Drum Group, the Bay Area's newest Drum. Let's hear again for this great drum." Another round of applause followed. "Dale Pepper and the Meadowlarks will now present a musical number," Od announced.

The Meadowlarks performed a medley of folk ballads. When the group finished, the audience responded with enthusiastic approval.

Od returned and, beaming at the gathering, proclaimed, "Today I have a marvelous bargain for each and everyone here." He removed a small bottle from a shoulder bag. Holding it up, he declared, "I'm offering bottles of Yerba Buena tea. Guaranteed to raise your consciousness. You can buy a bottle for one dollar or trade any item worth at least 50 cents for the nectar of paradise. Servers will take your orders." He paused and waited for deep quiet to fill the Inn. "Consciousness Drum will performed a number while the stage is set for the next act."

Stage lights dimmed. Two tables were moved on. The smaller table was located upstage. Two trays were set on it: one tray with a metal pitcher and four glasses and the other with four glasses. The larger table was positioned downstage with four chairs arranged around it.

Vibrant applause was given to Consciousness Drum while stage lights brightened. Od strode to center stage and announced, "Our next dramatic happening is Drinks for Four, starring Margaret Pepper as the waitress and John Ocean as the busser."

Margaret strolled on stage wearing a white blouse, grey skirt, black apron tied around the waist, and a small black waitress cap. She approached the edge of the stage and glanced around the audience. "Are there four people who'll assist me?" she asked. She selected from those who raised their hands. Once the participants were on stage, she introduced them–Art, Sally, Mike, and Betty–and invited them to join her at the table. After they were seated, she said, "In this dramatic skit I'll play a waitress and you are my customers. The menu is limited to five beverages: orange juice, tomato juice, cranberry juice, coffee, and tea."

She handed each customer a menu with drinks listed and a pencil. "Please mark the drink you want and write your name on the menu." After they had made their selections, she collected the menus.

Turning upstage, she nodded to the busser, wearing black trousers and shirt and standing by the small table. He picked up a tray with pitcher and four glasses and carried it to the customers' table. Placing the tray down, he returned to his station.

Margaret looked at the menus and put them in her apron pocket. She poured a different drink in each glass and served the glasses. The participants looked at the glasses she gave them, and then they all asserted they were given the wrong drink. Betty had ordered tea but received cranberry juice. Art wanted tomato juice but got coffee. Mike had asked for coffee but was given orange juice. Sally had selected cranberry juice but got tea. Several participants started to trade their drinks, but Margaret stopped them.

"Wait," she yelled. Quite flustered, she cried, "I'm so sorry. Please forgive me. I don't know how it happened. Let's start over." She picked up each glass and poured its contents into the pitcher. When she had finished, she turned to the busser and nodded. He picked up a tray with four glasses and brought it over to the table. Margaret took the four clean glasses from the tray and put one in front of each customer. Then she placed the dirty glasses on the tray the busser was holding. He returned to his station.

Margaret removed the menus from her pocket and read each one aloud. Smiling, she picked up the pitcher and poured tea into Betty's glass, tomato juice into Art's glass, coffee into Mike's, and cranberry juice into Sally's. When she had finished, she set the pitcher on the table. "Please pardon my mistakes, but it's my first day on the job and I'm nervous." The four customers tasted their beverages and expressed their approval. Margaret smiled and bowed to the four. The audience joined the participants in their enthusiastic applause. After she thanked each assistant, she again accepted the audience's appreciation.

Once tables had been removed and chairs set upstage, Od returned with Merle Leong beside him. Introducing him, Od remarked, "Merle is a creative artist who expresses his inner self through his art. His paintings are hanging on the Inn's walls, and Mary will guide your attention to each one as she strolls around playing her saxophone. She'll stop by each art work and perform a short musical impression of the piece."

When Mary concluded her musical tour, the audience filled the Inn with animated appreciation. After the applause Od sauntered on stage with an acoustic guitar and sang Woody Guthrie's famous ballad "This Land Is Your Land." When he finished, he called everyone's attention to their lifestyle. "My friends, renewing the earth requires us to renew ourselves. What are you burdening yourselves with at this moment? Free yourselves from carrying around loads of worries—those that possessions create. When you leave, deposit them in the Goodwill bins." A drumming rhythm accentuated his announcement.

Od walked upstage and retrieved a lectern stand. When the audience quieted, he peered about the Inn and then announced, "I'm proud to welcome here today Gordon Russell and Charles Freeman who will perform dramatic readings."

Gordon and Charles approached the podium, carrying printed material. Gordon stepped to the lectern and declared, "Today we will share with you readings from a few samples of LGBT literature. If your interest is awakened and you would like to learn more about our community and its creative talents, please stop by our table. We will supply background and perhaps personal comments before each presentation.

"We will open with two poems by Sappho, ancient poet of Lesbos, an island in the Aegean Sea." First Gordon read a poem followed by Charles. Continuing the alternating sequence, Gordon introduced and then read a passage from Thomas Mann's *Death in Venice*. After opening comments, Charles read a selection from James Baldwin's *Giovanni's Room*.

"These works were written before the Stonewall Rebellion of 1969," Gordon remarked. "The remaining works, with the exception of Allen Ginsberg's 'Howl,' were published after Stonewall. The next two works were published in the 1980s."

Offering background information, Gordon read a section of Nancy Garden's *Annie On My Mind*. Charles proceeded with Jeanette Winterson's, *Oranges Are Not the Only Fruit*. After completing his reading of Winterson's novel, Charles stated, "We now move into the 21st century. I've selected a fine passage from Patricia Nell Warren's *The Wild Man*, which came out in 2001."

After Charles had completed his presentation, Gordon displayed his dramatic skills with a passage from Michael Cunningham's *By Nightfall*, published in 2010.

When Gordon concluded, the partners looked out at the audience, letting silence envelope the Inn. Then Gordon spoke, "We've chosen verses from 'Howl,' published in 1956 and quickly banned in San Francisco, causing a remarkable lawsuit defending our freedom to write and read what we want, not to be shut up by those who are frightened by difference and try to force their attitudes on everyone else." Together they read from the poem that harkened the beginning of a new age. A work so fiery it opened minds and cast out demons of bondage.

When they finished the reading, they stepped away from the podium and, hand in hand, bowed to the audience's enthusiastic applause and cheers.

The Meadowlarks played a composition of soulful beauty that brought oohs and aahs from the audience.

Od approached the lectern and adjusted it so that it now functioned as a table. "Our next performer, well-known along Ocean Avenue for her spiritual counseling and intuitive powers, is Leila Lubec."

Leila approached the edge of the stage, smiled, and offered, "Today I'll give tarot readings to three participants. If you have a strong interest in psychic activity and would like to join me on stage, please raise your hand." She climbed down from the stage and moved among the audience selecting three from the many people who had raised their hands. Once they were back on stage, she introduced them—Natalie, Frank, and Peggy—and then asked them to be seated on the chairs on stage.

"Today I'll reveal the ever-present psychic force, not just once, but three times it'll be exhibited. Natalie, will you join me for the first event." Natalie rose from the chair and stood beside Leila, who pointed to the table. Leila picked up a tarot deck and fanned it, showing the faces to the audience. "Here is a tarot deck consisting of major arcana, the cards portraying mystical symbols which convey psychological and spiritual truths." She closed the deck and placed it on the table.

"Natalie, please cut the deck several times—three, four, or five." After Natalie finished cutting, Leila picked up the deck and spread the cards face down. "Please choose a card. Don't let me see it. I'll turn my back and you show it to the audience and memorize the image. When you've done that, let me know."

Natalie selected a card, and Leila turned her back to the audience. "I've shown the card and memorized it," Natalie affirmed.

Leila again faced her assistant. "Please put the card face down on top of the deck and then cut the deck." After Natalie finished, Leila picked up the deck. "Now we're ready for the test. Is my mind in tune with the psychic force and Natalie's mind?" Smiling at her assistant, Leila said, "Focus on the card's image and I'll try to locate it in the deck."

Leila spread the cards face up and scanned them seeking Natalie's card. She paused and stared at a card, then looked her assistant. Nodding in affirmation, Leila took the card from the deck, holding it up for all to see. "This is your card, Strength, the woman with the lion." Natalie sparkled with delight and agreed.

She gave the card to Natalie. "Please keep your card and rejoin the other two participants. Later I'll give all three of you a personal reading of your cards."

With subtle misdirection by varying the technique, Leila repeated the routine for the remaining two participants, finding their chosen cards. She then gave personal readings, indicating traits expressed by the images and their application to the individual assistant.

When she completed the readings, Leila thanked Natalie, Frank, and Peggy, and they all received the audience's warm and pleased approval.

A saxophone sang a lively melody accompanied by the heartbeat of the big drum. A clarinet answered the saxophone and they engaged in a cheerful duet. Deep strumming sounds from a bass enhanced the drumbeat. A guitar added its voice to the merriment.

Od walked on stage as the music faded into silence. He stood quietly until the applause ceased. Smiling, he announced, "What a fine musical introduction to our next act. Emma Leong and Shasta Garland will share some of their poetry. The poems are connected by a common theme: nature in all her moods and coloration. Here are Gaia's singers who will sing her songs."

Emma and Shasta came to center stage and placed their printed material on the lectern. Emma looked out at the audience and said, "Shasta and I will interweave our readings. Although I have tried many poetic styles, I have discovered certain verse forms that fit my personality and have become my signature. My first song is about a spring morning."

After Emma finished, Shasta stepped to the lectern and stated, "Like Emma I have explored many poetic styles and have found those best suited to my self-expression. Since I'm also a novelist, my writing is guided by my Muse and the direction she chooses at the moment. My first offering is based on an experience at Pescadero Marsh watching herons."

Alternating their readings, Gaia's singers wove together ten songs. When they concluded, they stepped to the edge of the stage and bowed to the audience's thunderous applause augmented by the drum's solid heartbeats.

Chapter 63

Consciousness Drum began softly, growing in strength until it reached a crescendo, then dropping to a gentle tapping. A Native American flute whispered its melody as a breeze blowing through leaves. The other members of Meadowlarks joined in and a rousing overture to the final dramatic event was performed.

Od was present on stage when quiet settled in. "Our last presentation, in three acts, is a joint venture by creative members of our community. I'm elated to unveil an awareness-raising adventure into the creative imagination." The floor to ceiling screen at the back of the stage lit up:

Consciousness Theater Presents
Renewing the World
Starring Real-Time Players
Act 1
Hopscotch
Starring
John Ocean as Buddy Zero
Rafé Courbet as Trixie

Buddy Zero, carrying a wicker basket by his side, saunters toward center stage. He is dressed in leisure clothes: walking shoes, tan trousers, T-shirt with a large zero printed on both sides, and a baseball cap. His hair is tied in a ponytail. He stops in front of a wall which has a hopscotch course painted on it. He studies the diagram and then looks at the ground where a duplicate course outline is drawn. A sign posted on the wall next to the diagram states: "Play time hopscotch. Toss your marker into the future moment and bring it back to the present."

Buddy places the basket on the ground and takes a stone from it. He tosses the stone at the course diagram on the wall. Stone floats to square one and sticks there. Buddy hops through the course drawn on the ground, turning at free zone sky and coming back to free zone earth. He takes stone off the wall diagram.

Buddy gets ready to make the second toss, but a voice breaks his concentration.

"Hi. I'm Trixie." She is wearing sandals, blue jeans, T-shirt with an infinity image on both sides, and a light blue beret. Her black hair is styled in a short bob with bangs.

Buddy looks at her. "I'm Buddy Zero."

"What are you doing?" Trixie asks.

"I'm playing time hopscotch."

"What's that?"

"The marker is thrown into the future and brought back to the present. Each of the eight squares is a future moment."

"So you go into the future and then back to the past."

"No, I come back to the present."

"But isn't your present the past of the future?"

Buddy stares at her. Feeling frustrated, he refuses to answer. He studies the course outline on the wall.

"Can I play too?"

"No. You can watch."

"Ok." Trixie spies the basket and peaks into it. Then she picks it up and turns it upside down, shaking it. "Don't you have any more stones?" She puts the basket down.

Buddy glances at her, then focuses on the course illustration, and tosses stone which floats to square two and attaches. As Buddy hops through the course, Trixie watches intently. When Buddy reaches earth, Trixie rushes to the course layout and grabs the stone from square two. She hurries to Buddy and offers him the stone. "Here. I'll help."

Buddy is furious. "Stupid. You've ruined the game."

"What! Why? I'm just helping." Trixie is confused.

"I have to get the stone. You watch. Don't touch."

Trixie holds the stone in her hand. When Buddy reaches for the stone, it vanishes. They're both astonished.

Buddy regains his poise. "I'll just go back and begin again." He reaches into the basket and extracts a stone.

Trixie is flabbergasted. "Where did you get the stone?"

"From the basket."

"But it was empty."

"I'm starting over, so it's ok."

Buddy aims and pitches stone, which hits square three and sticks. Trixie runs over to course layout and snatches stone and walks to the basket and drops stone into it. She turns basket over. She is stunned: the stone has vanished.

Buddy glares at her. "You freak. I told you not to touch!"

"You said you can start over," Trixie whimpers.

A skull, a serpent coiled around its top and a wand gliding around it, drifts to Buddy's left. The skull speaks, "I am Guardian of Lower World. What is revealed is now veiled."

Buddy and Trixie are shocked even more when a voice on their right announces, "I am Herald of Upper World. What is veiled is now revealed." Another skull, a wand gliding around it, floats toward them. The skull has an eagle perched on top.

A third voice catches their attention. They stare in amazement as a skull with a face mask resembling Buddy flies straight at them. The skull also has a wand swirling about it. "I am Presence of Middle World. Cover naked: bare self," the skull pronounces.

The three skulls, their wands gyrating rhythmically, circle Buddy and Trixie, chanting the litany. Each skull sings its chant twice, once in the female vocal range and then in the male range. The chant is repeat continuously. Guardian skull sings first as contralto and then as bass. Presence skull sings as mezzo-soprano and then baritone-tenor. Herald skull sings as female soprano and then male soprano. The sounds and 'words' intermingle and overlap, weaving a polyphonic texture.

"What is revealed is now veiled. Cover naked: bare self. What is veiled is now revealed."

Guardian skull floats to course diagram. Its wand points at square one. A stone appears stuck there. "What is revealed is now veiled," the skull chants.

Presence skull flies toward the chart, its wand waving at square two. A stone manifests there. "Cover naked: bare self," the skull sings.

Herald skull drifts to the layout, its wand aiming at square three where a stone materializes. "What is veiled is now revealed," the skull intones.

The skulls rotate and face Buddy and Trixie. The wands gesture at the basket. It vanishes.

Buddy and Trixie whirl toward the diagram where all eight squares have stones attached.

The chanting increases in tempo. Buddy and Trixie watch in astonishment as all eight stones vanish. The basket appears and floats toward them. Buddy grabs the basket and hollers, "The stones are here."

Trixie peers into the basket. "They're back," she yells and snatches several stones, holding them in the air.

The three wands float from the skulls and coalesce. The skulls move toward the revolving wands and rotate around them as their axis. The skulls chant in unison, "All has been revealed and veiled, covered and bared." They drift off stage in silence.

Applause erupts. Buddy and Trixie, holding hands, bow to the audience. Bravos are shouted and the drum beats mightily. The drum moves into a fanfare rhythm.

The stage screen lights up displaying:

Act 2
Grandmother's Tale
Starring
Rafé Courbet as Manabozho the Great Rabbit
Ralph Garland as Ktiti the Otter
John Ocean as Paisa the Forest Spirit
Od Tinker as Shkop the Cedar Tree

Manabozho the Rabbit, wearing light tan jeans and T-shirt with an image of a rabbit front and back, is standing in a clearing searching for potential danger. He is startled by a voice coming from the cedar tree beside him.

"I'm watching you looking at me, Manabozho," murmurs Shkop the cedar tree.

"Well, Shkop, I'm not looking at you as you but only gazing around, and you are in my field of sight," he replies.

"You're revealing a part of your hidden self when you speak," Shkop remarks.

"I'm not giving anything away. My secret is still veiled." A sly smile crosses Manabozho's face.

"You've ripped away the veil shrouding your secret, yet the secret is still undisclosed."

Manabozho moves around Shkop's trunk, studying the ground. He halts and peers at a hole in the ground next to the trunk.

"I see where you have a hideaway. What do you have concealed down there?" Manabozho thumps his foot next to the hole beating out a rhythm.

"You've discovered the location of my treasure and revealed the hiding place but not the treasure itself." Certainty fills Shkop's voice.

Manabozho peeks into the hole. "Well, if you have a treasure hidden down there, I'm going to find it." He hustles into the hole and vanishes.

"The treasure has revealed itself but not its secret. You've veiled yourself but are revealed for who you are," Shkop pronounces.

Manabozho sticks his head out of the hole and peers at Shkop. "I'm certainly not concealed and I know what your treasure is."

"What is it then if it's been revealed to you?"

"You're not using me to reveal you to yourself." He disappears down the hole.

Silence fills the clearing.

Ktiti the Otter, clothed in blue jeans and a T-shirt with an image of an otter on both sides, emerges from the woods into the clearing. He glances around as if expecting someone.

"Are you looking for Manabozho?" Shkop asks.

Ktiti, surprised, turns focusing on cedar tree. "Yes, I am. We're supposed to meet here. I hope I'm not too late."

"Manabozho has concealed himself and revealed a treasure more precious than all the gold in the world."

Ktiti, noticing hole, inquires, "Is he hidden down there?" Ktiti points to the hole.

"Manabozho unveiled the hole and descended into it seeking the secret concealed down there," Shkop whispers in the wind.

"Well, if he doesn't surface soon, I'm leaving. I've other things to do."

"If you leave before he reveals himself, you'll be covered with doubt and uncertainty."

"Wait. Do you hear something? Yes, a thumping from the earth itself."

"Manabozho will soon reveal himself, but the secret will remain unknown."

Manabozho crawls out of the hole. "Well, there you are," he remarks to Ktiti.

"What were you doing down the hole?" Ktiti asks.

"I was seeking Shkop's treasure trove."

"Did you find it?"

"No, it's still concealed, but I did discover its hiding place. Nothing was there though." Manabozho is disappointed.

"What did you want to talk about?"

"I've a message from the Great One. We're to instruct humans into the medicine way."

"I don't know much about the medicine path."

"I'll instruct you and then you help teach humans."

"Fine. Let's get started."

Manabozho points to a log and walks over to it and sits down on it. He removes a leather pouch hanging from his neck and, opening it, shakes its contents onto the log. Leaves, seeds, tobacco bundle, and a megis shell fall onto the log. He unfastens a hand drum and rattle attached to his belt and puts them on the log. Tearing a piece of tobacco from the bundle, he lays it on the ground while shaking the rattle and chanting "for Sukmukwe' grand-mother earth, our life source."

He reaches for the megis shell and discovers it's missing. "Ktiti, did you noticed what happened to the shell?"

Ktiti, surprised, surveys the log and the ground around it. "I don't see it. Where is it?"

Manabozho, his nostrils quivering, sniffs the air. "Ah, paisake are lurking about. I can sense them."

Ktiti stares at the surroundings searching for forest spirits. "Yes, there's a paisa in the shadows watching us. Has he been up to some mischief?"

Manabozho waves at the forest spirit, beckoning him.

Paisa, dressed in dark tan jeans and a green T-shirt, walks into the clearing and approaches them. "Greetings. What a fine day," he says.

"We've misplaced our megis shell. Maybe you can help us," Manabozho inquires.

"Yes, I've a talent for finding lost things. A megis shell, you say. Where did you last see it?" Paisa asks.

"Here on the log," Ktiti replies.

Paisa inspects the log. "Ha, yes, I know where it is."

"You do? Cool." Manabozho is delighted.

"Manabozho, hold out your right hand palm up," Paisa requests.

Manabozho follows directions. Paisa points at Manabozho's open hand. The megis shell is resting on his palm.

"Awesome," Ktiti exclaims.

Amazement fills Manabozho. "Thank you, Paisa. We're very grateful."

"What are you two doing? You have a secret, don't you?" Paisa inquires.

"Why would you believe that?" Manabozho is suspicious.

"Shkop was speaking about revealing and concealing things," Paisa responds.

"Shkop has treasure hidden down at his roots," Ktiti announces.

"Did you see it?" Paisa asks.

"Yes, I did," Manabozho declares.

"What is it?" Paisa is inquisitive and wants to know.

"It's a secret, isn't it?" Ktiti remarks as he looks at Manabozho.

"I know but I won't tell." Manabozho folds his arms, striking a defiant pose.

"I'll guess. It's a pot of gold," Paisa asserts.

Manabozho shakes his head. "No."

"Ok, I give up. What is it?" Paisa asks.

Manabozho shakes his head more vigorously. "I'm not saying."

"Well, if that's not rude. Here I revealed your missing shell and now you won't unveil the secret." Paisa is angry.

"It won't be a secret if it's revealed," Ktiti comments and then giggles at his own humor.

"You're insulting and I'm leaving." Paisa rises and starts for the forest.

"My leather bag–where is it?" Manabozho hollers.

"Stop, Paisa, wait," Ktiti yells. "Manabozho's bag is missing. Help us."

Paisa turns and frowns at the two. "Why should I?"

"It would be a very friendly thing to do," Manabozho says with humble voice.

"You two don't share secrets so why should I?" Paisa responds. He is very indignant.

"We'll tell you Shkop's secret," Ktiti answers and then looks questioningly at Manabozho.

"I know megis shells are important, but why is the bag important? Anyone can make a bag," Paisa inquires.

"The bag holds sacred medicine," Ktiti replies.

"The Great One has asked us to instruct humans in the medicine way," Manabozho adds.

"Humans are too foolish to learn anything," Paisa avers. A mischievous grin emerges on his face.

"The medicine way will improve them, give them more awareness of grandmother earth and all living beings," Manabozho responds.

"So what's in the medicine bag?" Paisa inquires.

Manabozho points to the objects on the log. Paisa studies them, nodding approval as he inspects each sacred item.

"Did you respect grandmother?" Paisa asks.

"Yes, we did." Manabozho points to the earth where he had placed a piece of the tobacco bundle.

"Excellent," Paisa comments. "Look," he says and points at the same spot. A tobacco plant is growing from the earth. He reaches down to the base of the plant and retrieves a leather bag. "Here, is this your bag?"

Manabozho brightens. "Thank you so much. I'm very grateful. Will you help us instruct humans in the medicine way? You have special talents that can be very beneficial."

Paisa sits in silence. The thought dwelling in quiet is now spoken. "First tell me Shkop's secret and then I'll help."

Manabozho nods in agreement. "Shkop's secret treasure is its roots."

"Everyone knows about Shkop's roots," Paisa affirms.

"Common knowledge conceals the true treasure," Manabozho retorts.

"Well, please reveal Shkop's true treasure to me," Paisa asks with some indignation.

"Shkop's roots are its life support system. If its roots were damaged or diseased, Shkop would probably die."

An aha arises in Ktiti's mind. "Yes, the life force resides in Shkop's roots."

Paisa nods in accord. "I understand. All life is the same. Our roots sustain us and supply us with life's sustenance. Fine. Now what is your strategy for instructing humans? How do we wake them out of their sleep?"

"I've a secret plan. Come close and I'll reveal it to you." Ktiti and Paisa circle around Manabozho.

A soft drum beat resonates in the clearing. The trio glance around seeking the rhythmic beats. In the center of the clearing, several feet from the log they're sitting on, a hand drum floats in a circle. A rattle rotates around the drum, adding musical texture to the rhythm.

Manabozho gasps. He stares at the levitating instruments and then at the log where he had placed them. Ktiti speaks first, "Your drum and rattle are giving a great performance. But what keeps them afloat?"

Manabozho eyes Paisa. "Is this your doing?" he asks.

"You want me to reveal a secret?" Paisa laughs.

"You don't have to unveil the mystery, only did you make the drum and rattle float?" Manabozho responds.

"Yes, are you the magician performing the levitation or is another mage present?" Ktiti asks.

"As far as I know, without incriminating myself, other spirits may be hereabouts."

"Who's causing the drum and rattle to float and play, is what I want to know?" Manabozho is very upset.

"I am."

They all stare at Shkop, who announces, "I've many more secrets than you'll ever discover."

In silence the drum and rattle drift over to Manabozho, who grabs them and attaches them to his belt. "The place is too spooky. Let's adjourn to a mundane site."

The lights dim and a drum beat is heard. Then singing interweaves with the beat.

Loud applause floods the Inn.

Chapter 64

The Inn quiets. The audience focuses on the stage in great expectation. The stage screen lights up displaying:

Act 3 in 9 Scenes
Journey to Deep Source
Starring
Ralph Garland as Ralph the Mage
Rafé Courbet as Ki
John Ocean as Adam
Shasta Garland as Eve

Scene 1

Ralph strides to center stage and bows. "Ladies and gentlemen, you are about to witness a strange and marvelous journey through the mystical landscape of consciousness. The dramatic happenings defy convention and free our minds to explore the universe with its many realities."

Ralph turns and walks to stage left where Rafé is waiting. Together they roll to center stage a large mirror–seven feet high and four feet wide. They revolve the mirror, displaying all sides, until it faces the audience.

"Look into the mirror and observe carefully the events that take place. What we see reflects our view of reality," Ralph proposes.

The audience see themselves in the mirror. Many find their own image and point it out to their neighbors. Gradually the mirror fills with sand from bottom to top. The audience sits spellbound as sand moves upwards.

"Here's the great sand mound of time that regulates the cosmos. Its steady flow is constant and unending," Ralph declares.

Ralph looks out to the audience and back to the mirror. "Notice the mirror is now filled with sand. Time has come to a standstill. But wait. What's happening?"

He gestures at the mirror. Sand is flowing downward from top to bottom. "Is time moving in another direction? Perhaps backward? Impossible we say."

Sand flows downward, but the level stays constant. Suddenly, the dry sand becomes liquid. Water flows over the edge of the sand mound. A waterfall has appeared.

The audience is stunned. "Ohs" and "ahs" are heard. Ralph gestures at the mirror. "A sandfall is now a waterfall. Reality has changed or at least our vision of it."

Ralph walks from one side of the mirror to the other side. As he does, the image of the waterfall moves, turning its face and allowing the viewers to perceive it in 3D, like they were walking around in front of it.

Ralph grasps a stone pendant attached to a necklace around his neck. He holds the stone up so the audience can see it. "The stone has power and is a guide to psychic energy sources. It alerts me to the presence of psi fields and detects the amount of energy."

As he speaks, drumming begins, increasing in strength.

Ralph turns toward the waterfall, listening. He nods his head in approval and pivots toward the audience. Drumming decreases into silence.

"Psi energy is strong. Waterfalls are known for their sacred power." Rotating to face the mirror, he steps into it and walks to the waterfall. Pausing, he waves at the audience and then walks beneath the waterfall and emerges on the other side. He strolls along a path into the forest. A Native American flute plays a bouncy melody.

While Ralph is seen leaving the waterfall, a figure emerges from the shadows of stage left. A partial mask covers its face: coyote-like muzzle and ears. The creature peers around scrutinizing the surroundings and sniffing the air, alert to any other presence.

Facing the audience, it says, "I'm Coyote, master of mischief and deceiver of innocence. There goes Ralph, silly clown, who believes he can find himself, his authentic being. Even mages can deceive themselves, constructing fantasy realities. We'll follow him. Delude him with our tricks. Lead him to failure."

Coyote starts toward mirror but stops. "If I'm going to act in Ralph's reality, I must disguise myself. Hide my true nature. I'll go in human form." With a grand gesture, coyote removes the mask and flings it into the air. It vanishes. Coyote steps into the mirror and turning its head to the audience says, "Just call me Ki."

Ki enters the mirror world and walks underneath the waterfall to the other side and follows Ralph's path.

During a musical interlude, stage darkens. Mirror is moved off stage and background scenery is displayed on the floor to ceiling screen.

Scene 2

Lights come on and music pauses. The scenery portrays a woodland.

Ralph steps into a clearing. He observes the setting. He has an uneasy feeling as if he's being watched.

Ki wanders from the woods. When he sees Ralph, he pauses and then calls, "Ho, friend. How are you?"

Ralph swivels and replies, "I'm fine. And you?"

Ki approaches and extends his hand. "I'm Ki. Out for a stroll. What a beautiful day." He looks around appraising the scenery.

Without much enthusiasm Ralph shakes Ki's hand. "I'm Ralph. It is a great day." He's a little suspicious about Ki's sudden appearance. He decides to keep his plans to himself.

"Which way are you heading?" Ki asks.

"To the east," Ralph remarks, "I'm going eastward."

"Why, that's cool. I've nothing planned today. Okay, if I walk with you?" Ki responds.

After a moment's hesitation, Ralph agrees to the proposal. As they amble along the path, Ki maintains a constant chatter, commenting on the landscape and the events of the day. Ralph preserves an inner silence, offering only a few grunts and nods of his head.

Stopping abruptly, Ki grabs Ralph's arm. "Look. What's that over by the ferns?" He hurries to the site. "My. These tiny pebbles glitter. See here." He scoops up a handful of shiny stones.

Ralph wanders over. "Well, it's certainly not gold," he remarks.

"No, of course not. But better than gold, if I'm right." Ki studies the tiny rocks. "I feel a strange sensation, an energy of sorts. Could these be psychic stones?" Ki asks.

Ralph, glancing at Ki's face, notices a subtle smile. A secret, he has a hidden agenda, Ralph thinks. I'll play along for the moment. "I'm afraid I'm unable to discern anything special about the stones. No, I don't believe they have psychic power."

"We don't actually know for certain, do we? We can test them. Go ahead, Ralph, and perform an experiment."

Ralph's wariness sharpens. He is picking up strong negative energy from Ki. He'll bluff. Putting on his magician's demeanor, he frowns in great concentration and gestures with his right hand. Nothing happens. He relaxes. "Either there's no psychic energy there or I can't control it. You try."

Ki laughs. "Your attempt is good enough for me." He throws the shiny stones on the ground. "Well, shall we continue our journey?"

An awareness touches Ralph. Ki, whatever his purpose, is a definite hindrance and not to be trusted. "You go on, Ki. I'm staying here for awhile. I like the vibes." Ralph goes to a towering redwood tree and sits down.

"The place does have good feelings. I'll join you. We can rest and get to know each other better before continuing." Ki walks over to Ralph seated beside the redwood tree.

Ralph stares at him. "No, Ki. I want to be quiet and clear my mind. If you want to stay here, that's your decision. But please sit somewhere else. Find your own banyan tree." Ralph moves into his inner chamber and becomes very still.

Displeased, Ki mumbles and sits down a few feet away. He peers around the grove of trees, studies his fingers, and grows impatient. Ralph is deep within and a serenity permeates the atmosphere. Ki realizes he must stay in tune with Ralph so he can guide him onto a false trail. But doing nothing is disturbing.

In his inner room Ralph reviews his options. Getting rid of Ki is the primary goal, and the method is the issue. Ki definitely has power of an unknown quality. One of the doors beckons him. It is room two. He enters the room and gazes about. There on the table is the answer. He walks over to the table and picks up a ball of string and a knife. Understanding fills him with hope. He breathes deep into his pelvic region several times. Seeing Ki seated a few feet away, he smiles and stands up. Without a word, Ralph leaves the grove and continues his journey.

Ki, noticing Ralph departing, gets up and follows quietly. The situation is serious, he realizes. Ralph has become aloof and reticent. Revised tactics are necessary. The path through the forest twists and turns. Ki maintains a small distance behind Ralph, often losing sight of him. When he spots Ralph again, he stops because Ralph is standing motionless.

Ralph waves at Ki. "Join me, Ki. I've a game we might play."

Ki hurries forward, wondering about the change in Ralph's behavior.

Ralph removes a ball of string and knife from his pocket. Cutting off a piece of string about a foot long, he holds it by one end. "Ki, here's the idea. Earlier, you indicated you have skill with psychic energy. I'll cut the string in half and give you both pieces. Hold the pieces end-to-end in your hand and fuse them together with your psi power."

Ki studies Ralph with shrewdness. "Okay. But you go first. You failed earlier. I want to see your psi power now before I try."

"Fair enough." Ralph cuts the string in two and grasps an end of each piece together and focuses his attention on them. After a few moments, he smiles and takes one end of the string and flings the other end into the air. The string is healed and all one piece.

"Excellent, Ralph." Ki applauds.

Ralph cuts the string again and gives Ki the halves. "Now it's your turn."

Ralph steps back away from Ki, allowing him space to apply his psi skills. Ki concentrates on the strings for several minutes. Opening his hand, he frowns in disappointment. The halves haven't fused. Ki stares at Ralph and closes his hand for a second attempt. Ralph slowly moves to the edge of the path. When Ki again opens his hand, Ralph vanishes into the forest.

Ki curses and, throwing the strings on the ground, chases after Ralph. "Damn you and your string theory, Ralph. Wait. Show me the technique." Ki disappears into the forest.

Getting on high noon, the sun shining on the path, Ralph stops every few feet to examine the flora along the trail. He has discovered a diversity of species all residing within their niche.

A voice conveying a message floats through the countryside. He listens and peers around searching for the source. Laughing to himself, he nods in agreement to the lyrics. Yes, what have I seen and heard on my journey? Someone is singing a favorite ballad "A Hard Rain's A-Gonna Fall." Whose voice is that? Ah, my distraction and adversary–Ki.

The crooning voice with a slight vibrato is becoming louder as he continues along the trail. Rounding a curve, he pauses before approaching Ki, who is sitting on a cedar log plucking a guitar and singing.

When the song concludes, Ralph claps with approval. "More talents sprout forth. That was a fine rendition," he commends.

"Thanks, Ralph. Yes, I've always had a knack for music, especially vocals. But hey, what say you join my ensemble. What instruments do you play?"

"I'm afraid I'm not much of a musician but I like to listen to music."

"How about drums? Anyone can tap on a drum."

"Well, yes, a drum. I can play the earth's heartbeat. When I find a drum, I'll perform with you." Ralph smiles and walks away.

"Wait, Ralph. I know where you can get a drum. There's a store up the road. Let's go." Ki stands up, holding the guitar around its neck, and starts to go in the opposite direction.

"Ki, you wait. I made a promise to myself to traverse the whole trail by sunset so I'm not going back." He takes a long step forward and quickens his stride. He is several paces away before Ki realizes the situation and runs after him.

"I can sing songs, traveling songs, while we're on the trail."

As he's moving along, Ralph considers methods for detaching Ki from his life.

By the time Ki has finished the fifth song, Ralph is becoming irritated. In the interim of silence he hears water sounds, moving falling water. Stopping so suddenly Ki nearly bumps into him, Ralph feels positive energy flow into his mind. Noticing a side trail, he follows it to an opening in the forest. Water is flowing over a rock ledge into a small pool. He searches for an outlet to the pool but finds none. So, he thinks, the water goes underground, surfacing somewhere else. Quiet in his thoughts, he doesn't sense Ki's presence.

The serenity is broken when Ki speaks, "Ralph, this is a lovely place. Why don't we sit down and I'll compose a song for it?" Ki locates a flat rock for a bench and sits. He begins to pluck the guitar humming a melodic line.

Now's the moment for decision, Ralph thinks.

Seeing Ralph stick his hand into the pool and agitate the surface, Ki stops strumming. Watching him for several moments, Ki asks, "What are doing, Ralph?"

An inner smile warms him–I believe I've caught a fool. Ralph twists and glances at Ki. "I'm creating water images."

Ki gets up, placing the guitar against the rock, and strolls to the pool. He scrutinizes the surface, observing images changing and morphing. Ralph withdraws his hand, and the surface quiets. They stare into the pool through the mirror-like surface down to the bottom. The water is clear, and the pool's inhabitants are visible. Ki squats and, following Ralph's lead, stirs the water.

Ralph comments, a soothing timbre to his voice, "A favorite art form—I can spend hours creating overlapping images. Notice the double and triple layers reaching down to the bottom of the pool. And the rippling effect on the surface. Ideas bubble through my mind—ideas about reality and the cosmos and the soul. Am I an image in someone else's mind? Is my basic self a series of morphing images? I can get lost in the pastime."

"It's really mesmerizing. I understand your meaning," Ki remarks. When only silence prevails, Ki looks up and then removes his hand from the water, producing a swirling pattern of forms. Ralph has vanished. Ki realizes he has been tricked again. Bitterness burns his pride. He curses his foolishness. Picking up the guitar, he wanders back to the main trail. A different strategy is the answer. His scheming flair will beat Ralph yet. He'll sabotage the foundation stone of Ralph's being.

Scene 3

Surveying the colorful flowers bordering the stone path, Ralph approaches the front porch. A sign hangs from its eaves: 'Eden House.' When he arrives at the front door, he notices a small sign attached to the wall below the doorbell: 'Please ring bell and then enter. –Adam and Eve.' Ralph, following directions, enters the house. He walks along a hallway, appraising the elegant furnishings. Reaching the corridor's end, he pauses. The door is the only other door in the hallway; none along the sides. He peers about for a sign giving directions or other clues about what he should expect. Should he knock first? Boldly enter or quietly slip inside?

He knocks gently and opens the door slowly. Standing in the doorway, he observes the room. It is a private chamber or suite. In the center is a large bed and two people are lying there. No doubt sleeping. The furnishings are appropriate for a well-appointed personal suite.

Ralph presumes the people are Adam and Eve, residents of Eden House. Should he approach the bed and waken them? Or– He is startled when the chamber door opens and Ki briskly swaggers in. "Well, well, we meet again," Ki remarks as he nods at Ralph and continues toward the bed. He takes hold of a long cord hanging down on Adam's side of the bed. Ki pulls the cord and chimes sound.

Adam wakens, rubs his eyes, and sits up. "Good morning," he says to the room in general. Then he notices Ki.

"Good morning, Adam," Ki replies. "Are we ready for today's pleasurable activities?"

"Oh, I guess." Adam stretches his arms in the air and then gets out of bed. "What's on the agenda for today?"

Ki removes a tablet from a jacket pocket and opens the calendar of events. As he reads a list of potential activities, Ralph moves back toward the wall on Eve's side of the bed. A cloud passes in front of the sun, darkening the bedchamber. Ralph remains in the shadows and watches in amazement, trying to grok the happening in all its many levels of meaning. Ki is acting like an advisor or more like a CEO's executive assistant. Ralph witnesses the clever and subtle techniques Ki applies to Adam. Ki, a veritable sleight-of-hand artist, has inflamed Adam's ego, which is now puffed up. As Adam and Ki leave the room, Ralph laughs to himself. Adam is strutting like a peacock, totally unaware of his foolishness.

Ralph turns his attention toward Eve who is sleeping, a slight smile on her lips. Should he wake her? Ki had slyly teased Adam about Eve, mocking their bond of love. The more Ralph learns about Ki, the more he dislikes him.

Ralph stands beside Eve, looking down on her. He speaks softly, "Eve, it's time to rise and shine." He smiles at the old-fashioned phrase. He speaks again, "Eve, it's a beautiful morning." Still, Eve sleeps. He listens to her breathing, a very quiet, slow rhythmic movement. He touches her wrist and feels her pulse, slow yet steady. She is in a deep sleep, and with that smile on her lips she is enjoying herself. He studies her, imbibing her exquisite beauty.

Enraptured, he bends down to kiss her, to savor the sweet smile and its hidden treasure. Hovering a few inches from her lips, he feels restraint and straightens. A kiss, however delightful, will break into her dreamscape. Instantly, he realizes she will be very unhappy if his disturbance should awaken her.

He decides to leave her to her dreams, yet commits himself to return. Her image shines in his soul.

Scene 4

The background scenery shows a map of the night sky with constellations illuminated. The night journey is depicted in lights on a star map.

Ralph comes to a meadow bordered by trees. Evening has arrived. He sits on a flat rock and observes the night sky. The sun has sunk below the horizon and Venus, the evening star, will set in a half hour or so. The constellations brighten against the darkening heavens. Soon their forms will be in high relief.

He locates Orion at the celestial equator. The constellation has always held mysteries for him. Shamans and other persons of power journey westward to visit the Upper World by following the same path souls travel on their way to the land of the dead. Ralph steps into the central room of his inner mansion. He is prepared to sail the cosmic ocean in a vessel that would make Phaeton jealous.

Because water possesses a sacred, mystical force that touches my inner being, I decide to voyage on River Eridanus, a constellation which will transport me to Orion, the gateway to Milky Way's galactic center. I'll start at Achemar, a hot, blue beauty, lying at the southern tip of River Eridanus, which flows south to north, and cruise to the River's northern tip at Beta Eridani or Cursa the footstool, second brightest star in the constellation. A short portage will carry me to Rigel, the brightest star in Orion.

Before I set sail for my destination, I look behind, recognizing the constellation Hydrus, and directly to my right is Phoenix. My journey has an auspicious beginning. Hydrus, the water serpent, conveys many meanings from the Sumerian saga *Gilgamesh* to S.T. Coleridge's poem "The Rime of the Ancient Mariner" to Native American archetypal images. The serpent has played varied roles in human culture. It frequently refers to life and regeneration. For many Native Americans the water serpent is the controlling power of the Lower World. Now it rests at the roots of my passage to the Upper World. Like the Ancient Mariner I'll bless water serpent of many colors for its healing power.

Phoenix is another positive sign. The ancient symbol evokes secret knowledge. My trip will involve a transformative process of rebirth and arising from the ashes of former self.

Leaving port, I sail north along the curving, twisting sky river. On my left is Horologium, the clock, a faint constellation, tracking time of my travels.

Next comes constellation Fornax, the furnace. Within the furnace lies the Hubble ultra-deep field, an image of the past, the universe 13 billion years ago. Perhaps it contains source data about the birth of our universe. Here also is the athanor of my soul applying its slow heat to digest the psi particles necessary for maintaining the soul's life.

Caelum, the chisel, to shape my soul and remove the encrustations is now within my visual field. I'm preparing myself for renewal at a higher level.

"Awesome," I exclaim, "it's true." I'm viewing Eridanus' Supervoid, a colossal emptiness—no lights, only darkness. Galaxies are missing. It's an astronomical enigma. Proponents of string theory and multiple universes propose the huge void may be a sign of contact with another universe, a quantum entanglement. The ocean of barrenness reminds me of Gilgamesh, ancient Sumerian hero, who crosses the Sea of Death on his quest for everlasting life. He has the rejuvenating plant in his possession but falls asleep and loses it. The subtle serpent steals it while Gilgamesh dreams. Gilgamesh arrives home an aging and mortal hero.

"Hey, there's Cetus, the sea monster or whale. Was it you who swallowed Jonah and hid him in your belly?"

As I sail by Epsilon Eridani, I remember scientific attempts to find extraterrestrial life. The search is now headed by SETI. The star hosts one if not two planets that may be hospitable to life and has been featured in sci-fi. Perhaps creative artists have better insights than astronomers.

The constellation Taurus is coming into view, north of my ship above the celestial equator. Ha, there's Pleiades, the Seven Sisters, an important stellar signpost, well-known in many human cultures. Famous Aldebaran, the follower, brightens the sky, as popular in human stories as the Seven Sisters.

My attention is called closer to hand as I pass 40 Eridani A, the star hosting the planet Vulcan, home of Mister Spock of Star Trek fame.

Ahead, not far, is my destination Beta Eridani, where I'll leave River Eridanus and portage to Rigel. Looking back over my journey, I wonder about the River's source. Some have suggested Eridanus flows from Aquarius. It's an intriguing thought.

I stop my travel at Rigel and survey Orion, another major sky-marker. Playing an important role in numerous stories, Orion has provided navigational assistance for eons. Many people intuit a mystical presence shrouding the constellation.

Looking south, I notice Lepus, the Hare, forever fleeing from Orion, the Hunter, who'll never catch the stellar Rabbit. And now I'm remind of the archetypal role Rabbit performs in human culture. Great Rabbit or Nanabozho for the Anishinaabe people is a cultural hero and teacher, trickster, and founder of Grand Medicine Society.

With deliberate care I inspect Orion, immersing myself in its entanglement with human culture and the Milky Way Galaxy of which we are a part. The constellation has conveyed numerous ideas and symbols to earth people. The night sky is a landscape for the soul's journey, a guidebook whose geography must be learned. Orion is the gateway to the Milky Way and its galactic center, which lies in the direction of Sagittarius. A bar, consisting of red stars, or perhaps two bars cross the galactic center where a supermassive black hole is located, a veritable star formation complex. Old stars are recycled and new ones birthed—a galactic transformative process that only the universal alchemist can perform. Are souls recycled here and sent forth for another incarnation? Is the portal a path to universal source of all things?

Orion's belt, close to the celestial equator, is a navigational and mystic signpost. A line drawn along the belt points to Aldebaran in the north and Sirius in the south. Hanging from the belt is Orion's sword, which contains Orion Nebula, another birthing chamber for stars.

A vision forms in my mind as I stare beyond Orion's Belt toward the galactic center: the Native American pictograph She Who Watches or Tsagiglalal located on the banks of the Columbia River in Washington State. The Native American leader has promised her people she will keep constant vigil and protect their welfare. The two enchanted eyes pull me toward her. The bear-like ears seem to hear my inner self. Her soft mouth speaks, "I am the gateway to the source." The icon vanishes as quickly as it had appeared.

My mind floods with thoughts.

Is Orion Nebula my home, my source, from whence I came? Where is the source of my soul and spirit, the cosmic field or channel that contains the basic human pattern and my individual Ralph form? My body comes from my mother whose body produced mine. But the self—where did the seed come from? The seed that grows into my individual self.

When I experienced my double, my true self, I had a mystical vision. I was filled with joy and understanding. Now my intellect questions. What is the double: a spiritual or eternal part of myself? Where is its source?

The night sky is a cosmic ocean. I was born here and came from the galactic center's birth canal. The Milky Way is the path and points to the entrance, the cosmic portal for my galaxy. As stars are born so too my spiritual being. The child of Humankind resides on a planet and grows into adulthood. Then the self migrates to another dimension.

At a certain time in life we look outward into the night sky, wondering and then searching for clues about our destiny and final home. Late in life we may venture and explore the night sky seeking the truth and the return-home path.

I'll internalize the night sky for meditation and use it like the inner mansion. My mantra: follow Milky Way to the self's source at galactic center.

A noise startles me, dissolving my rapture. Listening, I discern sounds like a coyote howling and turn toward them. Ah, yes, Canis Major, the Great Dog, but resembling a coyote rather than the family pet.

I'm again sitting on a rock seeking the coyote in the surrounding meadow. Physical reality captures my attention once more.

Chapter 65

A slow, soft drumming enhanced by a lyrical, songbird-like melody on the Native American flute pervades the Inn and then fades into silence. Scene 5 of Journey to Deep Source begins.

Rosy brightness breaks over the horizon as I stroll along the garden path to Eden House. Refreshed by my night sky journey, I'm ready for the day's adventures.

I enter the house and go to the bedchamber. Adam and Eve are sleeping, peaceful smiles on both their faces. Moving closer to the bed for a better view, I feel attracted to Adam. I must act now before Ki arrives and inflates Adam with more deceiving praise. Adam has become quite insufferable and, if Ki's sleazy adoration continues, will bury himself in egotism.

Focusing in my inner room, I allow a psi force to pull me into the bed and on top of Adam, enfolding him. The light of dawn brushes my eyelids, and I open them. A gentle breeze ruffles the curtains, and I smell the fragrance of flowers in the garden. I stretch my arms and then my legs. Feeling invigorated from the pleasant night's sleep, I rise and take my robe from the chair and put it on.

Ah, Eve is still asleep. Smiling, I start some coffee brewing and set a plate of fresh croissants on the table. Walking over to Eve, I admire her serenity and beauty. Bending down, I kiss her gently on the lips. A knowing smile caresses her mouth, and she opens her eyes. Grinning at me, she sits up. "What a wonderful way to awaken on this beautiful morning."

"Breakfast is served," I remark. Half bowing, I guide her gaze to the table with my hand.

She rises and, slipping on her robe, joins me at the table.

"Yum. The blueberry croissant is delicious," she declares and returns to nibbling it.

"What shall we do today?" I inquire.

"Something outdoors. It's too marvelous to stay inside."

"A walk along the river and through the redwood grove," I suggest.

"Yes. Let's."

An hour later we're ready for a nature hike. Before we emerge from the bedchamber, we hug each other with tenderness. With a gentle kiss on the lips we merge into each other becoming one.

Scene 6

Stepping out the front door of Eden House, I'm rejuvenated. The experience in the bedchamber was restorative. A magical healing salve had been applied to my mind, and I feel whole. I stride briskly along the path to the river's shore.

Observing the water's movement is very relaxing, my mind quiet. All my senses are open to the atmosphere and the special nuances discernible at the river's edge. The stillness is broken when a voice calls, "Ralph, it's good to see you again."

I know the source of the voice. My thoughts are shaping into speaking form as I turn toward Ki. "Good morning." I'm immediately aware of a darkness I had missed earlier. A shadow hangs about Ki's head, a lightless aura. I think 'tragic' when I perceive the divisions in Ki's personality, as if it were a bundle of fragments.

Ki breaks the silence. "I'm on my way to Eden House to visit Adam and Eve. Will you join me?"

Ah, I think, he's finally given himself away. I'm onto his game. "No thanks, Ki. I'll enjoy the morning beside the river. There's something stimulating about moving water, like it has a life of its own."

"Ok, then. Have a good one." Ki starts toward Eden House.

No more clues, I decide. Mum's the word. I saunter along the river trail, listening to bird songs.

Abruptly my awareness is heightened. An intuitive alertness signals I'm being watched and the observer is stationed out of sight.

I hear my name shouted, and when I revolve to look behind me, I see Ki running toward me, waving his arms. Reaching me, he pauses to catch his breath and then begins to speak rapidly and a little incoherently. "Ralph, something dreadful happened. At Eden House. Adam and Eve vanished. We got to call 911." He grabs my arm and starts to go back up the river trail toward the house.

I seize his wrist and pull him to a stop. "Whoa," I command. "Slow down. Tell me again what you saw."

Ki appears agitated but then regains his composure. "Ok. I went into the bedchamber calling out to Adam, as I often do. Nobody was there. Something bad has happened."

"Perhaps they went on a morning outing. What else did you notice in the bedchamber? Was there any sign of a struggle?" Now I can test Ki's accuracy. Note what he lies about and where the deception is.

Ki stares into space before answering. "No, no sign of struggle or violence. Actually, they ate breakfast. Dishes were in the sink, half empty coffee pot on the stove and a few croissants remained on a plate on the table. Their housekeeping standards have never been very high." He laughs at the joke.

I nod with approval, encouraging him to continue his report.

"Yes, I agree with your assessment. Obviously they've gone somewhere, maybe to town. I guess I jumped to a wrong conclusion." His smile in acknowledgement is weak.

I begin walking along the river trail again. Ki follows behind, asking, "What are your plans for today? Maybe we can do something together." His voice is entreating.

"I wish to be alone, Ki, but thanks for asking." I increase my gait. He sidles up to my right side. "You're not very sociable, are you?" he insinuates in a rude manner.

"Oh, I have my moments. There are times for socializing and times for solitariness," I remark. His clinging is beginning to annoy me.

I halt with a suddenness that leaves him off-balance. I pull the ball of string and knife from my pocket. "Would you like to try my theory of string restoration? You didn't mend it before, did you?" An ironic grin spreads across my face, expressing disdain.

"Well, okay, if you want me to. But you'll have to show me the method if I don't figure it out." Ki looks at me questioningly.

"I will. You must try first. I'll sit on the log over there." As I'm strolling over to the log, I notice a large rock further along the path and like its appearance. I decide to sit on the log for a bit and observe Ki fumbling with string and knife in his inept handling of the restored string routine. Then while he is immersed in his task, I'll go to the rock for a better inspection. The rock's aura evokes mystery.

Scene 7

Coming into a clearing, a meadow of blossoming plants, I intuit a peril, a lurking presence. A sense of disappointment envelops me. The conflict is appalling–blending danger and a carefree nature scene. Then I hear whining, more a high-pitched whimpering than anything else. Recognizing the threat, its source and meaning, I walk toward the sounds.

Several feet off the trail, Ki is bent over searching among the plants. "Oh, ye gods, help poor me. I implore you. Oh."

I stand watching. When at last he straightens and turns in my direction, I ask, "What's wrong, Ki?"

"Oh, Ralph, so good to see you. You can help me. I'm lost, forsaken. I don't know what to do."

"Why?" I realize the necessity to be sparse with words.

"I've lost my body. I can't find it." Ki moans.

I glare at him, shaking my head. "Of course, you're lost. You have your body. You're in it now. I can see it." My voice carries a touch of scorn.

"No, you don't understand at all, at all." Ki starts crying. "My corpus sidereum, my astral body, has just disappeared. What will I do?" He peers at me with a quizzical expression.

I bend over with laughter. "You've lost your astral body. Oh, Ki, that's impossible."

"You make fun of me–you who are whole. You're mean."

A wave of menace cloaks the site. I perceive fiery anger emerge from Ki's eyes. Yes, I realize, he is worse than I have imagined. The psi charm on my necklace gives an added warning. Ki has strong psi ability.

I begin exuding positive energy, transforming the negative. "Ki, please listen. I'm very sorry for laughing and making fun. Forgive me, but there's no way you can lose your astral body. It's only hiding from you because you're so upset."

"Really? I still have it?" Ki relaxes. Then very alert he inquires, "Can you see it, Ralph?"

Ooh, the situation could be a trap, I think. "We need a quiet place for the investigation." I look along the path toward my destination. Ah, a small hill with many rocks. Obviously a place of psi power.

I guide Ki to the hill and point at the top. "See, on top are several large boulders. We can unveil your astral body there. Come."

Reaching the hilltop, we rest on a large rock. I inspect the rocks around us and am amazed when I notice a large boulder with a pictograph on its face. I'll examine it later.

"Ok, Ki, I'll inspect your aura for your astral body." I sit in silence and, applying a special viewing focus, I scan Ki's aura. His astral body is readily visible. So that's your game, is it?

"Yes, Ki, I see your astral body. It appears in good shape to me. When you're in a quiet state, you should be able sense it." I stand and walk toward the pictograph rock. Ki jumps up and follows me, profusely filling the air with gratitude. I nod affirming his thanks.

The pictograph is an exact copy of Tsagiglalal or She Who Watches, the vision I had during night sky journey. A sudden awareness blossoms, eliciting a silent aha. I gesture at the image. "Isn't this marvelous, an indigenous work of art?"

Pensive, Ki studies the picture. "Yes, it's interesting enough, but what's the story?"

"Story?" I ask.

"Of course, Ralph. All indigenous art has a story attached to it."

"Tsagiglalal watches over her people eternally and will protect them when necessary."

"Hmm. Well, okay, shall we continue our journey?"

You never fail to give your game away, do you, Ki? I think but aloud say, "First I want a close up inspection of the image. Look here, Ki, her ears are bear-like. Now that's intriguing."

"What do you mean?"

"I'll show you." I walk up to the face of the boulder and step into it as if a doorway were there. Passing through the rock, I continue on my path down the hill and beyond.

Ki tries again and again to follow, but he doesn't find an opening. He's totally nonplussed. His bewilderment causes rage, and he howls at the coming of night.

Scene 8

A balmy breeze touches him with its refreshing curative power, bringing a tranquility to his spirit. The sun is moving closer to the ocean. As sunset nears, he approaches the end of his journey. The night will be delightful, the stars illuminating the sky. His pace is unhurried, and his mind is quiet as he observes the countryside from his inner room. He perceives a spiral staircase one hundred yards away. Its golden brightness beckons, offering fulfillment of his quest. Feelings of humility and satisfaction sustain him and, reaching the bottom of the stairs, he gazes up at the spiraling steps as they disappear into the heavens.

The moment is here. The sun will soon touch the ocean and begin to sink into its watery bedchamber. Smiling, with an inner balance, I mount the stairs. My confidence is strong and focused on achieving life's goal: attain access to my Self, the perfect nature of my being. The gateway is located at the top and, once I walk through, I'll be transformed forever.

The staircase is not as steep as it appears. The steps are mounted on an incline permitting an easy upward movement. The spiral enhances the journey. I'm able to view the terrain from a full circle. An exceptional clarity possesses my mind, and I perceive connections I was never aware of.

A sound bursts the inner silence. I turn and peer downward. A figure is at the bottom of the stairs, waving at me. Then I hear my name called. Has Ki gained access to the portal and followed, I wonder? The stranger hurries up the stairs to the first landing and pauses. "Ralph, wait. I've important information."

I recognize him now. It's not Ki but Carlyle. What's he doing here? A weirdness creeps along my spine. Something about Carlyle evokes Ki as if they were twins.

He yells, "Do you know about the secret that's never revealed? Let's talk." Carlyle starts up the stairs again.

Oh, oh, I think. Something's amiss. The paradoxical flavor of his query conjures wrongness. My mage persona surfaces and detects a superb misdirection. Glancing upward, I notice a landing only ten feet or so above. Hurrying up the steps, I pause at the landing and stare down at Carlyle, who has become a threat to my quest. The landing differs from the earlier ones. It is dark, lacking all illumination. Memories of black art routines arise in my mind. Smiling, I exploit the oldest deceptive cover ever used. I walk into the darkness and pull the shadows around me.

Carlyle is out of breath when he reaches the landing where he has last seen Ralph. He has always maintained his physical prowess, but the anxiety and stress of the last few days are taking their toll. Peering into the darkness, he hesitates. His ego is telling his body to stride forward and challenge Ralph and defeat him. An ancient fear agitates him. He shouts, "Ralph, it's important, a very serious matter. I must speak with you."

Stillness weighs upon him. He forces back the childhood memories which are slowly oozing from their prison. In a meek tone, he cajoles, "Please listen to me. We can help each other."

Carlyle is close to tears. The terror is too powerful, shattering its cell walls. Paralysis controls his mind, preventing him from entering the darkness. "Oh, Ralph, this is urgent." A pleasant thought pokes into his mind. No doubt Ralph has left or he would have answered. They've always been friendly. That's it, he believes.

He takes a last glance at the darkness, an ominous invitation to death, and starts down the stairs. Panicked, he quickens his pace. The voice of rage surges through his brain. He commences shaking as he imagines invisible, ferocious creatures descending upon him and ripping his flesh off. He nearly stumbles but holds onto the rail. When he reaches the bottom, he collapses on the earth, emptied, a hollow man.

Scene 9

I emerge from the black shadows and stare down to the bottom of the staircase. Carlyle is lying motionless on the earth. The trickster has finally defeated himself. I start my climb upward. Arriving at the top of the spiral stairs, I stroll toward the arched portal several hundred yards distant. At first I quicken my pace, feeling a refreshing vigor in my movement. But whatever dislikes haste speaks, and I slow my gait.

Engraved in the archway is the famous Delphic saying: "Know thyself." Pausing, I reconsider my status. Will I discover my true self if I go through the gateway? Or is such gnosis unattainable in this life? Only one way to ascertain the truth—carry on with the quest.

I cross the threshold. The path meanders through a meadow of wildflowers. The walk is pleasant and relaxing. Positive energy flows freely, increasing my happiness. I come to a small kiosk which is very inviting. Inside are a bench and a table with four boxes on it. Each box has an image engraved in its lid: dog, cat, horse, and cow. A sign beside the boxes states: "Select one box. Do not open the box until you leave the kiosk."

Even though the afternoon has been fine so far, I sense a foreboding in the air. I'm in a perilous place unknown to me and will definitely follow directions. Carefully studying the boxes–and I decide not to touch any until I make the selection–I hold the psi-detector over each box and choose the cat box. Its psi energy is most appealing, and then I'm a cat-person.

When I'm back on the path, I open the box. It contains a stone, the sun and moon tarot cards, a circle ESP card, a small cloth bag, and a small stick which is four to five inches long and notched on one side. The psi-detector purrs when held next to the stick, my psi wand I think. Replacing the items, I journey on toward the looming forest.

At the trees' edge the path diverges into four trails. A map of Golden Gate Park is sited at the trail head. Each trail leads to a different section of the park. I must choose one trail that will lead me to my journey's end. I scrutinize each trail with care. A strong urge surfaces from the depths of memory. The bison field–I'll visit one of my favorite hangouts in the park.

The park is one of the city's great attractions and a marvel of transforming sandy land into a forest of trees and flowers. The trail skirts the bird-fishing pond, a name I gave it as a child because herons, whites and great blues, frequented it for their fishing hole. Herons are such wondrous creatures. Based on their physical appearance and flying ability, I regard herons as a relic from the past and a herald of the future. With the heron time vanishes in the moment. During April Shasta and I visit Stow Lake in the park and watch the heron chicks nested in trees high above the lake. The heron flock normally births six to eight chicks yearly.

Luck is at my side. I spy a great blue fishing. Pausing, I wait for a few moments. Neither of us is disappointed. It catches a fish. Happy, I walk on, passing another pond which is too overgrown for fish to live in. Across Kennedy Drive is my next stop.

Arriving at the bison field, I sit on a bench facing the pasture. Indulging in reverie of the past, I recall facts learned as a child. Bison were part of the wildlife that had resided in the San Francisco Bay Area since ancient times. Like most large four-leggeds they were displaced by domesticated animals brought in by the Spanish. After the small settlement of Yerba Buena become the booming city of San Francisco, Golden Gate Park was established in 1870s. A pair of bison were introduced in 1890. Later more bison were added to the growing herd.

Having rested, I start to rise when I notice a boy about eight or nine years old at the fence observing the herd. When he turns around and walks over to the sidewalk, I realize he looks very much like I did at that age. Suddenly, the light flashes on: he is my younger self. Fascinated, I watch as he walks along the sidewalk and then moves onto the grass again and strolls toward the back of the fenced field. Suddenly, he rotates and peers at me sitting on the bench. Smiling, I comment, "Bison are such beautiful four-leggeds."

The lad nods in agreement and replies, "I love them. I'd like to touch one but Dad says no. They're dangerous. I wish I had something to feed them." He has been moving closer to me.

A memory of my father saying something similar pops into my mind. "Yes, that's good advice. Bison are quite peaceable when left alone."

The boy sits on the bench beside me and asks, "What's your name?"

I silently laugh before replying, "Ralph. And yours?"

"Wow. That's cool. Ralph's mine too."

Quiet, we two Ralphs observe the grazing bison. The late afternoon sun shines down warming the park. Young Ralph breaks the stillness. "Guess what I'm going to be?"

I respond, "You like animals, so maybe a park ranger or veterinarian."

Young Ralph smiles. "No. A magician. I like magic a lot."

I laugh. "That's cool. I dabble in magic myself." Retrieving the cat box from my jacket pocket, I open it and remove the small cloth bag. Turning the bag inside out and then restoring it, I remark, "You saw the bag was empty, right?"

"Yes, I did. What are you going to pull out of it?"

"Gosh. You already know the trick."

"I saw it before."

'So I can't mystify you. Ok, then, let's put something into it." Taking the stone from the box, I put it into the bag. Waving my left hand over the bag, I chant, "Sim-sala-bim." I open the bag and turn it inside out. The stone has vanished. I peer at young Ralph, who is surprised.

"And now for the encore." I reach into the air and grab a stone, placing it into the bag. "Well, young Ralph, what's your desire–is the stone in the bag or not?"

The youth frowns and then says, "The stone's gone."

"Your wish is my command," I answer and turn the bag inside out, showing it's empty.

"Bravo. That's awesome," cries young Ralph.

I the mage stand and hand the bag to my apprentice. "Here, please accept my gift. It'll help you become a great magician."

"Thanks so much, Ralph. I'll read about it in my magic book." He beams happiness.

The mage smiles and, waving goodbye, strides toward the ocean and the approaching sunset.

Have I initiated a great disaster for the future, even for my present moment? Have I disrupted time-space fabric? I don't remember ever having an experience like that as a child at the bison pasture. I did spend many hours wandering around the park and had favorite places. The bison were one. But I'm not going to fret and beat myself with uncertain guilt. Too much has changed since I began the project at the Institute. My reality has entangled with many others. The outcome is fluid, not to be set until choices are made.

Strolling along Kennedy Drive, I watch the rotating blades of Dutch Windmill situated on Great Highway. Ah, how Don Quixote would have loved to duel Dutch Windmill. Thinking of Jo Mora's 1916 bronze and stone sculpture of Don Quixote and his faithful companion Sancho Panza kneeling in reverence before the bust of their creator Miguel de Cervantes, located in Golden Gate Park, I visualize the quest I'm completing.

Arriving at Great Highway, I head north until I reach the southern boundary of Playland at the Beach, an amusement park torn down in 1972. Condos cover the land now, and San Franciscans must go elsewhere to play. Stepping into the inner room, I envision the old Playland, recreating it in my mindscape.

The rides, the shows, the food stalls, and gaming stands spread over ten acres. Hundreds of people crowd the grounds. I halt at the entrance and wait to purchase a ticket. When I reach the gate, the attendant asks, "Who are you?"

Puzzled, I show him my driver's license, which he doesn't accept as valid ID. My mind is dizzy and I'm uncertain.

"What type of ID do you want?" I inquire.

"Something that affirms your identity," he replies.

"My driver's license doesn't? The state of California believes it does," I counter.

"It only shows your public persona, not your authentic self," he says.

Taking a deep breath, I'm silent. A voice within whispers and I hear. Extracting the cat box from my pocket, I take out the three cards and shuffle them. Then I spread them face up–tarot sun, ESP circle, and tarot moon. Turning them face down, I shuffle again. When I spread them face up, the cards are now ESP square, tarot magician, and ESP star.

Staring at him, I assert, "You can see my true self here in the cards." I point to the magician card between the square and star cards. The gateman looks at the cards and then at me. "You may enter," he states.

I hand him the cards and walk through the arched gateway. I meander about the park, viewing the diversity of amusements. I stroll by a series of sideshows located on both sides of the path. Outside the shows barkers shout the attractions found within, beckoning potential customers with fantastic experiences awaiting them inside. Inspecting each sideshow as I amble along, I stop when a strange odor touches my nostrils. I sniff. A wry grin crosses my face when I recognize the smell of boredom, emanating from the sideshow on my immediate left. The barker, dullness in his eyes, gestures in a tedious fashion. I'm mesmerized. Buying a ticket, I go in.

Astonished, I gaze at a large framed glass construction. Sand is slowly filling the rectangular structure. I'm spellbound, fixed in time-space, while sand moves toward the top. Then sand begins to flow downward to the bottom of the structure. My mind blossoms when water flows over the sand mound. The sandfall has morphed into a waterfall.

I retrieve the cat box and remove the last item–the notched stick. With a smooth and slow motion I rub my index finger along the grooves, back and forth, gradually building the tempo. As I play the instrument, I walk to the platform where the waterfall sits. A low hum blends with the rhythmic flow of psychic energy. Pointing the stick at the waterfall as I continuing rubbing it, I climb onto the platform and with a graceful dancing gait step into the frame, vanishing under the waterfall.

A moment of silence until the audience realized the drama was finished and awareness broke upon them–then the Inn was filled with loud applause, cheers and the mighty drumbeats of earth itself.

Chapter 66

Once the room was empty, Lefty concentrated on restoring his mental alertness and physical agility. Lights remained on indicating he was being watched. He focused on breathing and calmness spread, saturating his mind and body. A fear gnawed at his soul, encouraging him to hurry and escape as quickly as possible while he had the opportunity. But recognizing the conditions of his imprisonment, he dispersed the fear and settled into inner silence.

He heard voices, feminine in tone, circling within his mind. He counted four different timbres and linked each to a woman he knew: his grandmother, mother, sister, and Kathy. The voices overlaid each other, repeating loops like a musical round. One word caught his attention–'earth.' He listened and recognized another word–'feet.' Gradually he discerned links to other words, forming a sentence in his mind: 'Be in your feet rooted in the earth.' Again more scattered words coalesced: 'Source is within yourself.'

Of course, his gifts–use them now. Grow the spirit-vessel. No time like the present. If he was going to die, he must be able to journey onto the next stage in his existence.

A new persona stepped forward. He realized it had been existing in the fantasy reality he had constructed as a child. More memories sprang up. Dinah Craik's *The Little Lame Prince* was such a fun story. His mother had given him the book for his seventh birthday, and he had treasured it. He had marveled at the Prince's magic cloak which permitted him to travel around the world. The Prince learned to develop his gifts and employ them wisely.

The Prince persona was seated in the captain's chair on the command deck, directing the action. Lefty felt strange. He had a bird's eye view of the corridor outside of his prison room. He noted three monitors which displayed the interior of the room. He saw himself sitting in the chair as if meditating. Surveying the corridor, he discovered it was empty of human occupation. A green glow caught his attention. The light above the door lock was green. Instantly, he understood. The prison was at one end of the corridor, and he zoomed in on the other end where a door was ajar. Everyone had gone.

Rising from the chair, Lefty departed from the room and strolled along the corridor to the other door. Opening it, he walked through a lobby, also empty, and out onto the street. The Ferry Building at the Embarcadero was the signpost. He was in familiar territory and on his way home.

The doorbell chimed.

Adele got up, went to the front door, and peeked through the spy-hole. She yelled, "Awesome." Yanking the door open, she embraced Marilynn. "Come in. We've been so worried." She stepped back, allowing Marilynn to enter, and shouted into the living room, "Marilynn's here. Alive and well."

The others gathered around the homecoming hero, hugging and congratulating her on her safe return. Everyone was speaking at once until Adele waved her hands in the air and hollered, "Quiet, everyone." The hubbub subdued and in the silence Marilynn smiled at everybody. "I've had a crazy couple days. I need to talk about it. I thought I was going insane."

"Let's all sit down and hear Marilynn's adventures. I'll fix drinks and munchies." Adele went into the kitchen. Eduardo introduced the newest member of the group, Tom Defoe. Sedna went to help Adele and soon beverages and snacks were served.

Marilynn sat on the edge of the chair as she recounted with great enthusiasm the adventures that had happened to her. When she had finished, she sank back into the chair, exhausted. Her friends rehashed the bizarre tale, adding their own comments.

Sedna was amazed Marilynn just walked out of the condo where she had been held prisoner without anyone stopping. Eduardo noted Marilynn had found the condo empty when her guards didn't appear in the morning as they always did. After a search of the condo, she had dressed and departed unhindered.

Adele began the story of their plans to rescue her after they had located her prison. Soon everyone was involved in sharing the group's agenda.

Lefty saved the document and leaned back in the chair. He was satisfied. The global novel would continue with new characters and adventures. His adversary had been vanquished. If Tau threatened again, Lefty would be ready with counter actions. His rediscovered talents would equalize their positions. He would no longer deny his gifts but would develop their full potential. His life now had a purpose.

Tonight Kathy and he were going to celebrate. Four bottles of Basa were cooling in the refrigerator, snacks for the whole night were prepared, and breakfast food was available. She would arrive in another hour, and he went to get ready. They both had stories to tell and a weekend to share.

Chapter 67

Shasta unfolded the garden chair and placed it near the living rock garden. She sat down and immersed herself in the sensory panorama of the backyard. She opened all her senses, especially her hearing. The gentle breeze soothed her skin. Smells from the flora pleased her. She listened to the symphony of nature's music and, focusing on the living rocks, heard their vibrant processes. Her songs for Gaia began here with Gaia's inspiration guiding her imagination. She channeled Gaia's voice in its full polyphony. The breeze sang a sweet lullaby as it rocked the branches of the trees.

The kitties were relaxing in the shade of the redwood tree. Ms. Anna Hummingbird was feeding on fuchsia flowers while Mr. Anna was sitting on a top branch of the fuchsia bush watching for danger. Mr. House Finch and his two spouses were busily searching for seeds.

Ralph placed a garden chair next to Shasta's and sat down. He looked at her, imbibing her happiness. Reaching across the small distance, he grasped her hand and gently squeezed it. He smiled at her and she smiled back, a gleam in her eyes. In silence their love is revealed.

Afterward and Acknowledgements

Many ideas derived from contemporary scientific disciplines are embedded in the story and influence thematic material. Those interested in the latest ideas and proposals in quantum physics, cosmology, biology, and psychology will find numerous fine books and articles, cogent and accessible, on these disciplines. The internet, our global Commons, provides extensive research facilities. The Institute of Noetic Sciences, University of Virginia, and University of Arizona are well-known for their parapsychology research. Scientific associations such as Parapsychological Association, Society for Psychical Research, and American Society for Psychical Research, offer opportunities for research and connecting with other people investigating the field.

The magical effects and routines described, portrayed, and alluded to in the story are either well-known in the craft or creatively derived from basic principles. The magical craft is an art and has been since the beginning of human culture. Like all the arts, it is based on a foundation of knowledge acquired and refined over the centuries.

Without the encouragement, assistance and advice from my friends this book could not exist. I am profoundly grateful for their part in the making of the story. Mary, my companion and partner, has been the greatest source of inspiration, and I deeply appreciate her support in designing the cover.

Note on the Author

John Caris has been a college teacher for thirty-six years, thirty-three of them at City College of San Francisco, where he taught Humanities and English. His previously published books are *Hermes Beckons, A Tale of Alchemy and Magic*; *Foundation for a New Consciousness*; and *Reality Inspector*, a novel set in San Francisco involving a world championship chess match and computer hacking at the Federal Reserve Bank.

John and his wife Mary have been residing in San Francisco for over forty-five years.

Visit their web site Ye Olde Consciousness Shoppe at westgate-house.com.

www.ingramcontent.com/pod-product-compliance
Lightning Source LLC
Chambersburg PA
CBHW070224260626
47160CB00002B/679